A Winning Betrayal

A Winning Betrayal

LOUISE GUY

LAKE UNION
PUBLISHING

Previously published as Fortunate Friends in Australia in 2017 by Go Direct Publishing Pty Ltd

Published by Lake Union Publishing, Seattle

www.apub.com

Amazon, the Amazon logo, and Lake Union Publishing are trademarks of Amazon.com, Inc., or its affiliates.

ISBN-13: 9781542016018
ISBN-10: 1542016010

Cover design by Sarah Whittaker

Printed in the United States of America

For Judy (Mum)
Your strength, independence and generosity are
truly inspirational. Thank you for always being so
supportive, interested and encouraging.

Prologue

The thump of music blared from the club's speakers and increased her longing to dance, to celebrate. She spun around, her heart racing as the significance of her win engulfed her. This was huge; it was life changing.

Laughing, she stopped spinning and accepted the champagne flute held out to her. Golden bubbles of Cristal tickled her nose as she brought the glass to her lips. She hesitated, doing her best to push away six little words that flittered through her mind.

Life will never be the same.

The same six words echoed across town as another family hugged, danced and screamed with excitement. They were winners too! Only suddenly it didn't feel that way for one. She'd stopped dancing, her breath shallow, her excitement stifled. Life *will* never be the same.

Chapter One

Shauna's breath streamed white into the night air as she tried to warm her fingers. Her watch confirmed it was two forty-five a.m., and instead of being fast asleep, she stood with at least two hundred others in a park across from the hotel.

The fire alarms had gone off twenty minutes earlier, yet hotel guests still peered out from the upper levels. Were they deaf? If the alarm hadn't been enough to shock them out of their sleep, surely the loud, recorded voice ordering them to evacuate would?

The temperature had dropped to six degrees, and while some guests had grabbed blankets from their rooms, others stood in skimpy pyjamas, and a few had nothing more than a towel wrapped around them. Shauna now appreciated the extra thirty seconds she had taken to throw on a pair of jeans and her long, wool-lined jacket, before grabbing her computer bag and dashing down the stairs.

The alarm continued and the noise level increased as two fire engines arrived. Six firefighters jumped out and raced into the building. Shauna was not in the mood to wait and watch. She shouldn't even be here. She should be tucked up in the guest room of Tess's Darlinghurst apartment. But with her best friend travelling through Europe and the States for work over the next three months, it hadn't been an option on this trip. Instead, with an important meeting at nine o'clock, she'd stayed up until midnight to put the finishing touches to her presentation. Now cold, tired and annoyed, she was grateful for the flashing neon sign of an all-night cafe a few doors down from the hotel.

Shauna pushed open the door and was greeted by a buzz of music and chatter. The majority of the patrons were in their pyjamas, laughing and ordering drinks, definitely making the most of the situation. She slid into a booth. As much as she'd prefer to be sleeping, she might as well use the time to go over her presentation once more. She pulled out her laptop and clicked through the PowerPoint slides. Her pitch to Tonacoal, a large mining company, was one she intended to win. Since she'd joined I-People in the role of business development manager twelve months earlier, she'd predominantly worked with hospitality clients. Tonacoal would allow her to expand her portfolio.

'You're keen.'

Shauna jerked her head up. A guy in his late thirties, dressed in a singlet and Mickey Mouse boxer shorts, stood next to her booth. She suppressed a smile. 'Sorry, are you talking to me?'

He smiled, dimples creasing his cheeks. 'You're dedicated to be working at this hour.'

'Figure I might as well fill in the time somehow.' She raised her eyebrows and looked him up and down. 'Interesting outfit, by the way.'

The guy stared down at his pyjamas and laughed. 'You never know when you'll want to impress some crazy workaholic in the middle of the night. I like to be prepared.'

Shauna felt her smile slip. God, he sounded just like Simon. He'd always called her a workaholic, and then forced her to choose between work and him. 'I'm not a workaholic.'

The guy put up his hands, his blue eyes piercing hers. 'Hey, no need to get defensive. It was a joke – a bad one, obviously. It's not a normal night for any of us. At least you had enough sense to grab your computer. I've left mine in the hotel. If it burns down I'm in huge trouble. I started a new job this week and I'm supposed to be wowing a client in a few hours, plus I'm meeting a colleague I've heard is a complete pain in the arse. If I turn up like this' – he indicated his clothing – 'I'm not sure I'll make the finest first impression.'

'No, probably not. The hotel will reopen soon so it probably won't be an issue.' Shauna's eyes flicked back to her screen. She was no longer in the mood to make small talk. This guy would be like the rest of them. Underneath the smile and charm he'd have another agenda, just like Simon had. She continued reading through the presentation, conscious he hadn't moved. Why was he still standing there? She looked up, noting his smile no longer reached his eyes. His eyebrows were raised. She didn't owe him an explanation. He clearly couldn't take a hint so she'd need to spell it out. She pointed at her screen. 'Sorry, but I need to go over this. So if you don't mind . . .?'

He continued to stare. 'Evacuations don't bring out your empathetic side, do they?'

'What?' Why was he still talking? Hadn't he got the message that she would like him to go away? Shauna gripped the edge of her seat. Was he planning to insult her again?

He folded his arms. 'You're not exactly friendly. I thought emergency situations were supposed to be a bonding experience.'

'Are you for real?' Shauna glanced at the clock on the cafe wall. 'Three in the morning and you expect me to be delighted that a loser in his underwear is hitting on me? Considering half the hotel guests came down in the lifts, rather than the stairs, I don't think this is an emergency situation.'

He shook his head. 'Loser? Really? That hurts. Cute, adorable, smart – they're all names I'm used to. But "loser"? Never been called that before.' He didn't wait for a reply, instead turned and retreated to the counter. The guy serving laughed at something he said.

Shauna averted her eyes. She knew it wasn't his fault that she was constantly on edge when it came to men. Even though twelve months had passed, trusting anyone after Simon was going to be hard. Unless it was for work, she found even talking to men difficult. She didn't know if she'd ever risk putting herself in a position to be hurt so badly again. The night she'd been expecting a proposal, and an ultimatum had been delivered instead, had been more than a shock – it had broken her heart. She pushed it out of her mind and spent the next thirty minutes engrossed in her presentation. The cafe was empty when she finally finished.

'Hotel's open,' a girl wiping down the counter called over to her. 'False alarm.'

Shauna smiled. 'Thanks.' She packed up her computer and dropped some coins into the tip jar on the way out, conscious that she hadn't ordered anything. It was nearly four already. Hopefully, she'd be able to get another hour or two of sleep before her alarm sounded.

'Graham and Michael will just be a minute.' The receptionist held up a piece of paper. 'Also, this phone message is for you. Why don't you take a seat while you wait?'

'Thank you.' Shauna took the message and walked over to the waiting area. She couldn't help being impressed by the spectacular views Tonacoal enjoyed of Sydney Harbour. She unfolded and read the message. It was from a Josh Richardson, who, according to the note, was running late.

Shauna went back to the front desk and smiled at the receptionist. 'I'm afraid this message isn't for me. I've never heard of this guy.'

'He definitely asked for you, Ms Jones. I do apologise if I got the name wrong.'

'I'm not meeting anyone. I think you'll find it's for someone else.'

Confusion clouded the receptionist's face. 'I'm sorry for the error. I'll sort out the mistake when he turns up.'

Shauna returned to her seat, closed her eyes and took a calming breath. This was a big contract and an important client for I-People to obtain. Their elaborate office space and million-dollar harbour views confirmed Tonacoal were doing well. She picked up a magazine from the coffee table and flicked through it. She barely looked up when the lift opened and a man carrying an overnight bag and briefcase walked out. Shauna's interest sparked when the receptionist spoke.

'She's in the waiting area, but I'm afraid she didn't seem to know who you are.'

'Oh, my interesting morning continues.' He smiled at the receptionist and came over to Shauna.

She was already on her feet. What the hell was going on?

'Josh Richardson.' He stuck out his hand. He was tall, at least six foot. His beautifully cut charcoal suit sat snugly across his broad shoulders. Freshly shaven, he smelled clean, musky. This was a man who knew how to present himself. Looking at Shauna, his smile extended from his lips to the furthest depths of his eyes.

Had he not recognised her? Shauna's arms remained crossed. 'I believe you already know me as "a complete pain in the arse".'

Josh's smile was replaced with a frown. He stared at her. 'Oh no.' He shook his head. 'Sorry, I didn't recognise you. You look a lot more professional during the day. Your hair wasn't that straight last night, was it? I kind of remember it being all messed up.'

Shauna's hand flew up to her shoulder-length bob. Hair? He was asking about her hair? She dropped her hand. 'Aside from standing around in your underwear in the middle of the night, who are you?'

The furrows in Josh's forehead deepened. 'Are you kidding?'

'No, other than being amused by the boxer shorts you choose to wear to bed, I don't know anything about you. Should I?'

'Craig didn't bother to mention I'm the new national marketing manager for I-People, and I'd be joining you for the meeting this morning?'

Shauna stared at him. 'Hold on, you can't turn up unannounced and join me at the last minute for a sales presentation. Do you have any idea how important this client is?'

Josh nodded. 'Yes, and that's exactly why I'm here. Craig wants me to accompany all pitches where the potential revenue is over a million dollars.'

'We're supposed to work together on the pitch if you're going to be part of the team. What the fuck is Craig thinking?' Shauna took her phone from her bag and walked over to the full-length office windows. A large cruise ship was preparing to depart from Circular Quay. Why on earth hadn't someone contacted her? She couldn't have this guy messing up her first opportunity to present to Tonacoal.

Josh followed her. 'Don't stress. I'm here to observe this meeting, nothing more. I'll make that clear from the start.'

Shauna scrolled through her phone contacts, searching for a number.

'Now what are you doing?'

'I'm calling Craig. This is ridiculous.'

Josh leant towards Shauna, his voice lowered. 'No time. The client's here. Go with it. Show me how good you are. Rumour has it you're a remarkable salesperson.'

Shauna took a deep breath. She needed to put the entire morning out of her mind and refocus. 'Really? A remarkable salesperson? That's a step up from complete pain in the arse.'

'Pain in the arse is obviously true, so prove to me you can live up to both reputations.' Josh winked and turned to greet the clients.

◆ ◆ ◆

'See, all went well.' Josh clicked his seatbelt on as the taxi drove out into the traffic towards Sydney Airport.

'It would have gone a lot better if you hadn't thrown me off at the start,' Shauna said.

'What? By turning up?'

'Yes. Your only contribution to the entire day is pissing me off at three a.m., and then throwing me off minutes before a huge presentation this morning.' She did her best to suppress a smile. Shauna had in fact been quietly impressed by Josh; not that she was going to tell him. He'd listened attentively throughout the presentation, adding value with some comments about additional marketing programs that would be undertaken for the direct benefit of Tonacoal.

Josh grinned. 'If I just witnessed you presenting when you were thrown off, I'd love to experience you at your best. You were bloody good. You'll win the contract.'

Shauna didn't respond. He was saying all the right things, but so had Simon. Both personally and professionally. Always stroking her ego to ultimately get what he wanted. She wouldn't let it happen again.

'Are you always this quick to decide you hate someone, or do you not like anyone? I'm just wondering if I should be offended.'

Shauna opened her mouth, ready to launch another sarcastic response, but closed it when she saw his face. His smile had been replaced with a frown. She was being a bitch. It seemed she couldn't help herself these days. A man just had to look at her the wrong

9

way and she felt her jaw clench. 'I'm sorry, okay? Lack of sleep and pressure to get Tonacoal aren't helping. Craig's heard talk of them absorbing LJR Mining's contracts. It could be worth millions. I wanted to be on my best game today, and with middle-of-the-night evacuations and surprise marketing managers turning up, I wasn't. I apologise if I've been rude.'

Josh nodded and they lapsed into silence.

After a while he turned to Shauna. 'How about we start again?'

'How do you mean?'

'We've never met. Today I'm some annoying guy you happen to be sharing a taxi with. Tomorrow, however, you'll be introduced to the new marketing manager of I-People. Not only will you like and respect him, you'll find him funny and charming. You'll be delighted when he turns out to be one of the best assets you've ever had on your team. Sounds like a dream man, doesn't he?'

Shauna felt the corners of her mouth twitching. 'Dream man? I'd say he probably only exists in *your* dreams. I'm not saying don't try. If nothing else, you might give me a good laugh.'

'Anything would beat the look of contempt I've been receiving.'

The reproval in Josh's voice was obvious. Shauna had been unfair, she knew that. 'Prove yourself to be as brilliant as you say and my expression might change.'

Josh laughed. 'I can't wait to see the respectful, awed version of Ms Shauna Jones.'

'Neither can I. Good luck is all I'll say.' As the taxi raced towards the domestic terminal, Shauna turned to the window in an effort to hide her smile.

Chapter Two

Frankie caught her toe in a crack in the footpath and stumbled. She righted herself just in time to hear Hope groan.

'Mum, you really don't need to come with us. We're not babies.' Hope's eyes avoided Frankie's and remained firmly fixed in front as they walked towards the school.

Frankie's gaze followed her daughter's. The street ahead was empty. What, or who, was she looking for? A tightness developed in Frankie's chest as she refocused her attention on Hope. Her ash-blonde hair was pulled into a tight ponytail, her face pinched and tired. Where had her gorgeous, fun-loving fifteen-year-old disappeared to? Only a few weeks ago they were laughing together, acting more like friends than mother and daughter. Now Hope was a stranger – a sullen, moody stranger. Had teenage hormones finally got the better of her? Frankie knew she'd been lucky up to this point to have had a very close relationship with both of her girls. She'd spent so much time nurturing, supporting and encouraging them. She hoped that this new attitude of Hope's would be short-lived.

'You look tired, sweetheart. Another late night?'

'What?'

'I said did you have a late night?'

Hope shrugged. 'No later than usual. Would you stop telling me I look tired all the time? I know I look like crap, I don't need to hear it from you, too. The next lot of exams are important and I have to be ready. Anyway, I'm going ahead. Walk with Fern if you think a thirteen-year-old needs a bodyguard. I'll see you later.'

Frankie watched as Hope stalked off down the street, her long, lean legs speeding up with every step. It was uncanny at times to realise how similar they were. Her height, her looks, even her stride mirrored Frankie's. Tom's dark hair, brown eyes and olive complexion had hardly got a look-in with Hope. Whereas her youngest, Fern, other than Frankie's green eyes, was all Tom.

She turned to face her younger daughter. 'I don't need to walk with you if you'd rather go on your own.'

Fern took Frankie's hand and squeezed it. 'Don't worry, I'm not embarrassed to be seen with you . . . yet.'

Frankie laughed, giving Fern a quick cuddle. 'That's good to hear. Give you another couple of years and you'll probably feel the same.'

'Maybe.' Fern stepped out of her mother's embrace and they continued walking. 'Hope's just trying to be cool. I don't need to try. I already am and everyone likes me. They're not nasty to me like they are to her. It's weird, isn't it? She's the pretty one, and everyone used to love her.'

'You're not just pretty, you're gorgeous,' Frankie said. 'But what do you mean, *used* to love her?'

'You know she was really popular, but this year it's all changed.'

'Why do you say that?'

''Cause it's true. She used to hang out with the cool kids, but now she hides in the library all the time.'

'Hides? Are you sure? She's probably studying. She's taking the exams pretty seriously.'

'Nah, she hides. Her only friend these days seems to be that weirdo, Hailey. You know, the one who dresses like a Goth.'

Frankie nodded. Fern was right. Hope used to be out after school a lot, either at friends' houses or at the park with her crowd. Now most nights she was either at the library or home straight after school, head in a book, studying.

They arrived at school a few minutes before the bell was due to ring. Frankie gave Fern a last hug. 'Have a great day, chickie.'

Fern hugged her back. 'Thanks, I'll see you later.' She turned and walked slowly across the courtyard towards the school building.

Frankie watched until she disappeared through the front entrance. She looked for Hope but saw no sign of her. She wondered if there was something other than exams worrying her eldest daughter. She sighed, knowing she'd have a better chance of winning a Nobel Prize than getting Hope to open up.

Frankie retraced her steps through the neighbourhood, taking in the character of the old houses that lined the streets. The majority were run-down, in need of repainting and repairs, but she delighted in imagining the houses when they were first built, freshly painted with proud owners. She rounded the street corner, her own house now in sight. The muscles in her neck tensed. A familiar figure sat on the pillar by the front gate. What the hell was he doing here? She was tempted to turn and walk the other way. Unfortunately, it was too late; he'd seen her. By the time Frankie reached the gate, her mouth was dry.

'Dash, why are you here?' There was no warmth in his cold, grey eyes. His pointed chin and permanent scowl sent a chill down Frankie's spine.

He spat on the ground in front of her. 'Is that any way to talk to your brother-in-law? What would Tom say if he knew his wife was so rude?'

Frankie crossed her arms. 'What do you want?'

Dash forced a smile. 'How about we go inside and chat.'

Frankie shook her head. Why on earth had she let this go on for so long? She should have told Tom when it had first happened. She had no reason to feel guilty; she'd done nothing wrong. 'No, we'll chat here. Tell me what today's blackmail threat is and then we can both get on with our day.'

'Fine. I'm here to give you a heads-up. Rod and I have a business proposition for Tom.'

'What is it?'

'Don't you worry your sweet little self about it for now. Just be aware, sometime in the next few days I'll be talking to Tom. When he discusses the idea with you, make sure you think it's fantastic. Okay?'

'I'm not promising you anything,' Frankie said.

'Really?' Dash raised an eyebrow. 'Do you think that's a good idea? Are you happy for me to finally share our little secret?'

Frankie's stomach churned. She was a grown woman, supposedly setting a good example for her daughters. Why did she continue to let him intimidate her? She needed to be strong, and this needed to stop. She pushed open the front gate. 'Do whatever you want. You'll ruin your relationship with Tom; make sure you realise that.'

Dash snorted. 'You reckon? Willing to risk it? Don't forget my mate Justin walked in on us, saw you on top of me, saw me saying no. He'll be happy to tell Tom every detail.'

Heat coursed through Frankie's body. Would he really have his friend lie for him? How could he? It was bad enough he'd tried to force himself on her. She clenched her fists. How she'd like to smash that smirk off his face. 'You wouldn't dare.'

Dash's lips curled up at the corners, the smirk replaced with what a stranger may have mistaken for a genuine smile. 'No, you're right. Of course I wouldn't. Look, I'm sorry, okay? That night should never have happened. I was drunk and I was stupid. I'm glad you stopped me before we really did have something to hide from Tom. How about we agree to never discuss it again?'

Frankie stared at him. From bastard to charming in less than twenty seconds. It could flip back the other way just as quickly. 'Fine. Now can you go? I've got heaps to do.'

Dash slipped off the pillar. 'Sure, but please listen when Tom tells you about the business idea and see it as the great opportunity it is. He'll listen to you. I don't think it's much to ask.' He flashed Frankie another insincere smile, shoved his hands into his pockets and began whistling as he walked back down the street.

Frankie blew out a breath. Her stomach was in knots. How Tom's beautiful parents had produced a manipulative, lying, self-obsessed dirtbag like Dash, she would never understand. The only positive to come from the tragic accident that had claimed their lives was they weren't here to witness any of his behaviour. How she loathed him.

The next afternoon Frankie felt herself blush as the old ladies fussed around her. For goodness' sake, she'd only written some emails. You'd think she'd invented the Internet the way they were going on. She'd never been appreciated or encouraged as much as she had in the four years she'd worked as a volunteer at the Birkdale Retirement Village. Expecting to do a bit of sewing for some of the residents, Frankie had been surprised and delighted to meet the wonderfully entertaining duo of Mavis and Betty. They seemed to run the social side of the village, ensuring the residents were provided with plenty of entertainment. 'We're not here to die,' Mavis had told Frankie on the first day she'd volunteered. 'We're here to live, and live well.'

'Or at least go out with a big bang,' Betty had added.

Now Betty looked at Frankie, her eyes full of admiration. 'Where would we be without you, dear? You should start up your own computer business.'

Frankie laughed as she switched off the screen. If only her high school computer teacher could hear these old ladies talk. Perhaps he wouldn't have been quite so keen to tell her that switching on a television was probably as far as she should push herself when it came to understanding and using technology. 'My knowledge is pretty much limited to writing emails, so perhaps not the best idea.'

'You know more than emails,' Mavis tutted. 'What about that Google program? You're an expert.'

Frankie clamped her lips together. She couldn't wait to relay this latest stream of compliments to Tom. If she ever needed a self-esteem boost, these were the ladies to visit. 'Just because I can type words into a search engine doesn't mean I can run a business.'

'Search engine,' Mavis said. 'Listen to her, would you, Betty? She's got the lingo down pat, operates the computer like a whiz. You must think about it, dear. We'd pay you, wouldn't we, Betty?'

'Of course,' Betty said. 'With the amount of emails I send, I almost want someone's help full-time. Don't forget Twitterbook. I need a profile set up so I can friend my grandkids. They're dying for me to tweet apparently. You could show me how to do that.'

Frankie touched Betty on the arm and smiled. 'If anyone could conquer Twitterbook it would be you, but I think you might be talking about Facebook or maybe Twitter. You seem to be forgetting that I am here to help you, and for free. Why would you want to pay me?'

The old ladies exchanged a guilty glance.

Frankie sighed. 'Listen, I appreciate you looking out for me, but we're doing fine. I'm busy enough with everything I do now. I'm out every day delivering leaflets and that's a perfect job around the girls' school hours.'

'You're a wealth of knowledge, dear. You need to use it to help yourself,' Betty said.

'I understand you mean well, but other than email, using the Internet and basic word processing, my skills are fairly limited. I'm not even employable. Believe me, I've tried.' Frankie cringed as she thought of the last job interview she'd attended. A nineteen-year-old had looked down her nose at her and informed Frankie that she did not have the skills for the position. A position that could be summed up as general dogsbody. 'Helping you send emails is a change from mending your clothes.'

'Maybe you should start a clothing-repair business,' Mavis said. 'There are so many people here who would pay for that service.'

Betty nodded in agreement.

Frankie closed down the computer. 'What is it with you two today? You seem very keen for me to turn you all into customers and charge you, instead of allowing me to do the volunteer work I happily signed up for.'

'A young girl like you deserves more,' Mavis said.

'Why? I'm blessed with a gorgeous husband and two beautiful girls. What else would I want?' Frankie was beginning to regret sharing information from her personal life with these two. Ever since she'd mentioned that they lived from week to week, the ladies had grilled her about Tom's job and presented her with money-making ideas. Yes, it would be nice to have more money, but jobs weren't growing on trees and they were in a good place right now. The old ladies didn't seem to appreciate this. Frankie shuddered as she thought back to eight years earlier. Tom had been laid off and was unable to get work for nine months. Providing for a young family had been incredibly stressful. Tom's wage might not be a lot, but he had a full-time position which gave them security and a regular income.

'Forget we said anything.' Mavis patted Frankie's hand. 'Your business is not ours to meddle in.'

A smile played on Frankie's lips. 'I think you ladies should concentrate on something more important, like afternoon tea.' She directed them towards the door.

'Will you stay for a cuppa, dear?'

Frankie checked her watch. It was nearly two o'clock. Tom and the girls would still be at the gardens. 'I won't today. My family are having a picnic and I promised I'd join them.'

Mavis sighed. 'Sounds lovely. You enjoy your afternoon and call or email if you need anything at all.'

Frankie chuckled as the two ladies made their way into the dining room, wondering what business ideas they would come up with between now and her next visit. She collected her belongings and walked quickly out of the retirement village towards the train station.

Frankie's delight at the vibrant explosion of red and yellow leaves that engulfed the magnificent elm and oak trees of Melbourne's Botanic Gardens quickly disappeared when she spotted her family at their regular spot on the lawns at Picnic Point. Anger instantly replaced her joyous mood. What was *he* doing here? Their monthly Saturday outing to the gardens was for their small family only. The time was precious, and it was an unspoken rule that neither Frankie nor Tom invited anyone to join them.

Fern was the first to notice her approaching as she stepped off the path and on to the lush green lawn overlooking Ornamental Lake. The freshly dug earth of new garden beds, coupled with the cool, fresh breeze coming off the small lake, would normally have Frankie stopping and inhaling large lungfuls of the crisp autumn air, but not today. Fern nearly knocked her down when she rushed over to hug her. Frankie did her best to push her anger aside and managed a laugh before hugging her close. She linked arms with her daughter and walked to the little group. The picnic rugs were spread in their usual place, positioned carefully to catch the afternoon sun. Hope glanced up and gave Frankie a brief smile before returning to the book she was engrossed in. A smile; that was progress. Hope had adopted a permanent glare whenever Frankie tried to question her about school and whether anything was wrong.

Tom's face flooded with relief when Frankie arrived. His dark hair was a mess, as if he'd been continually running his fingers through it, the way he did when he was stressed. He managed a smile. 'Hi, babe. Oldies happy?'

'Yep, fixed them up for another week or so.' Frankie turned her attention to Dash. 'I wasn't expecting you here today.'

'Good to see you.' Dash made motions to get up and hug Frankie, but she waved him back down. He would never touch her again.

'No need, relax,' she told him. 'So, what's been happening?'

'I was just telling Tom about a fantastic business opportunity that's come my way. Rod's too, actually.'

Tom gave Frankie a tight smile. 'Yeah, my brothers are looking for investors, and Dash is the spokesperson.'

Frankie laughed, sitting down on the picnic rug to join the conversation. 'I can't imagine we're on the top of your list of potential investors. I'm assuming you need people who actually have money. What's the business?'

'Charter fishing. A mate of mine is moving up north, so he wants to sell up. It does pretty well already and Rod and me reckon we could improve things heaps. We'd own two boats; one needs a bit of work but the other is in great nick. The deal includes everything – the gear, clients, future bookings. It's a once in a lifetime opportunity.' Dash hardly drew a breath as he described the business.

'Sounds wonderful,' Frankie said. 'I hope you find some investors. Can the bank help?'

'They'll give us most of the capital based on our current incomes, but there's a shortfall of a hundred and fifty grand.'

'That's where we come in,' Tom said.

Frankie laughed again. 'Dash, take a look at our beat-up rental house, our invisible car and our hand-made and op-shop clothes. Doesn't it give you some idea of our financial situation?'

Dash nodded. 'Yeah, but the manager said if you had an income, loaning you the money should be no problem.'

'Did you want Tom to be a partner, too?'

Dash averted his gaze. 'No. We didn't think it was up his alley and he'd probably need to stay in his job to guarantee the loan repayments.'

Guarantee the loan repayments. Did Dash honestly believe his bullying techniques the other day would have her agree to this? He must be out of his mind. They could hardly afford to feed themselves, let alone make loan repayments when Dash fell behind.

'Babe, they want us to go into bloody debt for them so they can run a business together that we have nothing to do with. Not up my alley? I've only loved fishing since I was three.' Tom's eyes flashed with a mixture of anger and pain.

Frankie tensed. Why did Dash always do this? She couldn't remember a catch-up with him when he didn't ask for something, causing anger and disappointment for Tom in the process.

'Don't be such a bloody drama queen,' Dash said. 'It'd only be a loan on paper. Me and Rod would pay you back.'

Frankie forced herself to look at Dash. 'If you can't make the repayment, are we responsible?'

'Well, yes, technically I suppose, but not with our plan. Blue Water Charters will only be profitable. We'd give you a percentage of the profit of course.'

'Most small businesses take a while to make a profit,' Frankie said. 'I've even read that a lot fail within the first few years. What if this happens?'

Dash didn't get a chance to answer.

'No.' Tom crossed his arms.

Dash scowled. 'What? You and Frankie need to discuss things.'

Tom glanced at Frankie. 'We already have an answer, don't we?'

Frankie nodded.

'We're not going into debt on your behalf, not when we can't pay it back,' Tom said.

'Oh, for fuck's sake, you wouldn't be paying anything. You aren't listening to me.'

'Don't talk like that in front of the girls.' Tom's voice was sharp. 'Why don't you go and hassle someone else for the money? We're trying to enjoy our afternoon, not be harassed by you. You still owe me five hundred dollars from Rod's twenty-first. That was eight years ago. As if I'm going to trust you with a hundred and fifty grand.'

Dash stood up. He looked as if steam would come out of his nostrils at any second. 'Fine. Be an arsehole,' he said. 'Rod told me I'd be wasting my time talking to you. He obviously knows you better than I do. And for the record, Frankie, the deal's off.'

They sat in silence as Dash stormed off, hands shoved deep into his pockets.

Tom finally spoke. 'What a nerve. My brothers are a piece of work. We only ever hear from them when they want something, yet they give nothing in return. I didn't see any presents at Christmas for the girls, did you?'

'Be fair,' Frankie said. 'Rod always makes an effort. Dash doesn't, but he's only twenty-five and doesn't appreciate family life. Let it go. There's no point getting worked up about it.'

'I'm not.'

'The vein in your forehead is bulging. It's a bit of a giveaway.'

Fern nodded. 'Be careful, Dad. I think you might explode.'

Tom sighed. 'Sorry. He constantly disappoints me. The last time I heard from him was when he moved and wanted me to lift all the heavy stuff. Before that it was bailing him out after the bar brawl. He's never offered to help us. My parents would be doing somersaults in their graves if they knew. Anyway, what was he talking about, the deal being off?'

Frankie's gut twisted. 'Who knows? I have no idea what he's talking about half the time. I don't think he does either.' She hated lying to Tom, but she'd made a promise to a dying woman. A promise that she would look after her boys and make sure they remained a family. She could hardly go back on her word, especially after all her mother-in-law had done for her.

She moved closer to Tom and put her arms around him. 'Try to forget about him. He's self-absorbed and probably doesn't realise how much we struggle. We've got each other; that's the main thing.'

'Yeah, Dad,' Fern joined in. 'We love you. Ignore him.'

'Second that,' Hope said, not looking up from her book.

Tom smiled. 'Where would I be without you lot?'

'Alone, like Mr Duck in the lake.' Fern broke up some bread and walked over to the water.

'They're good kids, aren't they?'

Frankie nodded. 'We're lucky.'

'Thank God they're not like Dash.'

'Yes, thank God.' Not only would Frankie ensure they were not like Dash, but they would never spend time alone with their uncle again. 'Come on, lie down and forget about him.'

Tom allowed Frankie to pull him down next to her on the picnic rug. They lay together watching as Fern coaxed the duck closer.

A short time later Frankie shivered. The sun had sunk behind the city buildings and the temperature had dropped. She got to her feet. 'As much as I'd love to keep lazing around, we'd better head home before we freeze. I'm pretty sure a train leaves in about fifteen minutes. We should be able to catch it if we hurry.'

Frankie was right, and it wasn't long before they were all sitting on the four o'clock express. The buildings flashed by as they moved further away from Melbourne's centre. The terraced houses quickly gave way to larger, more expensive homes. Frankie wondered how often the people left their sanctuaries to enjoy time at the gardens. Did they need to escape like her and Tom? Frankie let her mind wander, conjuring up stories about the inhabitants of these houses. The stories changed as they sped away from the inner-city suburbs and the neighbourhoods began to take on a tired, neglected feel. The beautifully manicured gardens were replaced with a mishmash of overgrown and even concrete allotments. At last they reached their station and piled out, ready to walk the short distance home. Frankie squeezed Tom's arm as Hope and Fern chatted companionably. She cherished the family time they spent together. The old Hope, the smiling, happy fifteen-year-old, seemed to have joined them for the afternoon.

As they walked down Lincoln Street, Hope moved away from Fern and picked up the pace. Two boys were standing at the corner ahead of them. They looked about the same age as Hope, who was now a good twenty metres in front of her family, her eyes firmly on the ground as she passed the boys. They said something to her and burst out laughing. Hope walked faster.

Frankie looked sharply at Tom. 'What was that about?'

'No idea, they're probably at school together.'

The boys sniggered again as Fern passed them, trying to catch up to Hope. She stopped, and for a moment Frankie thought she was going to say something but decided against it and kept walking.

Frankie's heart rate quickened. 'They'd better not be being mean.'

'Why would they?'

Frankie didn't respond. They were now level with the boys. She stopped. 'Afternoon.'

They exchanged a look and laughed harder.

'Something funny? Or are you being deliberately rude?' Tom asked.

'No, sir,' the taller of the two said, his cheeks colouring. 'Only having a bit of fun.'

'Okay, you make sure that's all it is.' He turned to Frankie. 'I'm going on ahead to check on the girls.'

Laughter spilled from the shorter of the boys as Tom ran on. 'He can run. Not a complete no-hoper, then.'

'Stop,' his friend hissed.

'Why?' the other said. 'I'd say, looking at those losers, Hope's probably got no hope at all, what do you reckon?'

Frankie jabbed a finger at the boy. She was furious. Even his friend had told him to stop. 'Like to repeat that?'

The boy looked Frankie up and down. 'Was talking to my mate. None of your business.'

Frankie stepped closer. She couldn't believe the cheek of this kid. 'You made it my business.'

'So what? You gonna run us down with your car? Oh sorry, I forgot, you don't have one. Bike maybe? Oops, silly me, you probably haven't got one of those either.'

Frankie shook her head, turned and started walking towards home. There was no point talking to this kid. The arrogance that spewed from him was putrid. Luckily, the others were out of sight and hearing. She ignored the increasing volume of a single voice chanting 'no-hopers' behind her. It wasn't hard to guess which of the two boys that was. She clenched her fists. Was this why Hope hid in the school library?

Frankie stopped in front of their gate and took a deep, calming breath. She sighed as she looked at their rented house. It was badly in need of repainting. Peeling paint and broken boards took away any charm it may once have had. The rusted iron panels on the roof were in desperate need of replacement, but as their leaks were minimal the owner refused to spend money on them. Frankie was sure that the removal of the wire fencing that separated them from the next-door neighbour would improve the aesthetics, but it was required to keep the neighbour's yapping dog in. She bent down and yanked at a weed that poked out through the front wall. She did her best to keep the garden tidy and the house as clean as possible, but overall the house, which at best would be described as a demolisher's delight, was virtually impossible to present nicely. The boys had touched a nerve. True, they didn't have a lot of money, but she'd never considered that they looked poor. Bloody kids. She pushed open the broken gate and walked up to the house. Tom and Hope were talking as she came in.

'They're idiots, Dad.'

'What else do they say?'

'Oh nothing, honestly. They tease everyone in the class and we all ignore them.'

'They called me "Mini-No-Hope",' Fern said. 'I hate them.'

Frankie came into the kitchen and embraced Fern. 'I think Hope's got things sorted. Don't waste any more energy on them.'

'They're just stupid boys,' Hope said. 'I've got homework to finish – I'll be in my room.'

Frankie let go of Fern and followed Hope.

'Are you sure you're alright, sweetheart?'

'I'm fine.'

'Are they the only ones being horrible? Is it because we don't have much money?'

'No, they use anything they can to be mean. The tall one, Hamish, he's not too bad. It's Pearce – the short, nasty one – who causes most of the trouble. I can't imagine why they're friends. He thinks he's hilarious calling me "No-Hope".'

Frankie walked over to where Hope lay on the bed and sat down next to her. 'You keep ignoring him. If he gets worse, or upsets you, come to me and I'll talk to the school.'

'It's fine,' Hope said. 'Don't worry about me. I'm not five. I don't need my mummy sticking up for me.' She got up and moved over to the small table she used as a desk. 'Gotta get this essay finished.'

Frankie knew when she'd been dismissed. She stood and stopped in Hope's doorway. 'If something else happens tell me, won't you?'

Hope rolled her eyes.

'I mean it. You don't need to put up with that kind of behaviour.'

Hope said nothing, her eyes now focused on her books.

Unease settled over Frankie as she hesitated in the doorway. The likelihood of this sullen, sulky version of her daughter discussing the problem with her was zero.

Chapter Three

Shauna leant back in her chair as Josh continued his presentation to Craig and the department heads. She was impressed. He'd had them eating out of his hands the moment he'd started speaking. Two weeks had passed since they'd returned from Sydney and Josh had shown he was keen to prove that he was an asset to the company. This was the second marketing meeting Shauna had sat in on and the amount of work he had achieved in such a short time was phenomenal. A new radio commercial would be airing the next day and an outdoor advertising campaign was under discussion now. Josh had mock-ups of the ads on display and Shauna could see from the directors' faces that they were captivated. So was she. He certainly knew his stuff. His passion and enthusiasm were contagious. A small smile played on Shauna's lips as she thought back to their middle-of-the-night encounter in Sydney. He probably wouldn't be thrilled if he knew she was picturing him in his Mickey Mouse boxers right at this moment.

'So, I would like a show of hands for your preferred ad,' Josh said. 'Once we've confirmed our choice with the agency, it will appear on the side of Kings' buses starting Friday next week.' He held up the artwork from the first version of the ad.

After a decision had been made – a clear majority in favour of the third choice – Josh wrapped up the meeting. Shauna stayed behind as the other department heads retreated to their offices. She clapped her hands together slowly. 'Clever, very clever.'

'What, the one they chose?'

'No, not the ad. I meant the way you manipulated them. I was told they would be deciding on the concept of outdoor advertising, a decision you helped them bypass altogether by focusing on the actual advertisement.'

Josh finished collecting his papers and winked. 'I hoped nobody would notice. I'm not waiting for a bunch of directors to make those kinds of decisions. That's my job. They approved the ad I wanted them to.'

'The other three weren't brilliant.'

Josh laughed. 'They were as dull as they needed to be. I made my choice yesterday and unfortunately the set-up here is I need to kiss everyone's arse and make them think they approved it. So I give them one good one and three mediocre, and guess what? I get my ad.'

'What if they'd chosen one of the reject ones?'

'Wouldn't happen. Now, moving on to more important matters, are you coming for a drink with us tonight?'

'Us?'

'Yes, the staff. You know, those other weird-looking people who hang around the office.'

Shauna rolled her eyes. 'Very funny. How on earth do you make friends so quickly?'

'Told you in Sydney. Funny, charming, adorable. Surely you remember?'

'You left out conceited. Seriously, you've connected with more of the staff in two weeks than I've managed in over twelve months.'

Josh shrugged. 'I make the effort to get to know people.'

'And I don't?'

'You tell me.'

Shauna laughed. 'No, I suppose I don't. I learnt my lesson in my last job. I'm trying to keep my social and professional lives as separate as possible.'

'So I can't twist your arm to come for one drink?'

'No, not this time. I'm having dinner at my mother's. Another night perhaps.'

Josh tapped his fingers on the table, not bothering to respond.

Shauna folded her arms in front of her. 'What?'

'What do you think? This is the second or third rejected invitation. I think I should be taking the hint. It'll save you coming up with any more excuses.'

'They're not excuses. I'm just busy. I have a history of cancelling on my mother and she won't be impressed if I do it again.' Shauna knew it would be quicker to just get dinner over with than have to listen to her mother complaining that Shauna didn't care about her.

'Not close with your mum?'

'It's a bit hard to be.' Shauna hesitated. She didn't usually discuss her mother with other people but something about the way Josh was looking at her made her feel like she wanted to tell him more. 'She has a few issues which makes it difficult to have a close relationship with her.'

'Oh,' Josh said. 'I'm sorry to hear that. What sort of issues?'

Shauna sighed. 'Mood swings, anxiety issues, impulsive behaviour. She can swing from being paranoid to being manipulative quite quickly. She's very self-centred. She's one of those people who likes a huge fuss made of her but doesn't reciprocate. Forgets my birthday most of the time.' Shauna gave a weak smile. 'Actually, I should be fair. She did remember last week, although I'm not sure if the three seconds it took to shove a lotto ticket into a card really counts.'

'She doesn't sound like much fun,' Josh said. 'Has she been diagnosed with an actual problem?'

29

Shauna shook her head. 'No. In her opinion she doesn't have a problem. If she's upset with me it's because of what I've done, there's no other reason. The same with her other relationships. She's never at fault if things go wrong. She doesn't believe her mood swings and behaviour are abnormal. I've tried to get her to talk to her GP to see if there is anything that could help her, but she won't.'

Josh's eyes were filled with sympathy.

Shauna cleared her throat. She shouldn't have spoken about her mother; it was better to keep that problem to herself. As much as she knew she should give up hoping things might change, there was a small part of her that just couldn't. Since her father had abandoned them when she was four, she'd craved a close relationship with her mother. She wanted her mother to show an interest in her, be supportive and proud. Even though she often wondered if her mother had undiagnosed issues, it was difficult to constantly overlook her behaviour because of them. Thirty years after her father had walked out she continued to find herself disappointed.

'Sounds like hard work,' Josh said.

Shauna nodded. 'I won't bore you with any more details.' She stood, collected her notepad and pen and walked towards the door. Letting her guard down with Josh was out of character and left her feeling a little unsettled. 'I'll join you all for a drink another night.'

Josh smiled. 'Not sure I should believe you, but I'll hold you to it anyway.'

Shauna sat down at her desk, her forehead creased in a frown. What was it about Josh that made her speak without thinking? Her mother was a topic she rarely discussed. She'd done her best to keep her mother separate from her life from a very young age. When she'd been at school, she'd only invited friends over if she knew for sure her mother would be out. She didn't want to have to explain her mother's moods and unpredictable rages to anyone, particularly as she hadn't understood them herself. As an adult it had been much easier to avoid bringing her friends into contact with her mother. Simon had, of course, met her, and to be fair, her mother had been on her best behaviour on the few occasions they'd had dinner together. *The few occasions.* It was more than enough in the four years they'd been dating but it saddened Shauna that she didn't have a close relationship with her mother, or any other family.

She sighed, reopening a proposal for Dark Depths, another potential mining client, and did her best to push all thoughts of her mother out of her head.

An hour later, as she emailed the finished document through to the client, the phone on her desk rang.

'Shauna Jones.'

'Now that's a voice I've missed.'

Shauna froze as the familiar, deep, smiling voice filled the line. *Simon.*

'Shauna?'

She cleared her throat. 'Yes, I'm here.' She willed her heart rate to slow down. She was over him. She could not let him have this effect on her a year later.

'How are you?'

Shauna closed her eyes momentarily before standing. She needed to switch on her professional self and find out what he wanted and get rid of him. 'Simon, why are you ringing? I thought you were off *seeing the world*.' She hated that the sarcasm was so evident in her delivery. But who could blame her? The night their relationship had ended twelve months earlier should have been one of the biggest nights of celebration in her life. Simon had been hinting for weeks that a proposal was looming and to top it off she'd been offered the position at I-People. Not only was it a great job opportunity, but it was also going to solve the issues she and Simon had developed by working together. He'd struggled to accept that her success rate with clients was higher than his and she believed at times he'd tried to undermine her, not only taking credit for her work but suggesting to clients they request him as their account manager rather than her. He'd denied doing either of these things, and she'd decided that working in different organisations would be the ideal way to remove this as a threat to their relationship. She loved him; they had fun together, shared the same interests and a wonderful group of friends. The solution around work had been obvious and, as it turned out, landing the role with the most prominent recruitment player in the Australian market had been exactly the right move for her. Or so she'd thought.

'I'm back for three months.'

Simon's voice snapped Shauna out of her thoughts.

'I've spent a lot in the last twelve months travelling, and getting work in London hasn't been as easy as I hoped. Tony, the new CTO at Recruit, has a three-month contract he wants me to work on.'

'And then?'

'*And then* I'll have enough money to travel for another twelve months at least.'

Shauna remained silent, waiting for him to explain why he thought he could ring as if nothing had happened. As if they hadn't broken up so abruptly and unexpectedly. Well, unexpectedly for her, perhaps not for him.

Simon cleared his throat. 'I thought you might like to catch up over dinner or a drink. I'd love to tell you about my travels and hear about your new job. I've missed you.'

Shauna shook her head. 'You've been gone for twelve months and this is the first time I've heard from you. The last conversation we had was you giving me an ultimatum that I throw away my career and follow you around the world or our relationship was over. I thought we were going out to celebrate that night, not end our relationship. You'd been hinting about rings and proposals for weeks.'

'The ring was in my pocket.'

Silence filled the phone line and a lump formed in Shauna's throat. How differently things might have turned out.

Simon's voice lowered. 'I never thought you'd choose your job over me.'

'And I never thought you'd make me choose.'

'Look, I'm not sure I handled it all that well but the one thing I do know from my trip is I've missed you. I've missed your enthusiasm for your work and the stories about your clients. I've missed telling you about my day too. I'm not looking to get back together, Shauna, but we were such good friends. I miss our friendship.'

So did she.

'Come on, let me buy you a drink at least. We parted badly last year so if nothing more we could at least part as friends this time.'

Shauna pictured the smile that was playing on his lips. The smile that she'd never been able to resist. She did hate how things had ended, but it was his fault. There'd been no reason to do things the way he had. She sighed; maybe catching up with him would be a step in the direction of forgiving him, or at least being able to move forward without constantly questioning how things had ended so badly.

'Fine. I'm free after work on Wednesday. Meet me at the Zee Bar at six.'

◆ ◆ ◆

Shauna followed her mother out to the kitchen, her hands stacked with dirty glasses and dishes. It had been an effort to enjoy the succulent roast lamb dinner when the conversation, that had initially been friendly, turned argumentative. 'I don't know why you invited me. He obviously can't stand me.'

Shauna's delight at finding her mother in a cheerful and friendly mood when she'd arrived at the townhouse had been short-lived. When Bob, Lorraine's latest boyfriend, emerged from the living room, Shauna's own good mood had instantly dampened. It wasn't going to be a night of enjoying her mother's unusually upbeat mood by herself. As the meal progressed, Lorraine's mood had changed to one of anger and accusation.

Plates clattered on the bench as Lorraine turned to face her daughter. The thick make-up she insisted on caking on each day did nothing to disguise her contempt. 'Always have to stir things up, don't you? You're the one causing trouble.'

Shauna moved to the dishwasher and began loading the dishes. 'Me? You're kidding? He hasn't stopped since I walked in. Sneering every time I try to say something. What's his problem, other than being drunk?'

Lorraine passed Shauna the glasses. 'His problem is you pointing out you earn at least three times what he's earned at any time during his career. It's disrespectful. You and your horrible attitude are why he's drunk more than usual.'

Shauna gasped. How could her mother misinterpret the conversation to such an extreme? 'Hold on a minute. He pestered me for over fifteen minutes to find out my salary and you encouraged him. I only asked if he ever aspired to be an engineer when he was working as a draftsperson. Showing an interest is not suggesting he was a failure.'

'Interest?' Bob stood in the doorway of the kitchen, using the doorframe to steady himself. 'Yeah, right.'

Shauna turned to face him. 'Do you need to be rude every time we meet? What's that about?'

Bob waggled his finger at Shauna. 'You're a troublemaker. Always in your mother's ear to get rid of me. Won't work, I love her and she loves me.'

Lorraine moved over to Bob's side. 'Come on, darl, let's go and sit back down. It's not worth wasting your breath.'

Shauna shook her head as her mother guided Bob back to the living room. Three would always be a crowd for Lorraine. She didn't seem to be able to handle more than one relationship at a time. If there was a man in her life, she took out every frustration on her daughter. Shauna took a deep breath, collected her bag from the kitchen bench, and made her way down the hallway towards the front door. She stopped briefly as she caught Lorraine's words coming from the living room. 'Even as a child she was incredibly jealous, hated having to share me with anyone.' Lorraine gave a bitter laugh. 'Didn't exactly help me with relationships. They often ended because of Shauna's outbursts. I sometimes wonder if that was the real reason her father left.'

A lump formed in Shauna's throat. She'd heard her mother say similar to this on other occasions and did her best to ignore the comments. Her mother was notorious for not taking responsibility for her own actions. As a result, Shauna would never really know why her father left them. Still, even if it wasn't true, the words still hurt. She couldn't listen to any more, so she slipped out of the front door and hurried down the driveway, blinking away the tears that threatened to fall.

Chapter Four

Frankie swung the leaflet-filled tote bag over her shoulder and walked away from the house towards the gate. 'Come on, girls. Time to get to school.'

Hope and Fern came out of the front door, bags casually slung over their shoulders.

Frankie raised an eyebrow at her youngest daughter. 'Fern, darling, as lovely as they are, you can't wear those shoes.'

Fern dropped her bag on the path. 'Why not?'

'Converse aren't part of the school uniform. And I know you love them, but they're too big. Erica was very kind to hand them down to you, but she should have checked your shoe size first. Quickly, go and change.'

'They're not too big.'

Frankie shrugged. 'Irrelevant. They're not part of the school uniform. Go and take them off.'

Shoulders slumped, Fern turned and dragged her feet back into the house.

Moments later Frankie nodded as Fern reappeared in her school shoes. She held out a pile of advertising leaflets to each girl.

Hope didn't reach out for hers. 'Really, Mum? Do I have to do this? It's embarrassing.'

Frankie stared at her daughter. 'Embarrassing? The job that puts food on the table is embarrassing? I'm sorry you feel like that.'

Hope had the good grace to flush. She said nothing more and took the leaflets from Frankie. They set off, posting them into every letterbox on the way to school. Twenty-five minutes later they reached the school gate and said their goodbyes.

A friendly voice spoke from behind Frankie. 'I'm surprised she'll still help you.'

Frankie turned around to see a mum she recognised from Hope's class. 'Sorry, what did you say?'

'That.' She pointed at the tote bag full of leaflets. 'Hope's fifteen. I'm surprised she's helping. Logan's the same age and she won't even talk to me. I'm Sheila. Sheila Matheson.'

Frankie shook the hand Sheila offered and smiled. 'I'm lucky. They're great kids. They understand the need to work.' Frankie tried her best to forget the look Hope had given her earlier. 'I'm Frankie, by the way.'

Sheila's huge hoop earrings jangled as she nodded her head. 'I think my kids need a lesson in hard work. They've had it good for far too long. We aren't rich by any means, but we're not in your situation. Perhaps I should take things off them and make them earn some money. Even get them into second-hand clothes like yours are.'

Frankie blinked. 'I didn't realise we looked so poor.'

Sheila's hand flew up to her mouth. 'Oh gosh, please forgive me, my feet seem to be permanently planted down my throat. Logan happened to mention you struggle from time to time, that's all. I think Hope might have mentioned a few things to her.'

'Really? Hope said something?'

'Oh, nothing much. Just that she envies Logan's wardrobe and can't even imagine what going to the races would be like.' Sheila smiled. 'I'm afraid Logan does have the tendency to brag, particularly about our racehorses. Just a hobby, of course, but dressing up and going to the track is something we love to do. My husband says I spoil her, but I don't think so. I like nice things and so does my daughter. If fact, we should take Hope with us one day. Get her out of her rut, give her something to look forward too. I'm sure Logan would have an outfit that Hope could borrow.'

Frankie took a deep breath, deciding to ignore Sheila's thoughtless comments. She found it hard to imagine Hope saying she envied Logan's clothes or lifestyle. Hope was a very private person, like Frankie.

'That's kind of you to offer. I'm sure Logan and Hope can work something out.'

Sheila nodded, her eyes travelling to Frankie's tote bag. 'How long have you been delivering the leaflets?'

'Close to eight years, I think. I started after Tom was laid off. Jobs I could do during school hours were pretty scarce so this one worked well for us.'

Sheila gasped. 'Eight years! But surely something else has come up in that time?'

Frankie laughed. 'Not that I've been suitable for. Jobs are still pretty scarce, especially those that require no skills and fit into school hours. As hard as this may be to believe, I enjoy my job. It keeps me fit, I'm outdoors and I explore the neighbourhood every day.'

The look of distaste on Sheila's face suggested she wasn't convinced. She forced a smile and patted Frankie on the arm. 'As long as you're happy. Now, as much as I'd love to stay and chat, I'd better go.' She held up a hand. 'Nails are a mess. Time to get to the salon.'

Frankie watched as Sheila hurried towards the car park. Frankie had been honest, she did enjoy delivering leaflets. Over the years, she had seen babies grow into toddlers, toddlers grow into school-age children and school-age children drive off to start lives of their own. She'd seen houses sold and new residents arrive, houses knocked down and rebuilt, and she'd enjoyed working out whose house the monthly book club was being held at. So much was going on in the streets where they lived.

As she turned to leave Frankie saw a familiar face. The short boy who'd been nasty to Hope on the weekend was talking to an older woman. She made a beeline for them. Before she reached him, the boy turned and ran towards the school building.

Frankie kicked the ground in front of her, stopping only a few metres from the woman. 'Little coward.'

'I beg your pardon.' The woman faced Frankie. 'Are you talking about my son?'

Frankie nodded, taking in the woman's appearance as she made eye contact. Her face seemed unable to show any expression it was so pumped full of something. 'Yes, I am. I wanted to talk to him, but he took off like a frightened rabbit the minute he saw me.'

The woman crossed her arms. 'And what is it that you've done that would cause my son to react that way?'

Frankie snorted. 'What I've done? That's a good one. He's been horrible to my daughter and I want it to stop.'

'Excuse me? Pearce is a decent, well-brought-up boy. Whatever your daughter's told you is lies.' The woman's voice and eyes were starting to show her anger, even though her facial expression remained unchanged.

Frankie hadn't finished. 'I witnessed your son and his mate harassing Hope on Sunday so I'm afraid you can't defend him. Her name is Hope and the constant teasing and calling her *No*-Hope needs to stop. It's disgusting to turn our situation into a weapon.'

'What are you implying? My son is calling your daughter names because of your financial situation?'

'Yes, and it's disgusting and hurtful.'

The woman put her hands on her hips, her eyes locking with Frankie's. 'Here's some advice for you. Get your lazy husband to go out and find a job and move yourself off Dole Street. Give your kids something to aspire to.'

Frankie gasped. How dare she? She knew nothing about their life. It was little wonder her son was a bully. Frankie opened her mouth to defend herself but was cut off.

'I haven't finished. Instead of giving me some pathetic excuse, stop thinking about yourself for just one second and think about how hard your laziness makes my life. I'm sick to death of watching my husband work himself into the ground to pay ridiculous amounts of tax so you can claim every bit of welfare under the sun. Get off your high horse having a go at my son, who's only pointing out exactly what you are, and do something about it.'

'How dare you make assumptions about my family?' Frankie's body shook as she spat out the words. 'You know nothing about us.'

The woman shrugged. 'I know enough. Now, I'd better get on. Some of us contribute to the community. You should consider trying it.' Looking down her nose at Frankie one more time, she turned, the click-clack of her heels echoing as she crossed the schoolyard.

Tom arrived home after working an early shift to find Frankie sitting on the couch, eyes red-rimmed, with a box of tissues by her side.

'She said what?'

'That we're dole-bludgers living off her husband's tax and her son was only being honest calling us no-hopers.'

'Bitch!' Tom paced around the living room. 'Who the hell does she think she is? We hardly get any help from the government and we pay tax.' He picked up a cushion and Frankie was worried he might rip it apart. She got up and took it off him.

'Come on, sit down. Us getting upset and angry isn't really going to help.'

Tom sighed, allowing Frankie to lead him to the couch. He took her hand. 'Stupid woman. First the kid upsets Hope and now us. We don't even know her name and she's managed to get us all worked up.' He pulled Frankie close and kissed her. 'Let's ignore her. We've had a tough time, but we're working hard and doing everything possible for our family. She was probably born with a silver spoon shoved right up her surgically enhanced butt.'

Frankie managed a small laugh. 'I'm not sure her kids would be in public school if that was the case. I think she was actually going to work.' She frowned. 'You don't think other people believe we're living off welfare, do you?'

Tom shook his head. 'They better bloody not. We work hard and the few benefits we get, like rental assistance and family tax benefits, most of them are getting too.'

'I wish we didn't even have to accept those,' Frankie said.

Tom hugged Frankie closer to him. 'Forever independent, aren't you? Remember when we first had Hope? You wanted to pay back every cent the government gave us as assistance and the same when I was laid off too.'

'I hate the idea of handouts.'

'Mmm.' Tom stroked Frankie's leg. 'I can think of something we could do to make us both feel a whole lot better.' He got up from the couch and took Frankie's hand. 'Come on, there's nearly an hour before the girls get home from school.'

Frankie smiled and allowed herself to be tugged up and led to the bedroom. Hopefully, Tom's plans would help stop the awful words replaying in her mind.

Frankie was calm and relaxed as she set about delivering her leaflets the next day. The girls had been in great form all morning. Even Hope had made an effort to act like a human being. She hugged a secret smile as she thought back to the afternoon before. After sixteen years the passion still existed between her and Tom.

Frankie wound her way around to Baar Street, with the pub on the corner and row of shops below. She stopped as usual outside the pub to chat to her beloved Pete. He was up on his feet, tail wagging the moment he recognised her. 'How are you, my beautiful boy?' Frankie scratched Pete behind the ears. He watched her adoringly as she stroked and petted him. She dug into her bag and pulled out a package of tin foil. At least once a week Frankie would try to save a leftover to give Pete a treat. Today was a sausage and he wolfed it down appreciatively. One last pat and Frankie continued on her way.

She stopped, as she often did, to pick up some rubbish blowing along the street. She threw the paper in the bin and kept going. Before she reached her next letterbox she'd picked up a can, an empty chip packet and what she assumed was an old lottery ticket. About to throw the lot into a nearby bin, the word 'Mega Draw' caught her eye. She'd only just walked past the newsagent, which had signage spilling out of the door promoting a twenty-million-dollar mega draw. She checked the date and discovered it was being drawn that night. Frankie made her way back to the store, stopping again to pick up a bottle lying next to a bush. As she picked it up her hand brushed a mud-covered piece of paper. She extracted it, a faint orangey-red shimmer glowing through the mud. It was a twenty-dollar note. She grinned – a lottery ticket and twenty dollars. People really were careless. She pushed open the door to the newsagent.

'What brings you in here today, Frankie?' Jim, the owner, gave her his big welcoming smile.

'I'm returning these.' Frankie put the ticket and the twenty-dollar note on the counter. 'Someone's dropped them outside.'

Jim picked up the ticket and ran it through his system. 'It's not registered to anyone, love.' He looked at the ticket again. 'It's a Quick Pick. Someone's just come in and bought it and probably dropped it on their way out. So I've no way of telling whose it is. Why don't you keep it? Might be your lucky day.'

'But what if the owner comes in searching for their ticket?'

Jim looked carefully at the ticket. 'This was purchased last Wednesday. I'd say whoever dropped it is long gone.'

'I wouldn't feel right keeping something someone else paid for.'

'Okay, I'll keep it here in case someone comes in for it, but you can definitely keep the twenty dollars.'

Frankie shook her head. 'No, it's not mine; it wouldn't feel right.'

'Looking at how caked in mud it is, that money was dropped a long time ago. Enjoy it. Buy yourself and the girls a treat for afternoon tea.'

Frankie shook her head again. 'No, you keep it in case someone asks for it.'

This time it was Jim who shook his head. 'You do so much for others, Frankie. Let the universe shout you afternoon tea.'

Frankie laughed. 'I'm fine as I am, thanks, Jim.'

She turned to leave but Jim called out to her. 'Wait a minute.' He printed out a lottery ticket and handed it to Frankie. 'I'm using part of the twenty dollars to give you this. Who knows, it might be your lucky day.' He held up his hand as Frankie went to object. 'No arguments. If you win something you can shout me a coffee. And that's only part of the twenty dollars you found, so in a few weeks' time when there's a really big mega draw I'm going to give you another ticket, and there will be no arguments then either. Do you hear me?'

Frankie laughed at the mock severity in his voice. 'I guess I can't argue with that.' She took the ticket and tucked it in her pocket. 'I'd better get moving and finish my deliveries.'

Two hours later Frankie arrived home and stuck the ticket on the fridge. After a quick bite to eat she grabbed the shirt she was sewing for Hope. She had made it as close to the one Hope had been admiring in the window of Just Jeans a few weeks earlier. Matching the exact stitch had been difficult, but Frankie thought she had managed it. She couldn't wait to see Hope's face when she gave it to her. It should guarantee a smile.

Chapter Five

Shauna looked up as Josh poked his head around the door of her office.

'Okay, I'm not taking no for an answer. You're coming for a drink.'

Shauna laughed. 'Bossy, aren't you?'

Josh came into the office and sat down across from her. 'Not much choice when I'm dealing with you or you'll think you're wearing the pants in this relationship.'

'Relationship?' Shauna hesitated. He wasn't serious, was he? She'd come to realise there was a lot to like about Josh, but he was a work colleague and therefore could never be considered as anything else. 'I didn't realise we were having a relationship?'

'By the mere fact that we work and converse together, we are having a relationship.' Josh grinned. 'Don't worry, though, when this turns into the type of relationship you're thinking of you'll be blown away.'

Shauna smiled, relieved he was joking. 'Cocky, too. Don't hold your breath on it turning into *that* type of relationship. Been there, done that. Never again with a colleague.' She was aware that Josh was waiting for her to elaborate, but she didn't. Simon was not a topic she wanted to discuss. Instead, she tidied some papers on her desk before making eye contact. 'I hate to disappoint you once again, but I can't come out tonight. How about I say yes to Friday night instead?'

'I think I'll need that in writing.' Josh handed Shauna a piece of paper and a pen. 'I'm not convinced you actually exist outside of work.'

'Fine.' Shauna scribbled on the paper and handed it back to him.

He read her note and burst out laughing. 'Drinks slave? This is all it takes?' He stood and bowed. 'Madam, I'm happy to be your drinks slave for the evening. In fact, I'd be delighted to be any kind of slave you like.'

Shauna pointed to her office door. 'Go. You can prove to me on Friday how irresistible and charming you are, but right now I've got a presentation to finish and plans at six that I'll be lucky to make.'

'Who's the client?'

'Mifflins in Adelaide. They're not big enough yet to need your expert marketing input.'

'Mifflins? I read something about them in *OzBuzz* the other day. Did you see it?'

Shauna shook her head.

'My copy's at home. You're welcome to come home with me.' He raised his eyebrows and attempted to flutter his eyelashes. 'There are other things I could show you at the same time.'

Shauna laughed and once again pointed towards the door. 'Go.'

'Mmm, you like it rough – my kind of woman.' Josh winked and disappeared.

It was after five thirty by the time Shauna finalised her presentation. Butterflies flitted in her stomach as she packed up her computer and the files she needed for her trip to Adelaide. She'd done her best to push all thoughts of Simon out of her mind since their conversation on Monday, but in less than half an hour she was going to see him. She glanced at the clock; she really needed to get a copy of *OzBuzz* before tomorrow. She wouldn't have time before meeting up with Simon, but there was a combined supermarket and newsagent in Richmond that stayed open late. She'd stop there on her way home.

Shauna was surprised at how nervous she felt seeing Simon again. She'd spent twelve months doing her best to move on, never really expecting to see him again. And now, here she was, sitting across from him, listening as he enthusiastically regaled her with stories from his travels.

Southbank and the Zee Bar were quiet for a Wednesday night; even the sports bar only had a handful of people watching the replay of one of the weekend AFL games. The patio heaters were on, and the lights of the city twinkled on the Yarra River.

Simon had been waiting at an outside table when Shauna arrived. His previously pale skin was tanned, and he glowed with health and vitality. He hadn't hugged Shauna, which was good as she had no idea how she would react to that; instead he invited her to sit and quickly ordered drinks for both of them.

Now, as he spoke, his eyes sparkled, and he seemed genuinely delighted to see her. His charm and the attention he paid her made it difficult to remember the amount of pain he'd caused her. The Simon sitting in front of her was the Simon she'd been in love with. The Simon who, up until the night of the unexpected ultimatum, was the one she knew so well and assumed she'd be spending her life with.

After finishing telling her about his luck in befriending a wealthy American in Athens and sailing around the Greek islands for three weeks on his luxury yacht, Simon reached across the table and took Shauna's hand.

'I'm sorry. That's one of the main things I wanted to say to you. I hate the way things ended between us when I left. I've missed you and think that perhaps this break was what I needed to make me realise how much you mean to me.'

Shauna snatched her hand back. 'We're not on a break; we broke up. You ended our relationship.'

Simon tilted his head to one side. 'That's a difference of perspective. I felt like you ended our relationship. You could have come with me.'

'You asked me to give up everything I'd been working for. It was hardly a fair request.'

'It was for me. I assumed it was a no-brainer. Who wouldn't want to travel the world? It's the perfect time before settling down and thinking about having a family.'

'So you said twelve months ago. It's just a shame you'd never thought to discuss these travel plans with me before that night. You presented it as an ultimatum. It wasn't an invitation to do something wonderful with you. Your exact words were "Come with me and see the world, or I'll go alone and we're over." It was hardly a romantic proposition. You also sneered at the job offer I had with I-People and told me I'd be a loser to choose a job over a relationship.'

Simon blushed. 'I guess I didn't exactly woo you. Travelling alone has given me the chance to grow as a person. See the world for myself. I'm not looking for a relationship now, but I do miss our friendship. I'm only here for three months so would love to spend some time with you. Having so many mutual friends we'll probably bump into each other anyway – I know Cath has a party this weekend and I was planning on going. I assume you are too?'

Shauna shook her head. 'No, I didn't know about it.' It wasn't a surprise she hadn't been invited. She'd drifted away from the group she and Simon had been so close with. Other than Tess, who'd moved to Sydney two years earlier, the majority of the group had been Simon's friends before she'd met him. They'd embraced Shauna, and she had developed friendships with some of the women, but when she and Simon had broken up, she'd decided to distance herself from them. She didn't want to hear about Simon and what he was doing, or have sympathy directed at her because of the break-up. At the time she'd thought she wanted nothing more to do with him. As a result, it had been a lonely year. Shauna had thrown herself into her work and the new role at I-People and worked long hours and most weekends. She and Tess caught up with each other when she was in Sydney or if Tess was in Melbourne for work, but that was only every month or two at the most, and with Tess now overseas those catch-ups were via Instagram, Messenger and the occasional phone call.

Simon raised an eyebrow. 'Really? You're not still hanging out with the group?'

Shauna shook her head. 'I've moved on, Simon. Time to make some changes in my life.' She glanced at her watch. 'I'm on an early flight to Adelaide and need to pick up a few things on my way home. It's been nice to say hello, and I'm glad your travels have been so successful, but I need to go.'

Simon grabbed her arm as she stood. 'Can we do this again? Like I said, just as friends. I'm going again in three months, but I'd like to leave on better terms this time.'

Shauna stared at him. Was there any point? He was the man she'd thought she was going to spend the rest of her life with and now he was offering her a couple of catch-ups before he left again. While the idea of being friends with an ex sounded very reasonable and mature on paper, the reality wasn't clear-cut. She knew from the way her heart had pounded when he'd first rung, and the nerves she felt around him now, that she was far from over him. She wasn't ready to let go, and therefore she couldn't just be friends, but she also didn't want anything else. She could never trust him again.

'Let me think about it. I'm not sure how I feel to be honest.'

Simon nodded. 'Okay, but if I haven't heard from you by next week, I might become impatient and contact you.'

Shauna smiled. 'I'll contact you regardless, okay? Even if it is a text to ask you to leave me alone.'

Simon stood and placed his hands on either side of her shoulders. He leant forward and kissed her gently on the cheek. 'You'd never do that.'

Shauna pulled out of his embrace and walked out on to the path that meandered alongside the Yarra and led her back to her car. She gave herself a mental shake. She'd overheard staff referring to her as 'a ball-breaking bitch', yet around Simon she struggled to assert that side of herself. She had no problem doing it at work with her colleagues, and even when necessary with her clients, so why did Simon's presence shake her confidence and have her questioning what she wanted?

Shauna wasn't convinced she could answer any of the questions that plagued her as she drove out of the city towards Richmond. The catch-up with Simon had unsettled her. She reminded herself that hearing from him and seeing him again was unexpected, and that was why she felt shaken. She pushed thoughts of her ex out of her mind as she pulled into Swan Street and saw that the supermarket and newsagent were still open. She needed to get her mind back on to work – the presentation to Mifflins the next day was important.

She entered the store and was relieved to see that they still had copies of *OzBuzz* magazine. She picked one up and, rummaging in her bag for her purse as she walked, took it to the counter. When she opened her purse, she noticed the lotto ticket her mother had given her for her birthday tucked into the note compartment. Taking it out, she checked the date of the draw. It was last night. She held it out to the salesgirl. 'Can you check if this won anything please?'

The girl ran the ticket through the machine, her eyes fixed on the screen. 'Oh!' Her hands shook as she checked the ticket.

'Are you okay?' Shauna asked.

'Yes . . . yes, of course. I might just need someone else to take a look at this.' She called over to another staff member.

An older woman smiled at Shauna as she entered the service area. She glanced at the computer screen. 'Holy crap, whose ticket is that?'

The salesgirl who'd served her was smiling and nodding but seemed unable to form words.

The older woman looked at Shauna. 'It's yours?'

Shauna nodded. 'Is everything okay?'

'Okay? It's won!'

Shauna smiled. 'Well, that's good news. How much?'

The woman's face broke into a huge smile. 'You might need to sit down. It's won first division.'

A bead of sweat ran down Shauna's back. 'Is this a joke?' She looked around the shop. Perhaps there was a hidden camera waiting to catch her reaction and then make fun of her. But all she saw was a man flicking through a magazine and a woman looking at birthday cards.

The woman started to laugh. 'I'm sorry, but you should see your face. I'm not playing a cruel joke. This is real. I'll get the manager; maybe he can convince you.' Shauna's heart raced as the woman called out to her manager.

'Is everything okay over here?' The manager made his way to the counter.

The woman handed him the ticket. 'This lady has won, but I don't seem to be able to convince her it's true. I think she's in shock.'

The manager raised his eyebrows at the grinning saleswoman and then ran the ticket back through the machine. He gasped before looking up at Shauna. His face broke into a huge smile. 'First division, now that was a good investment.'

'It was a present.'

'Bloody good present, if you don't mind me saying. First division is worth ten million dollars.'

Shauna's legs started to tremble as she watched the grin expand on the manager's face.

'Ten million dollars? You're kidding?'

'I'm not kidding,' he said. 'You're one of two winners from last night's twenty-million-dollar mega draw.'

Shauna's mouth dropped open as she stared at both the manager and saleswoman. Twenty million dollars! She'd won a share of twenty million dollars?

Half an hour later, heart still racing, Shauna slid back into her car. Her ticket had been registered by the store and she had been given all the information she required to claim her prize. She stared at the steering wheel and wondered what to do. Her original plan of an early night didn't feel right. She had to tell someone. Share the news. Celebrate.

Her thoughts shifted to Simon. What would this have meant for them twelve months earlier? Would it have changed her decision about travelling? Leaving a secure job when she was doing so well and about to move to a large organisation with the potential for further promotion and substantial pay increases was one of her reasons she'd said no.

She picked up her phone and dialled his number. As the phone rang, she mentally shook herself. What was she doing? Relieved that it clicked to voicemail before he answered, she hung up. Why on earth would she tell him? Yes, she still felt something for him but not enough to act on and certainly not enough to share this news with him.

She checked her watch, trying to remember what country Tess was in and whether she could interrupt her while she was working. It would be early- to mid-morning in Europe. She dialled. Tess's phone instantly connected to voicemail. She left a quick message asking Tess to ring her, sighed and hung up. Huge news and she had no one to tell.

An image of Josh drifted into her mind, which she quickly dismissed.

Her mum, of course; she was the one who'd bought the ticket. Shauna decided to get a bottle of champagne and surprise her. They hadn't spoken since the unpleasant dinner with Bob, but that suddenly seemed very trivial. Her announcement of a ten-million-dollar win was sure to clear the air between them.

Shauna danced from foot to foot, her stomach fluttering as she waited for her mother to open the door. She half expected to wake up any minute and discover this was all a dream. Come on, where was she? She knocked again.

The door flung open, her mother's scowl ageing her heavily lined face ten years. 'Geez, don't break the door down. Why are you here? I'm on my way out.'

Shauna grabbed Lorraine's hand and dragged her into the living room.

'What on earth?'

'Sit down.' Shauna led her to the couch, her cheeks beginning to ache her smile was so wide. 'You need to sit down.'

'Fine.' Lorraine glanced at her watch. 'Bob's expecting me in fifteen minutes. What's so urgent?'

'He can wait. I've got news.'

'Shauna, we've made plans. You can't turn up unannounced and expect me to drop everything.'

'Yes, I can.' Shauna held up her hands when she saw Lorraine about to object. 'You know the ticket you bought me for my birthday, the Gold Power Lotto ticket?'

'Did it win something?'

'Something? Yes, it won something. Mum, the ticket won ten million dollars.'

Lorraine's face paled. 'Ten million dollars? Is this a joke? Because if this is it's not funny and I'm going out.' She started to get up from the couch.

'Stay sitting. This is no joke. First division was twenty million and there were two winners. I'm one of them.'

They sat in silence staring at each other. Without warning Lorraine leapt up. 'We're rich! Oh my God, we're rich!' She grabbed Shauna and hugged her so tightly Shauna thought she might stop breathing.

'Okay, okay.' She laughed, untangling herself from Lorraine's grip.

'Where did you put the money?' Lorraine looked at Shauna's bag.

Shauna followed her gaze and burst out laughing. 'They aren't going to have ten million dollars in the store. The woman in the newsagent said I take the ticket and claim form into the offices of Gold Power Lotteries, and they'll pay me by cheque or direct deposit. I have to have a meeting with them first before they'll release the money. Something about their duty of care, whatever that means.'

Lorraine picked up her phone and started pressing buttons in a frenzy. 'This is so exciting, so exciting. I've got to tell Bob.'

Shauna grabbed the phone from her. 'You are not telling Bob. No way. This is nothing to do with him.'

'Oh, Shauna, don't be silly. I'm telling Bob; he'll be as thrilled as we are.'

'Mum, I don't want him to know. I don't want to listen to him telling me why I should give him money. Why can't you just share this moment with me, not make it about someone else?' Shauna sat down, the pleasure she'd felt only moments earlier gone. It was always the same; her mother could never make it about the two of them, enjoy something together. There was always some guy on the scene, who usually lasted only a few months, but was always so much more important to Lorraine than she was.

Lorraine laughed. 'Oh, come on, Bob can share our excitement. And anyway, how am I supposed to explain our change in circumstances?'

'This is my money and I'm not giving any to Bob.'

'What do you mean, *your* money?'

'The ticket was mine. Of course, I'll give you some, but tonight is about a celebration. I hoped you'd want to celebrate with me. Open the champagne, enjoy the moment. There's no rush to tell anyone or do anything but enjoy this moment.'

Lorraine faced Shauna, hands on her hips. 'Shauna, I'm going out. I'd love you to come and we can celebrate with Bob. But if you won't let me tell him, what's the point? Bob will be happy for you, too. I wish you'd stop being jealous for a moment. We're getting serious and you need to get used to him.'

Shauna rolled her eyes. 'Fine, whatever. You go out, enjoy yourself.' She picked up her bag. 'I'm off. Thanks for the birthday present – it was one of your better ones. Makes up for all of the years you've forgotten I actually had a birthday.'

Shauna slammed the door on her way out. Why couldn't her mother act like a normal person just this once? This was the biggest night of her life. It needed to be remembered.

◆ ◆ ◆

As she drove away from her mother's house, Shauna became acutely aware of how alone she was. No relationship; she'd deliberately drifted away from the mutual friends she'd had with Simon, and other than her girlfriend Tess, there really wasn't anyone to turn to. Thoughts of Josh entered her mind again. They were definitely becoming friends. And right now that was exactly what she needed. Joining Josh and the others from I-People would give her a chance to party.

The music throbbed as Shauna walked into the crowded bar. She waved to Josh when she spotted him at a table with a group of their work colleagues. He was listening intently to something someone was saying and when he saw her a smile spread across his face. His pleasure at seeing her was reassuring. Perhaps she wasn't as alone as she'd thought.

Josh jumped up and wove his way through the crowd towards her. 'I thought you weren't coming?'

Shauna put her mouth close to his ear so he'd hear her over the noise. 'I should be working, but I decided to come out. Felt like celebrating.'

'Celebrating? What are we celebrating?'

Shauna hesitated. 'Oh nothing, a bit of unexpected luck. What are they all drinking? My shout.'

Arriving at the table with a tray full of drinks, Shauna was immediately welcomed by the group. She couldn't help noticing two of the girls from sales raise their eyebrows at each other. No doubt they were wondering why the 'Ice Queen' had joined them. Months before she'd walked in on a meeting where she had heard herself referred to as that. Choosing not to socialise with the staff had earned her this label. Shauna smiled as the two girls happily accepted their free drinks and gushed unconvincingly at her generosity.

An hour later Josh stopped Shauna as she came back from the toilets. 'What's going on?'

'What do you mean?'

'Everyone says you never come out with work people and you hardly drink. You've got a huge day tomorrow and yet you're knocking back vodka like it's about to run out. What's happened?'

Shauna giggled.

'And I don't think you're the giggling type. Did you take something after I left you?'

Shauna laughed outright. 'What? Drugs?'

'Maybe? I don't know, you don't seem like you. If I had to fork out five or six hundred dollars on drinks I wouldn't be looking so happy.'

Shauna was silent for a moment. 'If I tell you something, will you promise to keep it to yourself?'

'Of course.'

'I won some money tonight and I want to share some of my good luck.'

Josh frowned. 'Hopefully your win was huge with the way these guys are drinking. We all appreciate you buying a few drinks, but it's getting a bit out of hand.' He turned towards the bar. 'They're doing shots now; you'll be up for close to a grand by the time this lot finish. Let me stop the tab. You want to keep some of your winnings for yourself.'

Shauna grabbed him by the arm. 'No, wait, don't stop them, they're having a good time.'

'At your expense.'

'I can afford it. Like I said, I won some money and yes, I won a huge amount.'

'How huge?'

Shauna started to giggle. 'Okay, but you can't tell anyone.'

Josh stood to attention, giving Shauna his best boy-scout salute. 'I solemnly swear all information will be retained only by myself.'

'Ten million dollars.'

Josh's hand dropped to his side. 'No way.'

'Yes way. Gold Power Mega Draw. I've been walking around with a winning ticket and didn't realise. Actually, it was because of you that I even remembered to get it checked. I couldn't find my copy of *OzBuzz* at the office so stopped at the newsagent to buy one on the way home. The ticket was in my purse. Now you can see why there's no need to worry about the tab.'

Josh's eyes searched Shauna's face. 'You're not bullshitting, are you?'

'Nope.' Shauna had surprised herself again by confiding in Josh. What was it about him that made her want to blurt out all sorts of things about her private life? She looked at him – it was those damned eyes. She was a sucker for beautiful eyes and his were trusting and sexy and she found herself drawn to him. Shauna shook herself; one minute she was thinking about Simon, the next Josh. The money, or alcohol, was making her crazy. He would make a good friend, nothing else.

Josh stared at her in disbelief. 'Wow, I don't even know what to say. What are you going to do with ten million dollars?'

'I have no idea. I only found out a few hours ago. For now, I think we drink!'

Josh grabbed her hand. 'Come on, this calls for champagne. A bottle of Cristal's in order.'

At a quarter to two, having had far too much to drink, Shauna called a taxi and went home.

Dreading the early morning wake-up and flight to Adelaide, fully clothed, she set her alarm and passed out.

Chapter Six

Footsteps made Frankie look up as she packed the last of the cleaning supplies back into the kitchen cupboard. 'Morning, sleepyhead.'

Hope yawned and stretched her arms above her head. 'Morning. I can't believe it's so late. Why didn't you wake me?'

'It's Saturday. You're allowed to sleep in, you know.'

'I've got plans, though. I'd better hurry up and get ready.'

Frankie studied her daughter as she continued to stretch. 'I was speaking to Logan's mum the other day.'

'Mmm, what did she have to say?'

'She mentioned you'd said a few things to Logan about us not having much money.'

Hope laughed. 'That's one way of putting the conversation.'

Frankie waited for Hope to elaborate.

'Logan talks a lot about her fancy house, cars, racehorses, outings to *the track*. She's completely superficial and ridiculous. She was talking about how upset she was that her father had said no to the two-thousand-dollar dress she wanted to wear to some event that's part of the Sydney Autumn Racing Carnival, whatever that is. They're flying up to it and staying in a suite at a hotel that has views of the Opera House from its four private balconies. From the sounds of it the suite costs more per night than the dress she wants! I suggested she borrow one of my dresses, that's all.' Hope grinned. 'I was thinking that one with the large hole in the side that you sewed that denim patch over – you know, the really cool one. The one Hailey says you should make copies of to sell, she loves it so much.'

Frankie stared at her daughter, not completely sure whether Hope was making fun of Logan or of her own clothes. Hailey had said she liked the dress, but Hailey dressed exclusively from vintage and second-hand stores by choice, not through necessity.

'What? It was funny. She's an idiot. Who'd spend two thousand dollars on a dress to start with. God, imagine what we could buy with that. We could live like royalty.'

Frankie nodded, deciding to change the subject. 'What have you got on today? You said you had plans?'

Hope got up from the stool and moved towards the fridge. 'Yep, study plans with Hailey.'

'Why don't you wear your new shirt?'

Hope opened the fridge, avoiding her mother's eyes. 'I'm keeping it for next weekend. Lisa's having a party and I want to wear something new.'

Frankie watched as her daughter shut the fridge empty-handed. 'Hon, if you don't like it, I understand. You won't hurt my feelings.'

Hope still refused to meet Frankie's eyes. 'I love it, don't be silly.'

Frankie wasn't convinced. There were too many mixed messages coming from Hope. 'I know it's not exactly the same as the shop one, but it's pretty close—'

Hope cut her off. 'It's perfect, okay? Like I said, I'm saving it for next week. Anyway, gotta go, I'll be at Hailey's until dinnertime. We've got an assignment due for English.'

Frankie gave her a hug. 'Okay, don't overdo the work and have some fun, won't you?'

Hope rolled her eyes and laughed. 'You're supposed to say the exact opposite. Tell me to study hard, not mess around.'

'I know you, you crazy, studious girl, and you'll spend the whole day with your head in a book and miss out on the glorious sunshine.' Frankie pointed out of the window. 'Look at those two.' Tom and Fern were outside sitting on the grass sharing an orange, with a pile of newspapers on the ground between them.

'I'll try not to study too much, okay?'

'Perfect.'

Hope reached for her books, ready to go.

'Wait a minute. Is that boy still hassling you at school?'

'No, Mum, don't worry, everyone's fine. He stays right away from me.'

'Really?'

'Yes, really. Just leave it, okay. I'm a big girl. I can look after myself.'

Frankie nodded. 'Okay. Now, off you go, enjoy the day.'

Once Hope was gone Frankie surveyed the kitchen. It was clean enough now to allow her to take her own advice and escape into the sunshine. She was about to walk out the back door when the lotto ticket on the fridge caught her eye. The draw would have been earlier in the week; she had completely forgotten. She'd better check the numbers in case she owed Jim a cup of coffee.

She went outside and sat down next to Fern, picking up one of the papers. It was Thursday's. She put it back down again. 'What papers have you got? I need to check the lotto ticket Jim gave me.'

'What date do you need?' Tom asked. 'I've got at least two weeks' worth here.' Tom collected day-old papers at work, bringing them home each week to read through. He and Fern would often sit and read the comics together on a Saturday morning.

'I need Wednesday this week.' Frankie watched as Tom worked his way through the papers, checking the dates. Finally, he pulled out the paper she needed and handed it to her.

'Perfect, the lotto result should be in it.' She flicked through the paper, found the page with the results and then handed it back to Tom. 'Can you read the numbers and I'll check the ticket?'

'Got a pen?'

'Yep. Now, there are eighteen lines, so go slow.'

'First number's four.' Tom waited while Frankie scanned the ticket, circling a few numbers. He read out the second and third numbers.

Fern checked what Frankie was doing. 'Ooh, three numbers.' She pointed to the fifth line of the ticket.

Frankie looked up at Tom. 'Does that win?'

Tom shook his head. 'No, I think it needs four. Fourth number is twenty-two.'

Fern gave a squeal. 'Ooh, four numbers.'

'You're right, four in a row. What are the others?'

Tom read out the next three numbers.

Frankie froze, her hand shaking. 'You're kidding?'

Fern screamed. 'Seven! Seven numbers! You've won!'

Frankie and Tom stared at each other.

Tom was the first to speak. 'Let's double-check, maybe we made a mistake?'

They pored over the ticket and newspaper, checking the numbers again – they had the seven numbers straight.

Frankie's legs trembled and she clung to Tom's hand as they entered the Gold Power Lotteries building on St Kilda Road. Once they'd triple-checked their ticket on Saturday, Frankie had immediately returned to the newsagent to see Jim and hand in the ticket. They couldn't keep it. It belonged to Jim or to whoever had lost the twenty dollars. She'd done her best to tune Tom out as he walked beside her, arguing, begging and pleading for her to think about it. *This was meant to be. The universe was finally smiling at them. She wasn't doing anything wrong. The ticket had been purchased for her.* Much to Frankie's surprise and dismay, Jim had echoed Tom's words.

'Frankie, this ticket belongs to you. No one has come in asking about the twenty dollars and probably never will. And even if they did, we'd be returning twenty dollars to them, not your winning ticket. They didn't choose to spend the money on a ticket, you and I did.' He'd taken the ticket from her and entered a range of details into the computer.

'But,' Frankie had tried to argue, 'it should be your ticket.'

Jim shook head. 'There's no way I would have bought that ticket at that moment if you hadn't come in with your twenty dollars. I don't need or want it. Frankie, I run the newsagent to keep me busy in my retirement and get me out from under Wilma's feet. We're very comfortable and she'd have a fit if I turned up with ten million dollars. She'd have no reason to spend her days searching for specials and loving the discounts she finds. We weren't blessed with children so even what we've acquired through our lives is too much and is being left to nephews and nieces we don't know very well. This money would give us ten million headaches we aren't interested in.'

He stared at the screen after finishing keying in some details.

'Now, I've registered the ticket in your name, so there is no arguing. You and Tom need to take it into the head office of Gold Power Lotteries to claim your prize. If you don't then the money will just be categorised as unclaimed winnings and no one will get to have it. That would be ridiculous. I recommend you embrace it and enjoy it. They have some conditions on releasing the money which they'll explain to you when you ring to make an appointment.' He'd handed them a printout with the number they needed to ring and the address to attend and winked. 'But Frankie, don't forget you do owe me something. One of those fancy coffees with the frothy milk in a large mug will settle your debt. Perhaps you can join me for one after you've been to Gold Power and you can tell me all about it.'

Frankie nodded, dumbfounded by the whole situation.

She'd operated in a daze when they'd returned home and shared the news with Fern and then Hope when she'd returned from Hailey's. The girls and Tom had gone crazy. They laughed and screamed and danced around the house. They made plans for the future. A new house, a car, a new computer for Hope, an iPad for Fern. It had been well after midnight when, exhausted and elated, they'd finally gone to bed and Frankie could stop pretending to be as excited as they were. She'd continued the pretence the next day, after ensuring the girls knew they weren't to tell anyone about the win, the whole time trying to shake the overwhelming sense of dread that had enveloped her the moment they realised they had the seven winning numbers.

Now, three days later, they were standing in the foyer of the Gold Power Lotteries building, waiting for their appointment with psychologist and counsellor Pamela Dickson.

'We can't keep the money, Tom.' Frankie's voice was a whisper as she gripped Tom's hand even tighter. 'It's wrong.'

Tom led her to the waiting area where another woman, dressed in an expensive navy suit, was absorbed in keying something into her phone. She frowned as her phone pinged with a message and continued typing into it without looking up. He pulled Frankie down on to a seat.

'Let's have this meeting and talk about it again after that, okay? If we don't claim the money, then as Jim said, it will probably be absorbed by Gold Power and no one will get it. At least if we claim it, we have the option to donate the whole lot to charity so it does some good.'

Frankie raised an eyebrow. Tom's arguments up to this point had been from a selfish perspective, about how they could use the money. This was a new line of attack.

'Frankie.' Tom's eyes were filled with love as he spoke to her. 'Having money isn't going to ruin us. I'm not your dad and you're not your mum. We're very different, very responsible people.'

A lump rose in Frankie's throat. She hadn't let herself think too much about her parents, but Tom was right. It was part of her concern. The day she'd found out she was pregnant she'd made a promise to herself and her unborn child that he or she would never experience what she had as a child. It was a promise that, no matter what was thrown at her in life, she was determined to keep. Money had ruined her family; she wouldn't let it happen again.

'Ms Jones.' The receptionist walked over to the waiting area and was addressing the woman in the navy suit.

She looked up from her phone.

'I'm sorry, but Pamela has double-checked and there has been a clash of appointments. She has an appointment now and then is in meetings for the remainder of the day. She apologises for the confusion but does insist that your appointment was booked for Thursday morning, not today.'

Frustration clouded the woman's face. 'I'll be in Brisbane on Thursday for work; I definitely didn't make an appointment for then.' She stood. 'Fine. Let's assume there's been an error made somewhere along the way and make a time for next week. To be honest, I can't see the point of this meeting anyway.'

The receptionist didn't respond but led the woman back towards the front desk to rebook her appointment.

Frankie stood and began to follow them. Tom grabbed her hand. 'What are you doing?'

'Being generous.' Pamela was the name of the woman Frankie and Tom were here to see. The woman in the suit looked a lot busier than they were. She'd be more than happy to delay their appointment and give the whole situation some more thought.

'Excuse me.' She approached the woman. 'I couldn't help but overhear that you had an appointment with Pamela. I assume that's Pamela Dickson?'

The receptionist nodded before the woman had a chance to answer. 'Pamela does all of our winner interviews and counselling sessions. Unfortunately, we've double-booked you today. Ms Jones will need to make a new appointment.'

'No, don't,' Frankie said. 'You look very busy. Take our appointment and we'll reschedule.'

The woman's eyes widened. 'Really? Are you sure?'

Frankie shrugged. 'We're in no hurry. In fact, I'd be happy to delay it. This is a strange situation for us.'

The woman in the suit lowered her voice. 'Did you win too?'

Frankie nodded.

'Big?'

Frankie nodded again.

'Me too,' the woman whispered. She grinned. 'Like ten million big.'

Frankie's mouth dropped open. This was the other winner. 'We won last week's mega draw. You too?'

'Yep.' The woman held out her hand. 'I'm Shauna, millionairess! And, other than incredibly generous with your appointment times, who might you be?'

Frankie grinned, taking Shauna's hand in hers. 'It appears we are sharing the same title. I'm Frankie, millionairess.'

'Reluctant millionairess, she should add,' Tom said, joining them. He held his hand out and smiled. 'I'm Frankie's husband, Tom. Congratulations.'

'And to you too.' Shauna returned his smile. 'It doesn't feel real, does it?'

The group were interrupted as a woman in a black pantsuit, with curly brown hair and a friendly smile, entered the reception area.

'I'm Pamela Dickson and straightaway I'd like to apologise to Ms Jones for the mix-up. JoJo, our receptionist, tells me that the Yorks would be happy to give up their appointment but I'm not sure if you've all decided on this as yet?'

Frankie looked at Shauna. 'Really, you're welcome to it. We can come back.'

Shauna shook her head slowly and turned to Pamela. 'I'm assuming the Yorks and I are here for the same type of appointment?'

Pamela nodded.

'Can I suggest we combine it? If the Yorks agree, that is? It seems silly to do two meetings when it could all be done in one.'

'Great idea,' Tom said. 'We're happy with that.'

Pamela frowned momentarily before nodding. 'Sure. It's a little unorthodox, but if you're all in agreement, then I can't see why not. The monies you've won will be disclosed during our discussion.'

'That's okay,' Shauna said. 'We shared the same mega draw; we know how much each other won.'

'Great. In that case, follow me.'

Shauna grinned at Frankie and mouthed *thanks* as they followed the counsellor towards her office.

Frankie glanced out of Pamela's office window as they were ushered to a meeting table that took up the centre of the modern office. Pamela's touches of colourful cushions and bright paintings gave the otherwise minimalist furnishings a lift. It was the quietness of the office that struck Frankie as such a stark contrast to the vibrancy of St Kilda Road below, where trams zipped through the central median, while cars crawled along the congested side lanes.

'Now' – Pamela pulled out a chair and sat down – 'as was explained on the phone, Gold Power Lotteries has a requirement that all winners go through this counselling session to give you advice on how to move forward from here – the type of legal and financial expertise we suggest you seek and also to make you aware of the potential pitfalls of winning a large amount of money. We want to help you think about the best way to maximise the opportunity you have and not succumb to the problems that others before you have had.'

Frankie shivered. This already confirmed that this money shouldn't be theirs.

Pamela, sensing her reluctance, reached across and touched Frankie's arm. 'Don't worry, it's not all doom and gloom, we just like to prepare you for the road ahead so you can hopefully enjoy every moment of it.'

Shauna laughed. 'I don't think anyone would consider winning ten million dollars doom and gloom. You're excited, aren't you, Frankie?'

Tom answered before she could. 'Frankie's reluctant to accept the money. The ticket was bought with twenty dollars she found outside a newsagent so she believes the ticket belongs to whoever lost the money, or to Jim, the owner of the newsagent who bought it for her.'

Shauna snorted. 'That's nuts. The ticket belongs to you. You can always give them the money they dropped back if they ask for it. No one expects to lose twenty dollars and be handed ten million back, and I'm sure the newsagent owner wouldn't expect a cut either. He'd hardly gift you a ticket and then demand it back.'

Tom grinned. 'Exactly. See, Frankie, that's what Jim said too. It doesn't matter how you look at this; the ticket does not belong to someone else.'

'I didn't decide to buy a ticket though – Jim made that decision for me.'

'An excellent decision,' Shauna said. 'I'd say go with it, Frankie. If you really hate having money you can always give it away. I'm sure there will be people lining up for it.'

'Which is a good point to start,' Pamela said. 'Shauna's right. It's possible that if people hear of your luck, they will be lining up for your money. For that very reason, we recommend you are discreet in who you tell about your good fortune. People can become incredibly greedy and unreasonable in their requests when it comes to large sums. They feel a sense of entitlement and at times have made past winners' lives very difficult.'

Frankie's thoughts immediately went to Dash. She could imagine him demanding money if he found out about their win.

Pamela continued to talk about the need to think carefully about who they told about their winnings, who they gifted money to, and also the recommendation that they seek advice from a reputable financial planner as soon as possible.

'You said at the start that past winners have succumbed to problems,' Frankie said as it appeared Pamela was beginning to wrap up the discussion. 'What sort of problems?'

'A mixture, to be honest. The most common being the greed of others and lack of self-control with the money.'

Pamela stood and took some documents from her desk before sitting back down and addressing Frankie. 'Here, take one of these.' She passed a flyer to Frankie that read:

*Friends of Lotto. An opportunity to mix and celebrate
with other lotto winners. Guest presenters will help you
navigate your way through this new phase of life providing advice to help ensure you avoid the common pitfalls
of a sudden windfall.*

Frankie looked up at Pamela. 'Common pitfalls?'

Pamela smiled. 'It's really an expansion on what we've discussed today but with real life examples from people who are
in your position. So yes, the pitfalls are often elaborated upon
to ensure you avoid them. Our guest speakers are a mixture of
past winners and professional advisors. Feel free to come along
if you like.'

'And you run this?' Shauna asked.

Pamela nodded.

'As an employee of the Gold Power group? So this is one of
their initiatives?'

'No, I was running the group before they approached me to
come and work in-house. They fully support Friends of Lotto but
it's my creation, not theirs. I was a lawyer in my previous life but
find this work a lot more fulfilling.'

'Why do you do it? Did you win lotto and lose everything?'

Frankie couldn't help but think Shauna's line of direct questioning was bordering on rude. But she was curious too.

'Yes, lotto did cause me to lose everything important to me.
Now I'm doing my best to make sure that doesn't happen to other
people and, if they do experience problems, they have somewhere
to turn.'

'That's amazing,' Shauna said. 'If lotto caused problems for me,
I don't think I'd be here working for them.'

'Winning lotto can be the most amazing thing that ever happens to you,' Pamela said. 'But some people need guidance on how

71

to make the most of it. Unfortunately I didn't seek out help when I won and, as a result, after winning I saw my marriage and relationships with most of my family and friends end. Add in a number of bad investments and within six years of becoming a millionaire, I was broke, in debt and needing to start again. And by then I was single and on my own. Only one good friend stuck by me and thank goodness for Annie, because, to be honest, if she hadn't I'm not even sure I'd still be here.'

Frankie stared at Pamela. A woman who seemed so together had really been through all of this?

Pamela smiled. 'It's hard to even say all of that out loud. It sounds like it must have been someone else's life. I founded the support group to try and prevent this happening to other people. To share stories and experiences and, if nothing more, make new winners aware that there are some very easy steps to put in place to ensure you keep your money and you enjoy it.'

'I'm so sorry your lotto win changed your life so drastically.'

Pamela smiled. 'Thank you. But Frankie, don't assume my story is your story. The point of me telling it to you is to encourage you to join the support group. The members are incredibly friendly. Most people only come for a few sessions but will often pop back to see us months or even years down the track. They'll sometimes be welcomed as our guest speaker on those nights to share their journey since winning. They are always incredibly interesting stories. We meet every Thursday night. The location details are on the flyer. Collingwood train station's only a short walk from the community centre we meet in so should be easily accessible.'

'I'll definitely be coming,' Frankie said. She turned to Shauna. 'How about you?'

Shauna looked from Frankie to Pamela, her eyes settling back on Frankie. 'No, sorry, it's not for me. And if I can be blunt, I think it might be the worst thing you could do.'

Frankie's eyes widened. 'What? Why would you think that? You don't even know me.'

'A gut feel. You've already suggested you hate the idea of winning the money, that it shouldn't be yours and is only going to bring bad things. You've lapped up Pamela's story.' She turned to Pamela. 'I'm not being disrespectful, but I watched Frankie's reactions and feel that it feeds her worries rather than helps them. I'm surprised that Gold Power Lotteries encourage you to share your story, actually. It's hardly a good advertisement for lotto.'

Pamela didn't respond.

'And I think immersing yourself in discussions that harp on about the pitfalls of winning lotto will make you miserable and spoil every exciting moment you should be enjoying over winning the money. I certainly think we both need to take on Pamela's excellent advice about seeing a financial advisor and, of course, being discreet with who we tell about our winnings and give money to, but I think a support group is really over the top.'

'The group doesn't *harp* on about the pitfalls, Shauna,' Pamela said. 'It reinforces why you should give thought to how you do things to ensure you have a positive experience.'

Shauna shrugged. 'Sorry, won't be attending. We've all heard the stories of doom and gloom when it comes to lotto winners losing everything a few months or years down the track, but I'm not going to be one of them. I've enough common sense to know how to handle this situation.'

Frankie stared at the woman in front of her. She seemed so sure of herself, so confident and in control. She was Frankie's polar opposite.

Pamela cleared her throat and rose from her seat. 'As I said, the invitation is open to all of you to attend the group at any time. You can just turn up, as we run every week rain or shine.' She turned to Shauna. 'I completely understand where you're coming from, and to be honest, before going through what I did, I would have agreed one hundred percent with what you just said. But, speaking from experience, I can tell you right now, don't get complacent. You never know what a win like this will bring out of the woodwork. I can guarantee you right now, you might be surprised.'

Chapter Seven

Shauna didn't ignore Pamela's advice; in fact she agreed with every-thing that had been suggested, other than the support group. She'd seen a financial advisor the next day, and still, two weeks later, hadn't told anyone other than Josh and her mother. Josh had prom-ised to keep quiet and with him interstate for meetings most of the past two weeks she'd hardly seen him anyway. On more than one occasion she'd had to sit down when the significance of what had happened hit her. Or she'd find herself logging on to Internet bank-ing at random times throughout the day to check the balance of her account. Her heart raced every time she did this. *Could it really be true?* When her statement appeared showing the money she'd find herself gasping in amazement or laughing at the absurdity of it. She, Shauna Jones, had won ten million dollars!

Her initial temptation to tell Simon had quickly tapered off and in fact she'd found herself ignoring his calls and texts. Her feelings were so mixed when it came to Simon, she'd decided the best thing was to stay well away from him. He'd be busy with his contract and she assumed would get the hint at some stage that she wasn't interested. The one person, however, she did decide she couldn't ignore any longer was her mother. She hadn't seen her since the night she'd told her about the win, and she wanted to set things right. Shauna checked her watch and continued to pace up and down outside her mother's house. Finally, the familiar blue car turned into the driveway.

'Where have you been?' Shauna's face was at Lorraine's window the moment it opened.

Her mother didn't smile. 'Hello to you, too, dearest daughter.'

'I've been waiting for ages. You're usually home by six on a Tuesday.'

'Not always. Next time ring if you want to come over, or let yourself in.' Lorraine opened the boot and took out some shopping bags. 'To what do I owe this special honour?' Her eyes shifted past Shauna and back out to the street. 'New car? Your latest purchase, I assume?' Lorraine nodded towards the Mercedes E-Class Cabriolet. 'Throwing around a bit of loose change, are we?'

Shauna ignored her mother's sarcasm. 'Yes, it's mine. Come on, let's go inside. I want to talk to you.'

Shauna followed Lorraine into the house and headed to the kitchen, while Lorraine took some bags into her bedroom.

'What are you doing?' Lorraine called as Shauna opened cupboards.

'Something we should have done weeks ago.' Shauna grabbed two champagne flutes and removed a bottle out of her bag.

Lorraine came into the kitchen and sat down on a bar stool across from Shauna. 'Mmm, Krug, I've always wanted to taste Krug. Fancy cars, expensive champagne. Nice for some.'

'Don't be bitchy. I wanted to celebrate the win and talk to you. There's a gift for you, by the way.'

Lorraine jumped up off the stool, her scowl replaced by a beaming smile as she flung her arms around Shauna. 'Why didn't you say so? Come into the living room and tell me all about what's been happening. You must be on cloud nine. When did you receive the money?'

Shauna had known the mention of a gift would change her mother's attitude. She followed Lorraine into the living room and perched on one of the chairs. 'The money went into my account about a week ago.'

'You were quick to get the car.'

'I put in an order the day after I won the money.'

'How much was it?'

'None of your business. It's extravagant, I know, but what's the point of having millions of dollars if you don't spend some of them?'

'I couldn't agree more. Cheers.' Lorraine raised her glass. 'So, what else have you bought?'

'Nothing, just the car. But I'm thinking about apartments.'

'You had plans to buy even before you won the money. I guess you're looking at something a bit more luxurious now? You won't be comfortable coming over here soon, you know. I'm afraid this is all a bit basic.' Lorraine swept her hands around, motioning to her furniture.

Shauna rolled her eyes. 'Hardly basic, Mother. You're not exactly living in poverty.' She opened her bag and removed an envelope. 'Now, I've got this for you.' She passed it to Lorraine.

'What is it?'

'Open it and find out.' A flutter grew in the pit of Shauna's stomach as her mother slipped her finger into the back of the envelope. She'd been planning this moment for over a week and couldn't wait to see her mother's face.

Lorraine pulled out a card, quickly dismissed the picture on the front and opened it. She sat staring at the contents.

Shauna took a deep breath, savouring the moment. Her mother speechless was not an everyday occurrence.

Finally Lorraine looked up. Her voice was low, practically a whisper. 'One and a half million dollars? You're giving me one and a half?'

Shauna got up and sat next to Lorraine on the couch. She put her arm around her mother. 'Yes, I wanted to surprise you.'

Lorraine shrugged her arm away and jumped up. This time she wasn't whispering; in fact she sounded almost hysterical. 'Of ten million, all you're giving me is a lousy one and a half?'

Shauna's mouth dropped open.

'Not only did I give you life, I raised you on my own and stupidly gave you that ticket for your birthday. This is the thanks I get?'

Shauna swallowed. From all of the scenarios she'd imagined when planning this moment, this reaction was certainly not one of them. 'One and a half million is a huge amount of money! How much were you expecting?'

Lorraine didn't hesitate. 'Half.'

'Half? Why on earth would you need five million dollars?'

Lorraine stood with her hands on her hips. 'Why do you need ten?'

'I don't. No one does, but I'm not giving it all away either.'

'I didn't say all, I said half. I bought you the ticket and I deserve an equal share. Bob thinks so, too.'

Shauna put her champagne down and stood up. 'Unbelievable,' she muttered as she went to get her bag.

'Where do you think you're going?' Lorraine followed her into the kitchen.

Shauna turned to face her. 'Home. Your attitude stuns me.'

'What do you expect? I'm supposed to be grateful you can only spare fifteen percent?'

'Yes, Mother.' Shauna sighed. 'Most people would be pretty happy right now. They're not all as greedy as you.'

'I'm not being greedy. I bought the ticket and I think I'm entitled to an equal share. You owe me.'

'What's that supposed to mean?'

Lorraine's voice was rising in pitch. 'I gave up everything for you. Protected you. I left my friends and family behind to make sure you were safe.'

'What the hell are you talking about?'

Lorraine hesitated. 'Nothing, forget it.'

'You told me you left Brisbane to be closer to friends in Melbourne after my father deserted us. Is that true?'

'Yes, of course it is.' She pushed her fingers into her forehead. 'I get muddled sometimes, that's all. It was a very hard time, one I'd prefer not to think about.'

'And family?' Shauna pushed. 'You've always said there was no other family. You had no siblings and your parents, my grandparents, are dead. What family?'

Lorraine sighed, her voice returning to a calmer state. 'There's no other family. Just the two of us. I guess I was referring to your father. He was our family. Until he took off, leaving me to raise you.' Her eyes hardened. 'You should show some gratitude. Try to understand the sacrifices I've made and do the right thing.'

Shauna stared at her mother. What sacrifices? Her mother had always done exactly what she'd wanted, put herself first and treated Shauna like an afterthought. Now suddenly she owed her?

She shook her head. 'If you don't want the money then return it. I'm not giving you any more. I'm going home.' She walked down the hallway and let herself out the front door. She could hear her mother pressing the buttons on her phone as she pulled the door shut behind her.

Shauna slammed the files down on her desk. Could the week get any worse? First Lorraine's lack of gratitude earlier in the week and now this.

Josh had seen Shauna storm out of the reception area and stopped in the doorway of her office. 'Anything wrong?'

She scowled at him. 'You tell me, you little shit. I thought you were trustworthy.'

Josh's face paled as he walked towards Shauna's desk. '*Little shit?* What's going on?'

'How do all the staff know I won ten million dollars?'

Josh frowned. 'I never said anything, I swear.'

'Who else would tell them?'

'No idea, but I promise I didn't say a word.'

'Yeah, well, I'm finding you hard to believe right now. People have been uncharacteristically nice to me this morning. And check this out.' She turned her computer screen around for Josh to see.

He sat down and read the email. 'No is the only answer to this.'

'How can I say no? Andrew's a colleague and I even met Stevie, his brother. He'll die without treatment. How could I look Andrew in the eye if Stevie died and I didn't at least try to help?'

'He's got cancer, according to this message. We have top specialists here. Medicare would cover most of the expense. He doesn't need to go to America and pay hundreds of thousands for treatment.'

'Read it again, Josh. He's got a rare form of cancer and according to Andrew if they get to some clinic in Texas he has a small chance. The drugs he's already been exposed to are damaging his kidneys so he might need transplants. The guy's a mess and I can help.'

'He's asking for two hundred thousand dollars.'

'A bargain if it saves Stevie's life.'

'Shauna, every man and his dog will be coming after you for money if you say yes.'

'No shit, Sherlock. That's why I wanted this kept a secret.'

'Hey, drop the attitude and stop blaming me for something I have nothing to do with.'

Shauna scowled at Josh, her arms crossed in front of her. 'I've told one person about the win and I'm staring at him right now. What am I supposed to think?'

'You're supposed to know me well enough to trust me and believe me when I tell you something.'

'Obviously I don't know you well enough, then.'

Josh stood up. 'You can be a real piece of work. I'm not sure I should even bother, but I'll prove it wasn't me.'

'Yeah, right.' She sat back down and reread Andrew's email once Josh left the room. She typed a message and suggested he contact her to make a time to catch up and discuss the situation. She spent the next hour returning client calls and emails. Her stomach rumbled, a reminder she hadn't eaten for hours. She contemplated asking one of the assistants to get her some lunch when Josh knocked on her door.

He waved a bag and juice container at her. 'Peace offering.'

'That's hardly going to earn you forgiveness, but my stomach will overlook that and accept the sandwich.'

Josh came in and put the food on Shauna's desk. '"Thank you" would have been enough. Like I said earlier, it wasn't me. I've done a bit of nosing around and worked out who leaked the information.'

'Who?'

'Turns out Jenni at reception opened your mail, which included a letter from a law firm.'

'Law firm?'

'Check your in-tray.'

Shauna sorted through the contents of her in-tray and stopped at a letter printed on gold-embossed letterhead. She sat down to read it. She finished and looked up at Josh. 'Do you know if Jenni told anyone what this says, other than the ten million?'

Josh cleared his throat. 'Um, yeah, I'm pretty sure she mentioned all of the details.'

Shauna picked up the phone and dialled reception. 'Jenni, it's Shauna. Get in here, now.'

'Should I go?' Josh asked.

'No, stay.' She looked up at Josh and swallowed. 'Sorry about before. Calling you a little shit and all that.'

'You should be.' A hardness replaced the usual warmth in Josh's eyes. 'You need to know I won't put up with you talking to me like that. Do it again and we're no longer friends. I mean it, okay?'

Shauna's face grew hot as she replayed what she'd said in her mind. 'I wasn't that bad, was I?'

Josh raised an eyebrow. 'I get it that you were upset and angry, but you don't treat me like that ever. Deal?'

Shauna blinked, surprised at how much it meant to her to keep Josh's friendship. 'Deal. And thanks for lunch.'

Josh's smile reached his eyes, and Shauna was relieved to know all was forgiven.

'What will you say to Jenni?'

'I'll be speaking to Craig to have her fired. This envelope is marked "private and confidential". Not only did she read the letter, but she's gone and shared the details with everyone. Stay. I might kill her otherwise.'

Jenni poked her head around the door. 'You wanted to see me?'

'Come in.'

Jenni approached Shauna's desk. 'Is there a problem?'

Shauna held up the letter. 'Thanks to you, there is. Why are you opening my mail and discussing the contents with the other staff?'

Jenni's eyes widened in surprise. 'I open all of the mail.'

'Even if it's marked "private and confidential"?'

'Yes, Craig and Allan's instructions are for me to open the mail – everyone's.'

'Do they also tell you to share any information you think is interesting?'

Jenni's face flushed red. 'No, I don't usually discuss the letters.'

'So, why did you with mine? Surely you could work out this was confidential?'

Jenni's surprise was genuine. 'But why? It's marvellous. I'm so happy for you.'

'Happy that my mother's threatening to sue me?'

'No, of course not. I meant happy you've had such a windfall. I only mentioned it to Sally, and certainly didn't mention your mother. At least I helped clear up the stories about your car.'

'My car?'

Jenni's hand flew up to cover her mouth. 'Me and my big mouth again.'

'What do you mean stories about my car?'

Jenni glanced at Josh and then down at the floor. 'A few people suggested you might have received a gift from someone.'

'Like who?'

'Um, well, a rich man perhaps.'

Shauna wasn't sure whether to be angry or laugh. 'And now I've got a sugar daddy, too?'

'No, no, that's what I tried to explain to Sally. I only told her you'd bought the car yourself because I felt bad about the rumours going around. She googled them, reckons they cost a packet.'

'Thanks for the good intentions, but how did the staff learn about my mother?'

'No idea. I put the letter in your in-tray last night. I'm sorry, Shauna.'

Shauna sighed. 'Fine, go back to work.'

Relief flooded Jenni's face as she turned and left the office.

Josh winked. 'No threats to fire her?'

Shauna shook her head. 'She's too naive and innocent. She seemed convinced she was helping me. Did you hear any rumour?'

Josh laughed. 'Yeah, I'd been told something along those lines. Figured you wouldn't care; help keep them off the track of the lotto win.'

Shauna nodded. 'Okay, but enough about Jenni and the rumour mill – can you believe this?' Shauna handed the letter to Josh.

'Outrageous.' He handed back the letter after he read it. 'You need to make an appointment with a lawyer. It's ridiculous. No way in the world could she be entitled to half the money. I'd be surprised if she was entitled to any at all. The money you've already given her is more than generous.'

'Yes, I'll make an appointment to see someone. This is crazy.' Shauna was still astounded that her mother had been to see a lawyer. This was low, even for her. But she also knew her well enough to realise she'd mean business. She'd push and push until she got what she wanted. Her chest tightened. Was it really too much to ask for a normal relationship with your own mother? Pamela's departing words replayed in her mind: *You never know what a win like this will bring out of the woodwork. I can guarantee you right now, you might be surprised.* Perhaps the support group wasn't as stupid as she'd originally thought.

'Hey.' Josh squeezed her arm. 'Don't let this get you down. Your win is an amazing thing. You just need to learn how to ride the problems that come with it. Now, why don't I take you out for a bite to eat tonight? We can talk more then.'

Shauna stiffened. 'What, a date?'

'No, two friends having dinner on a Thursday night. Actually, no. One friend taking the other out to apologise for accusing him of being a little shit.'

The muscles in Shauna's face relaxed. 'Okay, I think I owe you one. Meet me in reception at six and we'll go and get a drink first.'

Josh grinned. 'Six sounds good for our non-date. Now I'm out of here before you change your mind.'

Shauna looked up and smiled, expecting Josh, as her office door opened right on six. Her smile slipped as Simon's broad shoulders filled the doorway.

'Hey, thought I'd drop by as you haven't been answering or returning my calls.'

Shauna stood. 'And they just let you in?' Wasn't that what reception was for, to screen people before they appeared in your office?

Simon shrugged. 'It's six o'clock. The receptionist was leaving, and I convinced her that I was here to surprise you.' He winked. 'I guess she fell for my boyish charm.'

Shauna rolled her eyes. Simon never had any problem getting women to do things for him. 'What do you want?'

'That's not very nice. I came to see you. Mum wanted to know how you are and hoped you'd come to dinner with me tonight. Remember Thursday night's roast night with my olds. That's what my texts said if you'd bothered to read them. You did promise to get in touch when we had drinks the other week, remember?'

Heat crept into Shauna's cheeks. She'd deliberately ignored Simon's texts without reading them, hoping he might disappear and she could do her best to rebury the feelings she had for him. However, she would hate for Ellen, his mother, to think she was rude. She loved Ellen. It was one of the very sad parts about breaking up with Simon, breaking up with his family too. Ellen was such a contrast to her mother: rational, fun, supportive. Shauna adored her.

'So, are you coming? Dad and Cameron will be there too. They'd all love to see you.'

'I don't get why you're doing this. You're here for three months and we've broken up. What's the point?'

Hurt flashed in Simon's eyes. 'I thought you wanted to be friends? Yes, I'm going again in a few months but who knows what might happen before I go?' A cocky grin replaced the hurt. 'You might decide I'm irresistible and beg me to let you come travelling with me.'

'Not going to happen.'

'Fine, but does it hurt being friends? We have a history together. My family love you, and you love them. Mum's really missed you.'

A lump formed in Shauna's throat. She'd love to see Ellen, but what was the point? It would just remind her of what she was missing.

'And it's not like either of us is seeing anyone else.'

'Knock knock.'

Simon turned as Josh entered the office.

'Oh, sorry. Didn't realise you were with a client. Let me know when you're free, Shauna. There's no hurry.'

'Might have to wait until tomorrow, mate,' Simon said. 'We were just about to leave.'

Josh's eyes narrowed and he looked to Shauna. 'Change of plans?'

She shook her head, her mind instantly made up. 'Of course not. Simon, this is Josh, my colleague. Josh, Simon, my ex. He was about to leave.' She turned to Simon. 'Tell your mum I'm very appreciative of the invitation and I miss her too, but I have plans tonight.'

'Oh.' Simon looked Josh up and down. 'I was wrong then, about us both being free. Sorry, shouldn't have presumed.' He forced a smile to his lips. 'Another night perhaps? I'd hate to let Mum down.'

He was always good at guilt and manipulation to get what he wanted. Shauna shook the thought off as quickly as she had it. Where had that come from? Yes, Simon was persuasive, but manipulative?

She stared at him for a moment before responding. 'I'll let you know, okay?'

Simon smiled. 'I'll do you a deal. You answer my calls or respond to my texts and I won't just turn up again. Deal?'

'Deal. But Simon, don't promise your mum anything. I'm not sure that's going to happen.'

'We'll see!'

He clapped Josh on the back on his way past, and under his breath said, 'She's way out of your league, mate; I wouldn't waste your time.'

Josh raised his eyebrows once Simon left the office. 'Interesting guy. Now, you still owe me that apology dinner. Coming?'

Shauna nodded. 'Sorry about that. Let me get my bag and I'll meet you at the lift in five minutes.' She waited until Josh left her office before sinking into her chair. She was annoyed with herself. She would have loved to have seen Ellen tonight, been wrapped up in the warmth and caring of a family once again. She also knew that if it weren't for her dinner with Josh, she probably would have said yes. But she was smart enough to recognise that wanting to go to a family dinner had nothing to do with Simon or any attraction to him. It was the deep ache in her that missed the connection that his family had provided her with. That component of their break-up was almost harder to stomach than losing Simon.

◆ ◆ ◆

The waitress placed drinks in front of Shauna and Josh before retreating to the busy bar area. Music and laughter floated through the restaurant as tables continued to fill. Spirits was an increasingly popular spot for after-work drinks and early dinners.

Josh raised his glass. 'Here's to you finally agreeing to dinner.'

'I hate to burst your bubble, but you did force me to as an apology. This isn't a date, I hope you realise.'

Josh put down his wine and grabbed his chest with both hands. 'Oh, the pain! My poor heart! How can you be so cruel?'

Shauna laughed. 'Idiot!' She opened her menu. 'What do you suggest we order?'

'I think as you're paying, and you are officially a multimillionaire, I shall order the, ah, drumroll, the gnocchi.'

Shauna dropped her menu, the corners of her mouth breaking into a huge smile. 'Gnocchi? Really, that's what you plan to order?'

'No need to laugh.'

Josh's mock offence made Shauna laugh harder. 'How about the lobster or even the eye fillet? Go all out.'

'Gnocchi's my favourite, especially with a gorgonzola sauce. Doesn't get much better than that.'

Shauna put her hands up. 'Okay, whatever you want. Don't let me stop you.'

The waiter came and took their order.

'So, the ex, hey,' Josh said as the waiter retreated to the kitchen. 'What's he doing sniffing around?'

Shauna laughed. 'That's a pretty good description for him, actually. To be honest I don't know and don't think he does either.' She went on to tell him how Simon had given her the ultimatum twelve months earlier, gone travelling and retuned for the three-month contract.

'He returned for work then, not to try and win you back?'

'I'm guessing he's looking for familiarity and comfort while he's home,' Shauna said. 'Mind you, he has been talking about just being friends.'

Josh laughed. 'Guys never mean that. Friends with benefits maybe, but never just friends.'

Shauna raised an eyebrow. 'Really? So this invitation tonight, for two friends to have dinner, has an ulterior motive.'

Heat flooded Josh's cheeks. 'I didn't mean that. I meant that when you've had a relationship with someone it's unlikely you really just want to be friends. You and I are work colleagues; I respect that completely and wouldn't want to ruin our professional relationship.' He blushed an even deeper shade of red. 'And, according to your rather arrogant ex, you're way out of my league.'

'Way out of most men's leagues in fact.' Shauna stared at him, enjoying watching Josh squirm in his seat. She smiled. 'Gotcha. Sorry, couldn't help myself.'

Josh let out a long breath. 'Thought I was in trouble for a moment. Tell me more about the ex.'

Shauna shook her head. 'Long, boring story. Definitely don't want to be revisiting any of it.'

'Fair enough. But keep all the shitty things he did front and foremost in your mind if he does try to win you back. People rarely change. Does he know about the lottery win?'

'Not yet. Although with the office knowing and how that's turning out, I guess I should assume he might find out.'

'Possibly. But I'd suggest you don't tell him if you don't need to. I know you've said you're not planning on getting back with him, but if you change your mind and he knows about the money you won't know whether he's pursuing you for you, or for your millions.'

'Good point. I'm learning that you can't predict how people will react to the win, so I will take that advice on for now.'

The waiter appeared with a bottle of St Hugo Shiraz.

'One of my favourites,' Josh said as the glasses were poured. He held his glass up to Shauna. 'To you and your sensible approach to winning lotto.'

Shauna clinked glasses with him and sipped her drink. 'As you are the only person I can really talk to about this, what should I do about my mother?'

'First, explain to me why she would get a lawyer to contact you? Is your relationship that bad?'

Shauna took a sip of her wine, carefully considering her answer. 'It's a hard one. As I told you, my dad left when I was four and we never heard from him again. No explanation and no financial help. My mother's moods have always been erratic. Loving life one minute, in the depths of depression the next. I've always been aware of an underlying resentment in her. We'd be having fun and suddenly something would remind her of him, and she'd become angry. She'd take things off me, send me to bed or cancel plans we might have had. We've never been close. I'm sure she blamed me for him leaving. Apparently, before I came along they were completely in love and had a wonderful time together.'

Josh nodded. 'Perhaps, or it was her way of blaming someone else for her marriage failing?'

'Who knows? This is the story she's always spun. She makes out he couldn't handle being a father, they started arguing and when things got worse he left. The fact that I've never seen him again suggests she's telling the truth.'

Josh looked like he had something to say but changed his mind.

'You don't agree?'

Josh frowned. 'I'm thinking, that's all.'

'No. Come on, tell me.'

'I just hope your father doesn't suddenly appear if he finds out about the money.'

Shauna's mouth dropped open. 'How would he hear?'

'I'm only suggesting you be careful. The whole office knows, and you said you were thinking of giving Andrew money for his brother. Make sure you consider things carefully first.'

'Too late, I gave them the money.'

'What? Already?'

'Yes, I saw Andrew this afternoon. It might be crazy, but I can help someone, possibly give him back his life. It was an incredible feeling. In fact, I started thinking I should be giving more away to help people.'

Shauna had been overwhelmed when Andrew came into the office earlier. He had openly wept when she'd written a cheque for the full two hundred thousand dollars.

'It's a good idea to find worthy causes,' Josh said. 'You just need to make sure that you're the one finding them, not the other way around. Avoid the conmen who will be coming out of the woodwork.'

Shauna's cheeks burned. 'Andrew's not a conman. God, do you think I'm so stupid I'd give money away to anyone with a sob story?'

Josh put his hands up in defence. 'Whoa, calm down. I'm just saying the more people who find out you have money, the more who will come after it. I don't want you to get hurt.'

The waitress placed their meals down, interrupting their heated discussion.

Josh took the white cloth napkin off his lap and started waving it to and fro. It had the desired effect.

Shauna began to laugh. 'Sorry, this money is making me crazy. Let's eat. The food smells wonderful.'

'Phew, so you're not going to storm out?'

'Not this time.'

Josh smiled and took a bite of his gnocchi. 'Oh wow, this is delicious. How's your lobster?'

'Better than delicious.' Shauna attacked her meal. 'Told you to order one.'

'Lobster's not my thing but try this.' Josh held out his fork.

Shauna leant across the table, taking the gnocchi into her mouth. 'Mmm, sensational. Okay, you win.'

'Told you. Getting back to your mum, why does she want so much money?'

Shauna shrugged. 'She's probably jealous and no doubt annoyed because she bought me the ticket. Her boyfriend is most likely also encouraging her, hoping he'll get something out of it.'

'Can you imagine before winning lotto someone coming up and giving you over a million dollars? Would you be complaining and asking for more?'

'Crazy, isn't it?'

'Did you contact a lawyer?'

Shauna shook her head as she reached across and stole another piece of gnocchi from his plate. 'Not yet, but I'm thinking it's a good idea.'

'Good. Now, what about you? What are your plans with the money? Why are you still working, for a start?'

'What do you mean?'

'Most people say the first thing they'd do if they won lotto is quit their job.'

Shauna laughed. 'Yes, but that's because they hate their job to begin with. I love what I do.'

'But you could do anything. Take a holiday, start your own business. Anything you want.'

Shauna continued eating, thinking about what Josh had said. 'All I've really thought about so far is getting a new car and buying a house or apartment. I was going to give some to charity and probably invest the rest. I've never bought lotto tickets, so I haven't sat around dreaming about what I'd do if I won. What would you do?'

Josh thought for a moment. 'Probably very similar. Like you, I love what I do. I'd probably throw a bit around for the fun of it, a fast car and a boat perhaps. I'd enjoy planning some amazing holidays, but I'm not sure if I'd quit my job straightaway. I like the buzz it gives me. You could think about setting up your own business.'

'Mmm, maybe. I'm not sure if I'd want the responsibility that would come with it. I think I'll just enjoy a few luxuries for now. The money will be there if I want to do something different. One bit of advice I was told for lotto winners was not to make drastic changes in your life too quickly. Lotto winners are known to end up bankrupt and unhappy after a few years of bad decisions. I don't want to be one of them. So there you go – turns out we're both sensible and boring.'

Josh raised an eyebrow. 'Not sure if I'd go as far as saying we're boring, but then again I don't know all that much about you. Tell me about your childhood. It'll help me judge your level of boringness.'

Shauna laughed. 'What do you want to know?'

'The usual stuff. Where you grew up, went to school, music you like.'

'All the things you'd talk about if you were on a date?' Shauna teased.

'No, all the things you'd talk about on a non-date.'

'Fine, I'll bore you.' Shauna started talking of her childhood, her days at university and previous jobs.

'Sounds like a rough childhood,' Josh said.

Shauna shrugged. 'Maybe. Lonely is more how I found it. I only had Mum, and her mood swings were so extreme that I never really knew what to expect. She could be great, don't get me wrong.

93

We did have some fun, it was just her bad moods tended to over-shadow everything else. The best thing for me was meeting Tess. We met in high school and she was my saviour. I didn't have to pretend my mum was normal and everything was okay with Tess. She would roll her eyes if Mum was having a fit, tell me to grab my stuff and I'd sleep at her place. I became a pretty permanent fixture at their house.' She smiled. 'Her mum rang me one evening asking where I was. I'd been there so many nights in a row she'd just assumed I would be there again for dinner and was worried when I didn't turn up. I'd gone home, of course, but I think she thought I'd moved in. She was really easy-going too. Told me I was welcome anytime and if I ever needed any help with Mum just to let her know. They made my life feel normal because I had them to escape to when things weren't so good at home.'

Josh shook his head. 'I can't even begin to imagine what you went through with your mum. My mum is the one person I know I can always count on. It doesn't matter what I do or say, she's one hundred percent in my court at all times. I couldn't feel more loved. Dad's another case altogether but Mum is an absolutely rock. I'm sorry you don't have that.'

Shauna smiled. 'Don't be. Like I said, we had good times and still do from time to time. She's just very unpredictable. The one thing she did do was help me become independent at a young age. I moved out of home as soon as I got a place at uni and worked part-time all through my university years. With no other family I knew I had to be self-sufficient and so I made sure I was. Tess's family were my back-up when I needed them, so I wasn't completely alone.'

'Where is this famous Tess now?' Josh asked. 'She sounds like a great friend.'

'She is, but she's working and travelling in Europe and America for the next few months and she lives in Sydney when she is here.

I miss her like crazy, to be honest. Anyway, enough talk about me. Let's focus on you.'

Josh rolled his eyes. 'Boring! You're much more interesting. But feel free to ask me anything. I'm an open book.'

But Shauna found, as Josh repeatedly deflected the conversation back to her, that he was anything but.

'You know,' Shauna said as they left the restaurant just before midnight, 'considering how many hours dinner went on for, I hardly learnt anything about you. Are you hiding something?'

'What do you mean?'

'You managed to turn nearly every question into a question about me. I didn't learn anything about your family or your upbringing.' She raised her eyebrows. 'You know, the usual stuff friends discuss.'

Josh laughed. 'That's because you're more interesting, and it gives us the perfect excuse to go out for another non-date.'

Shauna smiled. 'We'll see about that.'

Josh rubbed his hands together. 'Want to get a nightcap? I could consider sharing some of my story with you.' He pointed at a bar across the street.

Shauna checked her watch. 'I'd better say no tonight. It's getting late and I've got an early appointment with a treadmill.'

'No tonight? Does that mean yes to another night?'

Shauna smiled. 'If you shout next time. I can't afford to carry you with such expensive gnocchi tastes.'

'Okay, but at least let me get you home.' Josh waved to a taxi driving past on the other side of the road. It slowed and turned back towards them. 'I'll drop you first and keep going.'

'Don't be silly, you live in the opposite direction. There's another one coming.'

Josh hesitated. 'Are you sure? I'm happy to come home with you.'

Shauna raised an eyebrow.

'Not that. Take you home to your door, not come in or anything.'

Shauna leant towards Josh, lowering her voice. 'What if I wanted you to come in?'

Josh's eyes were bright. 'Um, I didn't think you would want me to. Remember, work colleagues, too much respect and all that.'

Shauna winked, opened the taxi door and jumped in. She wound down the window. 'Thanks for tonight, I've had a lovely time. I'll see you tomorrow.'

Josh exhaled. 'Jesus, you had me going for a minute.'

'Scared you, did I?'

'No, aroused followed by frustrated would be a perfect description.'

Shauna laughed as the taxi slowly pulled away.

Chapter Eight

Frankie smiled at an older woman as she got herself a cup of tea from the self-serve stand. The woman returned her smile. 'You're new?'

Frankie nodded. 'First time. I'm a bit nervous actually.'

The woman laughed. 'I'm Helen and there's no need to be nervous. If you're new that means you've won recently. Congratulations!'

'Thank you. I'm Frankie.'

Helen smiled. 'I remember that feeling when you first win. It's amazing, isn't it? My heart practically fell out of my chest it was beating so hard. Where were you when you found out?'

'In the back garden with my husband and youngest daughter.'

'Did the neighbours hear your screams?'

Frankie laughed. 'They probably did hear a bit of commotion; my daughter let out a few shrieks. I think I went into shock.' Frankie wasn't going to elaborate on how she'd been filled with dread rather than excitement.

'You've come on your own. Was your husband unable to make it?'

'One of us had to look after the girls,' Frankie explained. She wished Tom had come with her, but he'd said no; he agreed with Shauna's summation of the group and thought it was a bad idea.

'It's not like we've told anyone or spent any money, Frankie. So what's the point? And anyway, due to your ridiculous phobia about the money and banning us from spending any of it, I have to go to work so we can afford to put food on the table this week.' He'd stormed off before allowing her to make any comment.

Helen patted her arm. 'Good on you for coming then. I'm just going to say a quick hello to Ivan before the group begins. It's lovely to meet you, Frankie.'

Frankie smiled as she lowered herself into one of the chairs that were predictably arranged in a circle. Helen was lovely and her nerves were settling. If she'd ever thought about attending any kind of support group, this is not the one she would have picked. If she'd followed her family history, she'd be more likely sitting at a Gamblers Anonymous meeting or a meeting for people with depression, or relatives of victims of suicide. She shuddered, grateful that her and Tom's life in no way reflected that of her parents. But that was partly why she was here. Money had only ever brought harm to her family. The more they'd had, the more her father had gambled away and the deeper her mother had slid into sadness and depression.

'Hi there.' A man in his forties sat down next to Frankie, interrupting her spiralling thoughts. 'I'm Todd. Nice to meet you.'

'Frankie.'

'Recent winner?'

Frankie nodded. 'Very recent.'

'Congratulations. I bet the excitement levels are high in your house at the moment.'

'Certainly with my husband and kids. I'm a little more cautious, so hoping to get some good tips tonight to ensure we don't lose all of the money.'

'You've come to the right place. I've been coming on and off for a few months. I find the information shared is a great reinforcement for me. Reminds me why I shouldn't go blurting out to every family member or friend that we went from struggling to pay the mortgage one day to being multimillionaires the next. Anytime I feel the desire to do something silly, and by that I mean open my big fat mouth, I come back here for a session. At least I can talk freely in this space as we're all winners.'

Frankie nodded. It was such a strange concept that something that most people would consider wonderful had happened, yet all the advice suggested not to share the information. She wondered if Todd had told anyone. Pamela entered the room before Frankie had the chance to ask.

'Frankie, so glad you made it.' She looked around the rest of the gathering. 'No Shauna, I see. Not really a surprise.'

Frankie smiled. 'I somehow doubt we'll see Shauna again. She seemed like she could handle herself.'

Todd laughed. 'That's usually the first mistake: not listening to the advice that's provided. What's the format tonight, Pamela? Anyone coming to speak to us?'

Pamela nodded and checked her watch. 'Mary, a past winner, is joining us tonight and hopefully will have some pearls of wisdom to share from her experiences. She'll be here in about ten minutes.'

'Did you want me to set the chairs up facing the stage?' Todd asked.

'No, she wants it to be very informal. She'll just join us in our circle so that people can ask questions as she talks. We'll get started now. It will give us some time to welcome Frankie and then we can give Mary the floor. It doesn't look like we have any other new members joining us tonight.' Pamela clapped her hands, calling the group together.

After being introduced, Frankie sat and listened as the group discussion began. She was the only new member and it appeared that fresh blood provided ample opportunity for advice. She wished Tom had come as some of what was being said was very useful.

'Each session we start with a brief run-down of what we call the five steps,' Pamela explained. 'We don't go into detail on each step every week as otherwise the information would become too repetitive and people would only come once. We do find most sessions end up concentrating on one or two of the steps. Basically, they are what we consider important for retaining your winnings and enjoying life. They include the importance of legal and financial representation, protecting your privacy, avoiding major changes in your life, self-control and being prepared for emotional turmoil.'

Frankie nodded. Pamela had covered these areas in their meeting at the Gold Power offices.

'You'll find our discussions are more relevant here, Frankie, as you'll hear real life examples of what people are doing to ensure these steps are working for them.'

The door of the community centre opened and a woman only slightly older than Frankie stepped into the room.

Pamela stood. 'Come and join us, Mary.'

The woman smiled, her heels clicking across the floorboards as she joined the group. Frankie couldn't help but feel impressed as she took in her glowing skin and happy, friendly expression. Her make-up was minimal and she exuded health. If this was what millions of dollars could do for you, she might embrace it, after all.

Mary was given a small round of applause after Pamela introduced her.

She looked around the group and grinned. 'How good is it that we get to be here? All of us, millionaires. And none of us probably ever expected to be. I won two years ago and my life has changed, but not many people realise how much. When I first won, Pamela suggested I come along to the group and I'm so glad I did.

There was so much to learn from others about what had and hadn't worked, so I thought I'd come and share that with you all today.'

Frankie found herself hanging off every word as Mary spoke about her cautious approach. 'I spent a few months working out what I would do with the money before I mentioned it to anyone at all. I won fifty million by the way.'

A ripple of whispers erupted. Even in a room full of lotto winners, fifty million was a lot.

'I engaged an advisor and a lawyer before I shared my news with anyone. I'm one of three siblings and my parents, while divorced, are both still alive. They were the only people I wanted to gift money to, but I was concerned about the possible ramifications that would have. So, on the advice of my lawyer, I had a non-disclosure agreement drawn up. I got the family together and told them I'd been lucky and come into some money and planned to gift a little bit to each of them, but it was on the condition that they all signed a non-disclosure agreement. The agreement means they can't disclose to anyone where they received the money from, and they had to agree to meet with a financial advisor as I knew how beneficial that was for me.'

'How did you give them the money?' Pamela asked.

Mary grinned. 'It was the highlight of winning to be honest. I hired caterers and put on a spectacular dinner for them, telling them I had an announcement. I'm single but they assumed it was to introduce a man or announce a promotion or something like that. I told them about my win, but the agreement needed to be signed prior to any more discussion. They all rushed to sign. I then told them collectively how much I was gifting them, which was one hundred and fifty thousand dollars per year for the rest of their lives.'

Frankie found herself smiling along with the rest of the group as Mary told her story. She could only imagine how wonderful Mary must have felt hosting that dinner.

'How did you come up with that figure?' Pamela asked.

'One of my advisors told me about a study that was done with thousands of people around the world that discovered that an income of one hundred and five thousand dollars a year maximised happiness. Getting more than that doesn't actually make people happier. The study was done in US dollars, so I allowed for the exchange rate and brought it up to one hundred and fifty thousand.'

'You don't think they would have preferred the money upfront?' Todd asked.

Mary shrugged. 'I wasn't going to give them that option. If I gave them millions of dollars upfront they'd be in the same position as most lotto winners. People coming after them for money or getting themselves into financial trouble. I led them to believe that that's how I have to access the money, so they have no choice if they want to keep receiving it.'

'How are the family now?' Pamela asked.

'Very happy,' Mary said. 'Only one of my brothers quit his job. The rest are pretty much living as they were before, but without the financial strain they were previously under. My sister sent her kids to private school, rather than public, my mum travels most of the year. The brother who stopped working isn't just sitting around. He was a high school teacher and passionate about working with troubled kids. He also loves horses, so he's using his money to run a riding school that offers equine therapy for troubled youth. Most of the kids can't afford to pay to attend but the combination of grants and Will's own investment means it can operate.'

Pamela smiled at Frankie. 'I told you it wasn't all doom and gloom. What Mary's story really shows us is that you can share your good fortune, but you need to plan it out and put safeguards in place.' She turned to Mary. 'What happens if any of your siblings or parents do disclose where the money came from?'

'The agreement says they are responsible to pay the money back. To be honest, I'm not sure I'd want to go about enforcing it and splitting up the family, but it seemed to be enough to have them all agree. My siblings and I have always been close. That's something to keep in mind if you are thinking this sounds like a good idea. We've always had each other's backs so I could possibly have done all of this without the agreement to start with. But if you aren't as close to your family or friends, be very careful how you go about giving out gifts.'

'I wish I'd had your foresight or your lawyer to advise me, Mary,' a man in his fifties said. 'I'm Ivan, by the way. I made the classic error of giving my two sisters a third each of my winnings. Our parents are no longer with us, so they are the two closest people to me in my life. One sister has done all the right things as far as getting advice, investing wisely and not making major changes in her life. But the other went on a three-year party. Spent the lot.' He shook his head. 'She went from having a secure job to being unemployed and in debt. She's just beginning to get back on her feet. I want to help her, of course, especially as I feel responsible for her downfall. Having listened to Mary's story I think I might set up a weekly or monthly payment to help her out. Not a huge amount, she'll still need to get a job, but enough to relieve the pressure. Not enough to party and go crazy though.' He turned to Mary. 'Thanks for sharing your story, it's a really sensible approach.'

Frankie drank in the rest of the advice as other members of the group added their own experiences over the next half hour. It was a fascinating group and world she hadn't even known existed.

'I hope we'll see you again, Frankie,' Pamela said as they stood to say their goodbyes. 'There's a lot of value to being part of the group as you navigate your way through this new start to your life.'

Frankie nodded. 'I'm sure I'll be back.'

'We'd love you to share with the group your plans for your money and how you've done things so far. If you're comfortable with that, of course.'

Frankie laughed. 'At this point, there's nothing to tell. It's all locked in a bank account. As positive as Mary's story was I've spent too much time googling all the disaster stories. Adding Ivan's into the mix makes me think I might donate the entire amount to charity. It might be less of a headache.'

Pamela laughed. 'Don't do anything hasty. Our "Don't Make Major Changes in Your Life" applies to the money too. If you're not ready to do anything with it then leave it in the bank or invested until you are. Like you've heard tonight, there are plenty of positive stories in amongst the negative. You'll hear a little bit of the negative side of winning when you're here, but that's part of the reason to come. To hear how the person handled the situation, what choices they made and what ramifications those choices may have had.'

'The difficult stories keep it real,' Frankie said. 'And that suits me. Money can be dangerous – very dangerous – and I'm wary of it.'

Pamela raised her eyebrows. 'Sounds like there's more to those words.'

Frankie nodded. There was, but it was far too personal to share. Instead, she leant across to Pamela and hugged her. 'Thank you for the invitation and for running this group. I can see why you do it and I can see how much everyone gets from it. I'll be back, hopefully next week.'

Pamela hugged her back. 'We'll look forward to seeing you.'

Frankie scrubbed the frying pan in an attempt to remove the heavily baked-on sauce. She silently willed Tom to leave the room before another argument unfolded. Every night this week had been a variation of the same theme. It was like a broken record. Now, having returned from the support group the previous night and sharing Ivan's story, she found it hard to believe he was still pestering her.

'Frankie?'

She placed the pan on the sink to drain and turned to face Tom. 'What?'

Tom put his coffee cup down on the table. 'Come on, hon, we're sitting on millions of dollars. Why can't we spend some?'

'The money isn't ours. When will you get it?' Frankie cursed the day she'd ever found the twenty dollars.

'Don't be silly, the money is ours. You won it.'

'I didn't win it. The ticket was bought with someone else's money. If anything, it probably belongs to Jim. But definitely not us.'

Tom sighed. 'Why can't you accept something good happened to us? We're living in this hellhole, we can't afford the electricity bill, we can't afford anything. We literally have millions in the bank. Why don't we just spend some? I'm not talking about a lot. Enough to find us a decent place to live at least.'

'Do you realise how unhappy people end up after winning lotto? Do a Google search and read the stories. If you do you'll be donating every cent of the money to charity tomorrow or burning it.'

'There are plenty of people living happily after winning too, Frankie. Of course news articles present the negative side, that's what news is. The more sensational, the bigger the disaster, the better. A story about a family living happily ever after with millions of dollars probably doesn't sell magazines. Isn't the whole point of attending the support group to learn how not to make mistakes? Tell me three of the positive things or tips you learnt.'

'Definitely see a financial advisor. If you're going to tell people you won or give them money, don't tell them how much you actually won. It leads to resentment when they think you didn't give them enough.'

'Good point. And?'

'And don't make major changes in your life. Take your time to decide what to do with the money and don't fritter it away on luxuries you never needed before.'

'All good advice.'

Frankie nodded. 'Yes, but there are so many stories online of people who've ended up losing friends, becoming depressed and going bankrupt a few years down the track. Some even take their own lives. Using the money will cause misery.'

Tom wrung his hands together. 'Misery? Hon, what do you think we live in now?'

'We aren't miserable. The money's already coming between us. Before the money we were so happy. Our problems never affected our happiness.'

Tom rubbed his face and sighed again. 'Do you honestly believe I'm not affected? How do you think I feel about the fact that I can't provide for my family? We're struggling to cover the essential expenses, let alone give the girls anything special. Rod and Dash think I'm a loser and my parents probably did, too. A total stranger told you she thinks we're dole-bludgers. Who knows how many people see us the same way?'

'Oh, come on. Neither your parents nor Rod ever thought anything of the sort and Dash isn't worth wasting energy on. The woman at school was one nasty person who we should ignore. The girls love our life. We spend more time as a family than any of their friends do. They don't ask for fancy clothes or new computers or phones; they need our attention, our love.'

'Fine, fine. I'm only saying our lives could be easier if we spent a little bit. Poor Hope's using that archaic computer for homework that hasn't got half the programs she should be using. It's crazy when we're in the position to buy exactly what she needs.' Tom yawned.

'Why don't you go to bed? You look done in.'

'I am. Think about the money, would you?' He stared at her for a moment before coming around and taking her in his arms. 'Babe, we're not your parents. I get that money scares you. That being poor and having nothing is actually easier for you than the alternative, but you need to trust me. I love you and I love the girls. I have no interest in gambling and no reason I'd ever be driven to it.'

'You never know what might happen, though.' Frankie's eyes filled with tears. 'My dad wasn't a gambler either to begin with. It was his escape when things got too hard.'

Tom kissed her forehead. 'I know that, but history isn't going to repeat itself, I promise. We have an opportunity to improve our own lives and the girls' too; we don't have to go crazy. In fact, I like the advice you heard tonight about not frittering away the money on luxuries. The things I'm talking about are basic human needs. A house that can be heated through winter, a car so we're not forever waiting for buses and trains. Clothes for the girls that aren't from the op shop. I'm not planning on buying a sports car or a racehorse and a two-thousand-dollar dress to wear to the track. Although I could give Logan a run for her money then.' He grinned as Frankie managed a smile. He kissed her again. 'I love you and I know you're wanting to protect us but this time I think you're right and wrong. Right to want to be cautious, but wrong to throw back the opportunity. Just think about it.'

Frankie stayed in the warmth of the kitchen after Tom went to bed. She made herself a cup of tea and sat down. As she ran her fingers over the cracks in the old wooden tabletop, she thought about Tom's words. He was exhausted trying to work as many hours as possible as a labourer and they were constantly going backwards with money. Frankie sighed, taking in the room through fresh eyes.

She had tried to make the house cosy, but the peeling paint, crumbling plaster, rotten floorboards and damp-soaked walls made it unachievable. Maybe Tom was right: they weren't her parents. It was her father's gambling that had caused unbearable pain and suffering for her mother, not actually having money in the first place.

In fact, whether her father had one dollar or a million dollars it was gambled away. It was an addiction, the root of which wasn't even to do with money. It was the constant need to try to fix what had happened. She'd learnt as the years passed that his desire had been to help her mother. To make things better after tragedy had struck. How wrong his approach had been. Instead the hole into which her mother had crawled had become deeper and deeper until it was so deep she couldn't find her way out.

The situation with her and Tom was different and she needed to start believing in that. She had listened to him tonight. The positive comments from the support group were inspiring and proved it didn't have to end in disaster. Perhaps she should, while continuing to be cautious, start enjoying the money. She finished her tea and put her cup in the sink. An uneasy feeling crept into the pit of her stomach as she flicked off the light and went to join Tom.

Early the next morning Frankie crept out of the house, careful not to wake the rest of the family. The sun had only just begun to rise as she pulled her jacket around her and, breathing in the crisp autumn air, strode briskly in the direction of the newsagent.

Jim looked surprised to see her outside his shop so early. 'What are you doing out and about at this time? I thought your early-morning visits were a thing of the past?'

When Frankie had first discovered the lottery win, she had gone to see Jim every day, checking if anyone had been back for the twenty dollars. Every time she'd asked, he'd reminded her that even if they had, he'd only be returning twenty dollars to them, not ten million.

Frankie smiled at Jim. 'Yes, they are a thing of the past, but I'm doing one last check before I spend some of the money.'

Jim took a step back. 'What? You haven't spent any of it?'

Frankie blushed. 'I've been too busy concentrating on the potential negatives to consider actually enjoying it.'

'You need to fill that glass of yours, Frankie. Walking around in life with a half-empty glass is never much fun. Why don't you go and treat your lovely family to a special breakfast?' He pointed towards the bakery.

'I don't think—' Frankie stopped herself. She would have to change her mindset that they could now do things if they were going to use the money. She smiled at Jim. 'Fantastic idea, thank you. And I'll bring you back that coffee I owe you.'

'Now you're talking my language! And I'll have mine completely full too, thanks. Never believed in this glass half-empty, half-full baloney.' He grinned. 'Like to have mine always filled to the brim. You should too, love.'

Frankie smiled. He was right. She was usually a positive person and encouraged the girls to be the same. The money had brought out the worst in her. She was lucky that Tom got it, that he understood why. Now it was time to show the family how to enjoy their newfound wealth in a responsible manner. That's the type of role model she needed to be for the girls, not a woman in her thirties hiding *just in case*.

A flutter of excitement came over her as she slipped back into the house, laying the table in preparation for a celebratory breakfast. For the first time since winning the money she felt exhilarated. They could do anything. Anything at all. They had ten million dollars in the bank! Tom and the girls woke up to the smell of warm croissants, muffins and fresh coffee. Fern squealed with delight.

'Does this mean what I think?' Tom grabbed Frankie by the waist and twirled her around the small kitchen.

Frankie laughed, her heart racing. For the briefest of moments she felt powerful, capable of anything. 'Yes, but on one condition. I want us to visit a financial advisor before we do anything else so we don't end up in a mess like some people do.'

Tom stopped dancing, tugged Frankie towards him and kissed her firmly on the lips.

◆ ◆ ◆

Three days later Frankie found herself sitting opposite John Wilton, Financial Planner. A giggle rose up in her throat. The whole situation seemed surreal and quite ridiculous. She, Frankie York, a millionaire. The financial planner was seated comfortably behind his large mahogany desk, wearing an expensive suit, slicked-back hair and a large gold Rolex on his wrist. Frankie couldn't begin to imagine her reaction if Tom ever came home looking like this.

'Frankie, Tom.' John Wilton put a file to one side and looked at them. 'Congratulations. A ten-million-dollar lotto win is not something I see every day. With some clever investments, we can turn this into a lot more money for you.'

'What sort of investments?' Frankie asked.

'It depends on your level of comfort, but for starters I would be suggesting a mixed portfolio. Invest a percentage of the money in high-risk, high-return commodities, some in medium-risk and probably at least half in low-risk investments.'

'High risk? I don't want to lose any money,' Frankie said.

John laughed. 'Neither do we, let me assure you. It's in all of our best interests to turn this money into an even larger amount.

We would recommend taking a large percentage of the overall sum to invest in low-risk funds. Funds that will pay more than a term deposit, though.' John pulled out a folder and handed it to Tom. 'Now, this should give you an idea of the sort of return on investments we've been having over the last few years.'

An hour later Frankie and Tom sat in a cafe across the road from John Wilton's office. 'Are you sure you don't want some cake?' Tom asked. 'Cake's affordable now, you realise?'

Frankie gave a tight smile. 'I know, but I still find eight dollars a slice excessive. I'm probably not cut out to be rich.'

Tom laughed. 'Don't be silly. Old habits will take a while to break. Let's start now. I'm going to get a piece of cake to share, not spend too much at once.'

Frankie tapped her fingers on the table as she watched Tom make his way over to the counter. The uneasy feeling in her stomach returned. She'd tuned out halfway through John Wilton's explanation of stocks and bonds and whatever else he was going on about. Did they really need to invest the money and make more? Surely ten million was enough for anyone.

'So, what did you think of our Mr Wilton?' Tom asked through a mouthful of chocolate mud cake.

'I didn't understand much. How about you?'

'Neither did I, but that's why we get experts in to guide us. I believe we'd be best to invest half with them and invest the other half ourselves. We can decide how much to give away, work out how much to use to live off and put the rest in a term deposit. I'm not sure whether we're best to have one term deposit or split the money into a number of smaller deposits. I'll find out.'

Frankie raised an eyebrow. 'Listen to you talking like a financial planner. You've been giving this some thought.'

Tom's eyes widened. 'Thought? It's all I think about. We've been given a chance to change our lives. The money's bought us freedom we didn't have before. We should make the most of it, but without losing any either.'

Frankie smiled and picked up a spoon.

'What? Why are you smiling?'

'You're sounding pretty sexy, Mr York. Talk money a bit more.'

Tom laughed. 'Turning you on, am I?'

Frankie slowly licked the remains of the cake from her spoon. 'Mmm, might be. Don't stop, keep talking.'

Tom groaned and shifted in his seat. 'Bloody hell, stop licking that spoon like that. You'll get us both arrested in a minute with what I'm thinking.'

Frankie stood up. 'Hold that thought. Come on, let's go; we've got a few hours before the girls come home.'

Tom didn't need to be convinced. Jumping up, he grabbed Frankie's hand and led her out of the cafe.

Frankie's pleasure built the next afternoon as she watched the anticipation on the girls' faces as they waited in the driveway for Tom. He'd rung ten minutes earlier telling them he had a surprise. Fern pulled herself up on to the pillar by the front gate. She craned her neck to be the first to see Tom come around the corner from Dorcas Street.

'If he comes that way, you idiot,' Hope said.

Fern stuck out her tongue. 'He always walks down Dorcas. Lionel, then Dorcas, then into our street. You're the idiot.'

'Okay, girls, enough,' Frankie said. 'Call out when you see Dad and we'll walk down to meet him together.' She leant down and tried to straighten a broken paver in the path. Another thing that needed fixing. They would have to start thinking about moving somewhere nicer. Frankie's thoughts were interrupted by the beeping of a car horn. A midnight-blue Honda CRV turned into the driveway. Tom waved from the driver's seat.

Fern jumped off the pillar, a shriek of delight escaping her lips as she ran towards the car. Hope followed closely. 'Is this ours, Dad?'

'Sure is. Jump in and we'll take a drive.' The girls climbed into the back. Tom got out of the car, making way for Frankie. 'Come on, babe, come and check out your new wheels. There's another surprise, too.'

Frankie was transported back to being a five-year-old on Christmas Day. The wonderful bubbles of excitement starting in her stomach days before and lasting for days after. 'It's lovely, Tom. What a surprise!'

'Are you sure? We can choose a different car if you prefer? This is for you.'

'Why for me? Won't you need to drive, too?'

'I think we could use one each, don't you?'

'Did you buy two?'

'No, I wanted to make sure you liked this one first before getting myself anything. We've been without a car for so long we're not in any hurry. I'm more than happy to make this one mine if you'd prefer to choose your own, by the way.' He handed Frankie the keys. 'Come on, jump in and take us for a drive.'

Frankie climbed into the driver's seat, admiring everything as she did. 'I love it, Tom. Absolutely love it! I've never had a new car before. In fact, I've never even had my own car. We had those old bombs you owned when we were first married, but we've used public transport for so many years now. I hope I remember how to drive.'

'Exactly why I got an automatic, easier to handle. It's an all-wheel drive too so we can go off-road. Nothing too extreme, but we can get to some places we couldn't in a regular car.'

Frankie thought of the national parks she had always dreamt of exploring.

Hope broke into her thoughts. 'Mum, the car's got sat nav and everything. I think you can even send text messages.' Hope was looking at the car manual.

Frankie laughed. 'Mmm, texting. Useful.'

'Imagine if you moved into the twenty-first century and bought an iPhone,' Hope said.

'Good idea,' Tom said. 'Let's talk about phones later. We need to go.'

Fern stuck her head through the seats to the front. 'What's the other surprise? Something for me and Hope?'

'Kind of. A surprise you'll get a say in at least. We're meeting a real estate agent in fifteen minutes. He's going to take us around a few nicer houses to rent.'

'Now?' Frankie asked.

'Yep. What do you think? Is this okay?'

'Of course. A house is the number one thing on our list.'

'He can show us properties for sale, but you said you'd rather rent in an area first before we commit to buying.'

Frankie leant across and hugged Tom. 'Thank you.' She lowered her voice and whispered in his ear. 'Remember what happened after the cake the other day?'

Tom nodded, his breathing becoming more rapid.

'Prepare for a repeat performance tonight.'

'Performance?' Fern said. 'What are you two talking about?'

Frankie pulled away from Tom and turned around to speak to Fern. 'Nothing, darling, just thanking him for being so thoughtful. I think your dad was right; having this money is only going to improve our lives.'

◆ ◆ ◆

Frankie moved around the kitchen island and looked outside to the leafy courtyard. Her family loved this house, but she still wasn't sure. They had been shown six properties, all a huge improvement on where they currently lived, and while she could have said yes to living in any of them, the expense was her concern.

She turned to face Tom, aware of the girls watching her. 'I know we can afford the rent, but do we really want to be spending four times more than we pay now?'

'We need to rent the quality of house we want to buy,' Tom said. 'These would give us a feel for a bigger, nicer house and they're still close to school, but in a better neighbourhood. This is where you've always dreamt of buying.'

'You're going a bit fast for me. As much as I love the idea of moving, shouldn't we sit down and work out what we need in a house?'

'We can work out the details when we buy or build our dream house. For now, our priority is getting out of the dump we're in. I don't even want to risk parking the new car in the driveway.'

Frankie smiled. 'The area's not that bad. Nothing's happened to us in the ten years we've lived there.'

'Only because there's nothing of value to wreck or steal.'

Fern interrupted their conversation. 'Can we choose our bedrooms now?'

Tom squeezed Frankie's hand.

Frankie turned to Hope. 'Do you like this one?'

Hope's eyes widened. 'Like? No. Love? Yes. You've seen the outdoor area. Imagine sitting out there for breakfast or lunch.' Her forehead creased. 'One problem, though.'

'What?' Frankie asked.

'Furniture. In addition to the open-plan living space, separate living, dining and media rooms, there're four bedrooms and an office. The master suite is huge and even has a balcony. I'm worried our furniture won't be enough.'

Tom laughed. 'You might want to consider a career in real estate, Hope. You're doing a better sales job than the agent. You're right, though. We'd need to go and do a bit of shopping before we move in.' He turned to Frankie. 'What do you think?'

Frankie had wandered from room to room, trying to imagine them living here. It was at least four, if not five times the size of their current house. 'You don't think this one is too big?'

She was met with three loud no's.

Of course, the girls would enjoy having their own space. She turned to her family and smiled. 'Let's vote, shall we? All in favour of moving, please raise your hand.'

Three hands shot up into the air.

Frankie nodded. 'Okay, decision made. Find the agent and we'll sign the lease.'

Chapter Nine

Shauna waited for her mother to open the front door, unable to shake the uneasy feeling that had settled in the pit of her stomach. It was a week since she'd received the lawyer's letter telling her her mother was suing her and until today she'd been uncontactable. Not answering her phone or door. Shauna had finally received a text message from her that morning saying that she and Bob had taken a holiday and were returning later that day. Now it was time to confront her. Her own mother suing her? It was crazy. But, based on Lorraine's erratic behaviours, not all that surprising. While it was unlikely speaking with her mother would make a difference, she'd decided to try and have a conversation before arranging to meet with a lawyer.

Lorraine opened the front door a fraction. 'What do you want?'

'To talk to you. I've been waiting all week. Are you going to let me in?'

'Fine.' Lorraine opened the door wider.

Shauna pushed past and walked down the hallway. Bob rose to his feet as she entered the living room.

'Hello, Shauna.'

'Bob.' Damn, he was the last person she wanted as part of this conversation. She turned to Lorraine. 'Can we talk in private, please?'

Lorraine folded her arms across her chest. 'No, whatever you plan to say you can say to both of us.'

Shauna was silent for a moment. 'Okay,' she said finally. 'What do I need to say to convince you to withdraw your claim on the money?'

Lorraine's laugh was bitter. 'Nothing. We'll fight until we get our share, won't we, Bob?'

Bob nodded.

Shauna turned to face him. 'Did you put her up to this? What on earth do you need five million dollars for?'

'Why do you need ten million?'

'I don't, but it's my money, not yours.'

'Debatable. Your mum bought the ticket for us.'

Shauna stared at Lorraine. 'What? The ticket was my birthday present.'

Bob laughed. 'Yeah, a present you got because she forgot to buy you one and had to quickly turn something into a gift. If only we'd had a spare bottle of wine, hey, love?'

Lorraine shrugged.

'You're kidding? You forgot my birthday again?'

'So? It's a birthday, big deal. It's hardly the end of the world.'

'You're unbelievable. How can a mother forget her daughter's birthday?'

Lorraine sighed. 'Oh, don't be so melodramatic. Listen to her, would you, Bob?'

'Ridiculous.'

Shauna tried to keep her cool. 'I'm right here you know. So you think you have a claim to the money because the ticket was yours and not supposed to be mine?'

'Exactly,' Lorraine said. 'And please note we're only asking for half, we're not expecting the entire winnings, even though the ticket should be ours.'

'My, how generous of you.'

'No need to be sarcastic. Bob and I would have given you half if we'd won.'

Shauna raised her eyebrows. 'Really? I can't quite imagine Bob handing over five million dollars.'

Anger flashed in Bob's eyes. 'You have no idea what I would do, but I can assure you you'll be handing five million over to us.'

'Why don't you save us all this unpleasantness and give us our share,' Lorraine said. 'Not waste a lot of money on lawyers.'

Shauna looked at her mother. 'You went to a lawyer before even speaking to me.'

'I spoke to you. When you gave me the measly one and a half million, I told you I expected half. Your response was to walk out and tell me to return the rest if I wasn't happy. I hardly thought talking to you again was going to make any difference. We spoke to Bob's friend Greg. He's a lawyer, and he said we were being extremely reasonable only asking for half, and he says we have a winnable case.'

Bob put an arm around Lorraine. 'Yeah, Shauna, he reckons we're entitled to the lot.'

Shauna shook her head. 'There's no point discussing this any further.'

'Don't be greedy, Shauna,' Lorraine called. 'You can prevent a lot of ill feeling by doing the right thing.'

Shauna walked out of the house and over to her car with mixed feelings. Sure, she didn't need ten million dollars, but being forced to hand it over to the likes of Bob? No way.

Sadness settled over her as she drove away from her mother's house. History was repeating itself once again, her mother siding with a man – a man who would probably only be around for a few months – instead of with her. Why wasn't she ever enough for her mother? She'd never understood why it couldn't be the two of them supporting each other. That Lorraine always had to have a man to fall back on. The men she chose were unreliable and usually after something – whether it be money, sex or a place to live. It was never true love. She wondered if her father was a loser like they had been. Her mother certainly talked as if that's exactly what he was.

Shauna sighed and checked the clock on her car as she drove aimlessly towards the city. It was nearly seven and she wasn't far from Collingwood. The support group met on a Thursday night. As much as she'd sneered at the very idea of it, Pamela was right about unpredictable things appearing out of the woodwork. No doubt the same had happened to other members of the group. She made a quick decision, turned left into Hoddle Street and headed to the community centre. It wasn't going to hurt to attend one meeting.

Shauna walked into the community centre and stopped. Jesus, what a cliché. Twenty or so chairs placed in a circle, a couple of long tables off to the side with a large hot water urn and tea and coffee supplies. They just needed a plate of doughnuts, and it would be straight out of a movie.

'Shauna!'

She turned to see a friendly face smiling at her.

'Frankie York! How are you?'

She was surprised when Frankie hugged her. 'Pleased to see you. This is only my second meeting and I wasn't sure about coming. It'll be nice to have a friend here.'

Shauna smiled. She'd been elevated to friend status already. 'How was last week's?'

Frankie frowned. 'Good and bad. I'm doing my best to try and take the inspiring bits from the meeting.'

'Hopefully there'll be a lot of those tonight,' Shauna said. 'The way my day's unfolded I could certainly use some inspiration. I've already made one of the classic mistakes Pamela advised us not to.'

Frankie raised a questioning eyebrow.

Shauna sighed. 'Put it this way. Don't tell anyone the amount you won. It's a really bad idea.' There was no time to elaborate as Pamela called the group together for the start of the meeting.

'We're welcoming Shauna tonight,' Pamela said, smiling at her, 'and also Barry and Ophelia, all recent winners.'

The group clapped to welcome them.

Pamela ran quickly through the five steps the group was based around, explaining, as she had to Frankie, that the discussion most weeks was aligned to one of the steps, as was the guest speaker they brought in. 'However, tonight's going to be a little bit different,' she said. 'We don't have a guest speaker joining us, so we'll be going around the group and asking everyone to contribute something significant that they've done since they won lotto that's impacted their life. Positive or negative. We learn from both scenarios. I'd like to start by having our new members share with us what's happened in their lives since they won.' She smiled at Shauna, Barry and Ophelia. 'Just a quick update, if you're happy to. It's certainly not compulsory.'

Shauna shuddered. This was exactly why she hated these types of things. Going around the group, introducing yourself and being expected to share private information with complete strangers. It was no one's business what was happening in her life. She listened as Barry and Ophelia, a recently married couple in their early thirties, spoke of their win. She couldn't help but smile at their excitement. They'd only won their money the previous week so hadn't had a chance to make many changes in their lives. 'Although I'm chucking my job in next week,' Barry said. 'I hate it so that's going to be the best thing that comes out of this.'

'What will you do if you're not working?' Todd asked.

'Windsurf, party. Who cares as long as I'm not chained to a desk all week.'

A concerned murmur went around the room.

'What?' Barry looked startled. 'Please tell me you aren't all still in your dead-end jobs?'

'I think you'll find the group's concern, Barry, is that we've had previous winners visit us who did exactly what you're planning to do. Some have managed to get through all of their winnings in a very short space of time. It's good to have a plan in place to ensure that doesn't happen. If you're not working, for instance, you might want to ensure the money is invested and you're living off the interest. Alternatively allocate a weekly or monthly amount from the winnings to live off, rather than having full access to it at all times.' Pamela smiled. 'You've just won lotto. It's exciting and no one wants to take that from you. The whole point of this group is to ensure you keep your winnings long term. One of the suggestions our guest speaker made last week was to take your time and not rush to make any decisions. Come along to these sessions a few times if you can. Learn from the experience of others and, of course, seek some outside advice.'

Barry nodded. 'Makes sense.' He turned to Ophelia. 'I'm still chucking my job.'

She laughed and squeezed his hand. 'You'd be mad if you didn't. But Pamela's right about seeing a financial planner.' She looked around the group. 'I was telling Barry about the Lotto Curse the other night. I couldn't help myself and googled stories about lotto winners. There are so many stories of disaster.' She blushed. 'It's one of the reasons we came tonight actually. I definitely don't want to end up bankrupt, or with friends and family hating me.' She lowered her voice. 'People have even been murdered over their lotto wins and others have killed themselves. It isn't all excitement and celebrations.'

Shauna glanced at Frankie, who'd visibly paled.

'What about you, Shauna?' Pamela asked. 'Would you like to share what's been happening in your life since your lotto win?'

Shauna shook her head. 'If no one minds, I'd just like to listen and learn from your stories.' She wasn't ready to share that life as a *winner* wasn't as rosy as she'd imagined. 'Although one piece of advice I'd appreciate is if anyone can recommend a good lawyer. I do have a family member trying to sue me for half of my winnings, so if you can recommend anyone?'

A woman with a long white plait laughed. 'Unfortunately, I have a lawyer I cannot recommend in those circumstances. Mine recommended I settle when a long-lost cousin came out of the woodwork and tried to sue me, and not knowing any better I did. Three million to a complete stranger.' She shook her head. 'If I could turn back time I'd hire a different lawyer and take that cousin to court. They had no claim over it whatsoever and I should have fought tooth and nail for the principle of the matter.'

'I have a lawyer I'd highly recommend,' Pamela said. 'Clare Spencer. She works at PJJ Law on St Kilda Road. I used to work with her, and she's dealt with cases similar to yours before and won. I'll give you her number after the session, Shauna. If you'd like me to contact her on your behalf, she might be able to see you quicker than if you make your own appointment.'

'That would be great, thank you.'

'If she gives you any advice you think would be useful for the group, it would be appreciated if you shared it,' Pamela added. 'No expectation, of course. Only if you're comfortable and are planning to come back.'

Shauna smiled in response. She didn't have a definite answer on either of those fronts.

'Does anyone else have news they'd like to volunteer tonight, or would you like me to get the discussion started?' Pamela glanced around the group.

'I have some news,' Frankie offered. 'As I mentioned to Pamela last week, I hadn't spent any of the money and thought donating it to charity might get rid of any potential headaches.' Her face coloured as she admitted this. 'I had a change of heart after the meeting last week and have since seen a financial advisor. We've even spent some money.'

Todd gave a huge wolf-whistle. 'Let me guess; you bought yourself a coffee and a muffin.'

Frankie's face turned an even darker shade of red. 'Have you been following me? Add fresh juice, croissants and a happy family, and you'd be spot on.'

The group, including Shauna, laughed. She thought of her own first purchase. A car that cost over two hundred thousand dollars; a slightly different take on splurging than Frankie.

'But since then we've bought a car. Nothing too crazy,' she admitted, 'but it's new and it's my favourite colour.'

'Not that Merc out in the parking lot then?' Ivan said. 'Was thinking I wouldn't mind one of those myself except I'm still following the "no unnecessary or frivolous purchases" strategy.'

Shauna shifted in her chair. She might have to park around the corner if she came again.

'No, a Honda, but it's new and beautiful. I'd be too scared to drive a Merc. God, imagine if I crashed that!' More laughter. 'We have also rented a new house.' The delight on Frankie's face made Shauna smile. She was beginning to realise Frankie didn't have much to start with, so the win was making a positive impact on her. 'We move in next week.'

'That's fantastic news,' Pamela said. 'I was worried after speaking to you last week that you'd been frightened off ever touching any of the money.'

Frankie blushed. 'I was, to be honest, and still am very wary of what disasters may be awaiting us. But I'm hoping that having seen the financial advisor and having my husband, Tom, agree with the advice of not telling people the amount we've won or doing anything too crazy, will keep us safe.'

Safe. That was an interesting choice of words. Shauna found her mind wandering as other people in the group shared stories of things that had impacted them since their wins. A similar theme seemed to run through each of their tales and it appeared that people finding out about their winnings rarely ended well. But it was Frankie who intrigued her most. She wondered what events, imagined or real, had Frankie worrying about keeping safe.

Just after eight, Pamela signalled an end to the group discussion. 'As we don't have a guest speaker tonight, feel free to stay and mingle over a coffee. We have the space until nine so there's no need to rush off.'

Shauna stood, her mind buzzing with her own thoughts. From everything she'd heard tonight, she'd definitely made the number one rookie error. People knew how much she'd won. Perhaps it was lucky that she didn't have a huge family or enormous number of friends who would try to get their hands on her money. She sighed. It was bad enough that one person, her mother, was doing this.

She turned to find Pamela waiting for her.

'Here are Clare's contact details. I've just sent her a text, and if you're free, she can see you at ten tomorrow morning.'

'Really? That's brilliant, thank you so much.'

'I'll text her to confirm. There is a condition.' Pamela's eyes twinkled. 'You have to come back at least one more time and give us an update. I gathered reading between the lines that you have a bit going on.'

Shauna nodded. 'I do. But I'm not a group sharing type of person. Happy to come back and pass on any advice your lawyer friend gives me, but I'm not guaranteeing I'll be sharing my problems.'

'That's fine. We'd like to see you back again anytime. Open door, remember.'

Shauna smiled as Frankie waved to her from across the room where she was speaking with Todd and the woman with the long plait. She said her goodbyes to Pamela and waited for Frankie to finish talking before joining her.

'How did you find the meeting?' Frankie asked.

'Interesting.' And it had been. The more problems that were arising in her own life, the more she felt she could relate, to a degree, to some of the people. 'You might even see me here again.'

Frankie smiled. 'Good, I'd like that. We have one thing in common, at least.'

Shauna nodded. They did. She hesitated for a moment before the words spilt out of her mouth. 'Would you like to go and get a coffee, or better still a drink?'

Surprise registered on Frankie's face, but she answered without hesitation. 'I'd love to.'

'Oh.' Shauna glanced at her phone as a text message pinged, just as she and Frankie sat down in the small bar they'd found around the corner from the community centre.

'Everything okay?'

Shauna glanced at Frankie. 'An ex-boyfriend trying to organise a catch-up.'

'What does the current boyfriend think about that?'

Shauna laughed. 'There isn't one, but I like that you assume there would be.'

Frankie frowned. 'I'd assume more than that. A woman like you would surely have your pick of any man you wanted.'

'Really? What makes you think that? Hold on.' Shauna stood. 'Before you answer I'll get us some drinks. What would you like?'

'Just mineral water or a soft drink. Anything non-alcoholic's good.'

Shauna raised an eyebrow. 'Are you pregnant?'

Frankie stared at her and then laughed. 'What, because I don't drink alcohol?'

Shauna shrugged. 'I can't think of any other good reason.'

'I don't drink. Nothing more than that.'

'One soft drink coming up then.' Shauna grinned and headed to the bar, reappearing a few minutes later with two mojitos over-flowing with fresh mint and lime. 'Virgin mojito for you.' She passed Frankie a glass. 'Rum in mine to make up for yours.' She held up her glass. 'Cheers!'

Frankie clinked glasses with her. 'Have you done a lot of cel-ebrating since you won the money?'

Shauna shook her head. 'Not enough, to be honest. Part of the problem of not wanting to tell too many people.' She grinned. 'Mind you, you'll often find me at work staring at my Internet bank balance and laughing like a maniac or doing a happy dance. There's part of me that still finds it hard to believe it's real. What about you?'

'My family have celebrated a lot. It's taking me a while to get my head around the benefits of having the money. Perhaps it hasn't really sunk in yet.' She smiled. 'Maybe when it does I'll be doing happy dances too.'

'Can I ask you something?'

Frankie nodded. 'Sure, or is this just to avoid me asking you about the ex-boyfriend and lack of current boyfriend, which was obviously going to be the next topic of conversation?'

Shauna laughed. 'You're getting to understand me already. Really though, in the session, you said that your strategy for using the lotto money should keep you *safe*. It seemed like a strange word to use. Are you worried that you're in danger?'

Frankie blushed and took a sip of her drink. 'Not the kind of danger you're probably thinking.' She took a deep breath. 'I grew up in a difficult environment. When I was four my mother gave birth to my brother, Anthony. He died two hours after he was born. From what my grandmother told me before she died, my parents grieved separately, not together, and it pushed them apart. My dad turned to alcohol and gambling for escape and comfort. He drank or gambled away nearly every cent that he and Mum earned. She was a teacher and managed to buy food, pay the mortgage and bills with her wage before he would demand whatever was left. He used all of his wage and any bit of hers he could get his hands on. When he won he was so happy and excited. He'd bring home presents, do anything possible to try and get my mum to smile. I loved it when he was like that, of course. At my age I didn't have any idea of what was actually going on. Mum slid further and further into depression to the point that she couldn't work anymore. Gran looked after me when she could, and my dad drank more and gambled more. Eventually, he was selling things – the furniture, the car – and finally the bank took the house. By then, Mum had been admitted into hospital for psychiatric evaluation. They weren't so big on depression back then and from what Gran said she didn't get the treatment she needed. Dad disappeared, which sent Mum further and further into a black hole.' Tears welled in Frankie's eyes.

Shauna reached across and touched her arm. 'Sorry, I wasn't trying to pry or bring up bad memories.'

Frankie took a tissue from her purse. 'You know, other than Tom, I've never told anyone this story.' She smiled. 'Our joint win must have formed a connection between us.'

'Was your mum okay?'

Frankie shook her head. 'No, she took her life when I was eleven. I saw her that day and for the first time in years she seemed happy. She hugged me, told me how much she loved me. I left the psych hospital with Gran on a high. Both of us thought perhaps she'd be well enough to come home soon. We got a phone call that night telling us she was gone. Her happiness earlier in the day must have been because she'd finally figured a way out.'

'You poor thing.' Shauna felt the backs of her own eyes prickle with tears. 'Did your dad come home?'

Frankie shook her head. 'Gran tracked him down, but she said she never knew if he understood what she was saying or not. He was so drunk that she doubted he could comprehend anything. She wasn't going to go to any effort to help him. She blamed him. She said that he should have been there for Mum when Anthony died. That the combination of not being there for her, and then making it so much worse with his drinking and gambling, was what killed her.'

'Do you think that's the case?' Shauna's words were gentle. She had her own thoughts on Frankie's father but wondered what Frankie thought.

Her new friend shook her head. 'I can vaguely remember my dad before Anthony died. He was the best dad ever. The man I remember after was a different man. The death of his son changed him beyond recognition. If it were now, there'd be all sorts of services there to help both him and Mum. But almost thirty years ago it just wasn't the same. I don't blame him, but it shows what can happen to people too. Alcoholism and gambling weren't in his DNA. It wasn't something genetic he inherited. Awful circumstances drove him to a place where not only was he unrecognisable, but he wasn't there to help Mum. I lost my mum and my dad because of terrible circumstances, and a baby brother too.'

'And that's why you worry you're not safe now?'

Frankie nodded. 'You've heard some of the stories. Yes, winning money should be fantastic, but it fills me with concern. All the what-ifs that come with it. What if we invest it and lose a large percentage and Tom decides to gamble what's left to try and recoup it?'

'Would Tom do that?'

Frankie smiled. 'No. See, this is part of the problem. The money makes me irrational. I spend so much time worrying about things that are unlikely ever to happen that I worry I won't be ready for things that *are* going to happen.'

'Now, that's a legitimate worry I can understand.' Shauna went on to tell Frankie about her mother suing her.

Frankie paled as Shauna explained the situation. 'This is exactly the type of thing that we could never foresee and that I worry about. Hopefully Pamela's lawyer will be able to give you some good advice.'

Shauna sipped her drink. It was lovely chatting with Frankie. From the little she knew about the other woman they lived completely different lives yet had an instant connection. She felt comfortable with her, like she'd known her for years, not just a few hours. 'Tell me more about your normal life,' Shauna said. 'Your girls, how old are they?'

It was close to ten when Frankie glanced at her watch. 'Oh God, I'd better go. Tom will be beside himself. I caught the train tonight and I should have been home an hour ago.'

'Wouldn't he ring you if he was worried?'

Frankie blushed. 'I don't have a phone.'

Shauna's mouth dropped open. 'Really? How can you function without one?'

Frankie shrugged. 'I've never needed one.'

'Do you have a home phone?'

'Yes, although we hardly use that either.'

Shauna took her phone from her bag and handed it to Frankie. 'Ring Tom and tell him I'll drop you home.'

'You don't have to do that. I'll get the train.'

'Are you crazy? Shit, you worry about all the bad things that might happen with the lotto win; I'd be worried about what might happen catching a train home on your own at ten o'clock at night. No arguments.'

Frankie smiled and looked at Shauna's phone, her eyes narrowing in concentration.

Shauna watched her for a moment then laughed and snatched the phone from her. 'You have no idea how to use this, do you?'

'Nope.'

'We're going to have to bring you into the twenty-first century, my new friend. What if I want to contact you? Do I send you a letter in the post or do you prefer it to be delivered by pigeon?' Shauna grinned. 'What's your number?' She keyed in the number Frankie recited and pressed the call button, handing it to back to her once it was ringing. She watched as Frankie smiled with delight as Tom answered, informing him she'd be home soon. The love Frankie felt for her husband was so transparent Shauna felt a stab of envy. They'd been together for sixteen years and adored each other. How lucky they were.

It was after Shauna dropped Frankie in front of a run-down old house in a north-western suburb Shauna hadn't been aware existed, that she remembered she hadn't responded to Simon's text asking to meet her for a drink the next night.

Nothing heavy, just a quick drink. Have some news I'd like your opinion on. Please say yes.

The message intrigued her. Wanting her advice? Simon usually knew his mind. He'd always told her about his decisions and the rationale behind them but rarely had he sought her help. She sent a quick text agreeing to meet him before beginning the long drive back to her Richmond apartment.

The meeting with Pamela's lawyer the next morning took less than twenty minutes. Shauna was surprised at the nervous energy coursing through her as she sat across from Clare Spencer. She still found it hard to believe that her own mother was putting her in this position. But then again, with Lorraine's changeable personality and extreme behaviours it really shouldn't surprise her.

Clare looked up from the letter Lorraine's lawyer had sent. She pushed it across the desk to Shauna. 'Your mother has no entitlement to your winnings. She gave you a gift and now that it's worth something she wants a share. I doubt any judge will rule in her favour.'

Shauna let out a breath. 'Even though they say they bought the ticket for themselves?'

'They would need proof. If they'd chosen numbers that were significant to their lives they might be able to put a case forward. A Quick Pick stuck inside a birthday card doesn't suggest this was any more than a present. Did she discuss sharing the winnings at any time before the draw?'

'She didn't say anything. She handed me an envelope at the end of dinner and wished me a happy birthday. That's all.'

'I'd recommend we draft a response to this on your behalf and see whether they choose to take the matter further.'

Shauna left the offices of PJJ Law feeling considerably more settled than when she'd arrived. Her phone pinged as she pulled into the underground car park of I-People.

*Just checking we're still on for tonight? That new bar opened
on Swan Street last night, near The J. I hear they do great cider.*

Shauna smiled. She'd met Simon at a cider-tasting in the Yarra
Valley wine region. She'd been at a friend's thirtieth and he'd been
on a buck's weekend, both following the famous Cider and Ale Trail
by minibus to numerous wineries. They'd started chatting and comparing notes over the ninth cider they were tasting and arranged to
meet for dinner the following night. They'd been inseparable until
their break-up four years later.

She sent a quick message back agreeing to meet him before leaving her car and heading for the lifts. Doubt once again plagued her
as she thought of Simon. She didn't need her heart broken again.
Advice, she reminded herself. He's asking me for advice, nothing else.

Back in her office, Shauna pushed all thoughts of Simon from her
mind and sorted through her mail and messages. She was surprised
to see a message from Lisa Gentville, a girl she'd gone to high school
with, and another from Miles Blauchamp, a neighbour from her
childhood. How bizarre to receive two messages in the same morning from people she'd not given a thought to in years. She smiled
as Josh came into her office.

Josh didn't return her smile. 'Seen this?' He held up a copy of
Empowered She magazine.

'No, I don't usually read trash mags. Why?'

'I think you'd better read this one.' He opened the magazine to
an article and handed it to Shauna.

Shauna felt her throat constrict. 'Shit, shit. How did this happen?' She was peering at a photo of her mother under a caption
which announced: 'Daughter Steals Mother's Lotto Win'.

She quickly scanned the article. It appeared Lorraine had sold her sob story to the magazine.

'It doesn't mention your name at least,' Josh said.

'No, but anyone who knows my mum will know about the lotto win.' Shauna paused. 'I had phone calls last week from this magazine, but I never returned them. I honestly assumed they were trying to sell me a subscription.'

'Appears not.'

'It also explains the phone messages I've received this morning,' Shauna said. 'Blasts from the past. They must have seen this and decided I'd be good to hit up for some money. What should I do?'

'Probably nothing. Don't return the calls, don't talk to any magazines or papers and just lie low. Possibly contact your mother and tell her not to give your contact details to anyone.'

Shauna nodded. 'I bet it's not the only story either. She'll be loving the attention. Although she's probably annoyed that she wasn't big enough news for them to do a new photo shoot. That photo's an old one. I organised some professional shots for her birthday last year. Anyway, as much as I'd like to kill her right now, there's not a lot I can do other than ignore any phone calls and tell her to shut up in future.'

'Good girl. Now, no arguments, I'm buying you a drink.'

'It's only four o'clock.'

'So?'

'So, my workday goes officially until five thirty, and unofficially until about ten if I want to get this presentation finished.'

'Due today?'

'No, next week, but I need to get a head start.'

Josh walked over and closed the cover on Shauna's computer. 'No, you don't. Presentations will wait, life won't. There's a bottle of Gewürztraminer waiting for us.'

Shauna snorted. 'Gewürzt-what-the-fuckier? Are you trying to impress me? Because it's not working.'

'Gewürztraminer is wine, you ignoramus. Next time I'll just say white wine, okay?'

'Or something a normal person would say, like Sav Blanc or Pinot Grigio?'

Josh folded his arms and towered over Shauna. 'Get your stuff, smart-arse, you're coming with me.'

Shauna's tongue rolled over her upper lip. 'Mmm, Mr Dominant. Asserting yourself, aren't you?'

Josh pretended to scowl. 'Stop talking. Don't spoil my moment. Now, come on, we're leaving.'

Shauna reached for her bag, then stopped. Shit. Simon.

'What's wrong.'

'I have plans tonight. I totally forgot.'

'Can you cancel them?'

Shauna thought about it for a moment then shook her head. 'No, if anything I need to get it over with.'

'The ex?'

Shauna nodded.

Josh pushed his hands into his suit pockets and retreated from Shauna's office. He stopped in the doorway. 'Fair enough, I get it. Unfinished business and all that. Just remember our conversation from the other night. People rarely change. Another time.'

Disappointment flooded through Shauna as Josh disappeared. Damn Simon and damn her for saying yes.

Shauna ran her finger down the icy glass of cider she'd ordered and glanced around Cool, Richmond's newly opened ale and cider bar. The back feature wall was filled with beer and cider bottles, ice packed around them to enhance the *cool* effect. She'd been lucky to nab the last tall table with its black-and-chrome stools as the bar was already heaving with the after-work Friday night crowd. The thump of music could only just be heard over the laughter and chatter that filled the venue.

She was ten minutes early, having found it difficult to concentrate after Josh left her office, torn between who she would rather be spending time with tonight. Simon still held a pull over her, even though she had no intention of allowing anything to happen between them, so why was she encouraging it at all? She tried to convince herself that she wasn't encouraging anything. They had a history together and he said he needed her advice. It was nothing more than that. And while she liked Josh, he was strictly friends material. But that was one of the major appeals about him. She could relax and enjoy herself in his company. She'd made it very clear that she wouldn't be having a relationship with a colleague again, so the boundaries were firmly in place.

'Hey.' A hand rested on her back and Simon gave her a light peck on the cheek. He sat down opposite her, his dark suit enhancing his tanned features.

Shauna smiled. He looked good, but then he always had.

'Let me order a drink and then we can chat.' He glanced at her half-full glass. 'Another one?'

Shauna shook her head. One was enough.

He disappeared and returned moments later with a large, chilled glass. He tapped it against hers. 'Do you remember the Cider and Ale Trail?'

She nodded, unable to stop herself smiling. 'Of course – it was quite a day.'

Simon laughed. 'I've never drunk so much cider in one day. I kept trying them so we could chat. I hope I sounded like the expert I was trying to be.'

Shauna thought back to their conversation. He had been very knowledgeable about cider, which had intrigued her as, while she quite liked the taste, she was more of a wine drinker. 'You were very impressive.'

He grinned. 'No, just lucky that you didn't know anything about cider, so I was able to make up a whole bunch of stuff that you thought was true.'

Shauna stared at him. 'You made all that up?'

'Mostly. I wanted to impress you.'

She laughed. 'It did, at the time. Not so much now.' She sipped her drink, trying to recall some of the expert knowledge Simon had imparted, but it was mostly a blur. She'd enjoyed far too many tastings that day.

Simon reached across the table and took her hand. 'I've missed this. I've missed you.'

Shauna swallowed. She didn't want this, did she? She opened her mouth, but Simon shook his head.

'Just hear me out before you say anything.'

Shauna retracted her hand from Simon's and cupped her drink in both.

He cleared his throat. 'I missed you when I was travelling but convinced myself I was doing the right thing. That we weren't ready to settle down and I needed to see the world. I wanted to contact you many times but knew it wouldn't be fair to either of us, so I didn't. Tony didn't offer me the contract; I contacted him to see if he had some work so I'd have an excuse to come back and see you. See how I felt being back in Melbourne and whether the feelings were still between us. For me, they still are.' He took her hands from her glass and squeezed them. 'Shauna, I still love you and I want you back.'

Shauna just stared at him. She'd spent twelve months getting over him, promising herself she needed to move on and now here he was saying he wanted to start again. 'What about your travelling? You said you were earning enough to go back travelling for another twelve months.'

'I don't need to travel; I need to be with you. I'd love it if at some time we did travel together, but it doesn't have to be for months at a time. We can take annual leave and go for a few weeks like we used to. I want what we had before. I want us again.'

Shauna continued to stare at him, trying to work out what she was feeling. Her emotions were all over the place. He was saying the words she'd wanted to hear twelve months ago. That he'd made a huge mistake, that he was sorry. But he hadn't said them when she needed to hear them. In fact, she hadn't heard from him at all the whole time he'd been away.

'You're scaring me by not saying anything.'

'It's a shock, that's all. I wasn't expecting this. I've spent the last year getting over you. If you really missed me so much why didn't you get in touch while you were away? It's a big risk to come all the way home if I'm no longer interested or I've moved on.'

'It's a risk I'm willing to take. I've picked up the phone heaps of times in the last few months to ring you, and started many emails. But each time I thought of how much I'd hurt you I was sure you'd hang up if I rang or you wouldn't respond to email. I spoke to Mum and her exact words were' – Simon did his best impersonation of his mother's singsong tone – '"Get your stupid butt back home and make this right. You've let the best thing that has ever happened to you go and you've got a lot of grovelling to do."'

Shauna smiled. She could just imagine Ellen saying this.

'I never stopped thinking about you, Shauna. Sure, I got to travel but I realised almost straightaway that I did it all the wrong way around. We could have done a lot of it together over time; there was no huge rush. I wish now I'd waited.'

Shauna's mind whirled. He sounded sincere but something didn't sit quite right. 'When we had that drink when you first got back, I got the impression you'd needed to spread your wings within the relationship, that it was about more than travelling. I assumed there'd been other women.'

Simon flushed. 'There were a few other women on the trip. Just a bit of fun, nothing that meant anything other than a good time.'

Shauna considered this. He'd disappeared for twelve months without contacting her, had flings with other women and was now saying what a mistake it all was and how much he missed her.

'I know it doesn't look like I was missing you, but I was. It was my way of filling the void of not having you around. I knew that I'd hurt you and doubted you'd ever take me back. I should have come back earlier; I realise that now.'

Shauna took a deep breath. 'Simon, I've moved on. I loved you, very much, but you broke my heart. I don't think I could ever trust you again. And I'm not sure if I want you back anyway.' Something had shifted in her. While the unexpectedness of their break-up had shocked her, it had also strengthened her.

'Over time I could earn your trust back.'

She shook her head. 'There were other problems before you left. Ones that at the time I was happy to make changes to accommodate, but I'm not now.'

'Like what?'

'Like work. You were never pleased when I achieved my goals or was seen to be doing better than you. I need to be with someone who's supportive, not competitive.'

'But we don't even work together anymore.'

'That's not the point. We work in the same industry and are both trying to achieve good results and move up within our companies – at least I assume you will be if you plan to stay?'

He nodded.

'I need someone who will encourage that and celebrate my successes with me.' An image of Josh flashed into her mind. She couldn't imagine him ever being jealous of someone else's success. He'd be the first to encourage and celebrate. He was like the male version of Tess. One hundred percent supportive. She'd rather not be in a relationship and have a friend like him by her side than be with someone who was self-centred and jealous.

'I want to be that person, Shauna. Give me time to prove to you that I can be that guy. Unless that guy at the office . . . is he your boyfriend?'

'He's a colleague and friend, but that isn't the reason I'm not interested in getting back together. I'm doing just fine on my own.'

Simon's jaw tensed and he shook his head exactly as he'd always done in the past when things weren't going his way. If history were any indicator of what was to come, he'd explode at any minute.

He wasn't going to get that chance.

Shauna stood. She'd heard enough. He'd completely upturned her life twelve months ago, and now it appeared he was trying to do it again. But this time she had a say in the decision, and she could protect herself from more hurt.

Simon grabbed her hand. 'Hold on. Just let me say this. I love you. I want to get back together, but I also respect that this is very sudden. Think about it. There's no rush.' He flashed his winning smile at her. 'I'm not going anywhere this time, Shauna. I'll be here for you and for us.'

Shauna's heartbeat quickened as she extracted her hand from his and, without speaking, turned on her heel and left the bar.

Chapter Ten

Frankie unpacked the last box for the kitchen before crushing it, ready to recycle. The thought of freshly brewed coffee convinced her to take a break. She made herself a flat white and sat down on one of the new stools that lined the island bench. She found herself looking around the kitchen and open-plan living area in awe that this was their new home.

'Hey, beautiful.' Tom came into the kitchen and went straight to the coffee machine. 'Coffee, definitely need coffee. I can't believe we survived this long without a coffee machine, can you?'

Frankie laughed. 'It wasn't really a choice before. Now we have more appliances than I realised existed.' Frankie had spent two days shopping for furniture, new computers and appliances before moving in. Most of their old possessions were now at the Salvation Army.

Tom poured his coffee and plonked himself on a stool next to her. 'Did I tell you Rod's moving?'

'Is he? Where to?'

'A new apartment. There's a pool and gym so he's pretty happy. I think Dash is hoping another one will come up in the same complex.'

'How can he afford to move?'

Tom was unable to meet Frankie's eyes.

'You've given them money?'

Tom nodded. 'Sorry, I was excited. I couldn't wait and we did agree to give them some. You should have seen their faces.'

'You told them we won ten million?'

'No, not the amount, just that we'd won enough to share some with them. I made a point of playing it down, in fact, so they don't know how much we have. I think the fact we're renting helps too. If we'd purchased an expensive house it would be a bit of a giveaway that we'd won quite a lot.'

'How much did you give?'

'Two hundred and fifty thousand each, like we discussed. They're blown away we're giving them any money.'

Frankie rolled her eyes. 'Yeah, right. I imagine Dash will be asking for more.'

'No, you're wrong. Dash couldn't stop hugging me and Rod was crying. They didn't expect anything.'

'Okay, let's hope that's the case.'

Tom drew Frankie towards him. 'Don't worry, this will turn out for the best. I might finally have a decent relationship with my brothers.'

'Because you gave them money?'

Tom shook his head. 'Not because I gave them the money, but because we're all better off, which is a huge stress relief for everyone.'

'I guess. At least they should be able to go ahead with their boat business.'

'Mmm, probably.' Tom moved his gaze back to his coffee cup.

'What? What aren't you telling me?'

'Nothing, don't be silly.' He got up from the stool. 'It's almost three. I'll go and pick up the girls. Might even take them for a milkshake or something as an after-school treat. Coming?'

'Wait. First tell me what else is going on with Rod and Dash?'

Tom continued to avoid Frankie's eyes. 'Nothing, okay. Now, do you want to come?'

'No,' she said. 'I'd better continue unpacking. But Tom, I need you to promise me something.'

'What?'

'If something's going on with your brothers, you'll tell me.'

Tom laughed. 'So suspicious. Nothing to tell. I promise you'll be the first to know when there is.'

Frankie slammed the document down on the kitchen table. The first to know? What a joke. Tea spilled from her favourite mug and splattered the wall and floor. Only two days had passed since Saturday morning when Tom had sworn nothing was going on with his brothers. The date on this document dated back more than a week. Tears pricked the back of Frankie's eyes and she lowered her head into her hands. How could Tom do this? They *never* lied to each other; they made decisions together. And this wasn't something small. It was huge. Her worst fear, that the money would drive a wedge between them, was materialising.

She took a deep breath, wiped up the tea, then picked up the phone and dialled Tom's new mobile number.

'Hey, beautiful wife.'

Frankie strained to hear Tom over the music and laughter in the background. 'Where are you?'

'At the pub, darls, what's up?'

'Darls? Are you drunk?' Maybe that was the explanation for what she'd just read. He'd been drunk and had no memory of it. Unfortunately Frankie was well aware this was wishful thinking.

Tom laughed. 'No, just having a beer or two with my brothers to celebrate.'

'Celebrate what?'

Tom hesitated. 'Oh, you know, nothing special. Life being good to us at last.'

'Shouldn't you be at work? It's Monday afternoon, not Friday night.'

'Work? No, I told them they could keep their job. What's the point of turning up to earn a pittance?'

'You quit?'

'Yep, it was a spur-of-the-moment thing. Rod and Dash both resigned, which motivated me to. We're millionaires. It's ridiculous to continue doing a job I hate.'

'I agree for you, but Rod and Dash? They quit their jobs? Why?'

'Hated old man McGregor. Wasn't a good place to work.'

Frankie shook her head. She'd only ever heard good things about Karl McGregor from Rod and Dash. 'Okay. So, what are you all planning to do?' Frankie knew from the documents in front of her exactly what they planned to do, but she wanted to hear it from Tom. Wanted to hear if there was actually any scenario in which he hadn't deliberately deceived her.

'Let's talk about this when I get home, sweets. I'd better go, it's my shout. I might be a bit late.'

Hope came into the kitchen as Frankie stared at the now silent phone. Not only had she not received an answer, he'd hung up. She gave herself a mental shake and mustered a smile for Hope, glad for the distraction. 'Everything okay?'

'No, it's bloody not.' Hope dropped her bag on the floor. She looked ready to explode.

'Hope!'

'What? It's not bloody alright, thanks to you.'

'What are you talking about?'

'You. What did you say to the school about Pearce?'

'Pearce? What, that horrible boy? I didn't say anything.'

Hope stared at Frankie, her anger replaced with surprise. 'Hold on, did you say anything to anyone?'

Frankie nodded. 'Yes, his mother.'

'What?'

'I spoke to his mother, mentioned how badly he had behaved that afternoon towards you. She was even ruder than he was. I didn't say anything to anyone else.'

'You shouldn't have said anything to her. I'm not four. Are you sure you didn't talk to someone else?'

'Of course I'm sure. Calm down and tell me what this is all about.'

Hope picked up her bag. 'It's nothing, don't worry about it.'

Frankie moved towards her daughter. 'No, it's not nothing. You don't come in here all worked up and then tell me nothing's wrong. Tell me what's happened.'

Hope forced a smile. 'Really, it's nothing. I got my wires crossed.'

Frankie stared at Hope. Why was it so hard to get a straight answer? 'Well, how are things at school? Is Pearce still hassling you?'

Hope hesitated before opening the fridge, her face now hidden from Frankie. 'Um, no. He's leaving me alone. It was actually Hamish, his friend, that I thought you must have said something to. He's been very nice. He apologised for not stopping Pearce that day.'

'Good. So why did you come in all worked up before?'

'Sorry. It's just, well, I thought he'd been put up to it. The apology, the being nice. It's a relief to know he wasn't forced.'

Frankie smiled. Hamish was now being nice to Hope? Perhaps he'd worked out there was an easier way to get her attention. Being a teenager certainly wasn't easy. She wanted to ask more but knew better. Hope had a smile on her face, a vast improvement from the past few months. 'Do you need any help with your homework?'

Hope closed the fridge, her eyes meeting Frankie's. 'No, it's maths, so please stay far, far away.'

Frankie laughed. 'Fair enough. Can I help with anything else?'

'No,' Hope said. 'Except I did want to ask you something. Can I go to a party on Saturday night? Susan Tillie's having a sixteenth.'

'Will her parents be home?'

'Her dad will be, but there might be alcohol. Don't worry, I won't drink any.'

'They're serving alcohol at a sixteenth?'

'Not her dad. Susan's boyfriend is eighteen and he and his mates might bring beer.'

Frankie hesitated. Parties. It wouldn't just be nasty kids they'd need to look out for now. Drugs and alcohol would be the next thing. She trusted Hope, but she also remembered being the same age. Experimenting was all part of growing up. She needed to be able to trust her daughter and that would only be by giving her some freedom and expecting her to do the right thing. 'Okay. Home by midnight, deal?'

Hope threw her arms around Frankie. 'You're the best!' She pulled away. 'The other thing I wanted to ask is whether I could buy some new clothes?'

'What about the shirt I made you?'

'I wore it to Lisa's party, so everyone's seen it. I'd love something new and we can afford it now, can't we?'

Frankie didn't respond.

'Mum?'

Frankie shook herself. Why did she clam up every time the money was brought up? 'Yes, of course we can afford new clothes.'

'But?'

'But I'm still uneasy about the money. Silly, I know. I'm not sure I'll ever feel it's ours to spend.'

'You found some money which bought a ticket. We have no way of finding who dropped the money and even if we did, they're owed twenty dollars, not a winning lotto ticket. Dad says we've been blessed and should enjoy ourselves.'

Frankie raised an eyebrow. 'Blessed? Interesting, as he's never set foot inside a church. Regardless, spending the money still doesn't sit right with me.'

'Why don't you put some of the money to good use?'

'What do you mean?'

'Find a charity, somewhere you can make a difference.'

'We've already given some to charity.'

'Yes, but they were handouts to big charities. Why not give money to something you're passionate about? You say the old people always complain they can't get out enough at the retirement village. Buy them a minibus and pay for someone to be employed to drive them.'

Frankie stared at Hope. 'What a wonderful idea. Why didn't I think of doing something for the oldies?'

Hope laughed. 'Because you're too busy hating the fact that we're millionaires and thinking of all the things that might go wrong. You haven't spent enough time thinking of the good money can do.'

Frankie gave Hope a hug. 'You are one extremely wise young woman. How about we go shopping after school one afternoon? I'll give you a budget and you can go nuts – a new wardrobe maybe?'

'Really? I can buy more than one thing?'

Frankie laughed. 'We'll go mad. Tell Fern and she can come, too.'

Hope flung her arms around Frankie again and squeezed her tight. 'Thank you, thank you, thank you.'

Frankie hugged her daughter, unable to shake the feeling of betrayal as her eyes travelled back to the document on the table.

Frankie allowed Tom to sleep late the next morning. He'd finally arrived home close to midnight and fallen into bed fully clothed, smelling like a brewery. She did her best to push away her childhood memories of her father coming home drunk, usually having lost all of his week's wages. She reminded herself that Tom was not her father and he'd been out celebrating, not gambling, and he didn't usually lie. Or at least she was fairly certain he didn't.

A little after ten she decided it was time for an explanation. 'Good morning.' Frankie spoke loudly. She couldn't help smiling as she heard the groan from their bed. 'Here, take these.' She passed Tom a glass of water and two paracetamol tablets. 'I need to talk to you.'

Tom dragged himself to a sitting position, washed the tablets down, then sank back into the pillow. 'I'm sorry, hon, I'm not sure what came over me. I won't be out drinking on a Monday again.'

Frankie sat on the edge of the bed. 'It was a celebration, wasn't it?'

A flicker of concern crossed Tom's face. 'Yes. How did you know?'

If she wasn't so angry, the look on Tom's face would have made her laugh. 'You told me when I spoke to you that you'd quit your jobs and were celebrating.'

Tom exhaled. 'I forgot you rang.'

'I don't understand how you and your brothers are suddenly best friends, when only a few weeks ago Dash was calling you an arsehole.'

'He was disappointed; he didn't mean anything.'

Frankie slowly shook her head. 'An interesting change of perspective. So now what? You're brothers, friends and business partners?'

Tom buried his head deeper into the pillow, his eyes focused on the ceiling. 'Who told you?'

Frankie waved the document at him. 'No one. This transfer of ownership of Blue Water Charters to Tom York, Rod York and Dash York gave me a hint. How could you, Tom?'

Tom glanced briefly at the paperwork. 'Sorry, I was planning to surprise you. Announce the new business once the paperwork was finalised and the boats were ready to show you.'

Frankie crossed her arms. 'Don't lie. You were scared to tell me, weren't you?'

Tom looked sheepish. 'Honestly? Yes. I thought you would try to talk me around and I didn't want to miss out on the opportunity.'

'According to the date on this application it happened over a week ago. You've had plenty of time to fill me in.'

Tom pushed his fingers through his hair. 'Yes, I'm sorry. Please trust me. It's a good thing. We want to work together in a real family business.'

'Trust you? Are you kidding?' Anger replaced the hurt and disappointment Frankie had felt since learning of Tom's purchase. 'When you've done something this huge behind my back how am I supposed to trust you? What else have you done without telling me?'

'Nothing. I promise.'

Frankie stared at her husband. It was like looking at a stranger.

His eyes met hers, pleading with them. 'Come on, hon. It's one thing. I know it's huge but in the scheme of what we won it isn't really. It's an opportunity, one that my mum and dad would be so happy about. Their three boys working together. Mum was all about family, you know that. And in his own way, Dad was too.'

Frankie swallowed. Was he really going to try to manipulate his way out of what he'd done?

'My issue is that you didn't talk to me about it. That you went and made this monumental decision without even bothering to mention it to me. Let me get things clear: Rod and Dash threw in their jobs and invested nearly all the money we gave them in this? Will they have any left over?'

Tom's eyes darted around the room. Finally he spoke, still unable to look at Frankie. 'They should be okay.'

A knot formed in the pit of Frankie's stomach. Had he given them more? 'What aren't you telling me now?'

'Can we discuss it later, when I'm feeling a bit better?'

'No. Explain now. You just *promised* me you hadn't done anything else without telling me and now we have another secret already.'

Tom sighed. 'Okay, so they didn't use their money to buy the business.'

'What do you mean? How can you all own a third if they didn't contribute?'

Tom shrugged.

Frankie's mouth dropped open. 'No. Please tell me you didn't pay the whole lot?'

'You're turning this into a bigger deal than necessary. It was only six hundred grand.'

Frankie stared at Tom. Was he kidding? '*Only six hundred grand*? On top of what we already gave them?' Surely she must have misunderstood him? 'Let me get this straight. Without even consulting me you handed over more than a million dollars to your brothers?'

'No, a third is still mine.'

'So, two hundred and fifty thousand each as a gift and then an additional two hundred thousand each as part of this business?'

Tom nodded.

'Nine hundred thousand dollars! Tom, I can't believe you would do this without first talking to me.' Frankie squeezed her eyes shut, willing the tears that threatened away. She let out a deep breath before reopening her eyes. 'When Dash hit us up for money in the Botanic Gardens you said you wouldn't dream of joining them.'

'Hold on, I said I was disappointed they only came to me when they wanted something, not that I wouldn't go into business with them if I could.'

'Why on earth didn't you buy the business in your name and employ them? You now have two business partners who've invested nothing but are entitled to two-thirds of the profits.'

Tom shrugged. 'They'll be investing a hell of a lot of hard work. Don't underestimate what it takes to make a successful business. Dash was right, being equal partners helps avoid any resentment down the track. If everyone works hard we should all get equally rewarded.'

Frankie sat down, taking another deep breath to calm herself. She spoke quietly. 'Agreeing to share the profit three ways, that would make sense, but instead you've given them an extra two hundred thousand each. If they decide tomorrow to sell up, then you'll get a third of the sale price.'

Tom was silent. 'They won't sell. We're going to turn this into a successful business.'

'Oh, Tom, you should have had a lawyer, or an accountant look over this before you agreed to anything.'

'We did. Dash's mate is a lawyer and he checked everything out.'

Frankie threw her hands up in the air. Sometimes she really wondered about Tom. 'Do you really think Dash's mate had your best interests at heart?' Dash, the one person she despised, had now been invited into their lives on a regular basis.

Tom rubbed his head and closed his eyes. After a few moments he opened them. 'Let's go down to the boats later this afternoon, take the girls. I'll show you everything and then you'll know why I'm so pumped about this whole idea. Please come. It's important to me.'

Frankie hesitated. Part of her wanted to scream at Tom, pummel his chest with her fists even. Tell him no, that he couldn't betray her like this and expect things to go on as normal. But she knew Tom. Knew that he'd craved a strong relationship with his brothers for years. That he'd do anything to honour his mum's memory, and keeping a close-knit family was one of the things she would have wanted.

He reached across and took her hand. 'I'm sorry, hon, I really am. I should never have done this without consulting you, but I knew you'd say no.'

Frankie pulled her hand away. 'You *knew* I'd say no and yet you went ahead anyway. Is that supposed to make me feel better or worse?'

Tom hung his head. 'I don't even know what to say. I was so excited about the opportunity and I thought once it was all there to show you you'd be as excited as me.' He glanced up and met her eyes. 'I hoped you'd overlook the way I went about it. If I'd asked and you'd said no then I would have resented you. You've been so anti spending the money I didn't want to take any risks on missing out. We have the money and it's an opportunity to build something wonderful for all of us.'

Frankie sighed. He was right, she would have said no. But it wouldn't have been solely due to her reluctance to spend the money; the reason would have been Dash. And, as she couldn't tell Tom what had happened with Dash, it would have been difficult to provide a convincing argument to exclude Dash from a family business. Especially as Dash was the one who had brought the business idea to the family. 'Okay. What's done is done and I'll do my best to be supportive, but I want you to promise me something.'

'What?'

'You don't spend large amounts of money, and by that I mean buying anything that costs more than a thousand dollars, without consulting me first. That works both ways, of course. I will consult you for any large expenses too. Either that, or we get the bank to change our account to both sign.'

'I promise,' Tom said. 'Of course I should have told you. This is the most impulsive thing I've ever done.'

'You said when you gave your brothers their money that you didn't tell them how much we won. Aren't they questioning it now that you've been able to put so much into the business?'

Tom nodded. 'Rod wanted to make sure we still had some left for us. He was worried that I'd used all of it.'

'And Dash?'

'He wanted to make sure that we had some left over too. Both of them have our best interests at heart.'

Frankie snorted. 'And let me guess, you told them not to worry, that we had heaps left over.'

Tom smiled. 'Not in those words, but yes. I didn't want them to feel bad that they'd ended up with all the money. They know we still have a little bit left. I'm not a complete idiot. They have no idea how much we won.'

Frankie swallowed. For the first time in their relationship she felt a niggle of doubt. Tom had broken her trust and while part of her understood his rationale for what he did, it didn't mean she liked it or believed that he wouldn't do it again. Her stomach churned. She needed to go outside for some air. 'Why don't you get some more sleep.'

Tom grinned. 'Okay, babe. I promise I'll come down showered and not hungover. I can't believe how the money is changing our lives.'

Tom's words played over in Frankie's mind as she left the bedroom and walked back down the stairs. 'Changing our lives,' she muttered. 'It sure bloody is.'

◆　◆　◆

Tom looked human again by the time they collected the girls from school. They drove towards St Kilda and the marina.

Fern hadn't stopped talking. 'Can we go out on the boat today?'

'Maybe,' Tom said. 'If Rod or Dash are happy to go, too. Until I get my marine licence we need one of them. Once I've got a licence we can go anytime we want.'

'Rod or Dash? I thought it was going to be the four of us?' Frankie really wasn't in the mood to see Dash.

'I mentioned we were coming down and they insisted on being there. They want to thank you and show you the boats.'

Frankie sat in silence. She would be interested to gauge how grateful Dash was. To Tom's face maybe, but to hers it was always a different story. She was jolted out of her thoughts as Tom pulled into a parking space at the marina.

'Uncle Rod, Uncle Rod!' Fern squealed and jumped out of the car. Frankie watched as Rod engulfed Fern in a gigantic hug and turned and did the same to Hope.

She smiled as Hope squirmed with embarrassment.

'Where's Dash?' Tom asked.

'Working on the boats. I wanted to be out here to greet my favourite girls.' Rod pretended to tickle Fern. She swatted his hand away, telling him she was too old for that. Rod turned to Frankie and before she had a chance to say anything he had her in a tight bear hug.

Frankie started to laugh. 'Help, I can hardly breathe!'

Rod released her, placing one hand on each of her shoulders, his eyes locked with hers. 'Thank you. What you and Tom are doing is life-altering for me and for Dash. I can't thank you enough and want you to know we will work harder than you could ever imagine to make sure this business is a success.'

Frankie smiled. Rod was genuine, she knew that.

'Come on,' Tom said. 'Enough of the warm and fuzzy stuff. Let's go and find the boats.'

Frankie freed herself from Rod and walked with the girls. As they rounded the corner of the building the marina spread out before them.

'Check out these boats,' Fern said as they wove their way along various jetties. 'Who owns them?'

'People with a lot of money,' Hope said.

Frankie couldn't get over the contrast from their lifestyle of only a few weeks ago. They passed some beautiful-looking craft. She could imagine going out in one of those. When Frankie thought of boats she tended to think of the aluminium tinny ones. These were real boats, with cabins, comfortable chairs, kitchen areas and toilet facilities. Wafts of petrol fumes and seaweed mixed in the salty ocean air. The gentle breeze whipped across her face, transporting her back to when she was pregnant with Hope and Tom had proposed. While they were legally too young to marry, he had insisted they have an *engagement honeymoon* before the baby was born. With no money between them their honeymoon had consisted of three nights in a tent down on Melbourne's Mornington Peninsula. As basic as the accommodation had been, Frankie would never forget it. Being five months pregnant at the time had not stopped them from making love at every opportunity, while Frankie's cravings for salty foods had been accommodated by a fish and chip shop across the road from the campground.

Other than the many hours they spent inside the tent, one of the more memorable events was Tom hiring a small tinny for a romantic sunset cruise. He'd packed soft drinks, chocolates and blankets and off they'd gone. Twenty minutes into their trip the engine had stopped working, a large puff of smoke erupting from it. At this stage petrol fumes had been combined with the stench of rotting seaweed. Within seconds Frankie had been retching over the side. Over an hour later another boat had come past and offered some help. The same smell now brought back fond memories of their engagement and a time in their lives when they had many exciting, yet frightening, events ahead of them.

Tom stopped in front of one of the older-looking vessels and Frankie was jolted back to the present. '*Get Reel* is the first of the fleet,' he announced.

'Fleet?' Dash's recognisable snigger echoed from within the boat. 'Not sure if you can refer to two boats as a fleet.' His head appeared from an opening in the deck. 'Hi, girls.' He waved to Hope and Fern but made no effort to acknowledge Frankie. 'I'm sorting out ropes down here. Will be up in a minute.' He disappeared below.

Tom helped everyone on to the boat and the girls headed inside the cabin. Rod followed and Frankie overheard him explaining each of the various instruments to them.

Tom turned to Frankie. 'What do you think?'

'It's older than I imagined.' Having walked past so many luxurious boats, the reality of the fishing charter was a let-down.

'She needs a cosmetic overhaul, that's all. We plan to get this boat out of the water in the next two weeks for maintenance. You'll be blown away at the difference a coat of paint makes. After we sort out storage compartments and a couple of minor repairs, you won't recognise her.'

'What about the other one? How much work is needed?'

Tom pointed to a smaller but more modern boat with the name *Fish Tales* written in fancy lettering on the side. 'Minimal.' The fishing rods were organised on the back of what appeared to be a very professional set-up. Frankie relaxed. 'That one seems nicer.'

'They both will be when we've finished,' Tom said. 'But *Get Reel* has room to take more people, so making improvements is a priority. I can imagine *Fish Tales* being hired out by one group at a time, whereas with this boat we can charge per person and allow twenty people on at once.'

'Is twenty the limit?'

'No, but the total we take depends on how many of us go out each time. We might get someone on casually if we start getting busy.'

'Come on, show me everything.' Frankie smiled. She knew nothing at all about fishing charters so decided to put her doubts aside and let Tom enjoy his moment. He showed her around the cabin and took her down through the hole in the deck Dash had appeared from. They found him down below sorting ropes and fishing gear.

In the small space meant for storage, Frankie felt the walls close in. She reached out to steady herself. The smirk on Dash's face wasn't worth responding to. 'I'm going up on top.'

'On deck, you mean,' Dash called after her. 'Learn the lingo, franks and beans.'

Frankie ignored him, grateful to be back in the fresh air. 'Sorry, not the right space for me.'

Tom squeezed her hand. 'Come with me. Time to visit *Fish Tales*.'

Rod and the girls were already enjoying the more modern of the boats. Fern sat in the captain's chair pretending to drive, while Hope lay back, eyes closed, on one of the bench seats.

Frankie laughed. 'Now, this is more my style.'

'Picture yourself on this one?' Rod asked.

'Definitely. It's newer, cleaner and nicer. I would enjoy a day out on this boat.'

'Don't worry, it will be as nice when it's finished. You wait.'

'Speaking of a trip, shall we motor out?' Tom looked at Rod.

Rod checked his watch. 'Sorry, bro, can't. I need to leave in five minutes. Dash might, though.' He called out to Dash before Frankie had the chance to stop him.

Dash jumped down on to the deck and agreed to take them out. After saying their goodbyes to Rod, they untied the boat and motored slowly out of the marina. Tom and the girls had moved to the front of the boat, leaving Frankie at the back, closer to Dash than she would normally choose to be.

Dash opened a can of beer and turned to her. 'I suppose you realise what a good idea this was now?'

Frankie looked across to Tom and the girls and lowered her voice. 'A few weeks ago you were happy to blackmail me into getting what you want. Now you're pretending it's all for the good of your brotherly relationship. Answer something for me. Are you actually interested in having a relationship with Tom, or just using him?'

Dash laughed. 'I think you're accusing me of being a gold-digger. How could you? I treasure my brothers.' He grinned and took a swig of his beer.

Frankie gritted her teeth, unable to respond. She turned and gazed towards the shoreline. He was so arrogant, so disrespectful.

'Don't be like that,' Dash said. 'I'm kidding. This is about family, not money. I really am grateful, Frankie. Tom made it very clear that he was using most of the money you won for the business and that blows me away. I never thought you'd be so generous. Putting everything else aside, thank you. This is life-changing for all of us.'

She turned back to face him, surprised to see the earnest look on his face. It appeared that he was actually grateful.

'Tom's hoping this will be a fresh start for all of us. I hope it will be too.' Her eyes drilled into his as she said that, making sure he knew exactly what she was referring to.

He nodded. 'Of course it is. Everything in the past is forgotten and we move on. I honestly never realised you could be so generous. I've had the wrong impression of you all along.'

'That's good to hear because you need to understand one thing. As excited as we are to be investing in this business, and as happy as we were to be able to gift you and Rod some money, no more money is being made available to the business, or to you. You'll be expected to work hard, and if expenses can't be met, you and Rod will contribute a third each.'

'Tom did suggest there was still a bit of money left from your winnings if we get into any trouble.'

'The money that's left over is to be invested for the girls' future. It won't be used for the business or for you or Rod if you suddenly need a loan.'

Dash took another swig of beer. 'Sounds like a sensible plan, but I'm not sure it's exactly what Tom had in mind. Look, I don't want to cause problems with you, but this is business. You can't start making up conditions on something that's already been agreed. I suggest you read the fine print of the contract Tom signed. Expenses aren't part of the deal for me or Rod.'

Pressure began building inside Frankie's head. 'Why?'

'The business is responsible for all expenses. In the case of no income the obligation to meet expenses falls to Tom. Ask Tom for the contract. A lawyer drew it up.'

'Who, your mate?'

Dash raised his eyebrows. 'Why is that a problem? He's a lawyer and he's only concerned with our best interests.'

'Your best interests, you mean.' Frankie turned away from Dash. She clenched her fists. How she'd like to wipe the self-satisfied smirk off his face, and again how she wished she'd never won the money. She wanted Dash far away from her and her girls and not in partnership with Tom. She could never trust Dash, never truly believe that he'd be working for the good of the business and family. She looked over at her husband. He was laughing at something Hope had said. Tom was too trusting. Too easy to take advantage of.

Chapter Eleven

Shauna took a deep breath before pushing open the car door and stepping out into her mother's quiet street. Leaves crunched underfoot as she crossed the front lawn and passed under the liquidambar tree that was now nearly bare of foliage. It was a week since the article had appeared in the paper and Shauna had made the decision to stay away from her mother until she had her thoughts clear in her head. She was angry, hurt and sad and needed some answers. History suggested she wouldn't get satisfactory ones, but she needed to ask anyway. She'd had a meeting earlier that morning in Doncaster, not far from her mother's house, and decided to stop in and see her.

Her phone pinged as Shauna walked up the path. She stopped, the edges of her lips curving into a smile as she read the message.

A ship without a captain gets lost at sea.
You're my captain and I'm lost without you. xx

At least one text a day had arrived from Simon since their drink the previous Friday night. It was corny, but immediately reminded Shauna of the text messages he'd sent her daily when they first started dating. All beautiful love texts she'd later discovered he'd copied from online sites. She imagined these new ones were no different. But they'd made her laugh, smile and feel desired then, and if she allowed herself to admit it, now too. She'd walked away from Cool the previous Friday night doing her best to push all thoughts of Simon from her head. And that was her problem: her head very clearly was saying no, she would not go there again, but her heart was a different matter. She'd loved him, thought they would spend their lives together and there was definitely part of her still attracted to him and still missing what they'd had. She just wasn't sure that that part of her was big enough anymore.

Shauna continued up the path and the curtain in the front room moved as she made her way to the front door. Lorraine was home. That was a good sign at least. She waited for the door to open; she knew her mother had seen her, but nothing happened. She knocked. 'Mum, it's me.'

The door opened a crack, and Shauna could see an eye staring at her. She began to laugh. 'What are you doing? Are you going to let me in?'

The door opened and Lorraine pulled Shauna across the threshold and quickly shut the door. Her mother usually dressed immaculately but despite the fact it was nearly lunchtime, she was in her pyjamas, her hair wild and no make-up on her face. This was a version of her mother she rarely saw.

'Are you okay?'

Lorraine shook her head and led Shauna into the living room. 'The bloody media keep showing up here, wanting to speak to me. It's driving me mad.'

Shauna narrowed her eyes. Wasn't that what her mother wanted? To be in the spotlight? To have all of the attention? Shauna pulled the copy of *Empowered She* from her bag and held it up. 'What did you think would happen after you did this?'

Lorraine glanced at the magazine. 'That bloody article should never have been published. I wouldn't be hiding in here all day if it hadn't been.'

'Why on earth did you do it then?'

Lorraine sighed. 'Shauna, I didn't. Bob surprised me with it. He thought he was being helpful. Come through to the kitchen and I'll make some tea.'

Shauna followed her mother. 'But the article reads like they've asked you questions, that they've interviewed you?' Shauna stopped, her mouth dropping open as they reached the kitchen. The cream wall behind the dining room table was covered with splotches of paint. It looked as if someone had blown paint through a straw and splattered the wall with reds, blues, yellows, greens and oranges. There were no drop sheets on the floor, and there was as much paint covering the polished boards as there was the wall.

'What the hell?'

Lorraine glanced at the wall. 'Oh that. I needed something to fill in my time during the week. I quite like it.' Shauna shivered as memories flooded through her. Lorraine had done this before, many times, when Shauna was young. Usually during a fit of rage after a break-up or when she had been fired from her job – which seemed to happen a lot – she'd start throwing paint. She'd often howl and scream and rage while she did it. On one occasion Shauna found her laughing and squealing, painting parts of her body and pressing them against the wall. She would have been about eight at the time and had joined in with her mother, having no understanding of why they were doing it but loving every minute of it. When it was done in a rage, she'd hide in her room. It had always been in rental properties though. She'd never known Lorraine to do this in this house, her pride and joy. The rentals had to be painted before each real estate inspection, or when they moved, which is why Shauna hated moving and kept her own apartment walls white.

'The floor's a bit of a mess,' Shauna noted.

Lorraine shrugged. 'Doesn't matter, I can clean it up at some stage.'

Shauna nodded, her thoughts switching back to the article. 'How did the magazine get all your information if you had nothing to do with it?'

'Bob organised for the magazine to email the questions and he answered them. Even went through my photos and supplied them with the one they used. It was from the photoshoot we did for my birthday.'

Shauna nodded. 'I wondered about that. Why would they publish an article without your permission?'

'I'm pretty sure Bob gave it. Just forged my signature on the agreement they sent through. He thought I was going to be elated.'

'But you're not?'

Lorraine shook her head as she switched on the kettle and took two cups from the shelf. 'Of course not. This is a very private matter. The last thing I want is everyone knowing that we have money or even where we live. I like to keep to myself.'

Shauna thought about her mother's words and realised they were true. While Lorraine liked to be the centre of attention if Shauna was around, she did generally keep to herself. She worked part-time and had a few friends but her main focus had always seemed to be having a man around. 'Where's Bob now?'

Lorraine gave a small smile. 'Too scared to show his face, I think. I gave him a real serve over this, Shauna. He has no idea of the potential damage he's done.'

The *potential* damage? Was her mother aware of what this could do to their relationship? 'I didn't think you cared about our relationship. I thought that was the whole point of you wanting half the money.'

'These are two very separate things. Yes, I am entitled to half the money, more if I go by what my lawyer believes, but the magazine article is a betrayal of my trust. Bob thought he was helping but has probably made things more difficult for me. For you too. I imagine you have people contacting you as well?'

Shauna nodded. 'Yes, looking for handouts.'

'Lie low, like I am. It'll blow over.'

Shauna accepted the cup of tea her mother pushed towards her. 'I'm confused. Are you still suing me for the money?'

'If you're not going to hand it over, yes of course.'

'You say that so calmly now as if it is completely normal to ruin our relationship over money. Last time you were yelling and screaming about it. I don't understand why you're doing this at all.'

Lorraine sighed. 'That's what you seem to be misunderstanding. You're the one happy to ruin our relationship. I gave you a gift that was never intended for you. Yes, I'd like the money, but it is the principle of the matter too. I would have given you half if I'd won.'

'If I give you half, Bob's going to take his share and probably disappear.'

'Bob loves me. The article proves how far he's willing to go for me. Yes, it was a misguided approach on this occasion, but it was done out of his love for me and wanting to make things right.'

Shauna shook her head. 'I'm not sure that going behind your back and forging your signature says that. I think it says that he was worried you wouldn't go ahead with it so did it without your consent.'

Lorraine threw her hands up in the air. 'Whatever! We can see the situation differently. You don't know Bob well enough to make any judgements of him.'

'You always need a man, don't you? Going right back to when I was little, there was always someone around. They never last very long, either. What if Bob's one of them and is gone in a few months. What then?'

Lorraine's eyes flashed. 'Stop needling me. If Bob leaves, I'll deal with it. You don't get to control my life, Shauna, any more than I can control yours.' The previous calmness drained from Lorraine's voice. She slammed her teacup down on the bench so hard it broke, flooding the benchtop with tea.

Shauna jumped. 'Jesus, what's wrong now?'

'What's wrong is I'm sick to death of you telling me how to live my life. Judging the men I choose to spend time with and denying me what is rightfully mine. You lord it over me with your fancy education, your well-paid job and that ridiculous car. How do you think that makes me feel? I'm your mother, for God's sake. I've done so much for you and this is how you repay me.' Lorraine's voice was now a high-pitched scream.

'Calm down,' Shauna said. The change in her mother from calm and reasonable to suddenly out of control was frightening.

'Don't tell me to calm down!' Lorraine screamed. 'Everything is your fault, Shauna. Everything. If it wasn't for you my life would be perfect.'

Shauna had heard these words before, and they'd always upset her. But this time there was an edge to Lorraine's voice, an edge that suggested there was more to this.

'What's my fault? Are we still talking about the money? How have I ruined your life?'

'EVERYTHING is your fault.' Lorraine turned to the kitchen table where she had four small buckets of paint lined up. She picked one up and threw the contents at the wall, laughing as a sea of blue covered the existing colours. She turned back to Shauna. 'Get out! Go or I'll throw one at you too!'

A lump formed in Shauna's throat. Without speaking she walked out of the house, closing the front door behind her and doing her best to ignore the squeals of laughter that came from the kitchen as more paint was probably being hurled at the wall. She'd seen this behaviour before, but not in a long time. It wasn't normal. Not at all.

Shauna closed her office door behind her and sank into the chair at her desk. What a morning. Visiting her mother had achieved nothing, other than reminding her how extreme her mother's behaviour could be at times. She wasn't sure whether to feel pleased that her mother had nothing to do with the article or not.

A knock on the door brought her out of her thoughts.

Josh opened the door and poked his head in. 'Just checking you're good for the two o'clock with Saddle Brothers?' His eyes widened as he saw the huge arrangement of red roses that had been delivered earlier that morning. 'Or are you too busy admiring your flowers? The ex, I presume?'

Shauna nodded. 'He's doing his very best to win me back. Daily love texts, the flowers. When he wants something, he pursues it until it's his.'

Josh folded his arms across his chest. 'I can't imagine you ever being *his* as such. You're very much your own, independent person. I take it you're considering getting back with him?'

'I'll need a lot more time to think about it. He's certainly doing his best to remind me of the things I loved about him, but it's hard to erase what he put me through. I'm not sure I can forgive him. But also, I've grown stronger in the last twelve months. My thoughts about the type of person I want to be with have changed.' Shauna sighed. 'Sorry, I'm not sure why I'm telling you all of this. We should be talking about the cowboys.'

'Cowboys?'

'Saddle Brothers. I'm still expecting them to be riding in on horses.'

Josh grinned. 'Mining, remember. Our focus is mining. Saddle is their surname, which the "Brothers" bit suggests.'

Shauna didn't return his smile. 'I'll be ready.'

Josh frowned. 'You okay? You don't seem your usual chirpy self.'

'Not sure anyone would ever describe me as chirpy, but no, I saw my mum this morning for the first time since the article came out. It didn't go so well.'

Josh stepped into the office and shut the door behind him. 'Want to talk about it?'

Tears pricked the back of Shauna's eyes. She cleared her throat. She was not going to let him see how much it had affected her. 'I'm good. She's just a bit out there sometimes.'

Josh nodded. 'That must be difficult. Did she have an explanation for the article?'

'It wasn't her; it was her boyfriend. She was surprisingly upset about the article and has been hiding out since it was published. She's been getting hassled by other reporters and for money too.'

'That's a good thing then; you're both on the same page.'

Images of Lorraine smashing her teacup and throwing paint at the wall flashed in Shauna's mind. Definitely not on the same page. 'My mother went from having a normal calm conversation in one breath to going crazy in the next.' Shauna explained what had happened.

'And she's done this before?'

'A lot when I was a kid. I moved out the minute I finished high school so haven't lived with her for sixteen years. She acts crazy from time to time and can be a complete bitch, but this was extreme and kind of manic. I haven't seen this in ages.'

'Possibly because you're not around her as much as you used to be.'

Shauna nodded. Josh could be right. Her mother's behaviour might not have improved at all; she just wasn't around her as much as she once was.

'It's not normal, is it?'

Josh shrugged. 'My mum's a psychiatrist, so I learnt at a very early age that it's hard to give anyone or anything a label, particularly one declaring them normal. Between you and me, I'd say no, it's not normal. Has she ever been treated by anyone for her moods?'

Shauna shook her head. 'No, she doesn't believe she has a problem.'

Josh picked up the phone on Shauna's desk. 'Why don't I ring my mum, see if she's free tonight. We'll invite her to dinner, and you can talk to her. She might have some ideas for you.'

Shauna stared at Josh. He always had a solution for her or a suggestion to help. 'Do you always go above and beyond to help people?'

'Of course, don't you?' He smiled and dialled his mother's number.

Shauna could instantly see where Josh's care and compassion came from. Tracy Richardson was full of warmth and genuine interest in Shauna's situation. Tracy hadn't been free for dinner as she volunteered once a fortnight at a local women's shelter and tonight was one of her rostered nights on, but she did have time to meet for a quick coffee.

'What do you think from everything Shauna's told you, Mum?'

169

Tracy ran her finger around the rim of her coffee cup, deep in thought. 'It is difficult to give any real diagnosis without spending time with a patient. Impossible, actually.' She smiled. 'But I know that's not what you're asking for. From everything you've described, it does sound like your mother is suffering from something. What exactly, I'm not sure. The swings in her behaviour from calm to irrational could suggest several disorders or even a hormone imbalance. That's why I'd need to spend time with her to get a better understanding of her condition. Do you think she'd come and see me?'

'I doubt it, but she's also very unpredictable so I won't completely discount the idea,' Shauna said.

'She might be bipolar,' Josh suggested.

Tracy frowned. 'Again, it isn't something we can assume or comment on without spending time with Shauna's mother. PTSD, bipolar, hormone imbalance and other forms of mental illness are just a few of the areas I explore with my clients. Has she suffered any trauma in her life, Shauna?'

'Not that I'm aware of.'

'What about her family? Her mother, father. Do any of them suffer from mental illness?'

'I have no idea. They're all dead.'

'You have no other family, just your mother?' Josh asked.

'My father is somewhere, but that's it. He might have extended family, I guess, but I'll never meet them. He deserted us when I was four,' she explained for Tracy's benefit. 'We never heard from him again.'

'I'd be more than happy to see your mother,' Tracy said. 'For a friend of Josh's, I'll squeeze her into my schedule.' She passed her card across to Shauna. 'See if you can convince her to come to an appointment. It sounds like she needs some help.'

Tracy stood and held out her hand to Shauna. 'It's lovely to meet you finally, Shauna. Josh has mentioned you a few times.'

Josh blushed as his mother leant down to kiss his cheek. 'And I hope we'll see you over the weekend at some stage? Dad needs some help putting up some shelves in the garage, and Kev's already said he's not available.'

'Sure, I'll pop in and help. Tell him to text me and let me know what times suit him best. I'm free both afternoons.'

'Great. I'd better dash. Second job awaits.' She flashed Shauna another smile and hurried out of the cafe.

Shauna smiled at Josh. 'She's lovely. Thank you so much for organising that.'

'You're welcome. I'm not sure if it really helped, but you can at least suggest your mum makes an appointment.'

'I'm not counting on her saying yes, but it can't hurt to ask.'

'Speaking of not hurting to ask,' Josh said. 'There's a rumour going around the office this afternoon that your ex is about to pop the big question. Just wondered if you were aware of this?'

Shauna's smile dropped. 'What?'

Josh nodded. 'Jenni's been swooning around the office all day going on about how a real-life Jane Austen novel is unfolding in front of our very eyes. She's a bit of a romantic.'

'She's a bit of an idiot! What makes her think he's going to pop the question?'

'The note with the roses, apparently.'

Shauna blushed. 'Jenni read the card?'

'Of course she did. As she explained when you were ready to rip shreds off her over the legal letter, part of her job description is to read all of the mail, regardless of whether it appears private or not.'

Shauna thought back to the message on the card.

Any plans for the rest of your life? I'm RSVPing YES right now.

171

It was one of the first messages Simon had sent her as a text when they'd started dating. Tess had laughed when Shauna shared it with her, reminding Shauna it was a line from one of her favourite screenplays, and while lovely, certainly not original.

'The message was an in-joke, that's all. Certainly not a proposal.'

Relief flooded Josh's face, which he quickly hid with a smile. 'I thought that might be the case. Just wanted to give you a heads-up in case you wonder why people in the office are gossiping about you.'

Shauna smiled. 'I've given them a lot to gossip about lately. At least this turns the focus off the money.'

'Kind of.'

'What do you mean?'

'Part of the discussion was that the ex might be after your money. Of course, they don't know he's your ex or of the history between the two of you so possibly assume he's a new boyfriend who heard of your win and thought he'd cash in.'

'Not that it's any of their business, but Simon doesn't even know about the money so that's not the case. He's genuinely wanting me back.'

Josh stared at her. He appeared to be weighing up whether to speak or not.

'You have an opinion on my relationship?'

'No, of course not. That's your personal business. I just worry about you. I've seen the impact the situation with your mum's having on you and I worry that the ex could create more problems.'

'Because he's after my money? Money he doesn't even know I have?'

Josh shrugged. 'Hopefully he doesn't know. I'm not trying to undermine your relationship with the ex or his desire for you. I worry about you. You've had all of these people contacting you trying to get money from you and the ex has gone from wanting to spend some time with you while he's back in Melbourne to suddenly wanting you back. If the money is his real incentive I'd hate to see you get hurt.'

'He does have a name you know. You refer to him as *the ex* the whole time.'

Josh smiled. 'That's how I prefer to think of him. It suits him. Just be careful, that's all I'm saying.'

Shauna swallowed, unsure how to respond. On the one hand, she hated him for pointing out that Simon's motives might not be genuine, but on the other hand she loved him for caring. She took twenty dollars from her purse and left it on the table. 'Coffees are on me. Thanks again for organising your mum.'

She felt his eyes on her as she turned and left the cafe.

Chapter Twelve

Frankie had spent the past two days doing her best to see the positive side in Tom's venture into a family business, and wipe the image of Dash's smirking face from her mind. She felt annoyed and on edge every time she thought of him. Unfortunately, Hope had caught the brunt of Frankie's irritation that morning. She'd dropped the girls at school only to arrive home to the phone ringing. It was Hope in a panic as she'd left her maths textbook in her room and needed it first period. After lecturing her about irresponsibility Frankie had driven back to the school and delivered it minutes before the first lesson started. The hug of gratitude Hope had given her immediately erased her bad mood.

'Frankie! Frankie! Hello!'

Frankie turned to find Sheila Matheson hurrying towards her as she made her way to the car park. She braced herself.

Sheila wiped the sweat from her forehead and smiled. 'I just wanted to say hello. How are you?'

Frankie tried to hide her surprise. They had had one conversation; they were hardly friends. 'I'm fine, thanks. You?'

'Good, all good, but it's you I'm interested in. So?'

Frankie tilted her head to one side. 'I'm sorry, I have no idea what you're asking.'

Sheila pointed at Frankie. 'You, the girls, the car, the move. I'm intrigued. Did someone die and leave you a fortune? I even heard Tom was starting a fishing-charter business?'

Frankie bit the inside of her cheek.

Sheila's eyes searched Frankie's, waiting for a response. Frankie remained silent.

Sheila smiled. 'I'm so happy for you and I wanted to come and tell you. Hope looked beautiful the other night at the party in her new clothes. Logan came home demanding I take her out to buy the same jeans. And you, too – your outfit is so stylish and your hair's lovely. The highlights suit you.'

Frankie touched her hair self-consciously. The T-shirt, jeans and boots she was wearing were what everyone wore. She certainly hadn't thought she'd stand out wearing them. 'I had no idea anyone was paying such close attention to us.'

Sheila leant towards Frankie. 'I keep my finger on the pulse.'

Frankie tensed. This woman really had no idea. She cleared her throat. 'I'm glad you find us more acceptable.'

Sheila nodded. 'Oh yes, you most certainly are. So, will you tell me the secret to your success? How do you go from a life of rags to owning luxury boats?'

Frankie hesitated before letting her muscles relax and started to laugh. No doubt Sheila thought she was being supportive rather than rude and offensive. She decided to give her the benefit of the doubt. 'I'm not sure I'd call our clothes rags, and as for the luxury boats they're part of a new business my husband and his brothers hope to make a success of. I hate to disappoint you, but fishing boats are hardly luxurious. The rest, well, I guess I would call it good fortune.'

Sheila clapped her hands together. 'Wonderful, wonderful. I suppose you can stop wasting your time with the leaflets, too?'

'That's where I'm off to now.'

'Oh. What a shame. I wanted to invite you out for coffee. A group of us meet every Thursday morning. They're all mums from Hope's class. I'm sure you'd love them.'

Frankie doubted that very much. 'Sorry, thanks for the offer, though.'

'Oh, there's Dianne.' Sheila pointed and waved as a woman crossed the courtyard.

Frankie recognised her immediately. Pearce's mother. The woman she'd had a run-in with not long ago. Dianne walked towards Frankie and Sheila, keying something into her phone. She stopped as she reached them, not bothering to look up.

'Frankie,' Sheila said, 'this is Dianne. Dianne, do you know Frankie?'

Dianne glanced up, her face flushing red as recognition dawned. 'Oh yes, sort of.' She put her phone away and gave a hesitant smile. 'Hello.'

Frankie crossed her arms.

Dianne shifted from foot to foot, unable to meet Frankie's gaze. 'I probably owe you an apology. I spoke with my son and I came to realise he and his friends had been a little mean. I think it was supposed to be in jest, but words can be misinterpreted. I'm sorry for being so rude. I believe Pearce apologised to Hope.'

Frankie shook her head. 'Not that Hope mentioned. I know his friend Hamish did but I'm not sure about Pearce. I do know he's leaving Hope alone though. So thank you. I appreciate how difficult this must be for you.'

'Yes. Things have changed, I suppose. Seeing people for their true selves does make a difference.'

Heat coursed through Frankie. 'You don't know me any better today than you did the other week when you called me a loser and a dole-bludger.'

Sheila gasped. 'You didn't?'

176

'She certainly did,' Frankie said. 'I'm intrigued as to why the sudden change in attitude?'

Dianne's face turned an even darker shade of red. 'Well, you. Your situation. You've obviously been making more of an effort than I realised. I was wrong to suggest you were lazy. I hope the new business is a huge success.'

Sheila beamed at the two women. 'Good, all sorted; all friends. Why don't you come, Frankie? The other mums would love you to join us for coffee.'

'Yes, come with us,' Dianne said.

Frankie marvelled at Dianne and Sheila's eager faces and attempted to calm herself before she spoke. 'Do either of you understand how rude you are?'

'What do you mean?' Sheila asked. 'We were just trying . . .'

Frankie put up her hand. 'No, let me finish. You've judged me purely on the assumptions you've made about my life. Neither of you made any attempt to talk to me in the past or include me in coffee mornings. You assumed my financial situation changed recently, and apparently I now fit into your version of acceptable, so you want to be friends. I'm sorry, but I'm not interested. Now, I'd better get on. I need to get to work.' The women's mouths dropped open as Frankie turned on her heel and strode towards the car park.

Later that afternoon, Tom arrived home to find Frankie at the kitchen table, engrossed in paperwork. She had a notepad to one side on to which she was jotting down ideas.

'What are you doing, hon?'

Frankie jolted upright. 'You scared me.' She pushed the papers aside. 'Just thinking something through. Working out the finances that would be involved.' She glanced at the clock. 'I'll have to take off soon for the support group, but how was your day? Get a lot done on the boats?'

'Day was great.' He opened the fridge and poured himself an orange juice. 'We decided to take a bit of a break this afternoon so went out into the bay and did some skiing.'

'Skiing?'

'Yeah, Rod bought all the gear last week. Dash came, too.'

'Does the boat go fast enough for skiing?'

'With the new motor she flies. It's not an ideal ski boat; I think Rod's planning to buy a proper one.'

Frankie opened her mouth then closed it. She remained silent.

'You should come next time.' Tom sipped his drink. 'Is something wrong?'

Frankie pressed her fingers into her palms. 'I'm trying to be supportive of this new business, but you make it hard when you choose a day of skiing over the work you should be doing. I thought the boats still needed a lot of work, so why aren't you working on them?'

'We are. *Get Reel*'s repairs to the hull are nearly completed. Once they finish cleaning her she'll be back in the water.'

'What about *Fish Tales*? You still have improvements to the cabin to do. Why isn't this happening?'

Tom's face hardened. 'We took one day off. Don't turn this into a big deal.'

Frankie sighed. Arguments were rolling from one into another at the moment and she didn't feel like instigating the next round.

Tom put a bunch of files on the table before sitting down with his juice. 'You'll be pleased to hear I met with the new lawyer you organised this morning before we went out.' Tom had agreed, somewhat reluctantly, to using a different lawyer from Dash's. 'He's looked over the paperwork and Dash's lawyer hasn't done anything dodgy. Every document is as we discussed.'

'Every document says you're putting in all the money and covering every expense, while Dash and Rod retain a third ownership each. That's the problem as far as I'm concerned. They aren't contributing anything, yet they'll receive a third of any profit.'

Tom pulled out a document from his file and handed it to Frankie. 'I agree, so I had him draft an amendment. Both Rod and Dash agreed with the terms.'

Frankie read through the details. 'Dash has agreed to this? He's actually said yes to investing fifty thousand dollars in the business?'

Tom nodded. 'They both did. Their money will go towards the start-up costs and for on-going maintenance. Once this first injection of cash dries up we all agree to contribute another equal amount.'

'Has he signed this?'

'Not yet. His lawyer is reading over the documents, but everything was approved in principle. So stop worrying about me being taken advantage of.'

'When Dash signs the document and hands over fifty thousand dollars I'll stop worrying.'

'Good. Now, how about you consider joining the business?'

'What do you mean?'

'Delivering leaflets is a waste of time when you can work with us. All sorts of jobs need doing. Organising a new website, business cards, brochures, accounts, answering the phones. There's so much more than just taking out the boats.'

Frankie's gut churned. In the last year she'd done her best to keep Dash at a distance. Working for the business would bring her in daily contact with him. She couldn't put herself in that position. She shook her head. 'Are you crazy? I have no experience, that's why I could never get a job other than delivering leaflets. I wouldn't know where to start.'

'None of us do. We're all learning. Dash knows a bit about the computers and the booking system. He could show you how that all works and then if you still needed help we could get someone else in for more training. Will you do it?'

'How do I continue running the household, looking after the girls?'

'The job would only be part-time, during school hours.'

Frankie bit her lip. Even if Dash wasn't involved in the business, she was the one who'd found the money that had led to them winning lotto, so surely she should be the one to decide what she wanted to do?

'What's wrong? I thought you'd jump at the chance to be a part of the team from the outset.'

'Then maybe you should have involved me from the outset. You know, before you actually decided to buy the business.'

The vein in Tom's head began to throb. 'Frankie, I know I hurt you and I'm really sorry. I've promised you I'll never go behind your back again and I mean it. You're everything to me and I can't apologise enough. It was a really shitty thing to do and the more I've thought about it, the more I wish I hadn't done it. I'd rather have lost the business opportunity than your faith in me. If I could go back in time I would, but I can't. I want us to move forward as a team which is part of the reason I want you working with us.'

Tom's face was full of regret as he spoke and Frankie knew he meant every word. She reminded herself that she was angry at him for his dishonesty, yet she was hiding a massive secret from him. It was to protect him, though, which in her mind was completely different. But he was right. They did need to move forward.

She sighed. 'Okay, let's agree to move on. I'm not saying I'm interested in working in the business, but it is what it is so let's just get on with things. There's something else I want to talk to you about anyway.'

'Mmm?' Tom took another sip of his juice.

Frankie referred to her notepad. 'I want to donate some money to Birkdale.'

'The retirement home?'

'Yes. I want to solve their transport problem for them. Provide them with a minibus and driver. The donation would need to cover the cost of buying and maintaining a vehicle, or leasing one, and a wage and the running costs.'

Tom looked sceptical. 'That's very generous.'

'We can afford to be generous. Look how generous you've been.'

'Rod and Dash are family. It's hardly the same thing.'

'Well, this is what I want to do. I don't have any of my own family to share the money with, but my old ladies are what I imagine grandparents would have been like; they're perfect candidates. I'll talk to Marg, the CEO, first and see if there's a particular way they want it structured.'

'They might prefer you to hand over a lump sum.'

'Maybe, but I want it used my way. The ladies are always complaining about the cost of getting out. Taxis and even Ubers are expensive and many of them don't have any family to take them around. A minibus service will give them back some independence and allow them to plan outings they can look forward to. Are you okay with me going ahead? I don't want to use the money if it's going to cause problems.'

'Like I did?'

The defensive tone in Tom's voice was one Frankie was getting used to hearing since they'd won the money. It seemed he was constantly needing to explain himself, defend what he'd done. They needed to get back to where they were before the win. Openly communicating and making decisions together. She took a deep breath. 'We just said we needed to move forward. I'm not looking for an argument, I'm looking for a way to embrace the money, see the good it can bring. This is something I believe in. It's not some faceless charity we're just handing money across to, and yes, I want to make sure you're in agreement with me spending the money. It'll be a lot. I want us to make the decision together.'

Tom's face relaxed into a smile. 'You're right, we should make decisions like this together and yes, I think you should do it.' He laughed. 'I should be focusing on your willingness to actually spend some of the money rather than questioning why. Hopefully you'll come around to the idea of the business, too.'

'I don't think I will, Tom. It isn't something I have any experience with. I'm better sticking to what I'm good at.'

'You're better using this opportunity we've been given to try something new. I'd love you to be working with the family business, but if you decide that's not what you want to do I think you should still be thinking about other options. Yes, we have the girls but they're teenagers and will probably both move out over the next six or seven years. You won't even be forty, Frankie. We have our whole lives ahead of us; we're young parents, not oldies about to retire.'

Frankie nodded. 'You're right. I should be thinking about other options.' She smiled. 'There's no hurry though, is there? The one thing the money has done is buy us the freedom to do anything we want.' And having anything to do with Dash would be incredibly low on that list.

'Now you're getting it.'

'And hopefully you are too, Tom. You've made a choice of what you want to do with the business but that's been *your* choice, not mine. I need to choose something that's good for me.'

Tom got up from the table. 'Yes, you do. But working together would be fantastic, babe. Think about it. I can't imagine a better life for us. Our old life had us going our separate ways during the day, me coming home exhausted and using the weekends to catch up on sleep. The business will keep us energised and excited, and doing it together means we'll have so much more to talk about and plan. We'd be living the dream.'

Frankie turned her focus back to the notepad as Tom left the room. Living the dream? Seeing Dash on a regular basis was something that she could describe in many ways. Dream, no; nightmare, yes.

Frankie grinned as Shauna hurried into the room ten minutes after the support group session had started. She'd assumed when Shauna wasn't there at the start that she wouldn't be coming and she'd been surprised at how disappointed she'd felt. Frankie hadn't had a close friend since her school days. It was hard to believe that, but it was true. Having a child at seventeen had seen her school friends drop out of the picture very quickly. They were interested in finding boyfriends, not talking about growth spurts and lack of sleep. Frankie had tried joining a mother's group, but some of the women in it were old enough to be her mother and she found she wasn't very welcome.

After that, she'd just got on with being a young mother. She'd met women who she got along with through the girls at kindergarten, then primary school, but the age gap between them had always seemed to be an issue. She was usually at least ten years younger. It didn't worry her; her family was the most important thing to her, and the time she spent with them and Tom, plus her volunteering, didn't allow much room for anything else. She'd felt a connection with Shauna, though. They were a similar age and from completely different circumstances, but she liked her. She was feisty and confident and made Frankie want to embrace those strengths.

'Thought you weren't going to make it,' Frankie said as they broke halfway through the session for tea and coffee.

'I wasn't planning to, but I had an awful day and didn't feel like going home.'

'Anything you want to talk about?'

Shauna grinned. 'Would Tom be okay with you getting home late again if we went for a drink?' She opened her bag, took out her phone and handed it to Frankie. 'You can ring him if you like.'

Frankie handed the phone back to Shauna, smiling as disappointment clouded her friend's face. She'd assumed Frankie was saying no. 'Of course, I'd love to; just get this thing ready to dial for me, would you?'

Shauna laughed, opened the screen with the keypad and handed it back to Frankie. 'I think you can work out how to key in the number and press the green button.' She strode over to the table with the coffee leaving Frankie to make her call.

Frankie joined her moments later having confirmed with Tom she wouldn't be too late. Pamela was getting herself a cup of tea.

'Thanks again for the lawyer's details,' Shauna said to Pamela. 'She was great.'

'Glad to have been of help. Was there any advice she gave that would be useful for the group? I'm sure we'd love for you to share.'

'Nothing to share as yet. Let me see how it all pans out with my mother and this case, and then I might be ready to talk.'

Pamela smiled. 'That's fine. We're a support group. You can do everything at your own pace, but remember, we are all learning from each other. Whatever you're going through, good or bad, as a result of your win, could help other people.' She looked across the room as the door to the community centre opened and a slim man with black hair and a huge smile poked his head in. 'There's Wayne, our guest speaker for tonight. I'd better go and welcome him.'

Frankie and Shauna both watched as Pamela greeted Wayne and shook his hand.

'I imagine his story's going to be interesting,' Frankie said. 'Setting up a charity would be huge.'

Shauna nodded. 'Very altruistic of him. Although I'm expecting there will be a very personal reason for why he's done this. I can't imagine you'd wake up one day and decide to set up a charity for kids with disabilities unless you'd had some experience in the area.'

Shauna was right, as the group found out with Wayne's introduction to what he was doing.

'My son, Levi, was born with cerebral palsy. In addition to intellectual impairment he has severe issues with his muscle control. It affects his speech and movement. He's been in a wheelchair all his life. Before having Levi, I had no idea what it entailed financially, let alone emotionally, to have a child with a disability. My wife and I learnt pretty quickly that all of our savings were going to disappear. It's estimated that raising a child with CP can approach fifty thousand dollars a year. That's direct expenses you pay for. It doesn't include indirect expenses such as lost wages for when you're taking him to medical appointments, or one of you having to give up work altogether or anything like that. There's government help, of course, but it doesn't cover the costs by any shot.'

A pain lodged itself in the back of Frankie's throat. To think that she'd thought they'd had it hard before winning lotto. There were so many families going through much tougher times.

'When we won, my wife Alex and I decided we wanted to do something to help other families in the position we'd been in. So we looked into setting up a charity. It took us six months from making the decision to actually opening the doors and beginning to offer help.' He smiled, his blue eyes twinkling. 'It's been the most rewarding experience of my life.'

'What exactly does the charity do?' Pamela asked.

'Levi's House, as we named it, brings together families with children who have CP. We offer a range of services from family fun days, support for parents, weekly after-school sports programs for the kids, to financial aid, equipment rental and loans. There's a really long list of what we do but the underlying goal is to relieve families of the financial strain that living with CP brings and provide them with a community where they are interacting with other families on a regular basis so they never feel alone. We took the advice of financial advisors and invested a lot of our lotto win. In addition to our initial donation to start the charity, we donate the interest earned on the money to cover the day-to-day running and we also run a number of fundraisers throughout the year. We're not-for-profit of course so we're also eligible for some government assistance.'

'What did you do before setting up the charity?' Shauna asked. 'Did you have experience already in doing anything like this?'

Wayne shook his head. 'I was a truck driver. I had no business experience at all. I employed expert help to guide me through the process of setting up the charity and employ experts now to help me run it.' He grinned. 'The lotto win was absolutely life-changing for me. It relieved so much pressure from our lives. The fact that I was away for days at a time with my truck-driving work was so hard on Alex. She had to do everything for Levi, only getting a break on the rare occasion her mother would drop by and look after him. It was exhausting. She was forced to give up work, which also meant we were living off one wage. We were down to one car and had to minimise expenses as best we could. Now we don't have to worry about money, we work together in the business and have the satisfaction of helping so many families. We've built a community. When Levi was first born I felt cheated, kept questioning why this had happened to us. Now I know exactly why. Everything happens for a reason. If our son didn't have CP and we'd won lotto I hate to imagine what we would have done with the money. I'd like to think we would have donated a lot of it to charity, but I doubt we would have thought to set one up and become so actively involved. We certainly wouldn't have realised how much it would enrich our lives.'

Frankie's eyes glistened with tears as she listened to Wayne talk. It was a wonderful, life-changing story. It reinforced that good could come from winning lotto.

'Now,' Pamela said. 'Wayne is going to talk us through the steps that were involved with setting up Levi's House. The legal requirements of a charity and of course the practical aspects he needed to consider.'

'Wayne's story was inspiring,' Frankie said as she and Shauna sat at the same table they had the previous week.

Shauna nodded. 'To go from driving trucks to making such a difference in people's lives is incredible. When you hear stories like his it makes you question what you're doing, doesn't it? I mean, we're all in a position to set up charities and make a huge difference, but it takes a special type of person to actually do it.'

Frankie nodded. 'And a personal interest makes a difference too. I know it's not the same as setting up a charity, but Hope, my oldest, suggested I use some of the money to help out the residents at a nursing home I volunteer at. She's sick of me harping on about the possible negatives that the money can bring and has pushed me to do something positive with the money. I'm hoping to provide them with a minibus and driver so they can get out and enjoy life more. I need to give more thought to who else I can help like that.'

'That's fantastic, Frankie. What a great idea. I should start thinking about who I can help like that too.'

'As we've learnt from the five steps, there's no rush to do anything, I guess, but if we plant positive seeds in our minds like this one we'll be more aware of opportunities as they present themselves.' She stood. 'But for now, it's my turn to get the drinks.'

Shauna shook her head. 'You're not even drinking. Mine costs twice as much as yours.'

Frankie smiled. 'I think we can both afford it.'

She returned a few minutes later from the bar with mojitos that looked just as delicious as the previous week. She sat down and sighed. 'I'm beginning to think I might need alcohol in mine too.'

Shauna raised an eyebrow. 'Really? What's going on?'

Frankie told Shauna about Blue Water Charters and what had been happening since she'd last seen her.

'You're kidding?' Shauna said. 'He bought a business without checking you were okay with the idea?'

'Yep. After having already given his brothers two hundred and fifty thousand dollars each, also with little discussion.'

'God, I'd kill him. Is Tom close with his brothers? Is that why he thought it would be okay?'

'No, and that's my main problem. They haven't been close for years. In fact, his younger brother, Dash, couldn't give a toss about any of us, other than our money. Rod's okay, but Dash is using Tom outright. Tom's so keen for a good relationship with them and to be one big happy family, he'll do almost anything. Dash won't put in the work required to justify his ownership. Time will tell, I suppose; it's still early days. But my prediction is things are unlikely to end well.'

'You never know,' Shauna said. 'The brother might surprise you. Having your own business and some money after many tough years might change him, give him something he's passionate about and enjoys.'

Frankie sighed. 'I'll be surprised if that happens. You'd have to meet him to understand how arrogant he is.'

Shauna nodded. 'I've met plenty of arrogant pricks in my time, so I can imagine what he's like. And what about you? You said it was a family business. Does that mean you'll be working in it too?'

'No, fishing's not my thing. Although Tom's trying to convince me otherwise.' She mimicked his voice: 'There's the administration side of things, running the office, organising the promotional materials, the website. The list is endless. Frankie, you'd be perfect.'

Shauna laughed. 'It's nice that he wants you to be part of it though. Is it the fishing that puts you off or the arsehole brother?'

Frankie smiled. 'You're getting to know me too well. The arsehole brother is the main reason and the fact that I don't have any skills to do that kind of job.'

'The skills aren't the problem, they can easily be overcome, but can you overcome the brother?'

'You think I should work in the business?'

Shauna shrugged. 'I work in recruitment so I can never help myself matching people to jobs, so feel free to ignore me, but yes, it makes sense. The girls are getting older and need less of your time now. Won't you get bored sitting around?'

'I spend part of my week at the old people's home helping out, and I also deliver leaflets. That on top of running the house and family keeps me very busy.'

Shauna coughed, nearly spitting out her drink. 'Leaflets? You haven't mentioned that before. I doubt many other lotto winners are out delivering leaflets!'

Frankie smiled. 'It helped make ends meet before the lotto money, but I've already given my notice. I'd hate to deprive someone else who needs the money. I'm just waiting for my route to be taken over.'

'What do you do for the old people?'

Frankie explained about the computer and sewing work she did at the retirement village.

'So, you're trained in computers?' Shauna asked.

'I wouldn't say trained exactly,' Frankie said. 'I took some courses at the library to learn to use email, the Internet and basic word processing. I learnt to touch-type in Year Eight at school, which has come in handy. The old ladies like to dictate emails for me to send, in between telling me their life stories.'

'What about sewing?' Shauna said.

'How do you mean?'

'Do you enjoy sewing?'

'Yes, I love it – particularly making clothes.'

Shauna nodded. 'It seems pretty straightforward. Either use your computer skills and go into business with your husband, or open a shop and make clothes or teach others to. You could turn it into a charity even – it might be the personal interest you're passionate enough about to consider doing something like that.'

Frankie's fingers tapped on the tabletop. 'It's too much change for me right now. Down the track perhaps but for now I'm happy just trying to adjust to our new financial freedom. We don't all have to be workaholics.'

Shauna's cheeks flushed red. 'Oh God, sorry! The recruiter in me rears her ugly head once again. I've spent too much time trying to fit people into the right job, so when I see someone wasting their time I feel obligated to try to help. Ignore me, I'm sorry.'

Frankie's eyes narrowed. 'You think I'm wasting my time?'

Shauna's hand flew to her mouth. 'Oh jeez, are both feet down my throat yet? Sorry, I have had an awful day, and I'm just making it worse. I probably shouldn't have come at all tonight.'

Frankie smiled. 'No, don't worry. I'm intrigued actually. Why do you think I'm wasting my time?'

Shauna took a sip of her drink. 'Okay, well, if you're asking. You've been given a chance to do something with your life. You've gone from having to scrape by to being able to do anything you want. You'll get bored doing nothing. You can keep visiting your old ladies, but you could make a difference if you chose to. You've got the funds to start up something new, something meaningful. Sorry, I'm just being honest.'

Frankie nodded. Part of her knew Shauna was right and listening to Wayne's story reconfirmed it. She did have the financial means now to do anything she wanted.

'But Frankie.' Shauna reached out and touched her arm. 'With all that being said, I also understand that the money scares you. The change it could bring; the worries from your past. I get that, I really do. You need to do everything at a pace you're comfortable with. I guess just being open to new things is a good idea. It's a shame you have someone like Dash to contend with, as otherwise I'd be suggesting to you that you try working with Tom. You're worried that he's started something without consulting you, but if you're working in the business, particularly in the administration side, you'll have a grasp of the finances and know what's going on. You can keep an eye on it all and have some control over it.'

Frankie sipped her drink and considered Shauna's words. 'You're right, you know. Rather than hide away from it, I probably need to step up and be part of it. Confront Dash at every turn if I need to.'

'Go you! That's exactly what you need to do.'

Frankie smiled. 'You're good for me. Your straight-talking is what I need. I'm so used to being a wife and mum; I need someone to remind me I'm Frankie too.'

'If you need any more reasons, think of your girls. You'll be an even more impressive role model to them when they see you taking the lead in the business and kicking some goals. You want them to achieve well at school and go on and have careers, I assume?'

'Of course. Jesus, the last thing I want them to do is follow my example and get knocked up at seventeen.'

'Hope's fifteen, isn't she?'

Frankie groaned. 'Don't remind me.'

Shauna laughed. 'The job will boost your self-confidence too. Make you realise that there's more to life than just getting by.' She held up her hands as Frankie was about to object. 'Don't take offence. I mean that up until winning lotto, survival was your main thing. Earning enough to give the family food, clothes and shelter. The basics are more than covered; now it's time to move up a step.' She grinned. 'I love my job, or I would have left the minute the money came through. It's not all about money; it's about being passionate about something and getting pleasure from it. I think you'll surprise yourself.'

'Possibly. Now tell me about your horrible day and let's work out what I can do to help turn it around for you.'

Chapter Thirteen

Shauna walked down to the Sushi Barn on Swan Street, glad it was Sunday and she had no commitments, and picked up a selection of the uramaki rolls her mother loved. She planned to drive over to her house just before lunch and cross her fingers that her mother's mood would be better today than on her last visit. After talking with Frankie on Thursday night, she'd spent a lot of time trying to work out exactly how to put the idea to her mother that she needed to see a doctor. She didn't want to say too much to Frankie as the moment she mentioned mental illness she saw Frankie shrink back in her chair. She couldn't begin to imagine what Frankie had gone through as a child, but then again, her own upbringing was hardly rosy. Her mother hadn't killed herself, though, and while Lorraine could be incredibly difficult at times, Shauna still loved her and couldn't imagine her not being around. She'd found her attitude towards Lorraine's apparent selfishness and moods softening as she came to believe it was highly possible her mother was suffering from mental illness.

She purchased the uramaki, enjoying the sunshine that was peeking out from behind the clouds. As she walked back to her apartment, she debated whether to call her mother or just turn up, deciding on the latter as it would be harder to reject her in person than over the phone. She smiled at this thought; her mother hardly differentiated between the two, so she was just as likely to be rejected in person.

Her phone pinged; another message from Simon.

How about a drink this afternoon? It's a beautiful day. We could take a bottle of wine down to the river or to the gardens? Would love to see you.

It had been over a week since Shauna and Simon had met at Cool for drinks and their only communication had been the multitude of messages Simon had texted. She thought back to Josh's comment about being careful that Simon wasn't after her for her money. He wasn't; she was sure of that. She doubted he even knew about it and if he did, he wasn't a patient person. He would have been demanding her attention and time by now, not being courteous and respecting her distance as she'd asked.

She considered his message momentarily. She'd probably need a drink after seeing her mother, and it was a beautiful day. She'd never really know how she felt about Simon if she avoided him and, if nothing else, she would like to prove Josh wrong. She was desirable for more than just her money, wasn't she?

She sent a quick message back suggesting they meet at a spot on the Yarra around three.

Fantastic, I'll bring a rug and wine, just bring yourself. S xx

Shauna collected her belongings from her apartment and slid into the front seat of her car. She took a deep breath and closed her eyes. Was it possible her mother might listen to her this once? Actually agree to see someone and get some help? This could be a life-changing moment for both of them and their relationship if she did. Shauna opened her eyes and switched on the car. A faint feeling of hope grew as she drove in the direction of her mother's house.

◆ ◆ ◆

Lorraine's reaction to Shauna's delicately put suggestion that perhaps she needed some help was met with peals of laughter.

'There's nothing wrong with me, Shauna. I'm sorry to burst your bubble, but this is just who I am. Yes, I get mad from time to time and do some impulsive things, but that doesn't mean I'm suffering from mental illness or whatever you've got stuck in your mind that's wrong with me.'

'Impulsive? Throwing paint at the walls and switching from calm to crazy in a matter of seconds is hardly impulsive. It's not right.'

Lorraine laughed again. 'I've always loved painting the walls, you know that. It's no big deal; you can't even tell that I did it. Come through and have a look.'

Shauna followed her mother through to the kitchen. The wall behind the dining room table was now painted a brilliant white, as was the rest of the dining area.

Lorraine took two plates from the kitchen cupboard and put them on the bench. 'Thanks for the uramaki! That was very thoughtful of you.'

'I'd like you to consider seeing this woman.' Shauna passed Tracy's card to Lorraine. 'You do have some pretty extreme mood swings which could be hormonal. She might be able to help you.'

Lorraine stared at the card. 'I don't need to see a psychiatrist for mood swings. There's nothing wrong with me. I'm sorry you don't like me trying to get my share of the lotto money, but this isn't the way to go about it either.'

'This has got nothing to do with the money.'

Lorraine rolled her eyes. 'Really? Don't you think I see your plan? Take me to a psychiatrist, have me declared crazy or unstable or something like that and suddenly the money is all yours. They're not going to give it to someone declared bat-shit crazy now, are they?'

'That's not the intention at all. I think there might be something wrong with you. Perhaps something that's gone undiagnosed for a long time. It could change how you feel about things if you got some help.'

'What's all this talk about help?' Bob entered the room. 'Who needs help?'

'I thought you guys had split up,' Shauna said.

'Shauna! Wherever did you get that idea from?'

'From you. You said he had no idea of the damage he'd done and that you'd given him a real serve; that he was too scared to show his face. I assumed you couldn't trust Bob anymore and would have ended it.'

'Bob's actions were done with the best intentions, Shauna. Yes, I was angry as he hadn't thought through the possible ramifications of the article, but I still love him for believing he was doing something wonderful to surprise me. His heart was in the right place.'

Bob groaned. 'Back causing problems, I see, Shauna. Can't help yourself, can you?'

Shauna bit the inside of her cheek. She didn't want to give him the satisfaction of even speaking to him.

'I overheard you trying to convince your mother she's unwell, that she's suffering from mental illness. That's a despicable thing to do. We both know that your motivation is exclusively related to the money.'

Shauna shook her head. 'It has nothing to do with the money. If you loved my mother, you'd want to help her too.'

196

Bob picked up one of the plates of uramaki and sniffed it. 'What the hell is this?'

'Give it a go,' Lorraine said. 'It's delicious.' She turned to Shauna. 'Bob does love me, which is why he would never suggest that I needed locking up or whatever you think this doctor is going to do to me.'

Shauna sighed. Everything was always taken to the extreme. 'She's not going to lock you up. She'll examine you and see if there's anything that could cause the extreme mood swings you tend to suffer from. That's all.'

'She's not examining anything. What she should examine is your bank account. When she sees how much is in it and how much you owe me, she'll understand your motivation, won't she, Bob?'

Bob grunted, his mouth full of uramaki.

'Thank you for lunch, Shauna. Now I suggest you get on with your day.'

A few minutes later Shauna found herself driving back towards Richmond realising she'd completely wasted her time.

Simon was waiting for her at their spot on the river, the picnic rug and basket on the ground, and a single white rose in his hand. She'd deliberately walked from her apartment as she didn't want Simon to see her car and question how she could afford it. He stepped forward to greet her, pulling her to him.

'It's so good to see you. I thought after the last time we had drinks we were done. But then you didn't send the roses back, so I figured maybe there was a chance still.' He handed her the white rose. 'Our second date, remember? That guy selling roses in the restaurant that you felt sorry for.'

Shauna smiled. She had watched a man selling roses walk from table to table being rejected by everyone. When he'd approached their table and she'd seen that Simon was about to say no she took charge and bought a white rose which she gave to Simon. She'd paid twenty dollars for the five-dollar rose because she felt so sorry for the guy trying to sell them. No one wants to do a job like that and if you are then you're pretty desperate for money. Shauna was tempted to hand him her card at the time and tell him to come and see her, that she could find him a better job, but she hadn't wanted to offend him.

'Aren't I supposed to give you the rose?'

Simon shook his head. 'Not this time. It was that gesture, what you did for that guy, that made me fall in love with you. You've got a very kind heart, Shauna. You've always been incredibly generous.'

In the four years they'd been together, 'generous' was not a term he'd ever used to describe her. He'd laughed at her reasons for buying the rose that night, had called the rose guy a loser even. He certainly hadn't fallen in love with her for her generosity.

Josh's words filled her head: *Simon has gone from wanting to spend some time with you while he's back in Melbourne to suddenly wanting you back. I'm just saying be careful.*

'Can I ask you something?'

'Of course.'

'Why this sudden change of heart? You were pleased to see me when you got back and were keen to be friends, then all of a sudden you've been missing me terribly and want me back. How did that happen?'

'I guess seeing you reignited all those feelings I have for you. I hadn't realised how much I missed you until I saw you again. I've caught up with some of our friends, too, since I've been back and it just isn't the same without you there. I sit chatting with them wishing every minute that I had you with me. I don't think I realised just how great our relationship was until now. I also hated seeing you with that guy at your office.' He gave a sheepish grin. 'The green-eyed monster rears its ugly head.'

'You don't need to be jealous of Josh. He's a colleague and a friend. Nothing more.'

'As long as he knows that.' Simon pushed the hair from her face and leant in and kissed her softly on the lips before pulling back. 'I'm sorry that I left the way I did. That I made you choose. I promise I'll never do anything so selfish again if you'll give me a second chance?' His eyes searched hers, causing her to look away.

He pulled her down on to the picnic rug. 'There's no rush to make up your mind. I understand that it will take time for you to trust me again and really believe this is what I want. But for now' – he opened a cooler bag and pulled out a bottle of Moët, one of her favourite champagnes – 'let's just relax and enjoy a beautiful Sunday afternoon.'

Shauna accepted a glass, her mind spinning. Would Simon really go to all of this effort just to get to her money? He had never been one to act subtly in the past. She would expect him to come rushing to her full of excitement if he'd learnt about her win. But Josh had planted a seed of doubt. She did her best to push all thoughts of Josh out of her mind as Simon chatted about the new contract he was working on.

'The best thing,' he said, refilling her glass, 'is I've met this really interesting guy, John Trickett, who owns Select Recruitment in South Melbourne. He's grown the business to be really substantial in the last five years and wants to offer me a full-time position once the contract with Recruit is up. I'm seriously considering accepting it. The money's fantastic and the opportunity even more so.' He grinned. 'What do you think about that?'

Shauna smiled; it was hard not to get caught up with Simon's enthusiasm. His grin and twinkling eyes were one of the things that had attracted her to him when they met, and they still did now. 'I think it sounds like a great opportunity.'

'I meant what did you think about the fact that if I accept a full-time position then I'm obviously staying here for good.'

Shauna raised an eyebrow. 'Getting a job isn't necessarily going to stop you from having the travel bug or quitting and going again.'

He took her hand and lifted it to his lips and kissed it. 'No, but if I have you it will. I promise.'

She pulled her hand away from him gently. She wasn't ready to restart the physical side of their relationship. She needed to get her head around everything he was saying and really believe he was genuine before she even considered going there again.

He reached into his backpack and retrieved an envelope. 'I got you something.' He blushed. 'You'll probably think it's silly but when we were together you often said how once you made it you were going to buy yourself a Louis Vuitton handbag. That it was a ridiculously extravagant purchase and if you ever bought one it would symbolise you moving into the next stage of your life. That it would mean you were richer and going places.' He handed her the envelope. 'Open it.'

She slid her finger along the back of the envelope, opened it and pulled out a card. Shauna's mouth dropped open. A two-thousand-dollar gift voucher! She stared at Simon. He put a finger to her lips before she could speak.

'I want you to use this to get that bag you've always wanted and let it symbolise the next stage of your life. The richness you talked about doesn't need to be about money, it can be about us enriching each other's lives just by being together. It would be a new start, a new chapter in our lives. I love you so much, Shauna.'

Shauna felt tears prick the back of her eyelids. His words were beautiful and the fact that he had remembered about the bag was touching. She loved that he'd assumed she was still at a stage where the bag was not affordable as it confirmed for her that he was genuinely trying to win *her* back, without any knowledge of the money.

She looked at Simon, remembering how much she'd loved him. *Loved*. As beautiful as everything he was saying was, it didn't elicit the feelings it would have four years earlier. Perhaps she was just still too wary after having her heart broken by him. Maybe he could win her trust back and those feelings would return? 'Thank you. I can't believe you've done this.'

He beamed. 'Just proving to you that I do love you and I am still that guy you loved before I left. We're good together, Shauna, really good.'

She nodded and sipped her champagne. When they'd been together she'd told him everything that was going on in her life. Now she had life-changing news and even though his actions today proved he didn't know anything about the money, she was still reluctant to share the news with him.

He reached for her hand and squeezed it. 'Is there any chance you'll take me back?'

She smiled. 'Let's just take it slowly, okay? What you've done today is just lovely but it's still early days. I'm not ready to rush back into a relationship.'

'But you're not saying no either?'

She shook her head slowly. This relationship wasn't finished. She definitely still had feelings for Simon – mixed feelings, but they were still feelings. 'No, I'm not saying no, just that I need time.'

He grinned. 'That's all I needed to hear. I'll win you back, you'll see.'

Shauna waited until the Monday morning staff meeting was over and the majority of her colleagues had returned to their desks before turning to Josh. 'You and the rest of the staff were wrong about Simon.'

He glanced up from the document he was scribbling notes on and looked around the room. A few members of staff were still chatting. He stood and gathered his belongings. 'Let's talk in my office, shall we?'

She followed him down the hall to his corner office which gave sweeping views of the city in one direction and Port Phillip Bay in the other.

She sank down into the chair across from his desk. 'Not everyone's out for my money. Simon knows nothing about it for a start. We were together for four years before we broke up and had planned our future together. He loves me for who I am, not for my bank balance. He proved that to me yesterday.' When they'd finished the champagne, Shauna had let Simon walk her home. He'd kissed her on the cheek when they'd said goodbye, which she was grateful for. The respect he was showing her was definitely going in his favour.

Josh frowned. 'I wasn't trying to cause problems, I just wanted you to be careful. It's a lot of money and will bring out the worst in people. That's great that you know he's genuinely in love with you. If that's what you want then I'm really happy for you. I'm sorry if it came across as anything else.'

Shauna hesitated for a second; Josh was pushing his hand through his sandy-blonde hair and looked anything but genuinely happy for her.

Her phone pinged and she checked the screen. 'Jenni's trying to find me. Hopefully she has the reports ready I asked her to photocopy. I guess I should get on with my day.'

She stood. 'I wanted to say thanks, by the way. You were great organising for me to see your mum, I really appreciate that. You're a great friend.'

Josh nodded, his lips turning up at the edges. 'Remember, I'm cute, adorable and smart. I told you that on day one. I should have added honest, trustworthy and a *great friend* to that list.'

Shauna smiled. 'Yes, you should have.' Her phone pinged again. She glanced at the screen. 'Bloody Jenni. I'd really better go.'

◆ ◆ ◆

Shauna stopped in her office on the way to reception, picking up a note Jenni had left on her desk. She held it up when she reached the reception area. 'Who's Don Rice?'

'I'm not sure,' Jenni said. 'It's why I've been messaging you. He's rung at least five times and every time I ask him for more information he says it's personal.'

Shauna scrunched up the message. 'Never heard of him. Another gold-digger no doubt. Do you have those letters for Tonacoal?'

'Sorry, the printer's jammed. Troy's fixing it. Is five minutes okay?'

'Yes, fine.'

Jenni poked her head into Shauna's office a few moments later. 'Shauna?'

Shauna looked up. 'What? Have you got the letters?'

'No, it's this Don Rice guy. He's in reception and wants to talk to you. Says he's happy to wait all day if necessary.'

'Really?' Shauna sighed. 'Fine, tell him I'll meet him briefly in about ten minutes. I'm not rushing out for a stranger.' Shauna sat down at her desk wondering who Don Rice was. She did a quick search on LinkedIn. Sixteen matches didn't help her. She replied to a few emails, and after ten minutes passed, went out to reception.

A man in his early sixties stood up the moment he saw her. He visibly drew in his breath as he scrutinised her appearance.

Shauna hesitated before approaching him. He was familiar. She couldn't quite place him, but she knew him from somewhere. She held out her hand. 'Don, I'm Shauna. How can I help you?'

Don took her hand in his. He didn't speak. His eyes searched hers.

A feeling of unease settled over Shauna. She pulled her hand back, crossed her arms and waited for him to speak.

'Sorry,' Don said. 'Do you remember me?'

Shauna shook her head, the unease growing in the pit of her stomach. 'Should I?'

'I hoped you might.' He looked around the reception area. 'Would it be possible for us to go somewhere more private to talk?'

Shauna hesitated.

'Are you sure you don't recognise me?' Don said. 'At all?'

Shauna couldn't shake the feeling of familiarity but struggled to place him. There was a warmth in his eyes that stopped her from dismissing him completely. 'Okay, come down to my office.' She led Don past the conference room and into her office.

'Impressive view. You've done very well.'

Shauna sat down and motioned to one of the visitors' chairs.

Don sat and locked eyes with Shauna. 'I'm not sure there's any good way to announce this, so I'll just say it outright. I'm your father, Shauna.'

Shauna drew in a breath. There was no way she could have anticipated this. She stared at Don. He looked nothing like the man her mother had described as her father. 'What are you talking about? My father's name is Lucas Jones. He has fair hair, not dark, and he looks nothing like you.'

Don shook his head. 'No, I'm your father. Your mother has done everything possible to keep you away from me, including changing her surname and my name by the sounds of it.'

'My father walked out on us when I was four and never attempted to make contact again. My mother didn't need to keep him away. We also lived in Brisbane at the time, so I imagine if he's alive, that Lucas Jones is still in Queensland somewhere.' Every muscle in Shauna's body was wound as tight as a spring. She couldn't believe the nerve of this guy.

Don took his head in his hands, shaking it to and fro. 'Oh God, is that the story she's told you?'

'Story? No, I'm telling you what happened.'

Sadness clouded Don's face. 'I suggest we get Lorraine in here and discuss the events of thirty years ago together. How I came home from work to find you both gone without any trace. I spent the next two years trying to track you down. I only gave up when the police convinced me you were probably both out of the country with false identities. Not to say I stopped looking, though. I kept in contact with her friends and her mother and rang them every week for over ten years, hoping to get some information of your whereabouts. I moved to Melbourne twenty-six years ago when I met my current wife, Sandy. To think we've been living in the same city all of these years without realising is even more heartbreaking.'

Shauna froze. This couldn't be true. Her mother would hardly win mother of the year, but she wouldn't have lied to her so consistently about something this important, would she? Also, her grandmother was dead; he could hardly have rung her every week for ten years.

'You don't believe me, do you?'

'No.'

Don pulled out his wallet and took out some photos. 'Familiar?' He passed them to Shauna. Shauna recognised the first photo of herself and her mother when she was about six months old. In the second Shauna guessed she was two. She held an ice cream in one hand and the other held hands with a younger version of Don.

She looked up at Don. 'Okay, this is definitely you, I get that, but this is crazy. Why would my mother go to such extreme lengths to hide from you? And how did you find me now?'

Don sighed. 'She did it to hurt me. Things were strained between us. I wanted us to meet with a counsellor. She thought I was rejecting her. Instead of a rational discussion about getting help to fix our marriage, she threatened me. I honestly didn't believe she'd go through with her threats. But then it was too late. She took you and left. She destroyed the most important thing to me – my relationship with you. I don't know what she's like now, Shauna, but I realised once she was gone that she was mentally unstable. She needed help and I'd failed to realise this until it was too late. There were so many behaviours she exhibited that in hindsight I realised were more than her just being moody. She had a problem that needed help. To answer your question on how I found you, I saw a picture of Lorraine in an article in one of my wife's magazines. I nearly stopped breathing. A private investigator helped track her down from the information we had, and he was able to find you quite easily.'

Shauna got up from her desk and fanned her face. 'I need some water. Be back in a minute.' She left the room and went straight to the staff kitchen. Thankfully it was empty. Could this man really be her father? If there was any truth to his story then her mother . . . She couldn't finish the thought. She filled a cup with water and gulped it down. She refilled it as the door to the kitchen opened.

'Hey, you.'

She turned at the sound of Josh's voice. His smile turned to a frown as soon as her eyes met his. 'What's wrong?' He moved across the kitchen and took her arm. 'You're white, and you're shaking, come and sit down.'

Shauna put down her cup and allowed him to lead her to a couch.

'What's happened?'

Shauna swallowed. 'There's a man in my office. He's claiming to be my dad.'

'What?'

'He saw the magazine article about my mum, and had a private investigator track me down. He's been looking for me for thirty years, apparently.'

Josh's jaw clenched. 'I'll bet. What a coincidence an article about winning lotto got his attention. Let me deal with him. I'll get rid of him for you.'

'No don't, not yet. He's got photos of me and him when I was a baby and if his story is real then my mother needs to be run out of town, not him.' Shauna repeated what Don had told her.

Josh nodded. 'I agree you need to speak to your mother, but what do you want to do about the guy in your office? Should I ask him to leave? You look like you're in shock.'

Shauna ran her hands through her hair. 'No, I will. But come with me.'

Josh followed Shauna back to her office, where she introduced him to Don. He stood to the side while Shauna spoke.

'I need some time to digest all of this. Can you leave me your details and I'll call you to meet up again?'

Don reached inside his jacket pocket and pulled out a card. He took out a pen and scribbled something on the back. 'Here are my numbers. Ring me as soon as you're ready to talk. I understand this is a huge shock, but when I saw the article it was one of the best moments in my life. To think I have an opportunity to reconnect with you. I've dreamt about this day for so long.' Tears glistened in Don's eyes as he passed his card across the desk.

Shauna felt a lump rising in her throat. This man could really be her father. She watched as Josh led him out of her office.

When he returned he sat down across from Shauna. 'How are you doing? Need a drink?'

She checked her watch and smiled. 'It's not even twelve o'clock, but the answer is yes.'

Josh jumped up. 'Come on, let's go for an early lunch. I'll get Jenni to cancel the rest of our days.'

'Really?'

'Definitely. This is a massive shock. A relaxing afternoon is probably the best strategy before approaching your mother, which I assume you plan to do next?'

Shauna picked up her bag and followed Josh out of her office to the reception area. 'I can't believe any of this. Don Rice is either a gold-digging liar, or I have the worst mother in existence.'

Josh pressed the button for the lift. 'Unfortunately, I don't think you'll be playing happy families with both of them. Come on, you can sort out how you feel while we numb the shock with a shot or two.'

Josh grinned as Shauna downed her third vodka and slammed the empty shot glass on to the bar. He put his empty glass next to hers. 'Feeling any better?'

Shauna returned his smile. 'Heaps, although I might not thank you tomorrow.'

'Why don't we end the shots and grab a bottle of wine? Go outside and enjoy the view.'

Shauna followed Josh to an outside table. The beautiful blue sky that greeted them contrasted with the icy wind that whipped the city streets. A reminder that they were heading into another Melbourne winter. Chester's prime position, overlooking the Yarra River and Southbank, ensured it was full of city workers every night by five, unwinding with drinks and spectacular views. Shauna took a seat closest to the outdoor heater, grateful it was the middle of the day and only a handful of people were scattered around the beer garden.

Josh sat across from her and poured them both a glass of wine. 'What's your gut feeling telling you? Do you think he's telling the truth? That he is your father?'

Shauna hesitated. There was a part of her that very much wanted him to be her father. 'I don't know. Part of me hopes he is. I'd have one parent in my life I could possibly depend on. It would kill any hope of salvaging a relationship with my mother, though. It'd be the final nail in that coffin.'

Josh nodded. 'Although, she might have had good reasons for what she did.'

'Stealing me away from him would be pretty hard to forgive. She'd want to have a good story.'

'Maybe she has.'

Shauna stared at the man sitting in front of her. He was always so positive. Always willing to give the benefit of the doubt. In her world, that only led to disappointment. He must have had a pretty easy life. Her face flushed with heat. Josh knew so much about her – the problems the lotto win had caused with her mother, her father reappearing – and she realised she knew very little about him. 'You see the good in everyone,' she said. 'Tell me, what's your real story?'

Josh shrugged. 'I don't know, I like to think people are decent. Hope they are at least. As for a story, not sure I really have one.'

'What about your family? I've met your mum and know what she does, but I don't know much more about you.'

'Oh, you know, usual stuff: Mum, Dad, brother and a sister. All pretty close.'

'And?'

'And what?'

'Where do they live? How often do you catch up? How old are your brother and sister? What was your childhood like?'

'God, you don't really want answers to all of those questions, do you? I'd rather talk about you.'

Shauna's eyes narrowed. 'Why?'

'Why? Because I find you interesting.'

'Not good enough. I hardly know a thing about you. You told me next to nothing when we last had dinner.'

Josh sighed. 'Fine, I'm the eldest, Kevin's thirty-four and Kayla's thirty-seven. We have dinner with my folks every month. You have to be overseas or dying to miss dinner. I meet the Ks, as I like to call them, every now and then for lunch or a drink. That enough?'

'No,' Shauna said. 'Where did you go to school?'

Josh took a sip of his wine. 'Scotch.'

Shauna raised an eyebrow. 'Scotch?'

'Yes, Scotch.'

'So, are you all networked in with the Old Boys' club?' Shauna was surprised when Josh flushed.

'I keep in touch with a few guys, but I left twenty years ago. School seems like a distant memory.'

'Did your brother go to Scotch?'

'Yep.'

'And Kayla?'

'She rebelled. Started at MLC but ended up dropping out in Year Eleven. She worked and earned some money before taking off to Europe. She was gone for three years. When she got back she started working in real estate, much to my dad's horror.'

'What's wrong with real estate?'

'Nothing at all, as long as you're buying it, according to my dad.'

Shauna stroked her wineglass, thinking about Josh's family.

'Why are you so quiet all of a sudden?' Josh asked.

'Just thinking.'

Josh raised his eyebrows. 'And?'

Shauna met his eyes. 'I'm making the assumption from what you've told me that your family is pretty well off?'

'My parents are. Mum's done really well with her practice and my dad's been successful too. Kevin works with my dad, but that wasn't really an option for Kayla or me.'

'Why not?'

'I had a falling out with my dad when I left high school. He was trying to control my life, have me do the university course he wanted, work part-time in one of his businesses and basically become a clone of him. I wasn't interested. I wanted to do my own thing. I was eighteen and finally could become independent and he wasn't happy about it.'

'Really? My mother couldn't wait for me to leave home; practically pushed me out the door at eighteen. What happened? What did you do?'

'I moved out and went to uni to do a marketing degree. He disowned me for three years and made sure I knew I was cut off from any financial help. It suited me. I didn't want to be indebted to him, so I worked my way through uni and got a job as soon as I graduated.'

'He must have respected you for doing that?'

Josh laughed. 'You don't know my dad. He's a successful guy who's used to people jumping when he says "jump". He probably never factored in kids who would have their own minds. When I'd been working for about a year, he contacted me and invited me to one of our Sunday dinners. Kayla reckons Mum threatened him and forced him to make peace. He's still never forgiven me for not joining the business, but we can at least sit around a table together and enjoy a meal.'

'He must be proud of you now. You've got a great job and you earn good money.'

Josh smiled. 'Mum is. Dad's not so impressed. If I owned I-People maybe he'd feel differently.'

Anger welled up inside Shauna. How could a father not be proud of a son like Josh? He was intelligent, hardworking and honourable. 'He sounds like an arsehole.'

Josh laughed. 'I've probably made him sound worse than he is. He's actually a nice guy overall; he just doesn't really understand why I want to be independent and successful in my own right. He's built up quite a business empire and Mum says he's disappointed that he can't share his success with me.'

'Empire?'

Josh nodded. 'Yeah, like I said, he's done okay.'

'So have you.'

'Not quite in the same league as my father.'

Shauna sipped her wine. 'Tell me more. Have you travelled?'

As Josh launched into stories of his adventures in Thailand and America, Shauna was aware of her body relaxing and her smile widening as she listened to his soothing voice. He was a genuinely lovely and attractive guy. Her chest tightened as an image of Simon entered her mind. She hadn't given him a thought all afternoon. Her absent father of thirty years had reappeared, and it hadn't even occurred to her to call the man who had openly declared his love for her and his desire to spend their lives together. What was wrong with her?

◆ ◆ ◆

The next evening, Shauna sat on Lorraine's front veranda, waiting for her mother to return. She'd taken the advice Josh had given her when he'd dropped her home the previous night. She'd not taken the day off and rushed over demanding answers first thing in the morning as she had planned. Instead, she'd allowed her workday to distract her and time to pass, ensuring she was calmer than she may have been otherwise. She let her mind wander back to the previous afternoon. They'd been sensible, ordered food and stopped drinking after the first bottle of wine. She'd enjoyed spending time with Josh but recognised she'd needed a distraction after Don Rice's revelation, and he'd been the perfect person to offer that. She had no history or complications with Josh like she did with Simon so hanging out was relaxed and fun. Shauna was also grateful she didn't have a huge hangover to complicate the discussion she was about to have.

Forty-five minutes after she arrived, her mother's car turned into the driveway. Lorraine climbed out, opened the boot and removed at least eleven or twelve shopping bags.

'Been on a spending spree?' Shauna called.

Lorraine flinched. She grasped the bags, slammed the boot and walked up the front stairs, her face contorted with anger. 'What are you doing here?'

'Waiting to speak to you.'

'Unless you're delivering a large cheque I'm not interested.'

Shauna shook her head slowly. 'No, Mother, this visit is not about money. We need to talk.'

Lorraine crossed her arms. 'Until the money's resolved I'm not talking to you. Don't even get started about me seeing a psychiatrist, I won't have it.'

Shauna inhaled, her fists clenched. 'This discussion isn't a choice. I'm here to talk about Don Rice. I assume the name rings a bell?'

Lorraine's eyes widened.

'Yes, Mother, Don Rice. I had a visit from him yesterday. You've got some explaining to do.'

Lorraine's hands trembled as she fumbled in her bag for her keys. She opened the front door and Shauna followed her down the hallway to the kitchen. Lorraine still hadn't spoken. She opened the fridge, pulled out a bottle of wine and poured herself a glass.

'Well? Are you going to say anything at all?'

'Wine?' Lorraine held up the bottle.

'No, I don't want a drink, I'm here for answers. Why have you lied to me for thirty years?'

Lorraine gulped down half the glass. 'What did he tell you?'

'He told me you threatened to leave him many times and how one day he came home to discover it wasn't an empty threat. You'd disappeared into thin air.'

'Anything else?'

'No, why? Is there more?'

Lorraine's eyes narrowed. 'A lot more. I'm not talking about this now. Come back another day. This is such a shock. In fact, I think I'd better sit down.' She walked into the living room.

Shauna followed. 'No way. You can't avoid this one. You let me believe my father didn't want kids, couldn't handle parenting and was a selfish bastard. The man I met yesterday grieved for years because he lost his child. He would give anything to get that time back again.'

'How did he find you?' Lorraine interrupted.

'He saw *your* magazine article.'

'Great. He knows you won lotto.'

'Is money all you think about?'

'Of course not, but he does. He'll be after a share. He couldn't care less about you, any more than he did thirty years ago. Ten million dollars, however, that's another matter. He's a charmer – believe him and you'll be handing over your winnings within a matter of days.'

'So, he'll charm it out of me rather than sue me?'

Lorraine waved her hand dismissively. 'Fine, give him a few million if that's going to make you happy. Your decision.'

Shauna's body tensed. She could hear Josh's words. *Try to be calm, have an adult conversation with her.* But it was almost impossible. 'This is not about money. You owe me an explanation and some answers. Why did you leave my father and then lie for all of these years?'

Lorraine threw up her hands. 'You really want to know? Fine. Undo all the work I've done protecting you.'

Shauna waited.

'Shauna, he was violent. We had one too many arguments over money. I spent too much feeding us and clothing you, which didn't leave enough for him to drink or gamble away. After yet another black eye and split lip, I decided to get out before you got hurt. I was terrified if he found me we'd both be in trouble, so I disappeared. Moved to Melbourne, changed our surname and maintained a low profile. I wasn't in touch with my mother anymore and the few friends in Brisbane had kept their distance once they realised he was knocking me around. Nothing like supportive friends.' Lorraine refilled her wineglass and gulped another mouthful. 'Now you know the real story.'

Shauna's stomach churned. The bitterness in Lorraine's voice was real. 'Why not tell me this before? Why lie about him not wanting me and moving away from us? He's been living in Melbourne for the last twenty-six years, by the way. He said he moved down here when he met his second wife.'

Lorraine's eyes widened. 'Really? Jesus, just the thought that we could have bumped into him at any time makes me want to vomit. I hate to imagine what he would have done to me. He was an abusive alcoholic and gambler. I couldn't risk him getting his hands on you. I was on edge for years, worried he might find us.'

She let out a breath. 'And to think he's lived here all this time. It's a worry to think what his second wife's been through.'

Shauna was reeling. It was hard to believe that the man who'd stood in her office was either of these things. He was fit, his face glowed with health. But then, thirty years had passed. He'd had plenty of time to clean up his act and change. 'Why didn't you speak to his mother, my grandmother?' Shauna said. 'He said she was devastated.'

'No point. She was a controlling bitch. Wouldn't believe a bad thing about her darling son. I had to get you away from both of them.'

'You've lied to me for thirty years; how can I believe what you're saying now's true?'

'What have I got to lose, Shauna? When you were little I could have lost you. He was a charmer, could easily have twisted things to get full custody if he'd chosen to. Then who knows what would have happened. He might have beaten you, or worse. You're an adult now. I don't need to protect you. You can do that yourself. Money is the obvious reason he's shown up. Just be careful.'

Shauna's mind was racing. Yes, Lorraine had lied to her on many occasions but this time her words seemed true. Her lies usually were to benefit herself and Shauna couldn't see any angle that this helped make Lorraine look good. If Don's treatment of her really had pushed Lorraine to the edge it certainly helped explain some of her mother's unpredictable behaviour. She went to the kitchen, grabbed a glass and returned. She filled her glass and took a large swig. 'I wish you'd told me this years ago.'

Lorraine sighed. 'What good would it have done?'

'Given me a better understanding of you, for starters. I'm so sorry you went through such an awful time.'

'You can show me your appreciation by not going near him again. He's bad news. I guarantee the money is the drawcard.'

'I'm beginning to wish I'd never won the bloody money. It's caused so many problems.'

Lorraine's eyes hardened. 'You can fix two problems instantly. Give me my half and stay away from Don Rice.'

Shauna stood up. 'Jesus, even during a revelation like this money is still the only thing on your mind. I'm going. I don't want another argument. I just wanted to learn more about Don Rice. Now I know.'

'Yes, you do. If he contacts you again tell him to go away and don't believe a word he says.'

Shauna nodded. For once she agreed with her mother on something. 'I'm going to head off. I've got a lot to think about.'

Lorraine didn't get out of her chair. Her hand shook as she took another sip of her wine. 'Be careful, Shauna. That man practically ruined me. I don't want the same to happen to you.'

Hot tears stung Shauna's eyes as she drove away. Her mother's story was unthinkable. Shauna didn't remember being four. She didn't remember leaving her father or Brisbane. Her childhood memories were of being in the way, of being told she was a nuisance. Of watching her mother with different men; men who were always more important than her. Why did a woman who'd done so much to protect her then spend the subsequent years withholding her love? It didn't make sense, but then Lorraine never had.

Shauna wiped her tears as she manoeuvred the Mercedes out into traffic. Regardless of her mother's motivations, she could take one thing away from tonight. She now had two parents in her life, neither interested in anything but her money.

As Shauna pulled up to her apartment block her phone rang. It was Simon. For once she didn't hesitate and answered his call. After the last two days of realising how awful her parents both were, she needed to talk to someone who cared about her.

'Hey, SJ!'

Shauna smiled. She'd always loved it when Simon had called her SJ. He said her initials in a sexy way, as if he couldn't wait to be with her. 'Hey, yourself.'

'Just ringing to see how you are. Sunday was really lovely. Have you used the voucher yet?'

'Not yet.' Shauna had put the Louis Vuitton voucher on her bookshelf in her apartment. It didn't feel right to be spending Simon's money when she had so much of her own, no matter how lovely a gesture it might be.

'Make sure you send me a photo of the bag when you do, or better still, bring it out to dinner with you and show me.'

Shauna laughed. 'Sounds like a fair deal.'

'I'm heading to Brisbane in the morning. Just wanted to chat to you while I was still here.'

'They have phones in Brisbane, you know. You'll probably even find your own phone works there.'

Simon laughed. 'Ha ha. You know what I mean. I wanted to talk to you while I was still close by. I was actually wondering if you had time for a drink tonight? I could meet you in about twenty minutes?'

This time Shauna hesitated. It would be the perfect opportunity to tell Simon everything. What was happening with her mother and her father's reappearance. She couldn't keep it from him forever and she was now at the point that she wasn't sure why she was keeping it to herself. Simon was bending over backwards to win her back, there was no question at all about that. Her thoughts however didn't match up with the words that left her lips.

'Not tonight, sorry. I've got a massive headache and just need to go to bed.' It was bordering on the truth. Her head had begun to pound as she drove home from her mother's. It was all too over-whelming. She should have paid more attention in the support group to the five steps. One of them was learning to protect your-self emotionally. She wasn't doing the best job of that.

'I can come over and look after you, if you like. A foot rub might be exactly what you need.'

He was certainly pushing the buttons of all her favourite things about him. His foot rubs were sensational, but from memory, rarely ended with the feet. Taking that next step with him physically wasn't something she was ready for yet. She was sure that once she had the issues with her parents sorted she'd have more energy to devote to Simon and whether they had a future or not. She just didn't have the brain space for it right now.

'I'll take a rain check,' Shauna said. 'Let's organise something once you're back from Brisbane. I really do need to have an early night tonight.'

A sigh came down the phone. 'You're not making this easy, SJ. This loving you thing is doing my head in, if you really want to know. How about we make a commitment that when I return from Brisbane you start loving me back?'

His tone was light-hearted, and Shauna laughed. 'How about we see where things are at. I'm about to drive down into the under-ground parking and there's no mobile reception. Have a great trip and I'll see you when you get back.'

'You'll hear from me before that, SJ.'

Shauna smiled as the call ended. He'd called just at the right moment. Reminding her that in amongst all of the turmoil she was going through, there was a guy who wanted her and was willing to put in the hard yards to get her back. She wasn't as alone as she sometimes thought.

Chapter Fourteen

The blare of the television and the raised voices of Mavis and Betty made it easy for Frankie to track down the old ladies. A heated discussion over which of *The Voice*'s contestants should move to the next round was taking place.

Frankie stood in the doorway of Mavis's room and cleared her throat.

The old ladies turned immediately, their faces breaking into wide smiles. Mavis picked up the remote and turned off the television. 'Frankie, dear, we weren't expecting you today. What a wonderful surprise. We haven't seen you in weeks. Is everything alright? Are you okay?'

Frankie returned her smile. 'I'm fine. I hope you got my messages?'

Mavis nodded. 'Yes, we did, dear. It was so nice of you to ring and let us know you weren't coming. We've had another young girl help us with our emails while you were away.'

Betty moved closer to Frankie. 'Just between us, you could teach her a thing or two.'

Frankie laughed. 'I'm sure she's doing her best to help. Now, what can I do for you today?'

Mavis glanced at her watch and exchanged a worried looked with Betty. 'I'm sorry, dear, but we have to attend a special meeting in a few minutes. All the residents have been asked to gather in the rec hall for an announcement.'

'Perhaps you could come with us?' Betty said. 'Then if you have time afterwards we could discuss the Twitterbook program.'

'I'd love to come. A cuppa and a biscuit would be rather lovely.' Unbeknown to Mavis or Betty, Frankie knew exactly what the meeting was about. She had visited Marg, the CEO, a week earlier, delivering a very large cheque and the conditions for which it was to be used.

Frankie noticed the women scrutinising her. Mavis was the first to speak. 'There's something different about you today, dear. Don't take this the wrong way, but you look wonderful.'

'Yes,' Betty added. 'Your lovely haircut and those beautiful clothes, and I don't know, you seem different. Doesn't she, Mavis?'

'Yes, more confident or something. Has something happened, dear?'

Frankie laughed and linked her arms through the two old ladies'. 'Come on, let's find that cup of tea. Your imaginations are far too active.'

Groups of residents were already gathered when they entered the rec hall. They took a seat as Marg motioned for everyone to sit down so she could make her announcement.

Gasps went up around the room as the residents were informed that an anonymous donor had provided enough money to purchase a minibus for the centre. A driver would be employed and a regular schedule set up for outings to the shopping centre, theatre and other destinations agreed upon by the travel committee.

'Travel committee?' Mavis asked. 'What exactly is that?'

'We'll need to elect a committee to help create the schedules and plan outings,' Marg said. 'We'll discuss how nominations can be placed this week.'

'Who donated the money?' one of the men asked.

'As much as I'd like to tell you so we could thank them, they've asked to remain anonymous. I can confirm, however, that this is an ongoing service. There are plenty of funds dedicated to ensure it runs for at least the next fifty years.'

There was another round of gasps.

'In addition, the donor has sent in a special afternoon tea, including champagne, for the occasion.' As Marg finished talking a group of waiters walked into the room, some carrying trays of drinks, others finger food. A cheer went up; this was unheard of.

Mavis turned to Frankie, her face beaming with excitement. 'Frankie, dear, what a day to choose to come and visit. Have some bubbles, won't you.' She took two glasses from a nearby waiter.

Frankie shook her head and reached for a glass of orange juice instead. 'You two enjoy the champagne, this is my preferred drop.'

'What a wonderful gift,' Betty said. 'I wonder who on earth would be so generous? Do you know, dear?'

'No idea,' Frankie said. 'How about a toast though – to new adventures and lots of outings.'

'Hear, hear.' Mavis and Betty clinked their glasses with Frankie.

'Tell us, dear, what have you been doing? How is your little family?'

Frankie spent the next hour enjoying afternoon tea with the ladies. She told them their luck had taken a turn for the better and Tom had been able to join his brothers in a business venture. She downplayed it, saying it was a new start and they'd see how it went. She then answered their many questions about the girls and listened to their own updates of their children and grandchildren. A little after five she excused herself, saying she really must get going.

Mavis and Betty hugged her tightly. 'Look after yourself, dear,' Betty said. 'And make sure you come and visit again soon.'

Frankie promised she would and walked out of the retirement village, her heart feeling incredibly full. She had experienced a wonderful afternoon, seeing the looks of surprise and delight on the faces of the residents. There had even been a few tears from those without family who rarely got out and now would be able to. Frankie crossed her fingers as she walked to her car. She could only hope that this feeling would stay with her and help her through the next day.

Frankie straightened her skirt and pushed open the office door of Blue Water Charters. It was her first day as office manager; she could hardly believe she was doing this. Tom's delight when she'd agreed to work in the family business had given her the confidence to start. Time to put her anger and resentments behind her and get involved. It would also give her the opportunity to keep an eye on Dash.

Frankie smiled as she thought of Shauna's surprise when she had rung her after the support meeting and their drinks to thank her for helping her make such a big decision. Shauna's directness had made Frankie think about her future.

She planned to do her best to be pleasant to Dash. Hopefully, he would be out on the boats most of the time and their interaction, beyond the initial training he was to give her, would be limited. She plastered a smile on her face and walked into the small office.

Dash stood as soon as she arrived. 'About time. I'm going out; just look after the phones, okay?'

Nausea swept over Frankie. As much as she didn't want to spend time with him, she needed training. 'Dash, I have no idea what to do.'

'If you'd come in earlier I would've shown you, but I'm too busy now, so we'll try again tomorrow. Get here at eight, not nine.'

Dash pulled on his jacket and stepped towards Frankie and the door.

Frankie put her hands up. 'Hold on a minute. The hours I agreed to are nine to two thirty. My work fits in around school.'

Dash snorted. 'No one listened to my opinion. The girls are old enough to take care of themselves, aren't they?'

Frankie forced herself to remain calm. 'That's not the point. The agreement is I work three days a week from nine until two thirty. You can't change this on day one.'

'If you want training you'll need to be here at eight. Now, can you move? I've gotta go.' Dash pushed past Frankie and out the door.

Frankie's heart sank as she stood in the empty office. This was hardly the start she needed. She walked over to the desk and picked up the phone. She needed to speak to Tom.

Tom and Rod were out on *Fish Tales* for the day with four American businessmen. Tom calmed her down. 'Don't worry, I'll sort out things later. Just poke around, read the files the previous owner left and make yourself as familiar with everything as possible.'

'What if someone rings? I don't know how much to quote or any information to give them.'

'No need to. Take messages and I'll call them tonight.'

Frankie felt relieved as she hung up. Tom had complete confidence in her managing the office. She slung her coat over the back of the chair and sat down at the desk. The small square room had enough space for two desks, some filing cabinets and a few chairs. The kitchen and bathroom were shared with the neighbouring bait shop. The sterile, sparsely furnished office was hardly inviting.

The computer in front of Frankie showed movie-screening times at the Dendy Theatre. Surely Dash hadn't rushed off to go to the movies? Would there even be one on this early?

She was relieved to find the phone was the same as the one at home so she could handle incoming calls without needing to learn a phone system. Frankie dug through the drawers and found herself a notepad and pen.

On top of two of the filing cabinets sat three in-trays. A large diary sat in the bottom one. Frankie read through the various bookings. As she flicked forward in the book she noted they only had confirmed business for the next three weeks. So much for the business purchase including all future bookings.

After familiarising herself with the diary, Frankie got started on organising the office. It was filthy and poorly laid out so she pushed open the door to the shared bathroom and kitchen and found a cupboard containing cleaning materials. Grabbing disinfectant, cloths and the vacuum cleaner, she got to work.

An hour and a half later every corner and surface of the office gleamed. With the floor and rug vacuumed, Frankie made a mental note to bring in the mop and bucket from home the next morning. She rearranged the furniture so the desk had two visitors' chairs in front of it, earmarking the far corner for small couches and a coffee table to give people somewhere comfortable to wait if she was busy with other customers. The walls also needed livening up. Frankie wondered what Tom would think of taking and framing some photos of the boats, perhaps a successful catch and smiling faces of happy clients?

With the cleaning and rearranging completed, Frankie decided to make herself a coffee. As she waited for the kettle to boil, the door from the bait shop opened and a man, who Frankie assumed must be at least in his seventies, came in. His deeply tanned skin was wrinkled and leathery, but the muscles bulging from the cuffs of his polo shirt suggested he had the fitness of a much younger man. He stopped when he saw Frankie and rubbed his white beard, holding up his finger, indicating for her not to speak. 'I've got it,' he said. 'You're the magic coffee fairy here to deliver my mid-morning brew?'

Frankie laughed and put out her hand. 'Frankie York, new office manager next door.'

'Ah,' the older man said. 'Good. Those boys need someone to whip them into shape.' He took Frankie's hand and shook it warmly. 'Josiah Jacobs.'

Frankie smiled and turned back to her coffee-making. 'I'm happy to make you a drink. How does this all work? Do we share the tea and coffee, or do we have our own?'

'The previous owner and I shared, but I'm happy to do separate supplies, too. Whatever suits you.'

'How about I come and visit you tomorrow and we work it out.'

'I'll look forward to it.' Josiah took the coffee Frankie made for him. 'Thanks for the brew, much appreciated. I'd better get back to the bait business. Lunchtime rush will be here soon.'

'Lunchtime rush?'

Josiah winked. 'You'd be surprised how many people sit on the pier with their lunch and a rod. I do small bait packs for them, even offer them use of the fridge if they catch anything they can't take back to work.'

The image of men in suits sitting on the jetty fishing stayed with Frankie as she took her own coffee through to the office and sat down.

The phone rang as she opened the top drawer, ready to tackle the drop file. Her stomach instantly contracted. She shook herself. It was a phone call, for goodness' sake. She picked up the phone. 'Hello, I mean, good morning, Blue Water Charters.'

'Frankie, it's Shauna.'

'Oh, thank God,' Frankie exhaled. 'You're the first person to ring since I've been here. I have no idea what I'm doing.'

'What do you mean no idea? I thought you were being trained today?'

'I was, but Dash is playing his power games with me and took off the minute I got here. Told me I was late even though I arrived fifteen minutes early.'

Shauna was silent.

'Are you still there?'

'Yes, sorry, just thinking. Tell me what you've worked out so far.'

Frankie told Shauna of her basic discoveries and the cleaning and rearranging of the office. 'Hopefully, Tom or Rod will be able to bring me up to speed tomorrow. I'm guessing Dash is going to enjoy making this as difficult as possible.'

'Mmm, I think you might be right. I'd better go. I just rang to wish you all the best for a great first day. How about we catch up for a drink on Thursday night after the support meeting, and you can fill me in.'

The next morning Frankie decided to call Dash's bluff and arrived at the office at quarter to eight. Tom had returned home late the previous night and was booked again by the American business-men from lunchtime. Frankie insisted he sleep in. She was perfectly capable of dealing with Dash.

An hour later there was still no sign of him. Frustrated, Frankie rang his phone, which clicked through to voicemail. She looked around, wondering where to start. A coffee seemed like a good idea so she got up and let herself into the shared kitchen.

As she was pouring her drink, Frankie heard the office door open and a familiar female voice call hello.

'Shauna?' Frankie went back into the office to find Shauna carrying a huge vase full of lilies, accompanied by a younger woman. 'What on earth are you doing here?'

'Visiting you and bringing you these, of course.' Shauna kissed Frankie and handed her the flowers. 'Happy job? Happy new start? Happy new life? I'm not sure which, perhaps all?'

Frankie was touched. 'They're beautiful, thank you.'

'You're welcome. Now, this is your real present.' She pushed the young woman in front of Frankie. 'Meet Makenna Finch.' Makenna smiled at Frankie. 'She's an administrative whiz. Makenna is yours for the next two days. She's here to train you, set up systems for you and will ensure you're running this office like clockwork. She'll also be available to you via phone at any time after she has finished and she'll be willing to come back in and help in an emergency. Sound good?'

Frankie stared open-mouthed at Shauna. 'I'm not sure what to say. Why would you organise this?'

'Because this business should be run in a streamlined manner. Whether this brother of Tom's has any clue or not is irrelevant. This is your baby, so let's make it yours. Learn from an expert. Use this week to implement Makenna's systems, next week to get on top of it all and then the following week I'm sending you Ryan Drysdale. He specialises in small business advertising and promotion. He'll help you map out the next six months' marketing campaigns.'

Frankie continued to stare at Shauna.

'Makenna will also test your computer skills and decide if you require extra training. Once she reports back I'll work out who to send in next.'

A soft giggle escaped from Makenna. 'I'm sorry,' she said. 'I don't think I've ever seen what I think my grandfather terms a stunned mullet before. You might need to give Frankie a shake.'

Frankie closed her mouth. 'Shauna, thank you. I'm blown away, but this is far too generous.'

'Don't be silly, I'm responsible – partially anyway – for pushing you into this job. I want to see you enjoy your work and turn this into a profitable business.' She checked her watch. 'I'd better go, I've got to be back at the office in twenty minutes. I can't make the support meeting tonight after all, I'm afraid. Are you going?'

Frankie shook her head. 'No. The new job's enough for this week. Hopefully next week. If you're there perhaps we can go for a drink after?'

'Definitely.' Shauna turned to Makenna. 'Call me if you find any areas you feel could use extra help.'

'Will do.'

'Good luck!' Shauna gave Frankie a quick hug and hurried out of the office.

Makenna smiled at Frankie once Shauna had gone. 'She's a bit of a whirlwind.'

Frankie laughed. 'Yes, she sure is. Thank you so much for agreeing to do this.'

'No need to thank me. Thank Shauna; she's paying good money. We'll get you up to speed in no time.' Makenna squeezed Frankie's arm. 'You are going to surprise yourself, I promise.' She put her bag down on the desk, pulled up a chair and sat down in front of the computer. She patted the seat next to her. 'Come on, let's get started.'

Frankie swallowed, a nervous smile on her lips as she took her place next to Makenna. This was happening. She was going to learn business management from an expert, not her condescending brother-in-law.

◆ ◆ ◆

A week passed and Frankie felt like she'd been doing the job for years. Tom joked she must have had a similar role in a past life. Frankie knew that it was Makenna, not a past life, who she needed to thank.

Makenna's employment had been extended by two days until Frankie was completely comfortable and on top of things. The booking system worked, the drop files had been cleaned out, and a proper filing system had been implemented. Much of the previous owner's paperwork was filed directly into the bin. The documents that appeared important were read and kept. Not only did Makenna bring Frankie up to speed with the basics of the computer, but she trained her in the accounts work she would need to do. The booking system linked to a website one of Makenna's contacts had been employed to create for the business. Blue Water Charters had a sleek, professional feel. Makenna didn't stop there. The office furniture had all been replaced with modern, attractive items. The small seating area Frankie had envisaged was furnished with a couch, two comfortable chairs and a coffee table, which would house promotional brochures. A small coffee machine finished off the welcoming environment.

The only negative aspect of the job had been Dash. On the few occasions he'd appeared in the office he'd been incredibly rude. He'd taken one look at the new office furniture and coffee machine and gone ballistic, not caring that Makenna was witness to his rage.

'Who gives you the right to spend the company's money? You've demanded I put fifty thousand dollars into this company and now you're throwing it about to make yourself comfortable. You're a disgrace, Frankie. You need to ask my permission before you buy anything.'

Frankie hadn't had the opportunity or inclination to respond. He'd slammed out of the office, deliberately smashing against the new couches on his way. Luckily he didn't do any damage.

Frankie had apologised to Makenna on his behalf, but it hadn't fazed the younger woman at all. 'His anger isn't our issue,' she'd pointed out. 'It's the money he's spending that is.'

As they'd worked through the files of paperwork, Makenna had unearthed a problem with the accounts. Dash had entered a number of transactions into the ledgers with no invoices to back them up. While the details he'd entered sounded like legitimate expenses, that he was unable to produce one invoice rang alarm bells with both Makenna and Frankie. Frankie scheduled a meeting with Tom and Rod and the three of them now sat in the new seating area discussing the matter.

Frankie bit her tongue as Tom was quick to defend Dash. 'Come on, Frankie, do you need to constantly stir the pot with Dash? He's authorised to spend money – we all are. We've needed a ton of equipment and repairs. There's nothing dodgy about what he's doing.'

Frankie tried to stay calm. 'Fine, then tell me why it's impossible for him to provide one invoice?' She held up a bank statement. 'We have fifteen unaccounted expenses totalling thirty-nine thousand dollars. That's fifteen missing invoices. This is in addition to twelve other payments totalling sixty-two thousand dollars.' She handed each of them a printed sheet. 'I've listed here every item the sixty-two thousand dollars was used for. The business name is in the second column and the detail of the equipment or repair is in column three.'

Rod rubbed his forehead. 'What's the point of this? The sixty-two thousand dollars shows our purchases so far.'

'Yes, I'm making it clear in order to stay on top of things. The point of this is to ask you whether the additional thirty-nine thousand dollars has been used for legitimate expenses. If yes, where are the invoices? If no, we have a problem.'

Frankie stared at the men, waiting for a response.

They sat in silence for a few minutes, looking through the expenses Frankie had listed.

Rod slammed his page down on the coffee table. 'Shit, this is pretty thorough. We understood the initial outlay to be around sixty grand, which this is just over. Thirty-nine thousand is a lot to spend without knowledge or receipts. I can't think of any big expenses, can you, Tom?'

'Not big expenses,' Frankie said. 'Fifteen expenses adding up to thirty-nine thousand.'

Tom glanced at Frankie then looked away. He picked up the papers. 'Leave this with me. I'll talk to Dash. Looking at some of the items, he might have preordered. A few of the items are for services, too, which have quite likely been carried out on the boats. I'm sure he'll be able to contact the suppliers and organise invoices.'

'That's not the only problem.'

Tom sighed. 'What now?'

'Dash still hasn't contributed his fifty thousand dollars. The money was due two weeks ago, when Rod paid his.'

Tom wrung his hands. 'We've discussed this already. His money is tied up in an investment.'

'Oh, come on. He can break an investment easily enough.'

'He'll get penalised if he does. There's no point losing money unnecessarily when the business is cashed up.'

Frankie held up the bank statements and waved them at Tom. 'It won't be cashed up for much longer.'

'He said he'll receive the money at the end of the month. That's only two weeks away.'

'Fine, I'll chase him up then.'

'Don't antagonise him, hon. This is supposed to be a family business, bringing us all closer, not driving a wedge between us.'

The pleading in Tom's eyes prevented Frankie from saying more. She knew Tom was sick of hearing her complaining about how rude and condescending she found Dash. Every time Dash set a foot inside the office, an argument started between the two of them. He was a master at creating a hostile work environment. Frankie stood and moved back to her desk. 'Okay, I'll do my best to be lovely to Dash.'

Tom smiled. 'We'd better head off. Dash is out doing some work on *Fish Tales*. I'll have a chat to him about the invoices and I'll see you later this afternoon.' He gave Frankie a quick kiss then slapped Rod on the back. 'Come on, mate, let's get ready for tomorrow – our first double booking. It's going to be a big day.'

Frankie watched from the office window as Tom and Rod walked towards the boats. Her gut churned as they laughed and chatted. Tom had managed to dismiss her findings for now. If he wasn't worried yet, everything in her gut told her he soon would be.

'Why on earth would you think I'm trying to steal money from the business, Frankie?' Dash stormed into the office slamming the door on his way in.

Frankie looked up from the document she was typing, her stomach immediately clenching when she saw the anger etched on Dash's forehead.

'I never said you were trying to steal money.' She'd thought it but she'd certainly never said the words.

Dash slammed his hand down on Frankie's desk causing her to recoil. 'Then why is Tom hassling me to provide invoices?'

'Dash, calm down; customers out on the pier can hear you yelling.' She took a deep breath. 'I need the invoices to balance the accounts. I'm happy to ring around and request new invoices if some have been misplaced, that's no problem at all. No one is being accused of anything. It is purely administration that needs to be kept on top of. If we get behind now it will be a nightmare at the end of the financial year.'

Dash's eyes narrowed as he considered Frankie's words. 'I'm not being accused of anything?'

'Of course not. We just need the invoices to match up against the expenses, that's all.'

Dash stared at Frankie, causing her to shift uncomfortably in her chair. He didn't believe her for one minute, it was written all over his face. But that didn't matter. If he produced the invoices then what she did or didn't think of him had no bearing on the matter at all.

'Fine. I'll get them to you in the next day or two. I'll ring around and get the ones that I might have misplaced, not you. I don't want you telling people I'm not doing my job properly.'

'I'd never do that, Dash.'

He turned and kicked the trash can across the room. 'You already did, Frankie. That's exactly what you told Tom.'

He stormed out of the office in the same manner he'd arrived.

Frankie was still shaking when Tom came into the office an hour later. 'Just need to check something for tomorrow's booking with the client.' He picked up the bookings file to find the phone number he needed. He glanced at Frankie. 'You okay?'

Frankie nodded. 'Dash and I had a little chat, that's all. He wasn't pleased that I'd brought up the invoice situation. Thinks I'm accusing him of stealing from the business.'

'He said he'd get the invoices to you though? We spoke with him out on the boat and he said it wouldn't be a problem.'

'Yes, over the next couple of days.' She sighed. 'I really hope he does.'

'But?'

'But nothing.' Frankie gave him a smile. No matter how revoltingly he behaved she'd give Dash the benefit of the doubt until he proved otherwise. He had a few days.

'I'm going to head home a little bit early tonight so I can get the girls sorted before I go to the support group. Is that okay?'

'You're going to keep going to the support group? I thought when you didn't go last week that you'd had enough.'

'No, I was just too busy last week. I like the group, there are some really nice people there. Shauna, of course, but Todd and Helen and Ivan too. Actually, I like everyone who goes. It's interesting to hear their stories and how they are managing week to week. I don't have a whole lot of friends, Tom, so it gives me a group of friends that have a common interest. For now I plan to keep going.'

Tom nodded. 'Okay. Drive though, don't catch the train if you're planning to have drinks with Shauna afterwards again. And Frankie, I bought you that phone to use, not leave in your desk drawer. It's charged up. Please spend some time learning how to use it and take it with you tonight. Right, I've got the number I need so I'd better get back out there. I'll call this guy from the boat.'

Frankie smiled as she closed the shop door behind him. She imagined Shauna's face if she pulled out her new phone, the latest iPhone on the market. Tom was right, she should probably spend ten minutes making sure she knew how to make calls, text and see what its other features were.

'Got yourself a good man there.' Frankie looked up from the iPhone she'd just taken from the drawer to see Josiah standing in the doorway of the kitchen, arm outstretched with a coffee mug. 'A real family man.'

She got up, accepting the coffee. From what Tom had told her he had only had a brief conversation with Josiah. 'Come and sit down.' She led him to the new seating area. 'What makes you think Tom's a real family man?'

Josiah tapped his nose. 'Instinct.' He smiled. 'And big ears. The walls are so thin between our offices it's impossible not to hear conversations, especially raised voices.'

'Raised voices?'

'Yes. I'm speaking out of turn here, I know that, but I also think you should know Tom's not taking his brother's side. He knows how badly Dash is behaving towards you.'

Frankie's face flushed with heat. 'Oh? He certainly doesn't give me that impression.'

Josiah sighed. 'Don't be embarrassed, love. If I knew him better I'd give him a swift kick up the behind. He's been on at Dash to be professional and stop the games with you nearly every afternoon after you leave.'

'Really? What does Dash say?'

'Says he's being nice and you constantly stir up trouble.'

Frankie's grip tightened on her coffee cup. The nerve of Dash. 'That's not the case at all, he . . .'

Josiah held up a hand. 'No need to tell me. I hear the way he speaks to you. His behaviour's appalling. Said so myself to him, I did.'

Frankie was taken by surprise. 'You spoke to Dash?'

'Yes. Just yesterday, in fact. Told him if I heard him raise his voice again I'd be in here with my gutting knife.' Josiah laughed. 'Should've seen his face. Didn't know whether to believe me or not.'

'Shame Tom doesn't realise what a troublemaker he is.'

Josiah sipped his coffee. 'Oh, he does, don't you worry about that. Your husband is a good man. He's doing his very best to get that rotten brother of his to wake up and make a go of this opportunity. Reminds me of myself. Wants to fix a problem before admitting there is one. Give him some time; he'll realise it's an impossible task with Dash.'

Frankie sipped her coffee. Josiah's words resonated with her. So Tom did believe her and was trying to improve the work environment. Why on earth hadn't he told her? Although Josiah was right, Tom would definitely try to make peace between everyone in his own way. 'Thanks for telling me, Josiah.'

Josiah winked. 'Hopefully Tom will turn him around, or better still realise he's a lost cause.'

Frankie nodded. 'That would be nice, but unfortunately I think there'll be bigger issues to come. The problem is no longer just about behaviour; there appears to be a lot of money missing. With any luck, it'll be accounted for.'

Josiah stood up. 'I hope so for all your sakes. Better be getting on. I've done my interfering for the day.' He winked again as he walked back into the shared kitchen, leaving Frankie deep in thought.

Frankie was still thoughtful as she drove home. She parked in the garage and walked through the internal access. Loud voices greeted her as she walked into the kitchen to find Hope and Fern arguing. They stopped as soon as they saw her.

'What's going on?'

'Fern wants to tell her friends we won lotto,' Hope said. 'I'm trying to explain why we don't want anyone knowing.'

Frankie put her bag on the bench and turned to Fern. 'I thought you understood. I know it's exciting, but if people know they'll start asking for money.'

'My friends wouldn't ask.'

Frankie pulled her close. 'I'd like to think that too, darling, but people spread stories very quickly. Your friends would tell their parents, they'd tell other people and before we know it we'd have a line of people outside the door begging for money. It's best if we keep this to ourselves.'

'But people are talking anyway.'

'What do you mean?' Frankie looked at Hope, who didn't meet her eyes.

'When I was at Cecilia's house the other day, I heard her mum talking to Jessica's mum. They were laughing, saying maybe Dad robbed a bank, or someone really rich must have died. They weren't being very nice.'

Frankie hugged Fern even tighter. 'Don't worry about what people are saying. They're curious, but they'll lose interest in us pretty quickly.'

Frankie turned to Hope. 'Are you hearing the same kinds of things?'

'I did a few weeks ago. I told a couple of people that you and Dad were shrewd investors and it had paid off. They must have believed me as no one has asked since.'

Frankie laughed. 'Obviously no one thought to question what we were using to make these investments with. Good for you. I wouldn't normally condone lying, but in this case you've handled it perfectly. Fern, if anyone asks you again, just tell them the same. That's the story we'll all stick to, okay?'

Fern nodded. Frankie could see she wasn't happy at having to keep this secret but knew she would.

'Now, tell me what else is happening at school? Hope?'

Hope shrugged. 'Nothing out of the ordinary. Lots of work.'

'What about Pearce and his friends?'

Hope blushed. 'The teasing's stopped, you don't need to worry.'

'Is he staying away from you?'

Hope picked up an apple from the fruit bowl. 'He's not annoying me if that's what you're asking.'

'So you're friends now?'

Hope polished the apple against her shirt. 'Sort of. More with Hamish than Pearce. Hamish is actually quite nice when you get to know him.'

'Just be careful, won't you? You've seen how cruel those boys can be.'

Hope refused to meet Frankie's eyes. 'Okay. I'd better finish my homework. Come on, Fern, I'll help you with your maths, if you like.'

Fern followed Hope out of the kitchen, leaving Frankie to consider their discussion. She hoped Fern would be able to resist the urge to tell her friends about the win. As for Hope blushing at the mention of Hamish – now that was a turnaround. The moody, sullen teenager of late had been replaced with a happier, more confident girl. No doubt that had something to do with the new and improved Hamish. Frankie couldn't help smiling as she thought of how horrified Tom would be.

Chapter Fifteen

Shauna found herself driving towards the support group despite her reservations about attending more sessions. It was Frankie who motivated her to attend the session. She was looking forward to seeing her and hearing how the week with Makenna had gone. She'd had updates from Makenna but wanted to check in with Frankie too. She had intended to drop into Blue Water Charters to see for herself, but time had got away from her. Going for a drink after the session would be a more relaxed way to chat properly.

Shauna's phone pinged as she pulled into the parking lot at the community centre. She checked it and couldn't help but smile. It was Simon.

Roses are red, it's really true, Shauna Jones, I love you.

The poems and texts had been arriving daily. He was in Brisbane until Tuesday for work but was making sure he stayed in touch. She had to admit, as reluctant as she was to be hurt again, she was enjoying the attention. She was also enjoying knowing that Josh and the other staff had been wrong about Simon's motivations. He was interested in her, not her money, and that made her feel good.

As she was getting out of the car, her phone rang. Her smile widened. It was Simon. His texts must be working as she realised she was happy to hear from him.

'Hello.'

'Hey, rose lady.'

Shauna laughed. 'Your messages are a little corny.'

'They're just my way of letting you know I'm thinking of you.'

'How's Brisbane?'

'Hot! No wonder people like living here in winter. I'm in a T-shirt whereas I bet you've got something warm on.'

'You would be correct. Actually, I'm going to have to go. I've got a meeting in a few minutes.'

'On a Thursday night? Who with?'

Shauna hesitated. She couldn't tell Simon where she was without telling him the whole story about the lotto win and she still wasn't ready to share the details with him.

'Just work colleagues.'

There was a momentary silence at the end of the line. 'Not that Josh guy?'

'You really need to get over this jealousy thing,' Shauna said. 'And no, I won't be seeing Josh tonight.'

'Let's forget about him then. I wanted to tell you that I received the official offer letter from Select today. I'll be letting Recruit know I'm not interested in extending my contract with them tomorrow.'

'Congratulations. That's great news.'

'It's great news for us,' Simon said. 'Means we have a reason to celebrate and once again confirms to you that I'm here to stay. Can I take you out for dinner next week when I get back from Brisbane? Somewhere romantic, of course. Donovans, if you like? I want to hear everything that's happening with you. You've hardly shared anything since I've been back.' He laughed. 'You always complained that I monopolised the conversations. Well now I want to hear all about you.'

Donovans was not only one of Melbourne's most exclusive restaurants, it was Shauna's favourite. It had been their special occasion restaurant when they'd previously dated. Shauna took a deep breath. 'I've got heaps going on at the moment, Simon.'

'Which is exactly why I want to take you out. So you can fill me in.'

'I know, but I need more time. I'm not ready to jump back into anything right now.'

'I'm not asking you to rush, just to give us a chance. It's just a dinner, Shauna.'

'Give me a ring when you get back from Brisbane and we'll sort out something then. I've really got to run.' She ended the call not giving Simon a chance to push her any further, opened the car door and made her way into the meeting room.

Frankie was already chatting with Todd, Ivan and Pamela and waved as she saw Shauna. Shauna returned the wave and walked over to join them.

'I believe from speaking to Frankie that her successful week is partly your doing,' Pamela said. 'You sound like an excellent friend to have.'

Shauna smiled. 'Just offering resources that are available to me. I'm looking forward to hearing how it's all going.'

'I'll leave you to it,' Pamela said. 'I need to get the chairs organised.' She turned to Ivan and Todd. 'How about you strong lads give me a hand.' The two men grinned and followed Pamela leaving Shauna and Frankie alone.

'I spoke to Makenna, and she's filled me in a bit,' Shauna said. 'But how's it going?'

'Are we going for a drink after the group tonight?'

'I hope so.' Shauna reached into her bag to get her phone; she assumed Frankie would want to let Tom know she'd be late.

She looked up at Frankie, who was grinning, holding a very new iPhone in front of her. 'No need for your phone tonight. I've moved into the twenty-first century.'

Shauna placed the back of her hand on her forehead. 'Oh my God, I think I'm about to pass out. How on earth did that happen?'

'You, the business, Tom. It's the start of my tech evolution.'

Shauna laughed. 'Text me your number, assuming you've worked out how to do that?'

Frankie rolled her eyes. 'What do you think I am? Of course I have.' She handed Shauna her phone. 'But can you put yourself in here as a contact first, I haven't worked out everything.'

Shauna laughed, taking the phone from her as Pamela called the group together for their session.

◆　◆　◆

'I wish you drank,' Shauna said, sliding a lemon, lime and bitters across the table to Frankie. 'I feel like we should be celebrating your new career with champagne.'

Frankie laughed. 'As I usually only drink tea or water, a sugary drink like this is the equivalent of champagne. I'll be buzzing all night.'

Shauna smiled, thinking perhaps she should have ordered the same rather than the glass of Cab Sav she'd chosen. But it was a chilly night, and a red was perfect. 'Everything's going well then?'

'As far as the running of the business, the office furniture and layout, and the website, it is going amazingly.'

'But?'

'But Tom's shit of a brother. Close to forty thousand dollars of expenses are unaccounted for.'

Shauna sucked in her breath. 'And he's responsible?'

Frankie nodded. 'I'm sure he is. Tom's trying to convince me they're legitimate expenses, yet he can't find any invoices. He's kidding himself.'

'Why would Tom believe him if there are no invoices? Have they received the goods?'

'Most of it appears to be for services and items that supposedly have been preordered for installation in the future.'

Shauna raised an eyebrow. 'Really? And Tom's not suspicious?'

'You'd have to meet Dash to understand. He can charm the pants off anyone. He's manipulative and a liar. He'll do anything he can to get his way. Blackmail is a speciality. He's not just an arsehole; he's a professional arsehole.'

'He sounds awful. What do you mean by blackmail? Has he blackmailed you?'

'He's tried.'

'With what? No offence, but I can't imagine you've ever done anything wrong that would allow him to try.'

Frankie hesitated, her eyes fixed on her drink. Finally, she spoke. 'There's something I haven't told anyone.' She kept her eyes down. 'He attacked me and then decided he could blackmail me.'

'Arsehole. I'll fucking kill him.' Shauna slammed her fists down on the table.

Her reaction brought a smile to Frankie's lips. She put a hand on Shauna's arm. 'Thank you, but don't worry; this happened over a year ago, and I don't think he'd try it again. He was drunk and, to be honest, scared me more than anything. Luckily a friend of his walked in and pulled him off me before anything happened.'

'Jesus! And you never told Tom, did you?' Shauna shook her head. 'Because if you had told him, there's no way the arsehole would be part of the business. You must tell him.'

Frankie picked up her glass and sipped her drink. 'No, I made a promise to Tom's mum that I'd look after her boys, make sure they remained close. If I told Tom, their relationship would be over forever.'

'So what?' Shauna said. 'He attacked you. You shouldn't have to spend time with him, let alone work with him. I'm sure Tom's mum wouldn't expect you to keep this secret. How did he blackmail you?'

'Before we won the money, he had the idea for the boat business and wanted us to go into debt to help him finance it. He threatened to tell Tom that I'd come on to him and wanted to sleep with him if I didn't support the business idea. His friend who walked in on us was going to back up his story.'

'Even though he pulled Dash off you?'

'Yep. I assume he was bribed.'

'But Tom wouldn't believe him, Frankie. He knows you wouldn't do anything like that.'

'I was worried it would plant a seed of doubt for Tom, especially if Dash's friend said it happened. I just wanted the whole situation to disappear.'

Shauna squeezed Frankie's hand. 'I don't blame you. When did you make the promise to his mum?'

'Tom's parents were involved in a horrific car accident. Ted died at the scene, but his mum was alive for about twenty hours after the crash. We all had a brief chance to speak to her. The doctors thought she might pull through, but with what she said to me she knew she wasn't going to.'

'Still, I don't think she'd expect you to honour your promise after what he did.'

'Tom was devastated when his parents died. I don't want to be responsible for breaking up the rest of his family.'

Shauna's mouth was set in a firm line. 'I'd say Dash's going to break up the family anyway if he's been ripping off the business.'

Frankie nodded. 'Yes, so there's no need to tell Tom if that happens.'

'What if it doesn't? What if Dash turns out to be above board, or he manipulates the situation to look like he is? Are you going to tell Tom then?'

'No. He won't ever try anything again. He couldn't risk Tom cutting him out of the business. Anyway, let's not talk about him. I don't want him to ruin the night, especially when there's so much to celebrate with the good that the business is bringing.'

Shauna sighed. 'Okay, enough about the arsehole brother for now. But it confirms that other people getting wind that you've won is the downside to winning lotto, isn't it?'

'Your mum?'

'And my dad. He's come out of the woodwork.' Shauna went on to explain the situation with Don.

'You poor thing,' Frankie said. 'I'm sad that I don't have parents around me and you're sadder because you do and they're awful. What are you going to do?'

Shauna sighed again. 'I think perhaps I should give my mum half of the money. I don't need it all, and if it makes things right between us, then I'd feel a lot better about everything. When I think of what she went through with my dad, I probably do owe her.'

'None of that's your fault, though. You don't owe her for the relationship she chose. It's not your fault he's your father or that he did those terrible things to her.'

Shauna nodded. 'You're right. I think I'll just lie low for the next little while. It's been one thing after another with my mum suing me, my dad appearing and my ex showing up. I think I need a holiday.'

Frankie raised an eyebrow. 'The ex is still on the scene?'

Shauna blushed. 'Very much so. He's taking things slowly, but he's keen to get back together. It's me that's been reluctant.'

'Because he hurt you or because of something else?'

'Hurt. I'm not sure I can trust him after what he did. It was so out of the blue. It would be like Tom turning up here and telling you your marriage was over. Everything's been going well; you have no idea that anything is wrong, and he suddenly ends it. You spend twelve months putting back the pieces and getting over him, and then he turns up again. There's part of me that loves him as much as I did before he left and there's part of me that hates him for what he did to me and wonders if I could ever fully trust him again.'

Frankie nodded. 'I completely understand that. I guess if you're not sure then take things very slowly. It doesn't sound like he's in a big hurry, which is good.'

'Mm.'

'What? You don't sound convinced?'

'Simon's always been very direct and very demanding. When he wants something he goes after it full speed until it's his. This slow and gentle romancing of me is a very different tactic.'

'Perhaps his travels changed him?'

'Maybe. Or he might just be trying to prove to me that he's a different, more considerate version of himself. I'm not sure. It's just unusual. He also seems to be remembering some of the things that happened in our past much more romantically than they actually were.' She went on to tell Frankie about the flower seller on their second date.

'One thing I've learnt from being married to Tom is you can't assume what the other person thinks or how they perceived an experience. Maybe laughing at the flower seller was romantic for him because you gave him the flower.'

'Possibly. Or he's just romanticising everything. Anyway, I'm in no hurry either, so I'll see how it plays out.'

Frankie's phone pinged with a message as she sipped her drink. She pulled it from her bag. 'Just Tom. Checking if I'm on my way home yet.'

She replied to the text and dropped the phone back in her bag.

Shauna laughed. 'Look at you, texting as if it was something you did every day. Watch out world; you'll be on Facebook and Insta before we know it.'

Frankie laughed. 'Makenna already set up the accounts. I like the idea of Instagram as we can post photos from the trips, catch of the day and that kind of thing. Apparently, I need to start thinking in hashtags. I always thought that was just for Twitter but it seems I'm learning a lot.'

'You sure are. I think I'd better get going too. I really should be working on a presentation tonight, not enjoying myself so much.'

The two women stood and walked out of the bar. 'Next week?' Frankie asked.

Shauna nodded. 'Sounds good. You know one night we could go out for dinner and skip the group altogether.'

Frankie smiled. 'We could always do that on another night and still go to the group.'

'Let me know how you go at work and if you have any more trouble with the brother. I'm sure there's someone I can send in to help you out if you do.'

Frankie grinned. 'Unless it's a hitman, I doubt it.'

Shauna turned her attention from her computer to her phone as it pinged with a text message. She'd already had a message from Simon that morning reminding her that he loved her, so she doubted it would be him. She grinned.

She was so excited for Frankie. With all the stories from the group of disaster and losing money, it was lovely to see a family's circumstances changed for the better. She just hoped the brother didn't ruin it for all of them.

She put her phone down, returning her attention to her screen when the intercom on her desk buzzed.

'Don Rice calling for you, Shauna,' Jenni announced.

Shauna hesitated. Close to two weeks had passed since her discussion with Lorraine, and she had ignored a multitude of messages from Don already. He was persistent, probably desperate to get his hands on her money.

She picked up the phone. 'What do you want?' She was met by silence. 'Hello?'

Don cleared his throat. 'Sorry. Your greeting threw me.'

'Surely you realised once I spoke with my mother I wouldn't want anything to do with you?'

Silence again.

'Are you there?'

Don sighed. 'I don't know why I expected her to tell you the truth this time. What did she say?'

'She started with your drinking problem, gambling problem and the fact that you're a wife basher. I can hardly blame her for leaving you. Now, I'm busy. Don't contact me again, and no way am I giving you any money, so maintain some dignity and don't ask.'

Josh's head appeared around Shauna's office door as she put down the phone. His smile disappeared the moment he saw her face. 'Everything okay?'

Shauna spoke through pursed lips. 'Bad morning.'

'Can I do anything to help?'

Shauna shook herself and forced herself to smile. 'Not unless you have the power to find me a new set of parents and erase my memory of the real two.'

'Did you speak with your father?'

'Yes, that was him. I told him in no uncertain terms to leave me alone.'

'How did he react?'

'He didn't get a chance, I hung up.'

'Good. Hopefully he listened and you won't be bothered by him again. Come on, I'll buy you lunch.'

This time Shauna managed a genuine smile, and collecting her bag she followed Josh along the corridor to the reception area.

'Feel like sushi?' Josh asked. 'Sushi Zone's supposed to be pretty good.'

The lift opened and before Shauna had the chance to answer, Don Rice stepped out.

Shauna took a step backwards. 'Are you kidding me? What are you doing here?'

Josh held the lift door open. 'Mate, Shauna asked you to stay away. I suggest you get yourself back down to the street and disappear.'

Don locked eyes with Shauna; the distress in them caused a rush of nervous energy to course through her. There was something about this man, something she thought she could trust – wished she could trust. If she hadn't seen her mother's anguish she wouldn't hesitate to talk to him further. But if she hadn't won the money would he be standing in front of her at all? She guessed that was a question she might never know the answer to.

'Please give me a chance to talk. I need to defend myself. Unfortunately your mother has chosen to lie to you again. I was outside the building when I rang. I'd been hoping to take you to lunch. I can't walk away until you hear the whole story. If you want me to stay out of your life after you learn the truth, I will.'

Josh turned to Shauna. 'Your call.'

Shauna's face was strained. 'Okay, five minutes. Come to my office.'

Relief flickered in Don's eyes.

'Why don't you join us?' Shauna said to Josh. 'We can go out for lunch as soon as he leaves.'

They filed back to Shauna's office. Josh pulled the door shut before taking a seat next to Don.

'Shauna, everything Lorraine has told you is lies. I need you to believe me. I never touched her. Nor have I ever had a drinking problem or any interest in gambling. She was hurt and angry at me. We were having problems. The writing was on the wall for our relationship, but she wouldn't admit there were any issues. Her mood swings were so erratic I never knew where I stood. However, appearances were too important for her. She couldn't stand the thought of her friends finding out we had split up – or worse, the embarrassment of them discovering I'd left her. She threatened me many times, saying if I was serious about splitting up she'd ensure I'd never see you again.'

'And you didn't believe her?'

'No. I'd spoken to a lawyer and been assured I would gain a share of custody. Probably not full custody, but at least fifty percent. He said not to worry until we got to court. Neither of us anticipated her disappearing act.'

Shauna rubbed her jaw. 'Why should I believe any of this? You seem as bad as each other.'

'I can prove my story. I contacted the police when I couldn't find her. They had you both on a missing-persons list.'

Shauna snorted. 'Hardly proves anything. She hasn't denied disappearing.'

'Give me a chance to prove I'm telling the truth. Please, you've got nothing to lose.'

'Just ten million dollars.'

Don flinched as the accusation left Shauna's lips. 'I'm not after your money. I'm quite comfortable in my own right. I'm after a chance to get to know you.'

Shauna stood up. 'Fine, get your proof. Show me you're a decent person and my mother is a compulsive liar and we'll talk.' She pointed to the office door. 'If I don't believe what you've got to say I want you gone, for good.'

'Okay, I'll be in touch in a day or two.' Don's eyes didn't leave Shauna's. 'Once I prove this to you I hope you'll change your mind.'

Shauna sat down again as Don left the office. She turned to face Josh. 'What do you think?'

'Hard to tell. He seemed pretty genuine, but if he's a con artist after your winnings he would do. Wait until he comes up with some proof.'

'I can't imagine how he'll prove anything to me except we'll find out what lengths someone is willing to go to for money.'

'Do you have his card?'

Shauna opened her business-card holder and flicked through it. She pulled out Don's card and held it up.

'Mind if I take it and do some digging? Check out Don the businessman?'

'Thanks, I'd love you to.' Shauna passed the card over to Josh. 'He's got a small vitamin business from what he told me. If they're in debt we'll have our answer quickly.'

Josh glanced up. 'Is he a doctor, too?'

'I don't think so, why?'

'The name of the company is D.R. Supplements. Might just be using his initials in a clever way.' Josh put Don's card in his pocket.

'Leave it with me. Now come on, my stomach is still demanding sushi.'

Shauna reached for her bag as Jenni appeared in the door, a huge bouquet of red and gold in her arms.

'Delivery from Romeo.' Jenni grinned and laid the bouquet on Shauna's desk.

Shauna's eyes widened. 'A chocolate bouquet?'

'Edible blooms,' Jenni said. 'There are exactly one hundred chocolates on that. It's the biggest arrangement anyone in the office has ever seen.' She passed an envelope to Shauna. 'This came with it.'

Shauna took the envelope and shook her head as she realised it had already been opened. 'You know, you can just leave the cards attached. No need to remove them or read them.'

Jenni winked at Josh. 'What would be the fun of that? We have a real-life love story playing out in front of us.'

Josh laughed. 'If you're comparing it to Romeo and Juliet then it won't have a happy ending.'

'Why don't you take the bouquet with you, Jenni. Offer it around the office – I'm sure everyone could use a pick-me-up.'

'Really?'

Shauna nodded.

Jenni picked up the bouquet. 'That's so lovely of you, Shauna. Thank you.'

Josh waited until Jenni left the office. 'That really was lovely of you. Won't the ex be upset?'

'You're assuming they're from Simon.'

Josh raised an eyebrow. 'I didn't realise he has competition.'

Shauna laughed. 'He doesn't. Just trying to keep you on your toes.'

'Flowers, chocolates, he's certainly pulling out all the tricks.'

'I think he's showing me how much he loves me and trying to win me back.'

'Do you think he's in with a chance?'

Shauna looked at Josh. It really wasn't any of his business and as she didn't know the answer to that herself she didn't want to discuss it with him. 'Undecided. Now, let's go and get that sushi and change the subject. If we're lucky there might even be a chocolate left when we get back.'

Not meeting his eyes, Shauna led Josh out of the office and towards the lifts.

The following Monday Shauna and Josh sat in a cafe following a presentation to a new client. Shauna had remained a hundred percent focused on the client during their meeting, however, her mind now was miles away. She took a bite of her sandwich. 'He says he's got proof and wants to see me at two o'clock. Do you want to come?' As the words left her lips she wondered why she was asking Josh. If she thought there was any chance of a relationship with Simon shouldn't he be the one accompanying her? She pushed away the thought. Other than the fact that she hadn't shared anything about what was going on in her life, Simon was in Brisbane. And anyway, it was much easier to talk to Josh. They were friends, so it wasn't complicated.

Josh didn't need to ask Shauna who she was talking about. 'Of course, if you'd like me to. I'll admit I'm quite intrigued.'

'The information your accountant uncovered proves he's unlikely to be after the money, so I'd say it guarantees to be interesting.'

Josh nodded. 'Maybe he implied he had a small vitamin company to downplay his success?'

Josh's research had uncovered that D.R. Supplements was Australia's largest exporter of vitamins and supplements. Don had grown their annual sales to one hundred and thirty-three million dollars in the twenty-six years since he'd established the business.

'Maybe,' Shauna said.

'What are you going to do if he's been telling the truth?'

'About him or my mum?'

'Both?'

Shauna let out a deep sigh. 'God knows. With him, easy – begin a relationship. With Mum, a different story altogether. I don't even want to think about her for now.'

'Fair enough. I'll get us a coffee and then we should head back to the office if you're meeting him at two.'

'No, I agreed to go to his office in Carlton. He has something to show me that he'd prefer to do there. It's only about five minutes from here.'

Shauna and Josh pulled up in a taxi outside D.R. Supplements a few minutes before two. Josh raised an eyebrow. 'Small business, huh?'

The building in front of them was massive. The signage suggested the entire complex belonged to Don's company.

Josh squeezed Shauna's hand. 'Come on, let's go in and listen to what he has to say.'

A pretty woman in her early twenties leapt up from a couch the moment they walked in and rushed over to greet them. 'Hello, you must be Shauna. It's wonderful to meet you. I'm Rose, Don's . . .' She hesitated. 'I guess assistant.'

Shauna shook Rose's hand and returned the warm smile. She introduced Josh and then took a moment to survey the impressive foyer. The only indication they were in a place of business was a long reception desk; the remainder of the space housed a meandering mixture of greenery and water features. 'This is beautiful.'

Rose nodded. 'Don wanted to create a relaxing and natural work area. He told the designer his vision was for a space as much like a creek and forest as possible. The couches are probably the only thing out of place in a forest, but he insisted on having them strategically placed around the area so you can meet by one of the water features without anyone being able to overhear your conversation.'

'He's certainly created an impression,' Josh said. 'The running water might be a bit too relaxing for getting any work done.'

Rose laughed, an infectious high-pitched sound. 'Don't worry, we get plenty of work done. With a boss like Don you can't help it.'

Shauna raised an eyebrow. 'Bit of a tyrant, is he?'

Rose's hand flew to her mouth. 'Oh gosh, no. He's too relaxed, if anything. Don't tell him I said that. I'm supposed to be impressing you. No, he's a great boss. He's created such an inspiring workplace and team, no one wants to disappoint him. I'm not sure how much you know about the company. Don started from nothing. He works harder than anyone but is the first to acknowledge and reward our hard work. Ask any of the staff; everyone loves working here.'

Shauna smiled at Rose's dedication and obvious respect for Don. 'You don't need to impress us, so don't worry.'

'Yes, but—' Rose stopped. 'Enough of me talking, I'd better take you up to him. He's probably still fussing over which coffee to serve.' Rose took Shauna's arm and whispered conspiratorially, 'Don't tell him I told you, but he's a bit nervous. He brought in four ties this morning for fashion advice.'

Shauna was touched. Her own nerves had been pushed aside when she believed her money was the attraction, but now she could feel them resurfacing.

Rose led them up a beautiful hand-carved staircase to the second floor. The sounds of laughter drifted from a meeting room. The office furniture resembled nothing like their own modern workplace. Beautifully carved desks, with a similar feel to the staircase, were scattered throughout the space, separated by plants. The cabinets, bookshelves and other furniture appeared to be hand-made, with intricate designs featured on each piece. At the far end of the area a ceiling-high water feature could easily be mistaken for a real waterfall.

Josh whistled. 'It's breathtaking.'

'Glad you think so.' Don's smooth voice spoke from behind them.

They turned to face him. Josh reached out to shake his extended hand.

'Thank you both for coming.' His eyes met Shauna's. 'I'm thrilled you've come.' He turned to Rose. 'Thank you, I'll look after our guests.'

Rose smiled and surprised Shauna by squeezing Don's arm as she walked past.

'Come this way. There's someone I want you to meet.'

They followed Don into his office. It was large and inviting. His desk faced a window that overlooked a beautiful garden on the same level. The rest of the office was dominated by a seating area where four couches surrounded an enormous coffee table. An older woman sat perched on the edge of one of the couches. She stood up as they entered the room. The moment Shauna made eye contact the old lady burst into tears.

Don rushed over to her. 'Come on, Mum, you promised you wouldn't do this.' He offered her a tissue.

Shauna's hand flew to her mouth.

Josh rested an arm on her shoulder. 'You okay?'

Shauna nodded and moved towards Don and his mother.

'Shauna, this is Madeline, your grandmother.'

Shauna looked at Don in surprise. 'Madeline? But Madeline's Mum's mum?'

He blushed. 'When Lorraine left we became close and Madeline became much more to me than an ex-mother-in-law. It seemed right to call her Mum.'

The older woman blew her nose, a small sob escaping. 'It did. And yes, Lorraine is my daughter.'

'I thought you were dead.'

Madeline wiped her eyes. 'She told you I was dead?'

Shauna nodded. There was no need to ask for proof of who Madeline was; she was looking at an older version of her own mother.

'I'm sorry to shock you,' Don said. 'But Madeline is the one person I know who can convince you my story is true. Why don't you come and sit down and I'll organise some coffee?'

Shauna sat on the couch across from Madeline. She realised Josh hadn't followed her and she turned to find he'd remained standing at the door.

His eyes searched hers. 'Would you like me to wait for you downstairs?'

'No, of course not. Come over and sit down. Meet my grandma.'

Madeline smiled at Shauna through her tears. 'This is the happiest day of my life. The pain Don and I suffered when you disappeared was unbearable. I still find it hard to believe Lorraine would do something so awful to us.'

'But . . .' Shauna hesitated, looking at Don.

Don picked up on Shauna's hesitancy. 'Why don't I show Josh the amazing roof garden while you two chat.'

Josh stood up and followed Don, who stopped as they reached the door. 'Please ask Madeline any questions you have. I've nothing to hide.'

Shauna nodded and watched as he guided Josh out to the garden, closing the door behind them.

Shauna and Madeline stared at each other. Finally Madeline spoke. 'He's a good man, believe me. The biggest mistake he ever made was getting involved with my Lorraine. You're the only thing he doesn't regret from their relationship.'

'But the story she told me?'

'About the violence, alcohol and gambling?'

'Yes, why would she lie? Are you sure nothing ever happened?'

Madeline sighed. 'No, it did happen, but not with Don. She's described my husband, her father.'

'How awful. I'm sorry.'

'Yes, it was awful. He died when she was seven. In many ways it was a blessing for all of us, but it was also when Lorraine's behaviour changed. She went from being a happy little girl to at times displaying extreme anger and sadness. I took her to see a psychologist about a year after her father died. He said her behaviour was normal for her age and the circumstances and she'd outgrow it. By the time she was thirteen she seemed to channel any anger or frustration into painting. I thought it was a wonderful outlet until I came home one day when she was about sixteen to find paint splattered all over her bedroom wall. It was as if she'd picked up a brush and repeatedly flicked it at the wall. It was a huge mess. She did it a number of times over the next three years and then she moved out. I tried to get her to see a psychologist again over those years, but she always laughed at me, told me I was ridiculous and that there was nothing wrong. The painting just made her feel better. When she disappeared I blamed myself. I should have taken her behaviour more seriously and realised that perhaps there was actually something wrong with her. Over time I've wondered if her father's death triggered some kind of PTSD. It wasn't something that was discussed as much, or even as well known, back in those days so unfortunately I didn't think of it at the time.'

Tears welled in Shauna's eyes. She thought back to Josh's mum. She'd also suggested that Lorraine's behaviour could be linked to PTSD, but not knowing her mother's background Shauna hadn't seen how that could be possible. This was all so overwhelming and explained so much about her mother.

'Oh, my dear girl.' Madeline moved next to Shauna and took her hand. 'Lorraine has no excuse for what she did to you or to any of us, whether she was suffering or not. Stealing a child away is a despicable act. She gave up her family and friendships purely to hurt Don. I never imagined she would turn her back on me, rob me of my granddaughter, any more than Don thought she would do it to him.'

'Why do you think she did it? It was so extreme.'

'Don's theory is she left him before he could ask her for a divorce. Things hadn't been good between them and her behaviour had become very erratic. She refused to get help and that was the final straw for him. He tried many times to help her, don't get me wrong, but she could be very nasty and unfortunately he saw too much of this side.'

Shauna nodded. She'd been on the receiving end of Lorraine's nastiness more times than she liked to remember.

'He assumed she was worried she'd lose custody of you and then she'd have nothing. The funny thing was she always seemed jealous of you when you were little. Jealous that you were taking up my time or Don's time and she wasn't the centre of attention. The fact she took you when she disappeared was as much of a shock as her actually disappearing. She was so selfish and self-centred that I would have thought she would have left you with us and disappeared. It was another indicator that I really had no idea what was going through her mind.'

'And she just disappeared? No note, no contact?'

'No. In thirty years she never contacted me.'

Shauna tried to process this information.

Madeline got up and retrieved a photo album from Don's desk. She handed it to Shauna. 'Have a look.'

She opened the first page to a photo of herself as a baby, only a few hours old, being held by Madeline.

'I was dying to see you,' Madeline said. 'It was one of the happiest days of my life.'

As she turned the pages Shauna was greeted by more photos of herself as a baby, each time being held by Madeline. Occasionally Don or Lorraine appeared in the pictures, but this was predominantly an album about her and her grandmother. The last photo showed Shauna on her fourth birthday sitting on Madeline's lap, a fluffy toy monkey in her arms.

'I remember that monkey. I loved him so much.' He was the one toy Shauna remembered from her early childhood. She realised he was probably one of the few toys her mother had allowed her to bring when they left.

Madeline smiled as Shauna turned the pages. Following the photos were birthday cards, one for every birthday right up to her last one.

'Even though there was nowhere to send the cards I still needed to write them. I've thought of you and your mother every day for thirty years.'

Shauna blinked her eyes, trying to contain her tears. 'This is beautiful.'

'You keep the book, dear.'

'Oh no, I couldn't.' Shauna passed the book to Madeline.

Madeline pressed it back on her. 'No, please keep it to remind yourself how much we've always loved you. I'm hoping I'll get to enjoy the real you now.'

Shauna reopened the album. After the last birthday card Madeline had stuck in a series of newspaper articles. The first nine or ten reported Lorraine's disappearance with her small daughter. Following these was a newspaper history of Don's success. Shauna didn't read them but turned the pages to reveal years of information on the success of D.R. Supplements, the charitable contributions the company made, and the opportunities given to young people. The last article had a picture of Don standing outside D.R. Supplements, his arm around a woman in her late fifties and three young adults crouching in front of them.

'Don's wife and children,' Madeline answered before Shauna had a chance to ask.

Shauna looked closer and then back at Madeline. 'Rose?'

'Yes, love. She's Don's youngest. She's twenty, Patrick is twenty-two and Lilliana is twenty-five. Don met Sandy in Melbourne three and a half years after you and Lorraine disappeared. Six months after he met her he moved to Melbourne. A second chance at happiness.'

Shauna fell silent.

Madeline was quiet for a few minutes before speaking again. 'Are you okay, love?'

'I'm not really sure. A brother and two sisters I have no knowledge of. How could she do this to me?'

Madeline drew Shauna to her and rubbed her back. The gentle rub transported Shauna back thirty-one years to when she was three. She had been frightened by her mother screaming at her father and leapt into Madeline's arms the moment she'd arrived to babysit. Madeline had comforted her exactly the same way. The simple gesture of rubbing Shauna's back brought back so many memories. A single tear rolled down her cheek, followed by another and another. They continued to flow as Madeline held her and rubbed her back. After a few minutes she finally pulled away and took the tissues her grandmother offered.

'I'm sorry.' She tried to pull herself together. 'I've no idea where all of that came from.'

'Don't be silly. This is a huge shock. I blubbered like a baby when Don told me he'd found you. He was terrified you wouldn't believe him. He's not after your money, which you probably already gathered.' She gestured to the magnificent offices surrounding them. 'He's done well for himself.'

'What about his wife and kids? Are they going to be okay with all of this?'

Madeline chuckled. 'If Rose had been allowed her way this morning you would have been greeted with a brass band and huge celebration. Don almost made her stay home for the day so she wouldn't go over the top. Patrick isn't contactable, he's serving in Afghanistan, and Lili, I think you'll find she's as receptive as Rose.'

'And Sandy?'

'You'll see for yourself. Don't forget you aren't a secret or surprise to any of them. They all knew you existed and Don always talked about you.'

'This is all so hard to take in. Mum told me we had no living relatives. Now I have a grandma, siblings and a father.'

Madeline laughed. 'I hope you'll get used to us quickly so we can enjoy each other. I insist you and your lovely young man come to my little cottage in Port Melbourne for dinner on Friday night. You can fill me in on the last thirty years. Sound good?'

'I'd love to, but not Josh. We work together, he's only a friend.'

'Oh.' Madeline raised her eyes in surprise. 'I assumed boyfriend. He's obviously in love with you.'

'What?' Shauna started to laugh. 'I can assure you we're just friends and you only saw him for about thirty seconds.'

Madeline tapped her nose. 'I may be old and decrepit, but I'm not blind, my girl. You mark my words, when you have the time to open your heart you'll see what I mean. For now though, we had better let them come back in.'

Shauna remained on the couch as Madeline walked over to the garden doors and called out to Don. There was so much to take in. Don, a new family, what her mother had done. And now Madeline suggesting Josh was in love with her? She dismissed the suggestion. They got along as friends, even flirted at times, but she still hadn't worked out what she was doing with Simon – and regardless, she wasn't going there again with a work colleague.

Don's face flooded with relief as Madeline whispered something in his ear.

Shauna stood up as he approached her. 'I believe you.'

A huge smile spread over Don's face and he moved towards Shauna and hugged her tight. She stiffened in his arms.

He let go immediately. 'Oh, I'm sorry.'

Shauna laughed. 'It's okay, you're my dad, I'm going to have to get used to the situation, that's all.'

The office door opened and Rose stuck her head in. 'Sorry, Don, you're needed for an urgent call. I know you asked not to be interrupted but this is an emergency.'

'Come in, you silly girl,' Madeline said. She turned to Shauna. 'You've just heard Rose's code talk for "Daddy, let me meet my sister properly."' They all laughed while Rose grinned and shrugged her shoulders.

A little after four, Shauna told them she and Josh must go as they still had work to do. Rose had bombarded her with every fact she could possibly think of about Don and her other siblings. Rose's enthusiasm and love for her father were contagious. Shauna found herself smiling and laughing.

She was quiet in the short taxi ride back to the office. Josh took her hand. 'You okay?'

Shauna smiled at him. 'Sorry, I'm in my own little world here. I'm fine, a bit overwhelmed, but fine. Thank you so much for coming.'

'I'm glad you asked me.'

'My grandma invited you to dinner on Friday night. She assumed we're an item. I told her we were just friends, but I'm not sure she believed me. Sorry.'

Josh stroked her hand. 'Don't apologise and let's not disappoint Madeline. I'd love to come if you'd like me to; unless you're planning to take Simon, of course?' Josh's eyes searched Shauna's for an answer.

She shook her head. 'I'd love you to.'

Shauna didn't go back to the office that afternoon; she had too much on her mind and found herself at home staring at the wall before five, which was unheard of. She lay on the couch, wondering who she could turn to for advice. The time difference wasn't going to work to ring Tess; also, she hadn't spoken to Tess in weeks, so filling her in on everything was going to take hours. She didn't feel like going back to the beginning. She wanted to talk to someone who was already partially up to speed. That left Josh and Frankie. She couldn't speak to Josh as he was part of the issue and she wasn't sure she could wait until Thursday to see Frankie at the support group.

She picked up her phone and considered texting her. Would she be free to chat? Even if it was just on the phone. They didn't have to meet up.

She sent a quick text.

How are you? Any chance you're free to chat? Having a difficult time.

Her phone rang immediately.

'You okay?' The concern in Frankie's voice caused a knot to form in Shauna's throat.

'I'm fine. Just a few things going on and I felt like I needed to talk to someone.'

'Why don't I come your way?' Frankie suggested. 'I can be in Richmond in about thirty minutes.'

'Are you sure? I realise you've probably got dinner to do, kids to deal with and all that. I could meet you halfway.'

'Nope, they can do it themselves tonight. You sound like you need a friend and I'm grateful that you've called me. If we make it in Richmond you can have a couple of drinks and walk. Sounds like you might need them.'

They organised to meet at Cool at seven.

Shauna was already halfway through her first drink when Frankie arrived. She hurried over to the table and sat down. 'What's happened?'

Shauna stared at her friend, incredibly grateful to see her. If she'd been here, Tess would have done the same: dropped everything and turned up ready to listen. She started to talk, watching Frankie's eyes widen as the details unfolded about her father, her grandmother and the rest of the family she hadn't known existed.

'That's amazing!' Frankie said. 'You must be the luckiest person alive.'

Shauna leant back in her chair and stared at Frankie. 'Really? That's your take on it?'

'Well, not the last thirty years of not having the family of course, but to be reunited with them now is amazing. You've got years and years ahead of you to get to know them. Aren't you excited?'

Shauna smiled. She was glad she'd rung Frankie as she'd been concentrating too heavily on the negative. Of her mother and the past.

'I know you've had a hard time with your mother, but from everything you've said your dad seems genuine, as does your grandmother. I think you need to do your best to approach them with an open heart. You're not used to having people care about you, Shauna, and it's time you got used to it.'

Shauna nodded. 'You're right. I might need you to keep on top of me and make sure I don't run a mile anytime I get scared.'

Frankie squeezed her hand. 'Sounds like there's a guy who might want to do that for you. You said your grandmother invited Josh to dinner. What about Simon?'

'I haven't told Simon anything that's going on. About the money, my mother, or my father appearing, whereas Josh knows everything. It makes more sense to take him.'

'Why haven't you told Simon?'

Shauna sighed. 'I don't trust him.' As the words came out of her mouth she realised they were true. 'He's being lovely, but some of his behaviour is out of character, and I'm not sure what his real motivation is.'

'The money, do you think?'

Shauna shook her head. 'No, he's done a few things that convince me he doesn't know about the money, but something doesn't feel right still. Look, it might be that after leaving the way he did I just can't let my guard down, I'm not sure.'

'Perhaps his motivation is genuine that he wants you back. You might need to give it more time to see if you can grow to trust him again.'

'Maybe, although I don't know if I want him back or if I'm just hanging on to the familiarity of what we had, too scared to let go completely.'

'What about Josh?'

Shauna smiled. 'Josh is lovely. He's perfect, in fact, but he's not for me. I said I'd never have a relationship with someone I worked with again and therefore he's a no-go zone. He's a wonderful friend though, and that's what I need at the moment.'

'As long as you're clear with him,' Frankie said.

Shauna thought back to Josh holding her hand in the taxi. That hadn't been more than friends, had it? She'd been through an incredibly emotional afternoon, and he'd been there for her.

'I think he knows,' Shauna said. 'He knows about Simon and that I haven't decided what I'm doing with him and he knows I won't date a colleague. I've been quite clear about that. I don't think there have been any mixed messages.'

Frankie didn't say anything.

'What? You don't believe me?'

'I'm hearing your words but I'm seeing your body language and listening to your tone as you talk about the two men. You need to work it out for yourself but don't completely dismiss the idea of Josh. If you let yourself, I think you might realise he means more to you than you're letting on.'

Shauna stared at Frankie, thinking of Madeline's words that weren't too dissimilar to Frankie's. *I may be old and decrepit, but I'm not blind, my girl. You mark my words, when you have the time to open your heart you'll see what I mean.* She shook her head. 'I'm not going there again with a colleague. It will end in disaster exactly like it did with Simon. Now, tell me about you. What's been happening since last week? Any more news about Dash or the business?'

◆　◆　◆

Friday night rolled around too quickly in Shauna's estimation. She still had a million questions she needed answered by Don and Madeline, she hadn't confronted her mother and had put Simon off when he'd rung on his return from Brisbane trying to organise dinner. She wasn't sure how she could even start explaining the situation to him.

She glanced across the back seat of the taxi to Josh. 'Thanks again for coming with me tonight. I really appreciate it.'

Josh smiled. 'I'm honoured to have been asked. I know this is a big deal for you. Just let me know anything you need me to do or say.'

Shauna's phone rang as the taxi wound its way around Albert Park Lake. She checked the screen. Simon. Even though she'd declined his dinner invitation he'd invited her to drinks at Southbank with some of their old group of friends. She'd said no and assumed he was ringing now to try and get her to change her mind. She glanced at Josh.

He glanced briefly at her phone before looking away. 'Answer it, if you like. I'll try not to listen.'

'No, that's okay.' She pressed the end button sending the call to voicemail. 'I'll speak to him later.'

'Does the ex know I'm going with you tonight? He might think it's a bit strange.'

'He knows we're friends, but he doesn't know about tonight so it isn't relevant.'

'But he knows about your dad contacting you?'

Shauna shook her head. 'I still haven't told him about the lotto win and my dad finding me is all tied up with that.'

'You said he's not after your money so why haven't you told him? Surely you want to share everything that's going on with your mum and your dad with him?'

Shauna glanced out of the taxi's window. She'd asked herself this same question many times and hadn't really settled on an answer.

'It's none of my business,' Josh said. 'You don't have to tell me.'

She turned to him. 'Honestly, I don't know. Simon and I had a wonderful relationship before he went off to travel. There's part of me that still misses that and wants what we had back. But there's this other part that thinks perhaps it was all for the best. I've heard a lot from the support group I've been to about people changing their attitudes towards you as soon as they know about the money. I guess for that reason alone I'm reluctant to tell him. If I did decide I wanted to get back with him I need to know it is one hundred percent about him and me and the money is just a bonus.'

'Aren't you worried that he'll be upset that you've kept all this from him? Wouldn't he want to be by your side to support you?'

'It's just not my biggest priority at the moment. If I'd jumped back into a relationship with Simon then of course I'd have told him everything, but I haven't done that. I'm still deciding what I want to do and with everything else going on it just isn't my biggest priority.'

Josh smiled.

'Why does that make you smile?'

'It just does. I like that technically he's still your ex. If he wasn't I'd probably have to call him by his name and personally I'd prefer never to have to do that. "The ex" suits him perfectly.' He held up his hand before Shauna could object. 'Seriously, you'll have to tell him at some stage.'

'When the time's right, I'll tell him.'

Josh opened his mouth as if about to say something then shut it again. He shook his head and looked out of the taxi window. Shauna imagined he was wondering why she'd even consider being with someone she didn't feel comfortable sharing the details of her life with. She wished she had a definitive answer to this herself.

They travelled the rest of the journey in silence, Shauna's nerves building as they drew closer to Port Melbourne.

The taxi dropped Shauna and Josh at Madeline's a little before six. 'She's old.' Shauna laughed. 'We'll probably be eating by six thirty and she'll be in bed by eight.'

Josh whistled as they opened the gate to Madeline's garden. Madeline's description of her house as a little cottage certainly underplayed the beautifully restored terraced house. The front garden boasted a glorious display of winter roses. Pale and dark pinks dominated with a spatter of white.

The door opened and they were met by Madeline's huge smile. Shauna debated whether to follow her urge to hug her. The decision was made for her as Madeline embraced her and practically squeezed the breath from her. Josh enjoyed the same warm welcome and laughed when Madeline eventually let go.

Madeline glanced to the back of the house and lowered her voice. 'I'm sorry about the next hour. A select few people heard about our dinner and demanded an invitation. I refused as this is my night with you, but Rose manipulated me quite craftily and they all arrived ten minutes ago for drinks. I hope you don't mind?'

Shauna smiled, her stomach flip-flopping. 'Doesn't sound like we're going to be given a choice. Don't worry, it's probably better to be thrown in the deep end. When you say a few people, who do you mean?'

'Don, Sandy, Rose, Lilliana and Graeme, Lilliana's husband.'

Rose appeared in the passageway. 'There you are, Grandma, we wondered where you got to.' She grinned. 'Hi, Shauna. Hi, Josh.'

Madeline waved Rose away before Shauna could ask why she'd called Madeline Grandma, and motioned for Shauna and Josh to follow. 'You watch yourself, Rose Rice, or you'll be leaving early.'

'Rose Rice,' Josh mouthed. A small smile played on Shauna's lips.

The long passage of Madeline's cottage opened up into a large open-plan kitchen and living room. Five sets of eyes stared at Shauna as she entered the room. Don was immediately at her side. 'Let me introduce everyone,' he said. 'This is my wife, Sandy.'

Sandy shook Shauna's hand warmly. 'You can call me Mum.' She laughed at Shauna's horrified face. 'I'm joking. I'm so pleased we finally get to meet you. You've been an important member of our family in memory and spirit since the day I met Don. It's wonderful to finally have you in person.'

Shauna felt herself relax a little, instantly liking this funny, quirky woman.

'This is Lilliana, my eldest daughter.' Don's face turned beetroot red. 'Sorry, my second eldest.'

Shauna smiled. 'This is going to take all of us some getting used to. I'm sure Lilliana has always been referred to as your eldest. You'd hardly be wanting to explain to every man and his dog what had happened to me.' Shauna stepped towards Lilliana with her hand out.

Lilliana showed less enthusiasm than the others. She limply shook Shauna's hand before introducing her husband, Graeme.

'What do you drink, Shauna?' Rose was busy opening a bottle of sparkling wine.

'Anything,' Shauna said. 'A big glass of anything, please. I'm a nervous wreck.'

Rose's laugh was infectious, helping Shauna relax further.

Graeme handed Josh a beer. 'This might be more up your alley, mate. Who do you barrack for? Please don't tell me Collingwood?'

Josh accepted the beer and started talking football with Graeme. Shauna caught his eye about ten minutes into Graeme's predictions for the game to be played later that night.

He winked and flashed her a smile.

Madeline busied herself in the kitchen, which allowed Don and the girls to monopolise Shauna.

'Can I ask a question?' Shauna lowered her voice and moved closer to her father and Sandy. 'I'm intrigued. Madeline's not related yet you'd think she was head of your family. Rose calls her Grandma, yet she's not actually related to her.'

Sandy smiled. 'She may as well be. When I met Don he introduced me to his mother, Madeline. It took a few months before I realised his own parents had passed on and she was his mother-in-law. We asked her to remain part of our family and be grandmother to the kids. We wouldn't have it any other way. Although she almost did.'

'What do you mean?'

'When Don asked me to marry him she suggested she should move on. She believed she represented his past – a past full of hurt. Thankfully we convinced her otherwise. We would have been lost without her.'

'And me without them,' Madeline interrupted. 'Sorry, my ears are burning over here.'

'One big, happy family,' Lilliana said. Shauna couldn't miss the hint of sarcasm in her voice and noticed the warning look Sandy gave her daughter.

The rest of the hour flew past. Everyone had questions and Shauna found herself laughing in the end when Madeline rang a little bell asking for silence. 'Enough. Seven o'clock, time for you to be on your way.'

'Oh.' Rose pouted. 'Can't we stay for dinner?'

Madeline handed Rose her jacket. 'Out now, missy.'

Rose was the first to hug Shauna. 'Any chance we could meet for lunch one day next week, or a drink after work?'

'I'd love to.' Shauna dug into her bag and gave Rose her card. 'Give me a ring or send me a text with what suits you.' She turned to Lilliana. 'Join us, if you'd like.'

'Another time, perhaps.' Lilliana picked up her handbag. 'I'm too busy at the moment. Come on, Graeme.' She removed a beer from his hand, leaving it half-drunk on the kitchen bench. 'Time to go.' Graeme gave a little wave to Shauna, thanked Madeline and followed Lilliana. Don and Sandy remained behind to say their goodbyes.

Sandy hugged Shauna. 'Don't worry about Lili, she's not as prickly as she's making out. She'll get used to the idea of you soon enough.'

Shauna hugged Sandy back, hoping she was right. She turned to her father.

He smiled. 'Thanks for putting up with us invading your space tonight. Everyone is so curious, I hope you don't mind.'

'No, I've loved meeting them.'

'Could we have dinner soon, the two of us?'

'Of course.'

'How about Sunday night or early next week?'

'Sunday's good.'

'Shall I pick you up?'

'No, text me the details and I'll meet you,' Shauna said.

Madeline shooed them down the passage to the front door, leaving Shauna and Josh on their own.

Shauna exhaled. 'Phew, ambush over. Sorry you got stuck with Graeme, was he okay?'

'If you like beer and football, yes.' Josh moved to the couch next to Shauna. 'He's a nice guy. How about you; approve of your instant family?'

'They're lovely, perhaps with the exception of Lilliana. She didn't seem very happy about my appearance.'

Madeline walked back into the room, apologising as she did. 'What a relief they've gone. I didn't mean you to face an entourage tonight. They mean well, but Rose is so excitable she's exhausting. Can I get either of you another drink?'

'Let me organise them,' Josh said. 'You come and sit down. You've been running around ever since we got here.'

Madeline didn't argue. 'What a lovely young man you are.'

Josh returned with three glasses of wine.

'Oh, would you prefer a beer, dear? I'm sure you'll find more in the fridge.'

'No, this suits me much better. Here's to two beautiful women.' He raised his glass.

Shauna sipped her wine and refocused on Madeline. 'Tell me about Lilliana. She didn't exactly seem pleased to be reunited with a long-lost half-sister.'

'Don't you worry, dear. She needs to get used to the idea.'

'Sandy said the same. What's her issue? As you said yourself, my existence wasn't a secret.'

Madeline paused, appearing to be searching for the right words. 'No, you were never a secret, which is why being reunited with you is so wonderful. However, I think Lilliana's preference may have been that you were a secret. She's always struggled with hearing about you.'

'Do you think she wished Shauna never existed?' Josh asked.

'I'd hate to upset you, but quite likely. Sorry, love.' Madeline's eyes were full of concern.

Shauna smiled. 'As much as I'd prefer everyone was happy to see me, if they're not, I'd rather know what I'm dealing with.'

'Yes, let me fill you in a bit more. Your mother disappeared with you, and three years later Don met Sandy in Melbourne on a business trip. He moved to Melbourne six months after meeting her. Sandy accepted he had a daughter and hoped, like we all did, that one day you would be found. Every Christmas Don bought you a present, just in case. On your birthday, not only did he organise a gift, but he made a cake. This continued once Don's children were born. As they got older, both Patrick and Rose joined in. They would make you cards, or sometimes they would buy a present or a unique candle for your cake.'

Shauna stared at her grandmother. She swallowed. 'But Lilliana?'

'She was jealous. Her siblings have always been close, but Lili kept to herself. She hated such a fuss being made of you and often complained that it wasn't fair. She convinced herself that no one cared about her birthday.'

'Her birthday wasn't celebrated?'

'They were over the top if anything. Still she believed you were more important to Don than her. I talked to her many times to no avail. Both Don and Sandy tried too, but nothing changed her attitude. We all decided to accept we couldn't change her and at the same time continued to mark your birthday.'

'What about Sandy? I'm not even her child.'

'The way she embraced you is one of the many reasons Don fell in love with her. She has one of the kindest, most generous spirits you'll ever find. Look how she not only accepted me but welcomed me as a family member and gran to her own children. She insisted I move down from Brisbane to be near them. Never did she show any signs of being jealous of you or Lorraine. She shared your father's sadness and lessened the pain for him.'

Shauna tried to digest all of this. 'How ironic that while my birthday was celebrated by a loving family every year, my own mother forgot half the time. The lotto ticket was a present because once again she'd forgotten. If she'd remembered and gone shopping, I certainly wouldn't be sitting here right now.'

'So, after thirty years we finally owe her a thank you.' Madeline smiled. 'Does she know you're with me tonight?'

Shauna shook her head. 'No, I haven't spoken to her about the lies she's told. I'm not sure what to say to her. I thought I'd deal with one thing at a time, get to meet all of you first.'

'Good idea.'

'What about you?' Josh asked. 'Are you planning to see her?'

Shauna looked at Madeline. 'Will you? I hadn't even thought about your relationship with her.'

Madeline took another sip of her wine. 'I would like to see Lorraine. Even after everything she's done she'll always be my daughter. However, I'm not sure I can forgive her. For now, I'll enjoy you and think about Lorraine later.'

Shauna nodded. 'I don't know if I can forgive her either, but she's still my mother.'

'Yes, she is, dear. Come on.' Madeline pulled herself up from the couch. 'Sit down at the table and I'll serve dinner. You must be starving.' She took Josh's arm. 'A growing lad, like you.'

Josh laughed. 'At thirty-nine I'm probably not a growing lad, but yes I'd love to eat. My stomach's rumbling. The smells coming from your oven are mouth-watering.'

As they sat down to dinner Shauna tried to focus her attention on Madeline and Josh, but her thoughts were invaded with images of her mother and the unpleasant confrontation to come.

After saying goodnight to Madeline, Josh suggested they take a walk along the Southbank Promenade. It was past eleven and the cafes and bars were packed. Music, laughter and glorious cooking smells surrounded them.

'Your grandmother is an amazing lady.'

'She is,' Shauna agreed. 'It's hard to believe my mother is related to her.' She stopped next to a crowd of people and held her breath as a street performer juggled with fire.

Josh took her hand and squeezed it. 'Look on the positive side. You now know who your father is and the people who make up your family. It's no longer just you and your mum.'

A cheer went up from the crowd as the juggler managed to juggle five fire sticks. Shauna smiled. She turned to face Josh, her hand still entwined with his. 'You always know the right thing to say, don't you?'

Josh took her other hand. 'Not always, but you're lucky and I want to make sure you focus on what's good.'

'I think I'm focusing on it right now.' Shauna's eyes locked with Josh's. He was right, she was incredibly lucky. Lucky to be here with him. He had the most generous heart of any man she'd met.

Josh pulled Shauna to him. She felt a shiver go through her as their bodies melded together. Lifting her chin, he searched her eyes with his own. She knew what he was asking and to answer his unspoken question, Shauna lifted her mouth, her lips brushing his. The pinging of her phone brought her back to reality very quickly, spoiling the moment. She pulled away. What was she doing? This was Josh. Had she drunk too much champagne?

She glanced at her phone, guilt flooding through her. It was Simon.

Love you SJ, please say we can get together soon.

Chapter Sixteen

Frankie manoeuvred the car into the driveway, her mind still at the office. For the first time since she'd started with Blue Water Charters, Dash had been pleasant to her. This turnaround in behaviour made her suspicious and anxious.

Dash had arrived at work to find Frankie involved in a job for the accountant. She'd been asked to send through copies of the original purchase documents for the business. The accountant needed information relating to their lease on the marina berths. When Frankie pulled out the purchase documents they had on file she read them to make sure she understood everything. The figures, however, didn't match up with what Tom had told her, and what the bank statements showed.

Tom had told her the purchase price of the business had been four hundred and fifty thousand dollars, to which Tom contributed another one hundred and fifty thousand to cover start-up expenses. The bank account reflected these amounts, yet the purchase document signed by Tom, Rod and Dash showed the business being purchased for only three hundred and twenty thousand. When she'd rung to check whether the document was correct, Tom assured her she was looking at the wrong copy and to contact Dash's lawyer for the current one. 'The lawyer had us sign three copies of the agreement when we bought the business, but the figures were wrong on one of them so they had to send through a new copy. I thought the one with three hundred and twenty grand was thrown out.' He laughed. 'Be nice if that was the purchase price. We definitely need the final copy on file.'

Dash arrived at the office just as Frankie had placed the call to his lawyer.

'Why are you calling Johnnie?' he demanded.

'I need a copy of the original purchase document for the accountant; I can't seem to find the final one,' Frankie said. 'Tom says the one I'm looking at had an error on it so we need the final. Why? Problem?'

Dash hesitated. 'Um, no, I guess not. Next time tell me and I'll call him for you.'

'No need, you'll be doing my job and I'm sure you've got a million other things to do.'

Dash smiled. 'Thanks, you're right. Lots to get on with.'

Johnnie Drowl was unexpectedly friendly when Frankie rang. She wasn't sure why she assumed he wouldn't be. His association with Dash had her automatically thinking the worst of him. As good as his word, he emailed through a copy of the signed agreement and offered to send her a hard copy. The figures on the document confirmed the purchase price of four hundred and fifty thousand dollars.

'Got everything you need?' Dash asked.

'Yes, I think so.'

'Let me know if I can help you with anything. By the way, I should get the funds from the term deposit at the end of next week. The bank has delayed things. No idea why. You know banks, such a pain.'

Frankie gave a tight-lipped smile. 'Tom will be pleased.'

'You know, Frankie,' Dash said, 'I'm quite happy to take the accounts work back from you, lighten your workload. I see how much you're doing and it's an awful lot. I could help.'

Frankie stared at Dash. Did he honestly believe she was stupid? 'Thanks, but I've finally got my head around the processes and it makes sense for one person to manage the admin. I appreciate your offer, though.'

Dash stood up. Frankie half expected him to get angry, demand she hand over the accounts and stop snooping about, but instead he flashed her another smile. 'You're doing a fantastic job. I know I can be a bit hard to work with and that's going to change. I'll show you how much I respect the contribution you're making. And, you know that other business, the stuff that shouldn't have happened.'

Frankie nodded.

'Well, I'm sorry. Truly sorry. Nothing like that will ever happen again. Now, I'd better get out to *Fish Tales*. Got some cleaning to do before tomorrow.'

Frankie watched as Dash strode out of the office towards the boat. She would have laughed at the insincerity of his speech if she wasn't so worried about what he was up to.

Frankie tried to rid her mind of all thoughts of Dash as she arrived home. The girls were helping themselves to afternoon tea.

Frankie hugged them and sat down to join them. 'So, what's happening?'

Fern quickly launched into an account of her day while Hope remained silent, nibbling on an apple.

'Everything okay?' Frankie asked.

Hope nodded. 'Yes, just a small problem.'

'It's about a boy,' Fern said.

Hope shot her a deadly look.

'Okay, Fern, let Hope explain what's happened.'

Fern poked out her tongue at Hope. 'Fine, I'll go. I need to ring Sally anyway and tell her about Hope's boy trouble.'

Once Fern was gone, Frankie turned to Hope. 'What's going on?' She suddenly had a flashback to sixteen years earlier, sitting in her grandmother's kitchen about to tell her she was going to be a great-grandmother. She inhaled. Hope had never even mentioned a boyfriend. Surely she couldn't be pregnant?

'I have to do my science project with a boy.'

Frankie exhaled and began to laugh. 'Oh, thank God.'

Hope narrowed her eyes. 'What did you think I was going to say?'

Frankie shook her head. 'Nothing. Now explain why this is a problem.'

Hope blushed. 'The boy's Hamish.'

Frankie hid her smile. 'Is that an issue? I'm sure you could ask to change partners.'

Hope's eyes dropped to the floor. 'I don't want to. I want to do it with him. I just didn't know how you or Dad would feel about it after the way he and Pearce behaved.'

'But that's all behind you now, isn't it?'

Hope looked up at Frankie. 'Definitely, he apologised. I think he was just trying to get my attention.'

'Well, he and Pearce certainly managed to get all of our attention. Okay, so you like him and have to do an assignment with him. Any other worries?'

'No, I just wanted you to understand and not make a big deal when he comes over.'

'He's coming over?'

'Yes, in about half an hour. I thought you'd prefer we work here.'

Frankie smiled. 'Of course, and I promise I won't be *too* horrible to him.'

Alarm flashed across Hope's face. 'Mum, you can't be horrible at all. You need to be nice. He's scared of coming over. He's worried Dad will shoot him.'

Frankie laughed. 'Okay, I'll behave, and I'll talk to Dad. How's that?'

Hope got up and hugged her. 'You're the best. Thanks. I'd better go and get ready, I mean get my books ready.'

Frankie felt a gentle tug on her heart as Hope's face flushed red. Her little girl really liked this boy. It was bound to happen; after all Hope was nearly sixteen. Frankie thought back to the talk she'd had with her a year ago. Hope had squirmed at the very thought of contraception, and at that time Frankie had known she had nothing to worry about. Now, even though she knew she could trust Hope, this wasn't something she was ready for.

Frankie let Tom relax with a beer before mentioning that Hamish was upstairs working with Hope. She had to stop herself from laughing out loud at his reaction.

He leapt up from the kitchen stool. 'What? He's in our house? Why didn't you tell me? I've got a few things I'd like to say to the little shit.'

Frankie pulled him back down next to her. 'Leave them. They're working on a homework assignment together. Hope can handle him, and I hate to tell you, but I think she quite likes him.'

Tom put his head in his hands. 'Oh no.'

Frankie laughed. 'Are you upset because it's Hamish or because it's a boy?'

Tom lifted his head. 'A boy, my little girl likes a boy.'

'Tom, she'll be sixteen soon. Think about what we were doing at sixteen.'

'That's why I'm worried. I don't want to be a grandparent just yet.'

Frankie shuddered. 'God, no! Imagine how your parents and my grandmother must have freaked out.'

Tom nodded. A knock on the kitchen door interrupted them.

Hamish appeared in the doorway. 'Excuse me, Mr York, Mrs York, could I talk to you please?'

Frankie noticed a slight tremble to his voice. 'Of course, Hamish, come in.'

Hamish walked towards them, his eyes focused nervously on Tom. Tom moved off the stool and stood, arms crossed, jaw set in a firm line.

'Sir,' he began and then stopped, clearing his throat. 'Sir, I want to apologise.'

'Go on.' Tom's expression remained unmoved.

'I shouldn't have stood by and allowed Pearce to say the things he did to Hope and to you and Mrs York. I'm very sorry.'

Tom nodded. 'Tell me, do you and your friends always tease people who're financially less fortunate than yourselves?'

Hamish couldn't meet Tom's eyes. He shifted from foot to foot, staring at the leg of the bar stool.

Tom raised his voice. 'I said do your—'

Hamish locked eyes with Tom, cutting him off mid-sentence. 'I heard you, sir. I like Hope, I've always liked Hope, but she wouldn't talk to me. To be fair, I've never said anything mean to her, but I've stood by while Pearce has. As stupid as this sounds, I was hoping she'd notice me.'

Tom exchanged a look with Frankie. She could tell that this was not the answer he'd expected. Frankie gave him a little smile.

Hamish watched the silent exchange. 'I want you to know I will never treat Hope badly or allow her to be treated badly by others again. I wanted to ask your permission to take her out on a date.'

'A date? You're asking us?' Frankie said.

Hamish's face turned a darker shade of red. 'Hope said she couldn't go out with me unless I explained myself to you and asked permission.'

Frankie noticed the corners of Tom's mouth start to twitch; he forced his face to retain a fierce look. 'Damn right, too.' His eyes bored into Hamish's. Frankie had to give the boy credit; he didn't flinch.

'I'll tell you what,' Tom said. 'If Hope agrees, you can take her out, but on the weekend during the daytime. Treat her with respect or you'll be having a chat with me.' Tom rubbed his hand against his clenched fist. 'Do you understand?'

Hamish nodded. 'Yes, sir.'

They waited until Hamish left the kitchen, listening to his footsteps on the stairs. Frankie burst out laughing. 'Wow, you're sexy when you're playing mean dad.'

'Think he got the message?'

'How could he not? He'll be too scared to hold her hand.'

Tom took a swig of his beer. 'Good. That was my intention.'

'You should give him some credit. Talking to us took courage.'

Tom sighed and sat back down at the counter. 'Doesn't change the fact that I still don't like him.'

Frankie raised her eyebrows at him. 'Would it make any difference who it was?'

Tom looked sheepish. 'Probably not. Although it's better that she likes Hamish than that Pearce kid. Imagine if they ended up together and we had to deal with that awful mother of Pearce's.'

Frankie shuddered at the thought. 'Another beer?'

'Thanks, babe.'

Frankie fetched another beer for Tom and a mineral water for herself, wondering if she should be drinking something stronger. Discussions with Tom about Dash rarely ended well. She passed Tom his beer. 'I got the lawyer to send through the purchase document today. You were right, I was looking at the wrong document.'

'Good.' Tom opened his beer, his eyes fixed on her. 'Why are you looking so concerned still?'

'Because Dash talked to me like a human being. In fact, he went out of his way to be friendly.'

Tom laughed. 'What? Why would that make you concerned? I told you he'd come around.'

Frankie shook her head. 'I'm sorry, but I'm sure he's up to something. He told me his money would be paid at the end of next week, and he told me I was doing a fantastic job. On top of that, he offered to take over the accounts work to lighten my load. That's what concerns me.'

Tom stared at Frankie. 'I don't believe this – he's bending over backwards and you still find a problem with him.'

'If Dash makes his fifty-grand contribution to the business, produces the invoices for the thirty-nine thousand, and then continues to treat me nicely, I'll change my opinion about him. For the moment his behaviour rings alarm bells. I know you want to play happy families, but I think you're being taken advantage of. You can't ignore this. If he's done nothing wrong, then he's got nothing to cover up.'

Tom sighed. 'What do you believe he's covering up?'

'Other than the missing invoices, my gut tells me there's a bigger issue with the purchase price of the business. It doesn't make any sense to find a document showing the purchase as so much less. I know you said it was a mistake but it seems suspicious that one document of the three you signed would differ from the others. Surely they would have all been printed out at the same time?

Also, the seller's signature looks like a scanned version has been used on all three documents. It doesn't look like an original signature to me.'

'What are you going to do?'

Frankie chewed on her bottom lip. 'I'm not sure at the moment. I think I need to find my own lawyer and get some advice. Don't be mad at me, I'm not doing any of this to deliberately cause problems.'

Tom took her hand. 'I know, but I'm confident you'll find the purchase price is right. We had a number of discussions with the lawyer present about the price. It was definitely four hundred and fifty thousand. And I know the outstanding invoices are a huge issue. I'm not ignoring them, just hoping he'll prove you wrong. He's promised we'll get them at the end of next week.'

Frankie nodded. 'Just so you know, there are company names on the bank statement that have nothing to do with boats or fishing. One is an investment company who when I rang them said they were unable to disclose the nature of the transaction or provide an invoice to me because they only dealt with their clients, and that was Dash. Their business, however, is investments in offshore gold mines. Two of the transactions also trace back to Dash's lawyer's company yet he says he hasn't engaged the lawyer for anything.'

'Really?'

'Really. He hasn't been very smart about what he's done. He must have known we'd see the bank statements and query all of this. Although the purchases were all made prior to me starting to work for the business. I'm beginning to wonder if he assumed he would be looking after the accounts and therefore no one would question the transactions.'

The nerve in Tom's cheek began to twitch. 'So much for my idea of a family business. Speak to a lawyer, see what else is going on and we'll make a decision from there. Hopefully in the meantime he'll surprise us and produce invoices that make sense.'

Frankie nodded. 'Hopefully, but if anything he's been doing isn't legit he has to go.'

Tom rubbed his forehead. 'Let's hope it doesn't come to that.' He pushed the beer away. 'I'm going for a run. I need to clear my mind.'

A lump rose in Frankie's throat as she watched Tom leave the room. His body was slumped, defeated. He had been so sure the money would finally give him the chance to fix his relationship with Dash. She hated that she was the one trying to end it for him.

The next day Frankie prepared the files to take to her meeting with Clare Spencer, the lawyer Pamela had recommended to Shauna and in turn Shauna had recommended to Frankie. Clare had offered to slot her in that afternoon due to a cancellation.

'Do you really think this is necessary?' Tom asked, shaking his head.

Frankie bit her tongue, determined not to start another fight. She closed the filing cabinet. 'I need to learn everything about the business and get to the bottom of the discrepancy with the purchase documents. I find Dash's lawyer difficult to get information from. I'm hoping this lawyer will make things a lot clearer for me.'

'As long as you're not on a witch-hunt to show up Dash.'

'I don't need a witch-hunt to show him up. Look, if everything is in order then we can move on. I need an explanation in non-lawyer talk.'

Tom laughed. 'What? You think a lawyer is the right person to do that?'

'Perhaps not normally, but the lawyer's going to answer my questions no matter how stupid they might sound.' Frankie put her hand on Tom's arm. 'We discussed this last night. There are some very strange transactions that need to be accounted for and the purchase price needs further explanation. If Dash hasn't done anything wrong then we'll sort out the accounts and move forward.'

Tom nodded. 'Okay. I'd better get out on the boat.' He rubbed his hands together. 'Another corporate group to cater for this afternoon.' He leant over and kissed her. 'I'm proud of you. The way you've taken to all of this office stuff and these fantastic marketing ideas you're having. This was probably always your forte. Still wish you hadn't picked up the twenty dollars?' Tom winked and walked out towards the boats.

Frankie checked her watch – enough time for a coffee before going to see the lawyer. She went through to the shared kitchen to find Josiah already making one.

'Was about to bring this to you, Frankie. Thought I'd wait until you'd finished talking to your husband.'

'You're very kind.'

Josiah tugged at his beard. 'More problems with the brother?'

'Yes, I think we have some much bigger issues to worry about, other than his rude behaviour.'

'Do you mind if I speak out of turn, again?'

Frankie's eyes widened. 'Of course not.'

'Always trust your gut. Don't be swayed by anyone else. Something doesn't feel right, trust your instincts.'

'We've certainly got ourselves into a difficult situation.'

Josiah tapped his stomach. 'Your gut is usually always right. Don't let up until you have proof.'

'I'm worried that Tom's relationship with his brother will be irreparable if I'm right.'

'Probably for the best. I've seen plenty of con men in my time, and he fits the description. Hopefully we're both wrong about him. Now, enough from me, none of my business.'

Frankie watched Josiah collect his coffee from the bench. 'Thank you. I appreciate your support.'

Josiah winked and walked towards his shop. He stopped at the door. 'You're a good egg, so I keep my eye out for you. It's the bad eggs we need out of our lives.'

Frankie nodded in agreement as he disappeared into his shop.

Frankie was surprised at how nervous she was meeting with Clare Spencer. Clare was lovely and immediately put her at ease, but until recently, Frankie's day had revolved around delivering leaflets, not dressing in suits and sitting across from lawyers.

'Okay, I'm ready to call Stuart Carbine,' Clare said, after they'd read over and discussed the documents. 'He's the lawyer for Lawrence Wilde, the guy who sold Tom the business to start with. We should be able to get some answers from him.'

The authority in Clare's voice as she spoke had Frankie sitting up, back straight, focused on every word. She wondered if Clare's manner would have the same effect on Stuart Carbine.

She listened attentively to Clare's side of the conversation, wishing she could hear the other lawyer talk and held her breath as Clare put down the phone.

Clare shuffled her papers together before making eye contact with Frankie. 'You were right, the contract sent through by Dash's lawyer is definitely not the original. It appears your brother-in-law's lawyer must have helped orchestrate this. Carbine's going to email some documents through in a minute.'

Frankie groaned. 'How bad is it?'

'Carbine confirmed the business was sold to Tom for three hundred and twenty thousand dollars. Included were the boats, equipment, marina lease and goodwill of the company. Carbine's documents show his client received no other payment.'

'Yet the documents Johnnie sent through show the purchase at four hundred and fifty thousand, a one-hundred-and-thirty-thousand-dollar discrepancy.'

Clare nodded. 'Yes, we need to find out exactly where the money went. Give me a few days to get the information together and then we'll call a meeting and invite your brother-in-law and his lawyer to come along. In the meantime, I would suggest we have another meeting to bring your husband and' – she checked her notes – 'his brother, Rod, up to speed. As owners in the business I feel you should all be given first-hand information. I'll give them some suggestions for retrieving the funds and dealing with their brother.'

'I want him gone.'

'I doubt there'll be any difficulty showing them what their brother has been up to. I think his days in the family business are numbered. So let me do some more digging and then we'll organise the meetings.'

Frankie smiled. 'I can't thank you enough for your help.'

'It's my pleasure. I'll need to thank Pamela for the recommendation, by the way. It's amazing how much business comes my way through her group.'

'If there's one thing that group has taught me,' Frankie said, 'it's that winning lotto is a magnet for bringing problems into your life.'

Frankie looked at the clock on the office wall. It was already past four. The meeting with Clare and travelling to and from St Kilda

Road had taken up a large chunk of the afternoon. She collected her glass and coffee mug from her desk and took them into the kitchen. After washing them, she did a quick tidy-up of the shared area and walked back into the office, ready to gather her things and lock up. She froze. Dash was sitting at her desk. 'I didn't realise you were coming in this afternoon. Do you need something?'

Dash's eyes locked with Frankie's. 'Need something? Yes, you could say that.'

Frankie waited.

Dash got to his feet and walked towards her. 'I had a call from my lawyer today. Wants to see me.' He sat down on the corner of the desk nearest to Frankie. 'Know anything about that?'

Frankie remained silent.

'What's the matter? Cat got your tongue?' Dash slammed his hands down on the desk.

Frankie jumped.

'I hear you've got a lawyer snooping around, asking all sorts of questions. What's the matter with you? I haven't done anything wrong.'

'Who said you had? My lawyer is helping me understand the business and explaining a few things.'

'Like what?'

Frankie's body straightened. She wasn't going to let Dash intimidate her. 'Like why two documents showing different purchase prices exist. Unless you can perhaps explain it to me?'

Dash's eyes narrowed. He stood up and moved closer to Frankie. 'If you know what's good for you, you'll call your lawyer and tell her you've made a mistake.'

Frankie's heartbeat raced. Dash was standing so close she could feel his breath on her face. 'If you've done nothing wrong, my lawyer will help me sort out the correct paperwork. It's no big deal.'

'No big deal?' Dash grasped Frankie's arm and squeezed it. 'You think destroying this opportunity for me is no big deal? The paperwork won't add up. We both know that.' His grip tightened. 'Now, I said call off your lawyer.'

Frankie trembled in Dash's grip and tried to pull her arm free. 'Let go.'

Dash's eyes remained locked with Frankie's. 'I'll let go when you promise to call off your lawyer and not mention any of this to Tom. We can add it to our stash of secrets.'

'No, you'll let go now.' Josiah's deep voice boomed across the room. He strode over to Dash, grabbed him by the shoulder and pulled him off Frankie. 'Are you okay?' he asked her.

She nodded, rubbing her elbow.

Josiah turned to face Dash. 'I suggest you leave. Now.'

Dash folded his arms and stared at Josiah. 'Really. Well, guess what, ol' timer, this is my business, so I suggest you get out before I call the cops.'

Josiah grabbed Dash's arm. 'I said get out.'

Dash tried to shake him off, but Josiah retained a tight grip and led him towards the door.

'Go!' Josiah pushed Dash firmly out the door.

Dash turned back to Josiah. 'You'd better watch yourself, old man.'

Josiah shut the door and turned back to Frankie. 'You okay, love?'

Frankie sat down at her desk, her body still trembling. 'Thank you so much. I'm not sure what he would have done if you hadn't stopped him.'

'Probably nothing. He's a coward trying to scare you into doing what he wants. Do you want me to ring the police, or Tom?'

Frankie shook her head. 'No, neither. He's gone and I'm not hurt, a bit shaken up but not hurt.'

'You are going to tell Tom, aren't you?'

Tell Tom? Frankie knew she should tell him, but she hated to think of how he might react. He'd probably want to kill Dash.

Josiah came over and sat opposite her. 'You can't let him get away with this.'

Tears welled in Frankie's eyes. 'It's not him I care about. It's Tom. He's going to be upset enough when it's confirmed Dash has stolen money from the business. Add this to it and I hate to imagine what he'd do.'

Josiah nodded. 'He'll give Dash exactly what he deserves, I should think.'

'Yes, and end up in jail himself. I honestly think he'd go crazy. I really don't want to find out. He'd be devastated if he knew Dash had threatened me. Let's leave it. My lawyer will sort things out in the next few days and then he should be out of the business.'

Josiah shook his head. 'I think it's a mistake, Frankie. If you were my wife I'd want the chance to knock his block off.'

Frankie smiled. 'With you looking out for me I think I'll be fine.' She glanced at the clock. 'I'd better go, the girls will be wondering where I am. Thank you again.' She leant over and kissed him on the cheek.

Josiah's face flushed. 'No worries, love. You take care of yourself, and if he comes anywhere near you again let me know.'

'Will do.' Frankie stood and hurried from the office, grateful there was no sign of Dash.

Frankie was still shaking when she let herself into the house. Tom was sitting at the kitchen bench reading a newspaper. He looked up, his smile dropping when he saw her face. He jumped up and hurried over to her.

'What's happened? Are you okay?'

Josiah's words filled Frankie's mind. *I think it's a mistake, Frankie. If you were my wife I'd want the chance to knock his block off.*

Tears filled Frankie's eyes as he took her in his arms. It was only now the ordeal was over that she realised how much it had affected her and the last thing she wanted to add to it was worrying about what Tom might do.

'Babe, you're scaring me. What's happened?'

Frankie pulled away and wiped her eyes. 'Sorry, I've just had a difficult day. The lawyer uncovered some information about Dash and he made it very clear that he wasn't happy about it just before I left to come home. It shook me up a bit, that's all.'

The concern lines on Tom's forehead furrowed deeper. 'Did he hurt you?'

'No, he was angry. Josiah stepped in and asked him to leave. I'm fine, really.'

'Stepped in? So he threatened you?'

'Leave it, Tom. I'm fine. Dash didn't touch me; he was just angry, like we've seen plenty of times before.'

Tom took Frankie's bag from over her shoulder and placed it on the bench. 'Why don't you sit down and I'll make you a cup of tea.'

Frankie sat down while Tom switched on the kettle.

'What did the lawyer discover?'

'Exactly what I feared,' Frankie said. 'The purchase price of the business was only three hundred and twenty thousand. Dash and his lawyer have stolen the rest in addition to the invoices he was unable to present. They were all personal expenses.'

The colour drained from Tom's face. 'You're kidding?'

Frankie shook her head. 'I'm afraid not.'

Tom picked up his phone. 'I'll call Rod, he needs to hear this too.'

He called his brother and went back to making the tea, his fist pounding the kitchen bench while he went through the process.

He handed Frankie her tea. 'I'm sorry, babe, but I might have to head out when Rod gets here. I need to do something. Hit something, or better still someone.'

'Don't do anything stupid, Tom. The lawyers will deal with him. He won't get away with it.'

Tom slammed his hands down on the bench top, his eyes flashing. 'He's ripped us off and from the sounds of it threatened you, Frankie. You're damn right he won't get away with it.' He leant across and kissed her forehead. 'I'm sorry, I love you but I have to go out. I'll wait for Rod out the front, go for a run while I'm waiting. I need to get rid of some of this anger. Don't worry, we won't do anything stupid.'

Frankie put her head in her hands as the front door slammed behind Tom. This was exactly what she'd been worried about and she hadn't even told him about the other incident.

Two hours later Frankie had gone through the motions of putting a meal together for Hope and Fern and cleaning up the kitchen and there was still no word from Tom. She'd tried calling his phone but it had gone straight to voicemail. A little after nine the front door opened and Tom appeared with Rod behind him. They both had the same determined, angry look on their faces.

'I'm so sorry, Frankie,' Rod said. 'I had no idea he'd do something like this.'

'What did you do?' Frankie asked. 'Did you go and see him?'

'We couldn't find him,' Tom said. 'He wasn't home or at any of his usual spots.' He clenched his fists. 'He'll keep. But for now, I need a beer. Rod?'

Rod nodded and sank down on a stool at the kitchen counter. 'What happens next?'

'We meet with our lawyer and Dash and his lawyer, probably on Friday from what Clare was trying to organise,' Frankie said. 'Clare will want to meet with us first to go over exactly what we want to get out of the meeting. It's a mediation, after which, if we can't work out an agreement, we sue him and take him to court. His lawyer's as bad, if not worse, than he is so they'll both be in massive trouble.'

Tom looked at Rod. 'Is that what we want? He'll probably go to prison.'

Tom and Rod sat in silence contemplating this.

'Jeez, Mum will be turning in her grave, for sure.' Rod broke the silence. 'Let's find out if we can just get rid of him for good. That's my priority. Obviously it's your money he's taken so it's up to you what you want to do about that.'

Tom nodded. 'I'll have a think about it. As much as I want to kill him, I'm not sure I want him in prison – he's still our brother. Although there's a part of me that wonders if that's exactly what he needs. Nothing we've ever done or said to him has ever made a difference. Maybe he really does need a huge wake-up call.' He looked to Frankie. 'What do you think?'

'I think Rod's right; your mum would be really upset by every-thing's that happened. I'd be happy if he signed over his share of the business to us and then stayed out of our lives. I doubt we'll ever get the other money back but returning his share of the business will make up for that.'

Tom took a long swig of his beer and paced up and down the kitchen. 'You're the one he's been awful to and here you are stick-ing up for him. He's bloody lucky you're so nice, Frankie. And he's bloody lucky we didn't find him tonight. I really need to hit something, and it would have been him.'

Frankie watched her husband. 'Please don't, either of you. Think of your mum and what she'd be asking you to do right now.

It wouldn't be to beat him up. It might make you feel better for a few seconds but it's not going to do any more than possibly get you into trouble.'

Rod sighed. 'Frankie's right.' He smiled. 'Lucky one of us is an adult.'

Tom came over to Frankie and put his arms around her. 'Yes, you're right, as usual. Just as you were the first day you said there was a problem with the accounts. I'm sorry I didn't want to listen.'

Frankie smiled. 'It's okay, I get it. He's your brother. You were hoping that he'd changed.'

'Hoping for a miracle,' Rod said.

'All that's important now,' Frankie said, 'is that we move forward. Make the most out of the business and working together.'

Tom sighed. 'I don't know if I'll ever be able to accept what he's done, but regardless, I'll raise my drink to moving forward and making this business work.'

He raised his beer and clinked it against Rod's before both men lapsed into silence, deep in their own thoughts.

Chapter Seventeen

Shauna's cheeks hurt she'd laughed so much listening to Rose tell stories of their father and her childhood. She was lovely and hilarious all rolled into one. Shauna found it hard to fathom that she and Rose were now related. They were sisters. Half-sisters maybe, but they were still sisters.

They'd met after work for a drink, which had turned into an early dinner.

'I hope we can do this more often,' Rose said as they paid the bill. 'It's been so nice getting to know you. Dad said the same after your dinner on Sunday night.'

Shauna smiled. She and Don had gone to dinner, just the two of them, and it had been lovely. It was the first time they had been alone together since she had discovered he was genuine about wanting to get to know her. It was hard enough wrapping her mind around the fact she had a half-sister, let alone a living, breathing father who was desperate to have her as part of his life.

'I'm looking forward to meeting Patrick,' Shauna said. 'Don, I mean Dad, I mean—' She stopped and laughed. 'Sorry, it's just so weird thinking of calling someone Dad. In time I'm sure I'll be comfortable with it but for now I think I'll stick with Don. Anyway, Don showed me some photos of him. He's incredibly good-looking.'

Rose beamed. 'I know. His uniform helps. Mum nearly had a fit the day he told her he was joining the army, but she's come around. I think she still worries every day that something's going to happen to him, but I don't think where he's serving is in direct fire or particularly dangerous. I'm sure he'll be alright.'

Shauna doubted Sandy would be able to be as relaxed as Rose about this. 'What about Lili? Are you two close?'

Rose shook her head. 'No, she's always been a bit of a loner. The black sheep of the family. Don't get me wrong, I love her, but we'd never do something like this, for instance. She'd probably just laugh at me if I suggested we go for dinner. I guess I've always been her younger, annoying little sister and that's how she still views me. It's a shame, but just how it is. I'm close with Patrick and who knows, now I have a new sister I might be close with her too.'

Shauna laughed. 'I'm definitely open to that. I've never had siblings before so this is all very new to me. If I do anything to offend you just let me know and I'll do my best to change. Have you got Lilliana's number? I might give her a call. See if I can get her to warm to me at all. I'd like to get to know her if possible.'

Rose scrolled through her phone and shared the contact with Shauna. 'Good luck with that. If you get to know her you can let me know what she's like.'

'We might all be able to go out one night. Three sisters out celebrating.'

'I think we'd need to get Lili very drunk to make it a good night.'

Shauna grinned. 'I'm always up for that. Come on, I'd better head off. As lovely as this has been I've got a report to finalise tonight and get off to a client.'

They walked back to where they'd both parked and Rose flung her arms around Shauna. 'See you, sis. Can't wait to do this again.'

Shauna was still smiling as she drove out of the city towards Richmond. How had she suddenly got an amazing sister? Her thoughts skipped to Lilliana. Would she be able to develop a relationship with her too?

She instructed Siri to call Lilliana and waited as the phone rang. Her stomach churned with nervous energy. What a contrast to how she felt about meeting up with Rose.

'Hello, this is Lilliana.'

Shauna took a deep breath. 'Lilliana, it's Shauna. You know, um, your sister.'

The line was silent for a moment. 'Yes, Shauna, I know who you are. How are you?'

'I'm good, thank you. In fact, I just caught up with Rose and was thinking of you. I wondered if you'd like to meet for a drink or dinner at some stage. It would be really lovely to get to know you.'

Lilliana cleared her throat. 'Shauna, don't take this the wrong way, but I'm just not ready for that. It's been a huge shock to me to know you're alive and will be part of the family.' She gave a little laugh. 'I'm not good with change and this pretty much trumps anything I've dealt with before. I know it shouldn't be about me and that you've had a really rough time, but I have a few things to come to terms with before I can try and embrace this new beginning.'

'I'm sorry that you're having to go through this, I really am.'

'God, you don't need to be sorry. I'm sorry that I'm not more like Rose and just excited for it all to be happening. Please know it isn't personal. It really isn't. These are my issues and I'll work them out. In the meantime, I'll see you at any family lunches or dinners. I'm sure between Dad and Madeline there will be plenty of those.'

'I'll look forward to it,' Shauna said. She ended the call intrigued by Lilliana's response. She believed her that it wasn't personal, and that it was her own demons she needed to deal with. Shauna imagined there was some truth to what Madeline had said about Lilliana having a difficult time accepting Shauna's existence as a child and now would be no different. That was fine. She hadn't known of Lilliana's existence for the past thirty-four years; there was no rush to bond with her. As she pulled into the underground parking of her apartment block Shauna recognised that the reality was they might never bond and that was fine too. It was just how it was.

Shauna rode the lift to the fourth floor where her apartment was situated thinking of how different her two sisters were. She guessed that was what was going to make this journey interesting. It wouldn't be much fun if they were all the same. She hesitated as the lift door opened and she stepped into the hallway. Simon was leaning against the wall, hands tucked in his pockets, a sexy grin lingering on his lips.

'Hey, gorgeous.'

Shauna forced a smile to her lips. She wished she'd been prepared for his visit. 'What are you doing here?'

'Texting and phone calls just aren't enough. I've got so much to tell you and wanted to do this.' He pulled her to him and kissed her firmly on the lips. It was nothing like the way she'd felt when she and Josh had so nearly kissed. This kiss was well practised, one that had been delivered many times before. Shauna pulled away. The attraction she once felt to him was gone. She'd felt nothing, other than the need to compare his kiss when their lips had touched. Her heart used to pound, her legs turn to jelly and now, nothing.

A lightness enveloped her as the realisation that Simon was her past, not her present or her future, filled her mind. How could she have even considered a relationship with someone she'd had no desire to confide in? She wasn't sad; she was relieved. It had taken more than twelve months, but she could finally move on.

Simon took her hand. 'Are you going to invite me in?'

'Of course, come in and tell me your news.' She'd let him talk first before she did.

Simon was already well into a monologue about an incredible business opportunity that had come his way by the time they sat down on the couch in the living room. 'That guy I told you about, John Trickett, has offered to sell me his agency. Originally he'd offered me a job, but when we got to talking about it more, he explained that he was looking to exit the business in the next couple of years and I realised I wanted to buy it. The client list is solid, the turnover reasonable and the potential enormous.'

Shauna had only listened to the last half of what he was saying. Was he actually considering buying a business?

'It would mean I'd be in Melbourne permanently. You wouldn't need to worry about me getting the travel bug. And the best thing' – he took her hand – 'is we could do it together. I know you said it was probably better if we worked in different organisations, but that was when we were working for someone else. Imagine if it was our own business. We'd be working together all day every day, building and expanding on an already great business. What do you think?'

Was he crazy? Did he really think she'd want to work with him again? It was the one problem she'd seen in their relationship before he'd announced he was moving overseas. It was why she'd taken the job at I-People. To separate their work and personal lives. Why would she consider this a good idea?

'How are you planning to fund this? I assume they're not just handing the business to you?'

Simon shook his head. 'No, it will require a large investment on our behalf. It will be worth it though. When you see the books, you'll see what I mean. We can do this.'

'I thought you'd spent all of your money travelling. How are you planning to fund the investment?'

Simon took her hands in his. 'Oh, come on, Shauna. I haven't wanted to say anything about the money because I've been waiting for you to tell me. To be honest I thought you'd want to celebrate with me, not keep it from me.'

Shauna pulled her hands back.

'Don't be like that. You're sitting on a lot of money, and while I'd never ask for any of it for me, I am going to ask you to invest in the business. It's a no-brainer. It gives us a secure income, a business of our own and the opportunity to be together so much more than we are now.'

'You knew about the money all along?'

He shook his head. 'No, I found out after we first caught up. Jenni, your receptionist, mentioned it to one of the guys at Recruit. I've been waiting for you to tell me, share the excitement. I still don't understand why you didn't.'

Bloody Jenni! 'I wanted to know that you wanted me back, not just my money.'

'I do want you back. I love you. This is just an added bonus. One we could do so much with.' He moved towards her, again reaching for her hands.

Shauna crossed her arms across her chest. 'If I say no to investing in this business, what are you going to do?'

'I don't know. Speak to the bank, I guess. I don't think they'll loan me enough to buy it though.'

'Okay, then what? Let's assume they say no. You can't buy it. Will you become an employee like you said you would?'

'Probably not. Honestly, if you say no I'll probably go back to London. I'll be too devastated to stay.'

'Devastated because I didn't invest in a business?'

'No, devastated that you don't think I'm worth investing in. If you won't invest in the business it tells me you're not going to take the time to invest in us either. There would be no point staying and trying to rebuild a relationship with someone who isn't fully supportive of my dreams.'

Shauna gave a wry laugh. 'This is a joke, right? Another ultimatum? Invest in this business or I'm going travelling? At least last time you were asking me to come with you. This time it's basically blackmail.'

'Of course it's not blackmail! I want us to do this together. I love you. This opportunity means we could carve out an amazing future for ourselves. Surely that's important to you too?'

She smiled. Thank God she'd already decided to end the relationship the moment he'd kissed her, or she might actually be upset at his blatant attempts to manipulate her.

Simon's brow furrowed. 'Should I be happy or concerned that you're suddenly smiling?'

'Neither. The last time you gave me an ultimatum I said no. This time's no different. It's finally clear to me that I don't want you in my life anymore. Not in business or my personal space. If you don't mind, I'd appreciate it if you'd leave.'

She got up, walked over to the bookshelf and picked up the Louis Vuitton voucher. She held it out to him. 'I assume this was all part of your plan to butter me up for this moment.'

Simon's mouth dropped open. 'Of course it wasn't. I meant every word I said about a new beginning. The business would be more than that for the two of us. Surely you can see what a great opportunity this is?'

'For you, maybe. I'm quite comfortable at I-People. Of course, you can buy it yourself and grow it. If you do that I wish you an incredible amount of good fortune.'

'Will you help me?'

'Financially?'

He nodded.

'No. We're over, Simon. We were over the night you gave me the ultimatum to travel with you. It's just taken me a lot longer than it should have to realise this.'

Simon's eyes darkened as he glared at Shauna. 'I can't believe what a bitch you're being about this. You've led me on for weeks. What was that about? Have you got any idea of how much work it's been convincing you I wanted you back?'

A short sharp laugh escaped Shauna's lips. 'The fact that it was *work* tells me straightaway that it was about the money and never about me. The change from "I want to be friends" to "I want you back" was way too quick. I should have realised then you had another agenda. I convinced myself you didn't know about the money and wanted me for who I am. You're not good for me, Simon.' She indicated to the door. 'Now, please leave.'

Simon snatched the voucher from her, shaking his head as he walked to the door. 'I can't believe you're doing this to me. This is an amazing opportunity and all we have to do is sign contracts and exchange a cheque. It would hardly even put a dent in your new fortune.' He didn't bother to even look at Shauna. He ripped open the front door and slammed it behind him.

Shauna sank on to the couch. Thank God for that. He was gone once and for all. It was hard to believe she'd even considered taking him back. Was she that bad a judge of character? Her thoughts immediately flicked to Josh and her lips meeting his. While the kiss had been cut off before they could really explore it, it should never have happened. She'd misjudged that situation – that they were only friends – too. When it came to men, she was beginning to realise she really was hopeless.

Since they'd kissed, Shauna had avoided Josh as best she could at work, feeling awkward in his presence. He, on the other hand, had been his usual friendly self, acting as if nothing had happened. Finally, on Thursday afternoon, he pulled her aside.

'You don't have to act weird with me. First and foremost, I'm your friend. I was honoured to be part of your journey with your family last week and would love to continue to be part of your life as a friend. Yes, if the timing were right, I'd like more than that, but it's not. That's fine. We're work colleagues and friends. We don't need to be weird with each other. If anything, everything that's happened should bring us closer together.'

'Really? That's how you feel? We kind of kissed on Friday night, if you remember?'

Josh smiled. 'Remember. It's something I'll never forget. Although I'd love to forget that stupid text message ruining it. Don't worry about it. It was perfect at that moment, and I'm glad it happened. Real life isn't that moment, so we move on. You make things work with the ex and I might get myself a cat to go home to each night.'

Shauna smiled. He was an amazing guy. Making light of it all to ensure they were still comfortable around each other. If he was willing to make that effort, then so was she. She wasn't ready to tell him she'd ended the relationship with Simon. She wasn't sure at this stage what that meant, if anything, for her and Josh.

She was, however, looking forward to seeing Frankie. She'd rung her at lunchtime suggesting they skip the support group and go out for dinner instead. There was a lot to talk about, and she didn't feel like making small talk with the rest of the group. In fact, Shauna realised, the only reason she was attending the group was for the opportunity to see Frankie. The group had its place, and the messages were good, but they were really only a reinforcement of what Pamela had told them in their initial meeting. Shauna didn't feel the need to hear any more true-life stories. Frankie hesitated only momentarily before agreeing to meet her at Délicieux in Carlton.

Shauna felt like she'd been transported to a French bistro as she soaked up the ambience of the French restaurant. French-themed posters lined the walls and laughter and music reverberated from the walls. A giant white chandelier created an impressive centrepiece.

'I love this music,' Frankie said. 'Do you know who it is?'

Shauna shook her head. 'Someone French, I would guess.'

Frankie laughed. 'I worked that bit out.' She pointed to the menu. 'French indie, according to this. Now, tell me everything. To get an emergency dinner call, something must have happened.'

Shauna told Frankie about the dinner with Madeline, the kiss with Josh, the break-up with Simon and the fact she still hadn't confronted her mother.

Frankie smiled when Shauna spoke of Josh. 'Told you – as did your grandmother.'

'He's still a work colleague,' Shauna said. 'Still out of bounds, in theory.'

Frankie raised her eyebrows. 'Theory is irrelevant; it's practice that matters, and it sounds like you've already started on that front.'

Shauna's cheeks flamed with heat. 'How do you think I should approach it? I've messed him around a lot, and he's been so good to me.'

'Go up to him tomorrow at work and tell him how you feel. Tell him you're nervous about starting anything with a colleague because of what happened with Simon, but you know he's worth the risk. Tell him you want to take it slowly and not ruin your friendship. See what he has to say.'

Shauna sipped her drink. Frankie was right, the ball was in her court now, and she needed to step up and show Josh that she did care and was interested.

'And then the next thing you need to do is go and see your mother. You can't keep putting that off. She doesn't even know you're spending time with your father and her mother, does she?'

Shauna shook her head. 'No, and as she told me her mother's dead, she might believe that. She'll get quite a surprise when she finds out that's not the case. I do need to deal with her, though, as much as I'm dreading it.'

'I'm dreading tomorrow,' Frankie said. 'If I can get through that, then you can get through this.' She went on to tell Shauna what Clare had discovered about Dash and how he'd threatened her.

'Thank God for old Josiah,' Shauna said. 'And I'm glad you told Tom, Frankie. It's bad enough you let Dash get away with blackmailing you. I'm sure Tom's mother wouldn't have expected you to protect him when he's been that awful to you. She'd be horrified.'

Frankie nodded. 'I know. But I think after tomorrow I won't need to worry about Dash anymore. I hope not, anyway.'

Chapter Eighteen

Frankie's stomach churned as she sat in the conference room with Tom and Rod, waiting for Dash and his lawyer to arrive.

'Don't worry; this won't take too long.' Clare handed Frankie a glass of water.

Frankie gave Clare a weak smile. She wasn't convinced Dash would even turn up after what had happened earlier in the week.

Moments later, the conference door opened, and a short, bald man, wearing an expensive suit and thick, gold chains around his neck walked in. Dash followed closely behind.

Frankie gasped. Dash's face was bruised; his left eye was black and half-closed, and his arm was in plaster. She immediately looked to Tom, whose face mirrored her shock.

'Rod and I had nothing to do with that.' He turned back to Dash. 'What the hell happened to you?'

'Your bitch wife can probably answer that.'

'Hey,' Tom said. 'Watch your mouth.' He turned to Frankie, his forehead creased in confusion. 'Why does he think you did this?'

Her thoughts instantly flashed to Josiah. It must have been him, but surely he wouldn't go this far? Would he?

Frankie shrugged. 'I've got no idea what he's talking about.'

Dash snorted. 'Ask her sugar daddy. I assume there's a payment plan to fulfil still.'

Tom slammed his hands down on the meeting room table and leapt to his feet. 'How dare you? After everything you've done to hurt the business and our family, don't you disrespect my wife too.'

Dash looked as surprised as everyone else at Tom's outburst.

'Your wife organised for her old thug to do this to me,' Dash said. 'I'm sorry if I can't show her the respect you think she deserves.'

'Frankie had nothing to do with it,' Tom said. 'She practically begged me to stay away from you because she knew what I would have done if I'd got my hands on you. And I can tell you right now if Rod and I had found you the other night, it's unlikely you'd even be sitting here right now.'

'Enough,' Clare said. 'Making threats isn't helping anyone at this stage. We have other important issues to discuss. Please take a seat.'

Tom glared at Dash before allowing Frankie to pull him back into his seat. She wasn't sure she'd seen him so angry before.

Once everyone was seated, Clare presented the proof she had that they had conspired to steal from the business. As her words sank in, she folded her arms and leant back in her chair. 'So, Counsellor Drowl, or shall I call you Johnnie? Is there anything you'd like to say in your defence?'

Dash's lawyer peered over the rim of his glasses, his mouth twisted in an ugly fashion. 'You can't prove anything.'

Clare laughed, throwing a copy of the documents at him. 'Interesting defence. I knew you were a crooked lawyer, but I didn't realise your skills were so bad.'

Johnnie got to his feet. 'Come on,' he said to Dash. 'Let's not waste our time with this.'

As they reached the door, Clare slammed her hands down on the table. 'Come back and sit down.' She glared at Johnnie and

Dash until they both retook their seats. 'You will listen to me. Don't speak until I instruct you to.'

Johnnie rolled his eyes in disgust but kept his mouth shut.

'"You can't prove anything" appears to be your defence. Terrible defence when I can prove you forged purchase documents for a business which robbed my client of one hundred and thirty thousand dollars. I can prove you took close to forty thousand dollars out of the company for personal expenses. I can prove you did not meet your part of the agreement and invest in the company.'

'Fine,' Johnnie said. 'Let's assume you can provide evidence to all of this. What are you planning to do?'

'I've advised my clients to take this to court. The outcome I predict is you will be struck off and never work as a lawyer again, and your client can look forward to jail time in addition to repaying all of this money and legal costs.'

Frankie was satisfied to see the colour drain from Johnnie's cheeks. Dash looked at Tom, his face suddenly looking young and scared. The cockiness had vanished. 'I'm sorry, Tom, really I am. I never meant this to happen. I wasn't thinking. Give me a chance; I'll pay the money back and make it up to you. We're family. You know Mum and Dad would be gutted if the family fell apart.'

Frankie watched Tom's reaction, wondering if Dash's words would get through to him.

'You constantly disappoint us, Dash. Maybe this is the only way you're going to learn.'

'You'd let me go to prison? Your own brother?'

'Jesus, you were happy to rip off your *own brother*, but now you can't handle the consequences? Maybe you should have thought this through a bit better.'

Dash nodded, his head hanging. 'You're right. I deserve everything I get.'

A lump formed in Frankie's throat. She wasn't sure if Dash was genuine or not, you could never tell, but she knew that Tom would be feeling like his heart was being ripped out right now. He'd tried for years to have a good relationship with Dash, and it had been thrown back at him time and time again. This being the ultimate betrayal.

'I figured you had so much money now that you could have afforded to give me a bit more to start with.'

Frankie glanced at Tom, who looked away. So he had told Dash that they'd won ten million after promising not to. She'd warned him. The support group had warned them. Would it have made any difference if Dash hadn't known?

'That wasn't your decision to make,' Tom said. 'That was mine and Frankie's.'

'And I hated that too,' Dash said. 'That it was you thinking you were so amazing handing out money. It wasn't like you even earned it. It was pure luck that you ended up with ten million dollars. How unfair is that?'

Frankie shook her head. It was unfolding exactly as it had for members of the support group. Resentment growing amongst friends and family members eventually causing them to act in ways they never normally would have. She guessed the difference was she and Tom had been lucky. They'd stopped Dash before he'd ruined them too.

Johnnie cleared his throat. 'If getting me struck off and sending Dash to prison's the plan, then why are we here? Is there a particular reason for this meeting?'

Clare nodded. 'Yes. As I said, I advised my clients on the path I believe they should go down. However, my clients, against my advice, are willing to consider settling out of court.'

'On what terms?'

'Your client will sign over his ownership of Blue Water Charters to Tom York with no future involvement in the business.'

'Anything else?'

313

'Your client will also agree to document the exact amount of money he has taken from the company and with whose help. This information will remain on file, and if your client ever tries to contact my clients or their children, you both will be taken to court.'

'Are you finished?'

Clare stood up. 'I'll give you five minutes to agree to these terms and your client will need to remain behind to complete the document. You may be present if you wish.'

Frankie, Tom and Rod stood and followed Clare out of the meeting room to her office.

'Relax.' Clare pointed to her couches. 'You don't need to go back in again; I'll sort out the details.'

'Do you think he'll agree?' Tom asked.

'Tom, he's got no choice,' Clare said. 'His lawyer can't fight this unless he wants to lose his licence to practise and go to jail. Your offer is incredibly generous. Mr Crooked Lawyer in there is well aware of this.' Clare left the group and went back to the meeting room to present the document Dash needed to sign.

Tom sighed. 'Not exactly the best start to our family business. I can't believe he'd steal money from us so blatantly.'

'His method wasn't very smart,' Frankie said. 'Still, better we found out now rather than a year or two down the track. Who knows how much he would have helped himself to.'

'No doubt the whole lot,' Rod said. 'Clare's right, Frankie. Your agreement to settle out of court is more than he deserves.'

'Don't thank me. Like you, I'm sad he didn't use the money and the business as an opportunity for a better life and a closer family.'

Rod hauled himself up from the couch. 'Let's not waste any more time talking about him. Come on, let me take you both out for lunch.'

Tom looked up from the loose thread on the carpet he had been staring at. 'What's the occasion?'

'We should thank Frankie for looking out for the company and us and enjoy the launch of a real family business. The one where all the partners care about each other and want to work together. We've had a bit of a false start, that's all.'

Tom nodded slowly. 'You're right. Although I don't feel like celebrating. He's our brother, regardless of anything else. I can't believe it's come to this.'

Rod flung an arm around Tom's shoulder. 'We've still got each other, bro, and that will never change. I agree a celebration isn't the right description, or what we need to do. We need to put this behind us and find a way forward. That might not happen today, but we can certainly work towards it.'

'Sounds good,' Tom said. 'What do you think, Frankie?'

Frankie smiled, knowing she could never vocalise the thought going through her head that she would be the first to celebrate seeing the back of Dash once and for all. 'I agree with Rod. There's no point looking back; forward is the only way to go.'

Frankie curled her hand around Tom's and pulled the doona over the two of them. 'How are you feeling?'

'Right now?' Tom rolled over on to his side, his fingers stroking Frankie's stomach.

Frankie smiled. 'No, the stupid grin on your face tells me how relaxed and content you are right at this second. I meant about Dash.'

Tom flopped back on to the pillows. 'Oh, him. I'll probably never understand why he did what he did, but I know that it's his loss, not ours.'

Frankie lay next to Tom and watched the rhythmic rise and fall of his chest. She knew it would take some time for him to accept that his relationship with Dash was over. She, however, wasn't going to deny the relief she felt. She'd used the excuse that she needed to collect some paperwork on the way home, in order to stop in and see Josiah. She needed to check that he was okay. He'd grinned and flexed his knuckles when he saw her. 'Hurt? Dash? Really?' was all he'd said. 'Know nothing about it, love.' She'd kissed him on the cheek, watching him blush, and raced home to join Tom.

Tom propped himself up on his elbow and with his other hand gently stoked Frankie's cheek. 'You know how sorry I am, don't you?'

'It's not your fault that Dash behaved the way he did.'

'No, I'm sorry for how I went about everything. Buying the business to start with. Dash would have been one of the reasons you said no to it, wouldn't he? You knew how rotten he really was.'

Frankie nodded. 'I suspected.'

'I'm angry with him but I'm angry at myself too. I didn't want to listen; didn't want to believe he would steal from us. I'm so sorry, babe. Putting you in a position where you had to put up with him and even be threatened by him is unforgivable.'

Frankie reached for the hand that continued to stroke her cheek and kissed it. 'There's nothing to forgive. I know how much family means to you and I know how desperate you were to make things work with your brothers. I understand that and I respect you even more for always putting family first above everything else. It's what your mum would want you to be doing.'

Tom's eyes filled with tears. 'I don't think Mum would be all that proud of me right now.'

'Of course she would. Look what you tried to do for your family. You can't control other people's behaviour, and any disappointment she holds would be towards Dash.'

'*Disappointment* is the word, isn't it?' Tom wiped his eyes on the sheets. 'I'm angry of course, but it's the disappointment that's really got to me.'

'It will take time to get over this. It's a huge betrayal. You've still got Rod, and you've got the girls and me but you need to allow yourself the time to mourn your relationship with Dash. He might change one day.'

Tom sighed and lay back against the pillows.

'I hate to tell you, but we'd better get up. The girls will be home soon.'

Tom groaned. 'You can't do those wicked things to me then have deep conversations and expect me to function afterwards. I need sleep.'

Frankie picked up a pillow and whacked him. 'Ten minutes, and then I want to talk to you about something completely different.'

'Deal.' Tom rolled over. By the time Frankie had put her clothes on and was walking out of the bedroom, she could hear his gentle snores.

An hour later, Tom made an appearance in the kitchen, dressed but groggy-eyed. He opened the fridge. 'Where are the girls?'

'Hope rang to say she was going to a friend's house to study and Fern is across the road. Apparently she's made a new friend at number thirty.'

Tom took a swig out of the milk carton and winked at Frankie. 'Back to bed?'

'Sorry, as irresistible as you are, I want to talk to you about the money.'

'What money?'

'The lotto money. I'd like to give it away.'

Tom dropped the milk carton on to the bench. 'What?'

Frankie laughed. 'You should see your face. Not all of it. I want to leave us comfortably off, but we don't need ten million dollars. Let's work out who we can help. Look at the oldies. The minibus has given them so much independence and enjoyment already.'

Tom nodded. 'Okay, so how much would we keep?'

'We still need to buy a house, and we want to have enough for the girls' uni fees, plus enough to live on. I'd also want to keep a bit extra for our future, just in case. So, I was thinking three million?'

Tom's face relaxed. 'Thank God, I thought you were going to suggest we move back to Poor Street again.'

'No, but from day one my gut told me something bad would happen with the money, and the situation with Dash proves my gut right. Shauna's experienced so many problems too. It's damaging relationships for all of us. Let's unburden ourselves. Help people.'

Tom came around the kitchen island and took Frankie's hand. 'You are such a good person. I'm so glad I knocked you up as a teenager.'

Frankie laughed. 'Mr Romance.'

'No, I mean it. You probably would've gone off to university and moved on from me otherwise. I never would have found someone as generous or as loving. I'm a lucky man.' Tom pulled Frankie close to him.

'You're happy with my idea?'

'As long as we keep enough to retain our millionaire status, I'm fine.'

Frankie smiled. 'I think I'm pretty lucky, too, Mr York.'

Tom leant forward and kissed her. His hand ran down the back of her dress and rested on her bottom. 'Any chance of showing me how lucky?'

Frankie felt Tom harden against her. She took his hand and led him back to their bedroom, locking the door behind them.

Chapter Nineteen

The soft murmurs of other diners and gentle sounds of a grand piano brought a smile to Shauna's lips as she and Josh crossed the restaurant floor to their table. The candlelit table was tucked in the corner, ideally suited for a quiet, romantic dinner. Shauna hugged her arms around herself, loving the care that Josh had put into booking this evening. When she'd gathered her courage earlier that day to speak to him, the combined look of shock and delight on his face had brought tears to her eyes.

'You mean it? You want to give you and me a go? Simon's in the past and you're ready to move on?'

She'd nodded, taking his hands in hers. 'And I'd like to do this properly too, with no phone and no interruptions.' She'd lifted her mouth to his, tentative at first, then their kiss had become more passionate, unlocking feelings for Josh she hadn't been aware were so deep. When she'd pulled away, tears had filled her eyes. His face was so full of genuine love she could hardly believe she'd considered going back to Simon.

He'd pulled her to him, asking if she was free for dinner that night before kissing her with even more passion.

'At last,' Josh said, once they were seated. He reached across the table and stroked Shauna's hand. 'Our first real not-just-friends date. I still can't believe this is happening, to be honest. I was sure you were going back to the ex.'

Shauna curled her fingers around his. 'I'm surprised you're here at all. My life has been crazy this last couple of months. I think most sane people would run a mile.'

Josh smiled. 'Confirming, therefore, I am in no way sane. And there's no need to apologise. It's not every day you're reunited with your long-lost father and discover a new brother, sisters and a stepmother.'

Shauna smiled. 'Don't forget a grandma, too.'

Josh continued to stroke her hand. 'How are things going with Don?'

'He's fascinating. I hate that I've missed so much time with him. He would have been such a good father.'

'He still can be.'

'Of course, but I'm thinking of my teenage years. Those years were spent avoiding a bunch of men my mother traipsed through the house. None of them lasted more than a few months. They were also pretty horrible – a good way to be put off men.'

'I'm sorry she did that to you. At least the lotto win brought your father back into your life, someone who wasn't after your money.'

'Definitely not after my money.' She leant closer to Josh, her voice low. 'You won't believe this, but he's bought property for all of his kids since his business became successful.'

'Even you?'

'Yes, he's organising for the titles to be transferred into my name this week. Four houses. He purchased two of them in South Melbourne over twenty years ago, one in Ascot Vale and one in Richmond. Imagine what they're worth now? Crazy, isn't it?'

'How do you mean?'

'For anyone else, this would be life-changing, but with the lotto money, they simply add more property to my assets.'

Josh shook his head. 'No, you're wrong; this is still life-changing. The houses are further proof of how much Don has always loved you.'

Shauna smiled. Trust Josh to point out something even better about her father. 'True. The other thing he showed me, which blew me away, were years of birthday cards and gifts. He has an enormous attic in his house full of the cards and some of the presents he bought for me over the last thirty years.'

'Only some? What happened to the rest of them?'

'He gave away the toys and children's books, anything I would have outgrown. Mind you, he photographed every present and put a photo in the card. He kept the adult presents. First editions of books, paintings and lots of jewellery.' Shauna fiddled with the diamond pendant on the necklace she was wearing. 'This is my present from this year.'

Josh smiled. 'Beautiful, like you.' He leant across the table and kissed Shauna lightly on the lips.

Shauna kissed him back before pulling away. 'I haven't told you what happened today.'

'What?'

'The lawyer I engaged over the lotto money rang. Mum's dropped the case.'

'You're kidding. Why?'

'I don't know. I'm going to go and see her tomorrow. I imagine she's trying to make up for lying to me for so long about my father. I'm not going to forgive her, but it's unheard of to see her show some sign of regret. This is a first.'

Josh's fingers entwined with Shauna's. 'See, I told you she might come good.'

'I don't know about good, but it's certainly unexpected behaviour. It might just be a new tactic; guess I'll find out soon enough.'

Josh leant across the table again. 'I can't help myself,' he said, drawing Shauna towards him.

The moment was spoilt by their waiter clearing his throat. Josh sat back and rolled his eyes.

'Your drinks, sir.' He placed two glasses on the table, pouring a small amount of wine into Josh's. 'Would you like to try the wine?'

'No, it'll be fine.' They watched as he filled both glasses before returning to the bar.

Josh leant back towards Shauna. 'Now, where was I?'

'About to order, if this is anything to go by.' Shauna laughed and pointed at the waitress standing next to the table.

'I give up.' Josh slumped in his chair. 'Actually, no, I don't. Listen,' he said to the waitress, 'I'll double your tip if you go away. I'll call you over when we're ready to order.' She disappeared, and Josh resumed his position. He kissed Shauna, gently parting her lips with his tongue. The warmth of his mouth had her melting into him. She lost all sense of time or where she was, until the crash of glasses breaking in the bar area brought her back to reality.

They pulled apart, Josh's frustration mirroring her own. 'This restaurant isn't the right place for us tonight. What do you think?'

'Perhaps it's the right place for dinner, but not the right time for other things? Maybe we should get the order right: eat first, other things later.' Shauna ran her tongue over her top lip.

This was too much for Josh. He stood up, threw fifty dollars in the middle of the table and grabbed her hand. 'Come on; we'll eat later.'

Shauna didn't object. She let Josh lead her out of the restaurant and into a nearby taxi. She heard him give the driver his address, before losing herself in another passionate kiss. They arrived at Josh's apartment building, and Shauna blushed as her eyes met those of the taxi driver in the rear-vision mirror. Josh paid the driver, jumped out and ran around to open Shauna's door. He put one arm around her and guided her to the lifts. He stopped as the lift arrived and searched her eyes with his. 'Are you sure you're ready for this?'

'Ready? Are you kidding? You're about to find out exactly how ready I am.' Shauna dragged Josh into the lift, leaving him in no doubt at all about exactly how ready she was.

◆ ◆ ◆

Shauna's body still tingled as the taxi drove from Josh's house to her mother's the next morning. She smiled, thinking about the passionate night they'd had. She had only had a few hours' sleep yet was full of energy. In a short space of time she'd grown closer to Josh than she ever would have imagined. He was so easy to be around, seemed to intuitively understand what she needed, and how to make her relax. A warm glow surrounded her. Their night together had her ready to face anything Lorraine might be about to throw at her.

Shauna paid the taxi driver and walked up the driveway to the house. She drew in a deep breath before knocking on the front door. She was going to do her best to remain calm and not get drawn into Lorraine's petty arguments or guilt trips. Moments later the door opened and a stranger faced Shauna.

'Can I help you?'

Shauna took a step backwards. 'Oh. Is Lorraine home?'

'She is, but she's not seeing anyone at the moment. Can I take a message and get her to call you?'

'Excuse me, but who are you?'

'I'm Wendy and I'm afraid I'll need to ask you the same.'

'I'm Shauna, Lorraine's daughter. Let me in please, I'd like to talk to my mother.' Shauna pushed past Wendy.

'Shauna, wait.'

Shauna stopped and turned back to face Wendy.

'Has your mother been in contact with you during the past few weeks?'

'No, why?'

'I must warn you, she hasn't been well and you might get a bit of a shock.'

'What's wrong with her?'

'She can tell you. Please keep in mind she tires easily.'

'Are you a friend?'

'No, I'm from Blue Cross. Your mother's in the living room. I'm sure she'll be happy you're here.'

Shauna hurried down the hallway. Blue Cross? What was going on? She stopped. Lorraine lay on the couch, pillows propped around her, a warm blanket covering her body. Her face was pale and drawn and she'd lost an enormous amount of weight.

'Hello, Shauna.' Lorraine spoke in a weary voice, void of any of her usual sarcasm. 'I wasn't expecting you.'

'Mum, what on earth's going on? You look terrible.'

'Thanks, I'd say the same to you, but firstly it wouldn't be true and also I wouldn't like to offend you. I've been a bit sick, not my usual self.'

'What kind of sick?'

Lorraine patted the edge of the couch. 'Come and sit down and I'll fill you in.'

Shauna moved closer and sat down. Lorraine was behaving out of character. Usually, when she had a head cold she'd call it the flu and insist Shauna bring her meals. It was unheard of for Lorraine to be ill and not deliver a list of demands.

'So, a few weeks ago, actually the day after you were here, I had a little incident.'

'Incident?'

'Yes, I slipped in the shower and hit my head pretty hard. Luckily Bob was with me so he called an ambulance.'

'An ambulance? The injury was that serious?'

Lorraine nodded. 'I was unconscious and dripping with blood. Bob had no idea what to do so he rang the ambulance. The next thing I found myself in hospital. They said I was out of it for about six hours. I had the biggest headache when I did come to.'

'Why didn't you call me?'

'After our last conversation I wasn't sure you'd want to know.'

'Of course I would. What happens now? Do you rest up for a while?'

Lorraine patted Shauna's hand. 'Wait, there's more. They ran CT scans and all sorts of tests in the hospital to make sure I hadn't done any internal damage.'

'And?'

Lorraine took a deep breath. 'And they found a large tumour pressing on my brain.'

A lump formed in Shauna's throat, restricting her breathing. She gasped. 'What? Can they operate?'

Lorraine forced a smile. 'Afraid not, the cancer is already in the final stages. Untreatable.'

'They can't do anything at all?'

'No, other than give me some pills to keep me comfortable until the end and supply help like Wendy to keep me in my own home as long as possible.'

Tears streamed down Shauna's cheeks as she stared at Lorraine. 'I can't believe you didn't call me.'

'Oh, darl.' Lorraine gave a little laugh and patted Shauna's hand. 'Selfish right up to the end I am. I didn't want you getting all upset and sad. I'm the cause of enough sadness in your life, believe me.'

'Nothing should have stopped you calling me at a time like this.'

'What's done is done. You're not even aware of some of the horrible things I'm responsible for.'

'You mean Don and the lies you told?'

Surprise flashed in Lorraine's eyes. 'You know? I hoped he'd be long gone by now. You get your stubbornness from him. I take it he wouldn't go without a fight?'

Shauna gave a little smile. 'I always thought I got my stubbornness from you.'

'From both of us, that's why you're so bloody stubborn. Now you know what a horrible thing I did to you and to your father all those years ago. To be honest, when I look back the only reason I can give you – and it's not a very good one – was that I was scared – actually terrified would be more accurate. We had a good relationship, your father and I, but I found myself sabotaging it at every opportunity. I pushed him away on the one hand and threatened him on the other. I couldn't help or seem to stop what I was doing. At times I felt like I had no control at all over my own thoughts or actions. It was like I needed to test him. Push every button to see if he was ever going to react like my father did, that way I'd know my fears were well founded.' She shook her head.

'The walls you've seen covered in paint aren't the only ones. I did a great job on the house Don and I shared. He must have thought I was nuts. Actually, I'm pretty sure he did. He kept trying to work out what was wrong and encouraged me to see a range of different doctors. Now that I think back my mum tried to get me to see a psychologist, Don did, and you did recently. I didn't listen to any of you. I didn't want to admit that maybe I do have a problem and I also didn't want anyone telling me there was something wrong with me. So rather than getting help, I took you and disappeared. Even though he never reacted with verbal abuse or violence to anything I did, deep down there was a part of me that truly believed he would turn out to be like my father and I couldn't live through that again.' Lorraine sighed. 'But in reality, Don was nothing like my father. He probably would have made an excellent husband and father, if only I'd let him. I'm not sure I have the energy right now to tell you about my own childhood. Another day, perhaps.'

'Someone else already has.'

'Who?'

'I met Madeline, your mother.'

Lorraine pulled herself up to sitting. 'What? How did you meet her? I thought she'd be dead by now.'

'No, she remained part of Don's family and he used her to help convince me he was telling the truth. She's wonderful.'

Lorraine nodded.

Wendy came into the room. 'Lorraine, I think you should rest, you're looking tired.' She smiled at Shauna. 'Could you finish this conversation later?'

'Yes,' Shauna said. 'I'll stay, so when you're ready to head off I can organise a meal and spend the night. Do you normally sleep here?'

'No,' Wendy said. 'I come in for four hours a day. Lorraine doesn't need full-time care yet, although we may need to increase the hours soon. Why don't we help her into bed and I'll show you what needs to be done regarding meals and medication?'

Wendy helped Lorraine off the couch and down the passageway to her bedroom. She returned to the kitchen moments later where Shauna was rummaging through the fridge.

'You won't find anything enticing, I'm afraid,' Wendy said. 'Everything's bland. Lots of easy-to-swallow foods.'

Shauna shut the fridge and turned to face Wendy. 'Is the cancer definitely untreatable? I can afford to send her anywhere in the world, to any surgeon.' Shauna's thoughts went to Andrew and his brother Stevie. She'd heard from Andrew that the treatment Stevie was receiving in Texas was going well, and the small chance of survival he'd originally been given had now been increased to sixty-percent. Surely there was treatment available somewhere that could do the same for her mother?

Wendy's face was full of sympathy. 'Unfortunately, we're too late. The cancer has progressed beyond help. It may have gone undetected if not for the accident. This is unusual but happens when people aren't showing any symptoms.'

Shauna sat down at the kitchen table.

'This is a huge shock for you and I'm sorry. I tried to convince your mother to ring you when she first came home, but she wouldn't. I honestly think she was hoping you would find out after she'd gone.'

'Surely she wanted to say goodbye?'

'She's spent hours writing letters, I assume to you and other people explaining and – from what she's told me – apologising for things she's done. She wanted to save you from the pain that comes from watching someone die.'

'A selfless act.' Shauna gave a small laugh. 'So unlike my mother.' Tears started rolling down her cheeks. Wendy put an arm around her, but Shauna gently shrugged her off and wiped her eyes. She was embarrassed to be so emotional in front of a stranger.

Wendy busied herself and made tea, handing Shauna a cup. 'Here you go. Can I ring someone to pop over and keep you company?'

Shauna thought of Josh. They had plans to catch up for drinks later. 'Thank you, but I'll be okay. Why don't you head off? I'll stay until Mum wakes up.'

'Be aware she may sleep for hours. The medication is strong.'

Shauna waited until Wendy left before bursting into tears. She'd planned to confront her mother; she'd spent hours planning what she would say, wondering if she would ever forgive her for taking her away from her father. Everything seemed so insignificant now.

She called Josh and explained the situation. He offered to come and be with her, but she needed to be alone. She needed time to digest everything.

Three hours later Shauna heard a bump in Lorraine's room. She went in. The bed was empty and she could hear her mother in the en suite. She waited until she came out.

'Oh, are you still here, darl? I thought you'd be home by now.'

'I wanted to check you'd be okay by yourself. I can stay the night.'

'Don't be silly, you go. You can come back and visit me again another day.' Lorraine shuffled back to the bed and slowly climbed in.

'Where's Bob? Is he helping out?'

Lorraine laughed. 'I didn't realise Bob could move so fast. The day after I was given the diagnosis, he high-tailed it out of the hospital never to be seen again.'

'What? The bastard! I thought you two were in love.'

'In hindsight, I think my bank account was the real object of his love. Once I found out the cancer was untreatable, I told him I was dropping the lawsuit. He was furious.' She smiled. 'It seems having cancer and no financial prospects made me less desirable to him.'

'Didn't he think you'd leave him money in your will?'

'No, I told him a long time ago my will was one thing I would never change and was also the reason I wouldn't get remarried or live with a man again. I wouldn't let someone have a claim on your inheritance. It's not much, but I do own the house. I've been a bad enough mother, I wouldn't add that to the list.'

'Really? Even though I don't need it?'

'Yes. I know it's hard to believe but it is true.'

Shauna smiled. 'You seem so different. Do you even care about Bob?'

Lorraine sighed. 'Yes and no. He's a disappointment, but that's all. I've had time to think. A lot of time to reflect on the things I've done badly and how self-centred I've been. You may not believe this, but I think since leaving Don and moving to Melbourne all those years ago, I went into a kind of self-preservation mode. There are so many things I wish I could change. The men, my relationship with you, the—'

Shauna cut her off. 'The only thing I want to change right now is your diagnosis. Are you sure there's no specialist in America? Or that guy in Sydney? He's always on the TV? He performs miracles all the time. We've got the money, we can afford anyone and anything.'

Lorraine shook her head. 'He's already seen my test results and even he agreed with the diagnosis. As hard and as horrible as this sounds, we have to accept there's no cure; we certainly can't buy one.'

'Did the doctors tell you how long you have?'

'A matter of weeks. They said six, maybe eight.'

Shauna recoiled with shock. 'Only six to eight weeks?'

Lorraine pulled her close and hugged her. 'Afraid so, and they gave me that information a few weeks ago.'

'Oh shit.'

'Yep, oh shit alright. Now, let's change the subject. Tell me about Don and Madeline. On a scale of one to ten how much do they hate me?'

A little before ten, Shauna rang Madeline's doorbell, grateful that she had somewhere to go after leaving her mother's. Shauna took one look at her grandmother and burst into tears. Madeline guided her into the house and down to the living room. It took fifteen minutes for the tears to subside and Shauna to be able to tell Madeline what had happened. It was harder than she'd imagined. Madeline's eyes welled with tears as Shauna explained the situation.

'She was a different person. Considerate, selfless, together, not like she normally is at all.'

'Death is a funny thing.' Madeline's voice was distant. 'People handle it in their own way. Sometimes it brings out the best in them. Robert, your grandfather, he died when Lorraine was only seven. You couldn't find a more selfish man than he was, but during the last three months of his life I didn't recognise him. He became selfless: worried about me, worried about Lorraine. The abuse stopped. If only he'd been like that all along.'

'That's how I feel about Mum. She's now a person I'd love to be around, but we only have a few weeks at the most. It's not fair.'

'I know, love. I know.'

'I dreaded going to her house today. I was planning to confront her for the lies she'd told me about my father. I also wanted to tell her how successful Don has been, about his family and about you. Before she got sick she would have hit the roof, made up some other story to get out of her lies, and most likely rushed over and demanded a share of his money. Instead, she can't apologise enough for her own behaviour and was genuinely happy when I told her about Don's success.'

Sadness washed over Madeline's face. 'All too late.'

Shauna yawned. Her eyes felt like they had sand in them. She couldn't remember the last time she'd cried so much.

Madeline stood. 'It's after midnight, love. Would you like to stay here tonight? You're exhausted.'

331

'Thanks, I think I will.' Shauna got up off the couch and hugged Madeline. 'I'm so sorry to drop this on you, but I thought you had a right to know. She didn't ask me to tell you, in fact quite the opposite. Mum's written letters to you and Don, which I'm supposed to deliver after she's gone. I don't agree with her. I think you should be given the opportunity to speak to her while she's still alive.'

Shauna searched Madeline's face for a reaction, but Madeline's expression gave nothing away.

Madeline showed Shauna to the spare room and offered her some pyjamas and a toothbrush. She hugged her grandmother again before saying goodnight.

When she awoke the next morning, Shauna found Madeline asleep in the armchair in the living room. She tiptoed into the kitchen.

The smell of fresh coffee woke her grandmother and she came into the kitchen as Shauna poured two large mugs.

'Perfect,' Madeline said. 'Exactly what I need.'

'Did you get much sleep?'

'A bit. It was daylight by the time I must have drifted off. I'd like to visit your mother, perhaps this afternoon.'

Shauna smiled. 'I hoped you would. Should I prewarn her?'

'Yes, I want her to be prepared. You go over first. Tell her I'm coming.'

Shauna stared at Madeline for a moment. 'You won't be too hard on her, will you?'

'Shauna! She stole you away from your father and the family who loved you. No contact for thirty years. Do you think I should just ignore that?'

'Of course not, but she's dying. We shouldn't upset her too much.'

Madeline smiled. 'Don't you worry, love, we'll sort things out. Things need to be said. She may have things she needs to say, too. We'll both say our piece and move on. How does that sound?'

'Terrifying.'

Madeline patted her arm and sipped her coffee. 'I'm going to finish this, shower and refresh myself. Why don't you do the same?'

'No,' Shauna said. 'I think I'll go home. I'm still in clothes from two days ago.'

She blushed as Madeline raised a knowing eyebrow.

'I'll get some fresh clothes and do a few things before going back to Mum's. I'll ring you this afternoon, okay?'

'Of course.'

Shauna watched as her grandmother walked to her room. Her shoulders sagged. Her body seemed to have aged ten years overnight.

Shauna hugged the phone to her. Just hearing Josh's voice gave her a much-needed boost.

'Are you sure you don't want me to come over and give you a hand, keep you company, bring you food? Anything?'

'No. I need to do this myself today,' she told him. 'Thank you, though. You're being so lovely.'

'Hey, I'm always lovely; you're realising this much later than most people do. Usually people realise it as soon as they meet me. That Josh Richardson, they say, he's so lovely. I get sick of hearing it they say it so often.'

Shauna laughed. She ended the call a few minutes later and went to have a shower.

A little before twelve Shauna pulled up outside Lorraine's house. There was so much she needed to say to her mother. She was instantly jolted from her thoughts at the sight of an ambulance parked in the driveway. She jumped out of the Mercedes and raced towards the house.

A paramedic met her at the door.

She caught her breath and searched the paramedic's face for news. 'What's going on?'

The paramedic didn't get a chance to respond. A voice called out from inside.

'Shauna, I'll fill you in.' Wendy met her at the front door.

'Why didn't you call me?'

'Calm down, I was about to.' Wendy guided Shauna back out to the driveway. 'I arrived fifteen minutes ago and your mother was finding it difficult to breathe. I called for an ambulance. I needed to make arrangements before I rang you. The ambulance only just arrived.'

At that moment Lorraine was wheeled out on a stretcher.

Shauna took her hand. 'Mum, I'm here. I'll come to the hospital with you.'

Lorraine squeezed Shauna's hand, her eyes shut.

The paramedic turned to Shauna. 'Why don't you meet us there. That way you'll have your car for later?'

'How long do you think she'll be in hospital?'

The paramedic's eyes filled with sympathy.

Wendy took her arm. 'I think this might be her final journey. She's gone down so rapidly. I'm afraid it'll only be a matter of days. Hopefully the doctor can tell you otherwise when you get to the hospital, but you should prepare yourself for the worst. I'm sorry.'

Shauna stared at Wendy. How could this be happening so quickly? She thought she had weeks. She pulled herself together. 'Okay, so do I need to take anything?'

'No, we've had her bag packed for a couple of weeks now. I added the few things Lorraine told me she'd need when the time did come.'

'She had her bag packed?'

'Yes, she was realistic about everything. Didn't want to be a bother, she kept telling me. She's a remarkable lady, your mother.'

Shauna thanked Wendy and climbed back into her car, ready to follow the ambulance.

An hour later Lorraine was resting comfortably in a private room at St Vincent's Hospital. The doctor had been in to examine her and confirmed what Wendy had suspected. She was into her final days, or perhaps even hours. Shauna had rung Madeline to tell her the news and expected her grandmother to arrive at any moment. Shauna felt her own eyes drifting shut when there was a gentle tap on the door and Madeline looked in. Shauna went over to greet her. 'She's still asleep. She hasn't woken up since they brought her in. They gave her a sedative.'

Madeline stood in the doorway staring at Lorraine. Shauna could only imagine what her grandmother must be thinking. Lorraine would have been twenty-nine the last time Madeline had seen her – young, healthy, so full of life. Now she was thin, her skin sallow, cheeks hollow. A terrible way for anyone to remember their daughter.

Shauna's eyes filled with tears. 'Are you okay?'

Madeline nodded, a sad smile on her lips. 'Yes of course, love. Why don't you go and get yourself a snack, or take a walk?'

'I didn't get a chance to tell her you were coming.'

'That's okay. We'll be fine. You head off and refresh yourself. You might have a long night ahead.'

Shauna turned back as she walked out of the room to see Madeline wipe a tear from the corner of her eye.

Thirty minutes later Shauna looked in to find Lorraine's bed tilted upright, and Lorraine and Madeline deep in hushed conversation. 'Everything okay?' she asked from the doorway.

Madeline looked up. 'All good, dear. We need a bit longer, if you don't mind.'

Shauna closed the door behind her but stopped as she heard her mother's tearful voice.

'I'm so sorry. I can't even really explain why I did what I did. I just knew I had to get away from Don and from everything in Brisbane. I had this feeling in my gut that something awful would happen. It was based on nothing other than a feeling.'

'You should have come to me. I would have listened, tried to help you.'

There was a silence and then Lorraine continued. 'I had it in my head that you would want me to see a psychologist and that you'd agree with Don that Shauna was better off with him than she was with me. I was acting crazy at times and if that was brought up in a custody hearing I assumed I'd lose my rights to my daughter.'

'Possibly,' Madeline said. 'One of my biggest regrets is not realising how much your father's death impacted you. I truly believe the acting crazy that you're talking about and the worries about Don all trace back to that. I knew it affected you, I just hadn't realised how badly. I think you needed professional help and I'll always blame myself for not forcing you to get it when you were younger.'

'Don't blame yourself. Don tried and Shauna too. I resisted everyone. Whatever's been going on in my mind might have been triggered by Dad's death, but I think maybe there was more to it. It's hard to explain how I've felt at times, but it's like all my emotions have been squashed up in a great big ball and are trying to strangle me. I don't know how to deal with any of it other than I want to lash out at something.' She gave a little laugh. 'I've gone through a lot of paint over the years. But I've lashed out at Shauna too. It would have been better for her if I'd left her in Brisbane and just gone myself.'

'To be honest, it always surprised me that you took her. I thought you would have found it easier to leave her with me or with Don and get on with your life.'

'There were times I wish I had,' Lorraine said. 'I was a terrible mother. There was part of me that had this idealistic picture of what motherhood should be like but I could never find that place. It was so tiring and such hard work looking after someone else. I don't think I did a very good job. She was left to fend for herself far too often. I took her because I'd failed at so many other things I wanted to prove to myself that this was one thing I could get right. Unfortunately, Shauna was the one that suffered from that decision.'

A lump filled Shauna's throat as she listened to her mother's voice break as she spoke.

'The Shauna I've met is an absolute credit to you, Lorraine. You can't have been terrible the whole time.'

Lorraine gave a little laugh. 'Shauna might disagree with you there. I'd say she came from good genes and luckily has inherited the best qualities of both you and Don. I don't think I've added any value to her life. The amount of unsuitable men I've dragged through our lives is enough to make my skin crawl. And then with this lotto money . . . suing my own daughter, what was I thinking?'

'That's the one good thing you've done,' Madeline said. 'If you hadn't we may never have found you.'

'Shauna said Don looked for us for a lot of years,' Lorraine said. 'And that he remarried. I hope he's happier now than he was with me.'

'He's very happy,' Madeline said. 'Happier now he has Shauna back in his life of course.'

Lorraine's voice cracked again. 'I can't believe it's taken cancer for me to realise how much I love her, Mum. I've been so selfish and stupid for so long and now it's too late.'

Tears streamed down Shauna's cheeks as she sank against the wall. It was so unfair that the mother she'd always wanted seemed to finally be appearing.

'It's not too late to ensure she knows you love her,' Madeline said. 'We'll look after her when you're . . .' Her grandmother didn't complete her sentence. The lump in Shauna's throat was so large now she felt like she might choke.

'I hope you can forgive me,' she heard her own mother say. 'I know what I did to you was unforgivable but one day, I hope you'll find it in your heart.'

Madeline sighed. 'Me too, Lorraine, me too.'

Shauna closed her eyes. She knew her mother wanted to hear the words that all was forgiven but it was just too big an ask.

Her grandmother spoke again. 'I can't promise forgiveness, but I can certainly work towards trying to understand. Regardless of anything, there's one thing that you do need to know and that is I never stopped loving you. Every day you've been gone I've thought of both you and Shauna. I've raised a glass on every birthday of yours and have spent many days sitting in my armchair thinking back to your childhood and teen years and the fun times we had.'

A sob escaped from Lorraine.

'I will always love you, Lorraine. You're my daughter and I'll always be very proud of that. Shauna will live on through you and I can't wait to spend more time getting to know her.'

'Look after her, won't you, Mum. Make sure she knows she's loved.'

Shauna couldn't bear to listen anymore as gentle sobs, which she assumed were Madeline's, floated out into the corridor. Her mother and grandmother were being reunited after thirty years and they might only have a matter of hours left together. It was absolutely heartbreaking.

She went in search of a ladies' room to wash her face and pull herself together. When she returned Madeline was quietly closing the door.

'She's sleeping,' she whispered. 'Come down here and we'll talk.'

Shauna followed Madeline down the corridor to a waiting area. It was empty so they sat down.

Madeline's pale face confirmed the visit had been difficult.

'Are you okay?'

Madeline smiled. 'Yes, I'm fine but exhausted. We had a good chat.' Madeline patted Shauna's leg. 'I'll fill you in another time, love. I'm drained. I'll call a taxi and go home, but I'll be back in the morning. What are you going to do? The nurse said she'd probably be asleep for a few hours.'

'I'll stay. I haven't spoken to her properly since she was admitted.'

Madeline hugged Shauna. 'Call me if you need anything or think I should come back in.'

Madeline gave her a final wave as the lift door shut and Shauna turned and slowly walked to her mother's room.

The room was bathed in moonlight by the time Lorraine opened her eyes. The day had been a blur for Shauna, and for the past four hours, since Madeline had left, she'd sat next to her mother's bed, caught up in her own thoughts. Regardless of the arguments and problems their relationship had suffered, she'd realised she would miss her mother terribly.

'Hey, darl, what are you still doing here?' Lorraine managed a weak smile.

Shauna put down the magazine she'd been flicking through. 'I had no other plans, so I thought I'd stay. Do you need a drink?' Shauna reached for the cup of water.

'No, just sit me up, can you?'

Shauna pressed the buttons on the bed until Lorraine was raised to a sitting position.

'Thanks, love.'

'How are you feeling?'

'Honestly?'

'Yes.'

Lorraine gave a little laugh. 'Like I'll be meeting my maker sooner than expected.'

'God, don't say that.'

Lorraine took Shauna's hand. 'I'm sorry, but we need to face facts. I don't think I have much longer.'

'You seem a lot better right now.'

'Must be the drugs. They're giving me a new lease on life.'

'How was Grandma's visit?'

Lorraine smiled. 'Grandma, that has a nice ring to it. Her visit was weird, horrible and lovely. She's a hell of a woman. Make sure you become part of her life, won't you.'

'I think I already am. Did she forgive you?'

A range of emotions played over Lorraine's face, sadness being the final one to settle.

'Sorry, it's none of my business.'

'Don't be sorry, of course it is. You're the main part in this and what I did.' Lorraine considered her answer. 'I'm not sure about forgiveness, but we've made a kind of peace with each other. We talked for a long time. I think she needed me to realise how much I hurt both her and Don, but also wanted me to understand that she's never stopped loving me and never will. She also wanted me to know how sorry she was that she hadn't realised that I was suffering at the time, that I needed help, and she feels that she failed me by not getting me that help.' A tear escaped from Lorraine's eye. 'Like I said, she's a hell of a woman.'

Shauna handed her a tissue. 'I wish you'd realised this years ago.'

'Me too, but I'm also realistic. I would never have stopped and looked at myself and the hurt I've caused without some kind of huge wake-up call. It doesn't get much bigger than this. My biggest regret though is not listening to Don, and even you in your adult years. You both suggested that I might need some help and I dismissed you. Perhaps you were right, perhaps things might have been different.'

She managed a weak smile. 'Now, tell me something sensational, something to take my mind off this. How's that guy you're seeing? Anything serious?'

They spent the next two hours chatting quietly. Shauna told her mother about Josh, about her job and the wonderful friendship she had developed with Frankie. She spoke more about her current life in those two hours than she had done in the previous two years. Close to midnight Shauna noticed how quiet Lorraine had become.

'Are you okay? Do you need to sleep?'

Lorraine could only nod. Her eyelids sagged heavily and the colour had drained from her face.

Shauna lowered the bed, leant down and kissed her.

Lorraine spoke softly. 'I love you, and if you do nothing else just remember this one thing. I love you more than I've ever loved anything, and I'm sorry.' Lorraine tried to smile but the effort was too much and her eyes closed.

A large tear fell from the corner of Shauna's eye; it would only be a matter of time now. She sat next to her mother's bed until the early hours of the morning when she stopped breathing. The doctor came to confirm that her mother was gone. Shauna remained next to her, not knowing what to do. After some time, a hand rested gently on her shoulder. She turned to see Josh's kind, concerned face looking at her.

'How did you . . .? I mean, how did you know?'

Josh didn't answer, he just pulled Shauna up out of her chair and held her tight. 'I'm so sorry.' He spoke softly in her ear. The unexpected kindness opened the floodgates for Shauna. One tear followed another as she buried her face in Josh's chest.

The Funeral

Shauna was pleasantly surprised by the turnout for her mother's funeral and wake. People were gathered in the Dragonfly room of Grey's Funeral Home. Now that the service was complete, they were being served finger food and drinks. The presence of Frankie and Tom was comforting. She walked over to where they were enjoying cups of tea. 'Thank you so much for coming.'

'Don't be silly, we wanted to be here for you,' Frankie said. 'How are you doing?'

Shauna forced a smile. 'Okay. Everything's been a bit of a shock. I'm not sure if it's hit me yet.'

Frankie nodded. 'Promise you'll ring us when it does. That will be the perfect opportunity to visit you with an expensive bottle of wine.'

This time Shauna's smile was genuine. 'Which I'll have to drink all on my own.'

'I'm happy to help,' Tom said.

'Josh is popular,' Frankie said. Shauna looked across to where Josh was talking to a group of women.

'Does he know those people?'

'No.' Shauna was unable to hide her amusement. 'Although he'll have had intimate conversations with everyone in the room by the time we leave. He's a special man. He helped me organise every detail of the funeral.'

'You did your mum proud,' Tom said. 'I might do Josh a favour and go and rescue him.' The two women watched as Tom headed over to Josh.

'What happened with Tom's brother? Did you sort him out? I'm sorry I haven't been in touch to ask.'

'Don't be silly, you've had all of this to contend with. And yes, he's gone forever.'

Shauna grinned. 'That's fantastic news.'

'I need to thank you,' Frankie said. 'If you hadn't pushed me into changing my life and getting involved with the business, Dash might have stolen a lot more. You should have seen his lawyer, he was disgusting. The sort of man you can only imagine will be single for life. He didn't possess one redeeming quality. In fact, he oozed repulsiveness and I couldn't stand the sight of him.' Frankie started to giggle. Her hand flew up to her mouth. 'Sorry, I shouldn't be laughing, not at your mother's funeral.'

'Laughter is good for the soul, my dear.' The women turned to find the kind eyes of an older lady smiling at them. She took Shauna's hand. 'So, are you going to introduce me to your friend?'

'Of course.' Shauna nodded. 'Grandma, Frankie. Frankie, this is my mystery grandmother.'

'I'm very sorry for your loss, Mrs Budd,' Frankie said.

'Thank you, dear. Call me Madeline, though. It was a lovely service, wasn't it?'

'Yes, although most of the people here are acquaintances, not real friends,' Shauna said. 'Mum didn't have many friends.'

Madeline squeezed Shauna's hand. 'She found it hard to maintain friendships when she was younger; with everything she's been through that might not have changed.'

'Mmm.' Shauna was deep in thought. She looked across to where Don was talking to two men. 'Can you believe my father came today? Not every man would be so forgiving.'

'He loved her very much once.' Madeline's eyes became distant. Shauna wondered what memories she was reliving. 'She had problems he couldn't find solutions for, and he's always blamed himself that he didn't do more to help her. In spite of what she did, I'm sure a part of him still loved her. If nothing else she gave him you, something he'll always be thankful for, as will I.'

Shauna's eyes misted over. She took the tissue Frankie offered.

Over the next hour the few guests in attendance began to leave. As the last guest departed, strong arms slid around Shauna's waist. She turned to face Josh. 'You've been wonderful.' She tugged him close.

Josh lifted Shauna's chin up so he could look into her eyes. 'You know why I've been like that, don't you?'

'Because you're the nicest guy alive?'

Josh smiled. 'One valid reason, of course, but no, a more important reason. I love you. I am completely in love with you.' Shauna wasn't given a chance to respond as Josh leant forward, his lips meeting hers.

Six Months Later

The sun's soft glow as it slowly disappeared behind the hills threw a beautiful light on the garden and wedding guests. The waterfall and majestic weeping willows provided a stunning backdrop for the ceremony, and sounds of laughter and music filled the air. Fairy lights strung through the trees added to the magic of the day.

Frankie and Tom stood together and admired the beautiful setting.

'Oh my God, I think I'm going to cry again.'

Tom put his arm around Frankie and passed her a tissue. 'I don't think I've been to a more superb wedding.'

Frankie dabbed her eyes. 'It's like a fairy tale. Being walked down the aisle by her long-lost father to marry such a gorgeous man. And she was crying. So much for the hard-nosed businesswoman.'

'Oh, I think she's still pretty hard-nosed.' Josh came up behind them and smiled. 'I was lucky to find the softer side to her, too.'

'Congratulations.' Frankie kissed Josh on the cheek. 'We're so happy for you.'

'Thank you.' Josh beamed, shaking Tom's hand. 'Did you see my stunning wife, by the way? Here she comes now.' Josh held out his hand, which Shauna took as she glided towards the group.

'Simply lovely.' Frankie continued to dab at her tears. 'The most magnificent wedding I've ever been to.'

'Thank you,' Shauna said.

'Seriously,' Frankie said. 'You're dazzling and the service was perfect. Your sisters are striking, too.'

'Two sisters for bridesmaids; how unbelievable.'

'Very! How did that happen? You said Lilliana said no. When did she change her mind?'

'She surprised me this morning,' Shauna said. 'Turned up with Rose to get hair and make-up done and asked if I'd still like her to be part of the bridal party. I nearly fainted! Apparently, a few weeks ago she decided she wanted to do it so got Rose and Tess to help organise the dress without me knowing. She wanted to see my reaction.'

Frankie squeezed Shauna's arm. 'She's accepted you.'

Shauna smiled. 'So it seems. It was a really lovely gesture. We've been slowly getting to know each other but I wasn't expecting anything this big from her. Rose said they'd had a lot of fun organising the dress so it seems that their long-lost sister might be helping them form a bond too.'

Frankie's tears began to flow again. 'Sorry, I'm so emotional today, it's ridiculous. I just know how much that would mean to you. I'm so happy for you. It's been so lovely to finally meet Tess too. I spoke to her earlier and she said she was heading back to New York on Monday. How wonderful that she came back for the wedding.'

'I would have killed her if she hadn't,' Shauna said. 'It's bad enough that she's accepted a position over there. So much for three months away. It's been almost twelve already and it doesn't sound like she'll be coming home permanently any time soon.'

Frankie squeezed her arm. 'You'll have to put up with me as a substitute for a bit longer.'

'Substitute? Are you kidding me? Frankie, I adore our friendship. It has nothing to do with whether Tess is here or not. One of the best things about winning lotto was meeting you.'

Happy tears continued to flow down Frankie's cheeks.

'And did you see my aunt, Dad's sister?' Shauna pointed to a woman deep in conversation with her father. She was so like Shauna it was uncanny.

'Oh my God.' Tom laughed. 'Incredible. Imagine if you'd bumped into her in the street before reconnecting with your dad. At least you know what you'll look like in thirty years.'

'She's really lovely, actually,' Josh said. 'Hopefully, my beautiful wife will be as gorgeous when she's in her sixties.'

They continued to stare at Shauna's Aunt Sharon until Frankie broke the silence. 'Who's the guy in the suit talking to Hope?'

'Patrick, my brother,' Shauna said. 'He came back from Afghanistan so he could be here today. I finally met my little brother, and check him out, he's gorgeous. Mmm, Patrick and Hope are very cute together.'

'She's only sixteen,' Frankie said.

'He's only twenty-two.' Shauna grinned at Frankie's horrified face. 'Okay, perhaps a bit too old for her. She looks beautiful, by the way. I love her hair.' At that moment, Hope looked over at Frankie and gave her a little wave. 'And her dress.'

'It seems that all the boys at school agree with you. Her phone never stops ringing.'

Shauna fanned her face. 'Oh my God, you mean she was allowed a phone too? Your tech evolution must nearly be complete.'

Frankie blushed. 'Ha ha, very funny. Now, be quiet.'

'Hey, this is my wedding, I can say what I like.' Her smile faded. 'On a more serious note, how are things with the business? When we spoke a couple of weeks ago you said Dash contacted Tom and wanted to see him. Did they meet?'

'They did and of course he was after more money. He had a sob story prepared about how he'd never really realised how important family was to him until now and that he'd do anything to change the past so he could still be a part of the business and Tom's life.'

'What did Tom do?'

Frankie blushed. 'Flattened him. Not straightaway but when Tom told him he wasn't getting any more money and really wasn't welcome, Dash made the mistake of saying this was all my fault. That I was a bitch for stirring up so much trouble. He then referred to the night he'd tried to force himself on me. I guess he was going to suggest that I'd wanted it, but Tom didn't give him the chance. He was so upset when he came home.' Frankie's gut twisted remembering Tom's despair at learning the truth – the overwhelming guilt he'd felt over purchasing the business without her consent and then pressuring her to join a team that included Dash. 'I should have told him when it happened. I was ashamed, though. Of course Tom believed my version of that night. He won't allow Dash near any of us ever again.'

'Good,' Shauna said. 'And remember you had absolutely nothing to be ashamed of. I'm just glad that Tom made sure he realised that. Your old fisherman friend gave him a small taste of what he deserved but, in my opinion, he deserved more, which it sounds like Tom's delivered. Anyway, that's enough about him. We have many reasons to celebrate and never seeing the brother again is definitely one of them.'

She turned to Josh. 'Sweet husband, would you mind finding a waiter and getting us some drinks, please?'

Josh kissed Shauna and went in search of the waiter.

'He's the happiest man alive right now,' Frankie said. 'Married to an intelligent, funny, sexy, rich woman. He's also the luckiest man alive.'

Shauna nodded. 'He is and at least he's not marrying me for my money.'

Frankie raised an eyebrow. 'Oh?'

'Turns out our Josh was hiding a secret of his own. See that guy over there?' Shauna pointed to a silver-haired man who had just thrown back his head and was roaring with laughter at something someone said. 'He's Josh's dad, Lloyd Richardson.'

Frankie sucked in her breath. 'What, the billionaire? You're kidding. How come you didn't tell me before?'

'I only found out when we had a family dinner last week so that my dad and grandmother could meet his family. Turned out he and Dad had done business together in the past.'

'How did Josh explain?'

'He never denied having money. Ages ago he told me about his family and how successful his dad was. He made it very clear that he'd lived independently since he left home at eighteen and refused any handouts or help. He just didn't let on who they were or the extent of the family empire. He wanted to make sure I loved him for who he was. He's never used the family's position to benefit him, always done things on his own terms, but he can't deny the fact that he has a rather large trust fund and a ridiculous inheritance to accept one day. Our lotto win pales in comparison. Mind you, he'll probably donate the lot to charity. He's adamant about making it on his own. Anyway, I'd better stop, he's coming back.'

Josh returned with the drinks.

'Looks like your house will be the next big celebration,' Shauna said.

'What will?' Tom rejoined the group, putting his arm around Frankie.

'Our housewarming,' Frankie said. 'I mentioned to Shauna the new house should be ready in a couple of months. I still can't believe we're going to own our own home.'

'A party to look forward to.' Tom squeezed Frankie. 'Hopefully you'll still be up for a late night. Have you told Shauna yet?'

'Told me what?' Shauna demanded.

Frankie patted her stomach. 'We'll be introducing someone new in about five months.'

Shauna threw her arms around Frankie and Tom. 'That's such brilliant news!'

Frankie struggled out of Shauna's grip and laughed. 'Let's just say it's been an unexpected but welcome surprise.'

'Do you know what you're having?' Josh asked.

Tom rubbed Frankie's stomach. 'Can I tell them?'

Frankie laughed. 'You'll burst if I say no, so you might as well.'

'A boy. Can you believe we're having a boy? I was sure we'd have another girl.'

Josh raised his glass. 'This calls for a toast. To Frankie, Tom and Tom junior.'

They all raised their glasses and toasted the new arrival.

Frankie turned to Shauna, a gleam in her eye. 'You two will need to get a move on. Tom junior here is going to want a playmate.'

Shauna feigned shock. 'Don't hold your breath. Imagine me as a mum! I'd be a nightmare. Now,' she laughed, 'check out the guys from the support group.'

Frankie looked over to where Pamela, Todd and Ivan had formed a small group and were following Helen's energetic dance moves. 'I'm kind of surprised you invited them.'

'Really? How come?'

'I just am, that's all. Actually, I'm surprised you returned to the support group at all. It doesn't really seem like your kind of thing.'

'It wasn't initially. I was just coming to see you as I was enjoying our friendship but the idea of supporting others has grown on me. As have those regulars over there.' Shauna had surprised herself, let alone Frankie, when she'd called Pamela and explained she'd like to become more involved in the group and that she'd realised if she'd followed the advice of the five steps that was given from the start, her journey may have been quite different.

'They were blown away when you got up and told your story last month.'

Frankie still found it hard to believe Shauna had opened up. She'd kept the group on the edge of their seats as she told the story of her mother suing her and eventually succumbing to cancer, of Simon doing his best to manipulate his way back into her life and money, and then of her father and extended family and what an amazingly positive thing had risen from the negative. She'd reinforced the importance of following the five steps to the new people attending the group in the hope that they wouldn't have to experience anything like the upheaval she had.

Frankie frowned. 'I just realised you left out how lotto brought you and Josh together when you told your story.'

'I'm not sure it did.' She turned to Josh. 'We'd already met through work, hadn't we?'

Josh nodded. 'Frankie's right though. It was you confiding in me about the winnings, your mum and letting me be part of the journey in getting to know your new family that really built the trust between us. You've dealt with some exceptional circumstances this year, Shauna.'

She grinned and took his hand. 'And snagged myself an exceptional husband into the bargain. One who is about to show me how exceptional his dance moves are.' She dragged Josh towards the dance floor.

Frankie and Tom watched them go.

'Want to dance, Mr York?' Frankie tugged Tom to her.

He kissed her.

'Mmm, what was that for?'

'Just thinking how lucky I am. A beautiful wife, two awesome girls, a baby boy on the way, good friends, freedom to do whatever we like. I'm scared it's a dream.'

'Don't be scared,' Frankie said. 'Like a very wise person said to me many months ago, *embrace it and enjoy it.*'

'And live happily ever after,' Tom added.

'Sounds good to me.' Frankie allowed Tom to guide her to the dance floor.

◆ ◆ ◆

Josh stood in front of Shauna in the early hours of the next morning. The wedding guests had all been farewelled and finally he was able to undress his wife. 'You don't really believe you'd make a terrible mother, do you?'

Shauna placed a hand on her belly. 'I hope not. I just wanted to put them off the scent. Couldn't upstage Frankie's news now, could I? Trump her with a wedding and a pregnancy; it was her moment, not mine.'

Josh laughed. 'Wow, you're a big softie, aren't you? Where's the ball-breaker gone?'

Shauna slipped her hand inside Josh's pants and took a firm grip. 'She's still here, and don't you get the wrong idea now.'

Josh groaned. 'Hey, be careful, you might want more babies after this one. Although from memory, I think this is what got us into the baby situation.'

Shauna parted her lips. 'You may be right, Mr Richardson. Now, it's time to move on from all this baby talk and make slow, romantic love to your wife.'

Josh drew Shauna to him and kissed her. He didn't need to be told twice.

ACKNOWLEDGMENTS

I'd like to send a sincere thank you to the many wonderful people in my life who continue to encourage and support each step of my writing journey. Having friends and family who are not only interested but love to talk writing and reading is a dream come true.

A very special thank you to Ray and Judy for your constant encouragement, support and enthusiasm for my writing, coupled with your willingness to read early versions and proofread final drafts.

There are many people to thank who helped me with the original version of this story, published as *Fortunate Friends*. Maggie, Sarah and Tracy, thank you for the invaluable feedback provided at various stages of the original manuscript development. To Alexandra Nahlous, Bonnie Wilson, Laila Miller and Louise Cusack – thank you!

For both the original version of the story and the new, a huge thank you to my wonderful writing friend Robyn. Our daily chats, laughs and encouragement sessions are something I treasure, as is your friendship.

To the Lake Union Publishing team, in particular Sammia Hamer; I am incredibly grateful to be working with true professionals. Thank you for making this an exciting and enjoyable experience.

A very special thank you to Celine Kelly. Your editing brilliance has helped strengthen this manuscript, while at the same time added depth to both the characters and storyline. It has been an absolute pleasure to work with you.

And lastly, to the wonderful readers who continue to comment, review and message me about my books, an enormous thank you. Your enthusiasm and support is incredibly uplifting.

ABOUT THE AUTHOR

Louise has enjoyed working in marketing, recruitment and film production, all of which have helped steer her towards her current, and most loved, role – writer.

Originally from Melbourne, a trip around Australia led Louise and her husband to Queensland's stunning Sunshine Coast, where they now live with their two sons, gorgeous fluffball of a cat and an abundance of visiting wildlife – the kangaroos and wallabies the most welcome, the snakes the least!

Awed by her beautiful surroundings, Louise loves to take advantage of the opportunities the coast provides for swimming, hiking, mountain biking and kayaking. When she's not writing or out adventuring, Louise loves any available opportunity to curl up with a glass of red wine, switch on her Kindle and indulge in a new release from a favourite author.

To get in touch with Louise, or to join her mailing list, visit: www.LouiseGuy.com